Romantic Suspense

Danger. Passion. Drama.

Mistaken Identities
Tara Taylor Quinn

Find Her
Katherine Garbera

T0359532

MILLS & BOON

MISTAKEN IDENTITIES
© 2024 by TTQ Books LLC
Philippine Copyright 2024
Australian Copyright 2024
New Zealand Copyright 2024

First Published 2024
First Australian Paperback Edition 2024
ISBN 978 1 038 93903 6

FIND HER
© 2024 by Katherine Garbera
Philippine Copyright 2024
Australian Copyright 2024
New Zealand Copyright 2024

First Published 2024
First Australian Paperback Edition 2024
ISBN 978 1 038 93903 6

Published by
Harlequin Mills & Boon
An imprint of Harlequin Enterprises (Australia) Pty Limited
(ABN 47 001 180 918), a subsidiary of HarperCollins
Publishers Australia Pty Limited
(ABN 36 009 913 517)
Level 19, 201 Elizabeth Street
SYDNEY NSW 2000 AUSTRALIA

Cover art used by arrangement with Harlequin Books S.A.. All rights reserved.

Printed and bound in Australia by McPherson's Printing Group

Mistaken Identities

Tara Taylor Quinn

MILLS & BOON

A *USA TODAY* bestselling author of over one hundred novels in twenty languages, **Tara Taylor Quinn** has sold more than seven million copies. Known for her intense emotional fiction, Ms. Quinn's novels have received critical acclaim in the UK and most recently from Harvard. She is the recipient of the Readers' Choice Award and has appeared often on local and national TV, including *CBS Sunday Morning*. For TTQ offers, news and contests, visit tarataylorquinn.com!

Books by Tara Taylor Quinn

Harlequin Romantic Suspense

Sierra's Web

Tracking His Secret Child
Cold Case Sheriff
The Bounty Hunter's Baby Search
On the Run with His Bodyguard
Not Without Her Child
A Firefighter's Hidden Truth
Last Chance Investigation
Danger on the River
Deadly Mountain Rescue
A High-Stakes Reunion
Baby in Jeopardy
Her Sister's Murder
Mistaken Identities

The Coltons of Owl Creek

Colton Threat Unleashed

Visit the Author Profile page
at millsandboon.com.au for more titles.

Dear Reader,

Would you pretend to be someone you aren't for good reason? The question came to me, and the answer was a no-brainer. Of course. But what if you start to care for someone while you're busy doing good by pretending to be someone you aren't?

And multiply that by two.

Savannah and Isaac are good people on different missions. One prompted by love. The other by a career bringing down bad people. Both are dedicated, respected in their fields. And one of them is wrong. Or they both are.

I didn't know how this book was going to end until they took me on their journey and we got there. It was so worth the trip! I hope you'll let them take you along, too. They're very much worth the time. And they might leave you with some deeper thoughts about life, too.

Another little tidbit—while this book is a complete stand-alone story all on its own, if it leaves you wanting more, you have options! *Mistaken Identities* is part of the Sierra's Web series, *and* there's a direct sequel to this story, too.

I'd love to hear what you think. You can find me on socials or at tarataylorquinn.com.

Tara Taylor Quinn

For my two siblings, the one I lost and the
one I am so lucky to spend my life knowing.
Chum, you are always loved and never forgotten.
Scott, I cherish every single memory we make.
I love you, little brother.

Chapter One

Anxiety slid through her like a snake. One Savannah Compton mentally beheaded as she neared the airport turnoff. She watched her rearview mirror as much to find a clear path to get over as to remind herself that the make and model of the black sedan that had kept distance with her since she'd left the Grand Rapids neighborhood was as common as they came.

And the woman behind the wheel bore no resemblance to the driver of the blue SUV that she'd thought she'd seen a few times the day before.

Being a partner in a nationally renowned firm of experts that spent a lot of time fighting crime took its toll. One she'd handled without a blip until her partner and friend, Dorian Lowell, had been kidnapped the year before. The medical expert had been found unharmed and had come through harrowing days lost in the mountains, running from high-powered killers, managing to keep a newborn baby safe the whole time.

But that kidnapping...plus, just months before—Dorian being taken off her normal hiking trail, just around the corner from her home, to be found days later unharmed. Savannah still had moments of residual stress.

Mostly when she felt her most vulnerable, emotionally alone, as she did pulling into the Grand Rapids, Michigan, airport on her way to San Diego, California.

Not back to the Sierra's Web home office in Phoenix, where she'd spend a day or two with the friends who'd become her only family. Or on to another job. Her norm.

No, she—savvy, smart, sophisticated expert lawyer that she was—had decided to fly off willy-nilly into an abyss layered in darkness. Beneath the glaring California sun.

Alone.

Kelly Chase, the firm's expert psychiatrist, had official names for the butterflies that swarmed Savannah's stomach when she let herself think about certain things.

Or when she imagined she was being followed.

And if Kelly had been with her right then—or even knew what she was about to do—her friend would most definitely understand the slight presence of paranoia continuing to ride on Savannah's shoulders as she dropped off her rental car and headed into the terminal.

Certain that the black sedan had been at the rental return two down from her.

After Dorian's kidnapping, all seven of the Sierra's Web partners had reached a mutual agreement to undergo training for things like noticing tails and awareness of their surroundings in general. They'd pledged to visit the gun range on a regular basis, too. Savannah had been first to vote. To sign up. And to master the course.

And the whole thing had made her afraid of her own shadow sometimes.

Thankfully not all that often. She had it under control. Went days or even weeks without a single moment of anxious discomfort.

But when she was out of her comfort zone…

The airport wasn't the problem. She flew almost as often as she drove. Once inside, Savannah dropped off her bag, headed through her priority security line, and stopped for a glass of wine before heading to her gate. Without once looking over her shoulder.

Where she was headed, what she was about to do wasn't the most logical choice she'd ever made. Far from it.

She remembered backward two and a half decades, to the

murder and kidnapping that had changed everything—a terror Dorian's much more recent abduction had brought back full force.

It didn't take an expert psychiatrist or even an expert lawyer to figure out that moments of anxiety were to be expected and dealt with accordingly.

Maybe all it took was an acknowledgment of the seven-year-old girl she'd once been, who still lived inside her. The one who'd held on to what was, refusing to let go while moving forward with absolute focus, one step at a time.

Fear wouldn't win. It wouldn't rob her of joy. Of life.

Or of the chance to see her baby sister again.

No matter how big the two of them had grown.

The timing wasn't up to her.

The determination, the refusal to quit, the never-ending search...those had been within her control. Choices she'd made. They were part of the person she'd become that day so long ago.

And why there was no choice but to board the plane when her flight was called, in spite of her tension, then buckle herself in.

And wait.

"Seriously, Isaac. I've been doing these guest lectures since way before you came on board. There's no reason for you to tag along..."

Behind the wheel of the black limousine in which they were traveling, undercover FBI special agent Isaac Forrester figured himself as the driver of the situation, not the follower, but sent the beautiful, soft-spoken, wise-beyond-her-years suspect a shrug and easy smile. "Much less inconvenient standing in the wings hearing about women's studies than appearing in front of your father to explain why I wasn't standing in the wings," he said to her.

"Daddy doesn't have to know."

But somehow the older man would—know, that was. Every movement his daughter made. And, more recently, every movement her bodyguard made as well.

He'd suspect his cover had been blown. Except that there was no way the powerful businessman would leave Isaac alone with his precious Charlotte, let alone charge him with keeping her safe, if Eduardo Duran had even a hint of an inkling that Isaac wasn't who he said he was.

But to that end, he didn't have a second to waste. He'd been in Duran's employ as personal protection director and lead personal guard for Duran's only child since late fall—a long two months—and could feasibly continue on far into the spring. But he had no intention of being that bad at his job. He'd spent nearly a year in and around the transplanted Salvadoran, building trust, laying groundwork so that when Duran's previous personal protection director had suddenly had to leave his post, Isaac had been the obvious choice to step in.

"Please, Isaac?"

Stopped at a light, Isaac turned to see Charlotte's big brown eyes staring at him with more than just a casual desire to not have her bodyguard attached to her back during the morning's university lecture.

Every nerve in his body shot to attention, every muscle honed, as, light turning green, he pulled into a small cul-de-sac not far from their destination. And pinned his charge with a look most often reserved for the interrogation room.

To her credit, Charlotte didn't look away. Or even seem to blink. Her long dark hair pulled into its usual bun gave her unlined face no cover.

And as hard as he looked, he saw no subterfuge there.

They had proof that the woman's unique coding signature had been used on a suspicious bank transfer from a US investment group to an untraceable source outside the states.

With three doctorate degrees at twenty-five, one of which was in information technology, Charlotte had already made a name for herself in the field with a program she'd written to help monitor generative AI use and inconsistencies.

She swore, though, that she had no interest in a career in technology. Her true love was ethnography and autoethnography—or, as she put it when breaking it down in her lectures to undergrads, studying individual cultures and how women's personal experiences connected with a global picture of social meanings and understandings.

Studies that were mostly above his pay grade. Or typical intellectual pursuits, at the very least.

Isaac's brain didn't trust anything Charlotte Duran said. His gut, though... When she met his gaze so sincerely, she reminded him of the little sister who'd once adored him.

And had grown to hate him.

"Tell me what's really going on," he said. They were early for her lecture. Early everywhere, always, so he had a chance to check out the surroundings to his satisfaction.

She knew he'd take the time to sit there until she grew nervous about being late and opted to talk.

And could be, in that very second, concocting some smoke screen to distract him.

"I plan to feel really sick right as the event is starting— something I ate—and slip out the side door before anyone in the audience is aware that the lecture is about to be canceled."

She was telling him she was going to ditch him, whether he liked it or not? The woman was scary smart. Intelligent enough to know that he was far better at, and more knowledgeable of, his game than she'd ever be. That he had skills she didn't even know about.

Which told him that it wasn't him she was running from.

Or...that was what she wanted him to think she was telling him.

"And you were going to go where? To do what?" he asked. Curious, engaged in her determination in spite of himself.

She continued to hold his gaze as she told him, "I was going to wait in the women's restroom in the lobby of the dormitory half a block away and make my way back to the auditorium in time to meet up with you and catch my ride home."

"To what end?" He had to know.

He *wanted* to know, too. Two months living in the woman's back pocket and he still didn't have a workable profile of her.

He hadn't found an iota of hold-up-in-court evidence to arrest her and, through her, bring down one of the largest international criminals around. Eduardo Duran had ties to everything from arms dealing and illegal art sales to large-scale shipping thefts.

"Arnold Wagar is going to be there."

Another name on Isaac's list. He forced himself to continue to appear relaxed as he tuned in with every sense he had.

"To report on your lecture to your father?" He didn't for one second think that was the reason. But because he had no idea why on earth a banker who had ties to a high-profile, disgustingly wealthy international criminal would be at a women's studies lecture, he played ignorant. Hoping to find out.

"No. To see me."

Ah. Forcing his breathing to remain normal, Isaac fought the urge to grab the woman's hand and try to convince her that if she came clean, he could help her.

No way he was risking his cover. Not without the ability to guarantee her father would be locked away for the rest of his life.

Nor was he in the habit of making promises he didn't intend to keep.

"My father told me last night that he expects me to marry the man," Charlotte said, her brown eyes seeming to darken further as she slowly shook her head. "I'd do almost anything for my father, Isaac," she said then, her voice not quite breaking but sounding like it might at any second. "My whole life, it's been just him and me." Her gaze implored him to understand.

He wasn't sure if she was honestly seeking to have him see the relationship or hoping that he'd agree not to see things that could hurt her beautiful life.

"He was always there for me. Always. Every Christmas he spent with me. Whether at home or traveling, we were together. There was always a tree. And he always managed to get me the one thing I wanted more than anything but hadn't mentioned. When he was in town, we ate together, at least one meal a day. And when he was gone, no matter how important his meetings, even with heads of states, he called me every morning and every night." She barely took a breath as she continued to unload on Isaac, who didn't take his eyes off her. "I got my first doctorate degree in technology because that was what he wanted," she said then, stabbing at Isaac with another piece of the proof that showed him the truth of what so many knew—without giving him tangible evidence to take to court.

Duran had been one of the first to use Bitcoin, a highly technological form of payment, and had grown even wealthier from the intricate tunnels of virtually untraceable means he'd used to amass his fortune there.

Untraceable unless, say, the daughter who'd devised them gave them up.

"I've agreed to live at home, for my supposed safety and his peace of mind, even though I'm technically free to move out at any time. And agreed to a bodyguard when Daddy explained that he'd rest much easier if I'd do that for him. I do most of my various work projects online, as I did a lot of my schooling as well, also for security purposes. And I let his people—you now—vet the few real friends I have before inviting them into our midst. I have never once even tried to sneak out to party. I don't do drugs. And the few times I've actually liked a guy enough and he liked me enough to put up with my father's overbearing protectiveness, I always insisted on condoms during sex..."

TMI. Issaac almost looked away at that one. Thankfully his nearly forty years, and two decades of police work, had prepared him to keep a steady expression no matter what he heard.

"But this..." Charlotte's gaze was definitely moist when she paused, wringing her hands for a second before clasping them together. "I will not marry a man I don't love," she said. "Not even for Daddy. I don't care how decent and kind and rich he is. I don't even care that he adores me. The thought of Arnold Wagar's hands on me makes my skin crawl. The man's practically old enough to be my father." Wagar was only four years older than Isaac's thirty-seven, but who was counting?

"And besides—" Charlotte finally looked away, her gaze pointing out the front windshield "—I'm not even sure I want to *get* married," she spoke into the silence of the car, surprising Isaac. "I'm beginning to realize that I've been under Daddy's thumb for so long, I'm not ever sure I know what *I* want."

In the two months he'd been walking practically hand in hand with the only Duran offspring, he'd never seen her show a moment of doubt. Of weakness. Or vulnerability.

She was sass and teasing and brimming over with confidence. The perfectly well-adjusted child of a very bad man.

A man Isaac had yet to be able to arrest.

He'd found a lot of substantive evidence that he and his team were on the right track. As had other teams before them, both foreign and domestic, including the CIA. But now that Duran was a US citizen and a very important piece of forensic work had pinpointed Charlotte's technological coding signature, Isaac had been charged with doing what no others before him, including Salvadoran compatriots, had been able to do.

Bring down an international nightmare.

Even if it meant taking the precocious twenty-five-year-old genius down with him.

Having graduated with a law degree at twenty-two, Savannah was used to relying on her mind for all important learning. She was a critical thinker. Made decisions based on logic, not emotion. But when she heard the announcement that the nonstop flight she was on from Michigan to San Diego was suddenly making an unscheduled landing at the Denver airport, she nearly allowed her fear to convince her to cancel her secret plans.

What was she thinking? Flying off to San Diego without a word to anyone? Lying to her best friends, who were the only family she had, about taking a long overdue vacation to cruise the Bahamas in an expensive suite for which she'd paid months before—and that was currently sailing empty on a very large ship filled with revelers. Her would-be vacation mates.

But while ordinarily the lie would have been a shock to her system, in the one instance before her, it was not. From the age of seven, she'd lived with one particular lie. A matter of life and death, as proven by her father's murder.

A lie put upon her by the people who little-girls-whose-fathers-had-died were taught to trust above all others. Her mother. And the police.

National statistics, she'd been told, understanding even then what that meant, showed that in the history of witness protection not one person who followed all guidelines was breached. They were all safe. She and her mother and sister—in absentia—were in the program for being associated with a witness on a case, but her father had been a witness. And he'd broken protocol to stop by Nicole's daycare and tell the one-year-old goodbye...

She thought that the flight was perhaps landing to tend to someone with an emergency. Though, looking around her, she couldn't see anyone in distress—nor had the attendants made any announcement about a medical emergency. Normally they would call for any medical personnel on the flight who could possibly assist until the plane was on the ground. Savannah was fully engaged in talking down her own paranoia by the time the wheels actually did touch down.

"Ladies and gentlemen, we need to ask all of you to leave your belongings and deboard the plane as efficiently as possible, starting with row one." As soon as she heard the steward's voice, Savannah pulled her purse onto her shoulder and reached for her phone, finger on Kelly Chase's speed dial icon. Just in case.

In the event she had a full-blown panic attack and needed her friend's expert advice.

Or...more likely...there'd been some kind of report of a bomb or other dangerous material on the plane. Sierra's Web would be able to access accurate information within minutes, which would put a stop to Savannah's over-the-top anxiety.

She never should have lied to her partners.

But how could she tell them that she'd had a hit on her own familial DNA, submitted under an assumed name and a fake email, which indicated a sibling match. She couldn't confess without possibly putting herself, her partners or, just as bad, her sister in harm's way.

Until she knew that Nicole was safe—hopefully having been sold in a black-market kidnapping to a desperate but loving couple who'd tried every other way to have a child—Savannah couldn't let anyone know who she was. Or who Nicole was, either, for that matter.

Witness protection protocol, and the best hope of keeping them both safe, demanded it.

Which meant when she got to San Diego, she couldn't approach her sister. Or even let it be known that she knew who Nicole—going by the name of Charlotte Duran—was.

All passengers had been led to an empty gate area at the far end of the terminal. There were bathrooms just across the hall for their use. They were instructed not to leave the area or risk missing what was expected to be a very quick reboard process.

Phone still in hand, Savannah took a seat along the back wall. She needed to be able to see any and everything that might be taking place among the members of her flight—crew and passengers alike.

Were any of them suspicious looking?

Or watching her suspiciously?

Had there been a bomb scare? That's why no one had been allowed to bring their carry-on luggage?

A man about her age, dressed casually in shorts and a button-down shirt, sat across and down from her, turning to the woman next to him—his wife, Savannah surmised, based on the identical wedding rings—and proceeded to spend the next full minute or more detailing a fairly complicated plot devised by someone to steal all of the valuables from the bags the passengers had been ordered to leave behind. The tale grew so far-fetched, and yet television worthy, with every counterpoint his wife brought up to his suppositions that Savannah might have been distracted from her own uneasiness long enough to rediscover her calm. If not for the two uniformed law enforcement officers she'd noticed taking away first one and then another of her fellow fliers.

Had they been surly looking characters, she might have felt relieved—safer, even. But so far the four parties she'd seen led away had been an elderly gentleman with a cane, a woman with two little children, a guy in professional dress who looked to be in his twenties, and one of the flight crew. None of them had returned.

Two middle-aged women, obviously traveling together, were approached by one of the officers.

Had all the people being carted off come from some other airport, just transferring planes in Grand Rapids? Could be there was a problem with transferred luggage. They all had to have something in common. Maybe they'd already been on the plane when she and the others in Grand Rapids had boarded…

"Miss, can you come with me, please?" Savannah's head

swung toward the deep voice. She'd been so stuck on the two women being escorted away to her right that she'd missed the officer coming up her aisle on the left.

"Me?" she asked, heart pounding, phone in hand. She didn't know any of those people. Hadn't done anything.

Except be the recipient of a report from a public DNA family-finder source. And then use a public computer in Grand Rapids, logged in only as an anonymous guest, to look up the address that the donor had permitted to be given only to a close familial match.

She stood when the officer stopped in front of her, waiting, and followed him down the terminal to a smaller hallway.

Savannah hadn't made the choice to have her information known to anyone when she'd submitted her DNA. No way. After more than a decade with Sierra's Web and in courts all around the country, she knew far too much about the criminal portion of the world to put her information out into the ether. She'd submitted anonymously.

Had checked the database without any expectation of finding something. Had done so just to rule out the possibility, so she'd quit thinking about it.

A little work from there had gained her the rest. Only because this person, a woman who called herself Charlotte Duran, had permitted her information to be shared.

Savannah had discovered that the woman's father was a successful businessman with a conglomerate of companies he'd amassed through buyouts over the years.

"I haven't done anything wrong," she said the second she was shown into a small room with a table and chairs and asked to take a seat.

She didn't sit. "I'm a lawyer," she said next, keeping the understatement in that message to herself. "And don't intend to say anything until I call my own attorney."

It wasn't like her to start out on the defense. At all. The reminder came a little late. Still, she paid it heed. If she'd somehow triggered something to someone from a quarter-of-a-century-old murder just by looking up an address she'd been given, she had to be at the top of her game.

Not losing it.

On the other hand, if there'd been a bomb scare—or any other type of threat, for that matter—she and her firm of experts might be able to help.

Savannah took a seat at the table.

Chapter Two

Isaac wasn't at all surprised when he got a summons to report to Eduardo Duran's home office. He'd made an executive decision that morning, doing the job he'd set out for himself—to build trust with the daughter to get to the father. He'd taken Charlotte to the lecture and had whisked her offstage immediately afterward, citing a potential safety risk, getting her to the car and heading off the lot before Arnold Wagar had had a chance to get out of the audience and out to his car.

And he'd ordered her not to answer her phone. That one had been a no-brainer. Her father had told her, explicitly, to do whatever Isaac said to do. Charlotte was off the hook.

Isaac had, in one small move, won more of the young woman's loyalty than he'd been able to gain in more than two months of guarding her every move.

Facing the wrath of a man he despised was a small price to pay for the large step toward putting a man he believed to be a cold-blooded killer, among other heinous crimes, away for life.

Isaac had seen names on accounts that all disappeared into the same ether. Had recognized one of them as a hired assassin.

He stood ready to give a detailed account of the bogus threat he'd supposedly seen in the theater that morning because he couldn't use the true threat—a forty-year-old man buying his way into illegal wealth while sacrificing a young genius. He waited in front of Duran's impressively large solid-wood desk, in his standard black pants and jacket, hands on top of one another at his beltline. His gun was invisible beneath the suit coat but fully accessible to Isaac.

A position of docility and readiness at the same time.

The older man, in his usual suit and tie—blue that afternoon—remained seated and, with a nod, dismissed his own protection detail. Isaac caught a hint of the steps of two of the men he—as head of protection detail—managed, on the soft carpet behind him. And heard the heavy pine door close with an authoritative click.

So it was going to be personal.

And Isaac had some kissing up to do. He couldn't afford to lose the job. It wasn't like his little trust-building exercise that morning was going to bring Charlotte Duran running in to confess all of her and "Daddy's" illegal deeds once Isaac was back at his Washington, DC, office.

"Have a seat," Duran said, his tone all business but...more respectful than Isaac had expected. With no obvious hint of animosity in verbiage, delivery or even body language. The man nodded toward one of the two oversized wooden chairs on either side of where Isaac stood.

Bracing himself for the unexpected, not relaxing his guard even a little bit, Isaac sat. Elbows on the arms of the chair, hands on his thighs.

"I have reason to believe that someone is poking around in my daughter's business," the man started in, and Isaac nodded, remaining silent out of seeming respect. Waiting to hear what the man had to say.

While trying to guess how Duran was going to bring the conversation around to Wagar. And, more, how he'd attempt to manipulate Isaac's support in his plan to see his daughter married to the man of his choice.

The latter was most important to Isaac. He'd be skating a slippery slope. To hold on to his job—and his cover—with the man who was, for all intent and purposes, his boss, he'd have to agree to Duran's mandates. And to continue to build the loyalty that was his surest bet of doing his job and making the world a safer place, he had to protect Charlotte from the unwanted attention.

"I'm a powerful man." Duran's tone had grown darker.

A reminder issued.

"This gives me the ability to provide my only offspring with the best of the best. But it also makes her vulnerable to any number of evils lurking in this world."

A pot calling the kettle black, if ever Isaac had heard one. He had no trouble maintaining his facade. He'd faced more than his share of wealthy, powerful despicable men in his decorated career. Including a politician who'd greased a lot of homegrown hands, but ones in other worlds as well, before Isaac had been finally able to get evidence that the man couldn't buy his way out of. His compatriots had come swarming like flies to testify against him rather than be caught in his web.

"My intel says that a client of a woman is looking to prove that my Charlotte has a biological relative here in the States. This woman, Savannah Compton, is a lawyer, a partner in a firm of experts out of Phoenix—Sierra's Web. Further investigation shows that the firm has worked with various law enforcement agencies around the country, including the FBI..."

Isaac's outward demeanor didn't change. But he was suddenly thankful for the jacket, which hid the fact that he was sweating. Wagar out; nationally renowned firm of experts in.

He'd never personally worked with Sierra's Web, but he'd certainly heard of them. And had to call his superior immediately to warn the firm away from the Durans lest they lose over a year of work and create untold future risk to national security.

A call he couldn't make while maintaining the cover that would allow him to prevent, or at least greatly lessen, that risk.

Which made it a hell of a lot harder to sit there. One client out to scam a wealthy man versus arms dealing? He'd get the firm off Duran's back.

And maybe win himself a gold medal or two with the older man.

"I had a law enforcement friend of mine call the firm. They claim that Ms. Compton is on vacation. My friend talked to another one of the partners, someone she worked with personally, who swore that Savannah is not working a case for Sierra's Web."

So much for the phone call. "Did your...associate...believe that?"

"She did," Eduardo Duran said. "She worked a particularly tough child-abduction case with the firm and has an excellent rapport with them. She went on to say that this Savannah hasn't been herself in the past year or so, which is why the partners were all relieved when she booked the cruise."

A partner gone rogue. From burnout?

Or buyout?

Either way, while the woman posed a potential inconvenience to Isaac, she wasn't the problem he'd at first thought.

Rogue, he could handle.

Maybe even use to his advantage if the woman's supposed threat created a way for Isaac to get more access to Duran's day-to-day business dealings. He would need to be present during Charlotte Duran's classified conversations, for instance.

His mind spun with possibilities as he listened to the older man's theory that the expert lawyer was working a case outside the firm, probably because it had criminal overtones and she'd known the firm wouldn't agree to take it on.

"The phone call I received this morning indicated that this Compton woman's client is intending to mooch millions from me through Charlotte."

Millions. Even if the lawyer made just a quarter of that, it was one case, a week or two, that would pay Ms. Compton far more than she'd make in a year or two at the firm.

"I assume you're issuing a payoff with a stringent noncontact order and nondisclosure document attached to it..."

"I was going to. Changed my mind until I know more," Duran stated, but the furrow in his brow did not bode well. "I had an *interrogator* at the Denver airport this morning. Savannah Compton isn't on her way to board a cruise. She's on a flight to San Diego. One that had an impromptu layover in Denver. During which she claimed that she'd taken a short leave from her firm, and from her career, to vacation at the ocean."

"So your intel was wrong." Which led Isaac to wonder why

he was taking part in this conversation. What did Duran really want from him?

How was he being manipulated?

And did the man own the entire country? Who had large enough clout to bring down a plane to question one passenger for his own personal business?

"No. My information was spot on," Duran said. "I had a search engine designed to pick up any search of this address and alert my team in real time when it happened. This time we got lucky enough to have a camera nearby," he finished, turning around a thirty-two-inch screen to show Isaac a grainy security-camera image of a woman in expensive-looking gray slacks and an orange sweater seated at a computer screen. Obviously, Isaac was to assume that the woman was Savannah Compton. A man like Duran would have verified that before bringing a lower-level employee like Isaac into his confidence.

When Duran enlarged the image, Isaac could see the Duran address, listed under Charlotte's name, in the search field.

"Charlotte owns this place?" Isaac's question was probably not the first one he should have asked.

"I have right of occupation for life," Duran told him, sliding his screen back around. "I moved her here when she was in her teens. She had dual citizenship as her mother was American born and traveled back and forth between the States and our home in El Salvador to take care of the elderly grandparents who raised her. Charlotte favored her mother in looks and had always yearned to live in California. When she turned eighteen, she sponsored my own citizenship."

That part Isaac had known.

"And what about her mother?" While he had no idea why Duran was being so uncharacteristically forthcoming and had his guard up, with full sensory reinforcements, he couldn't waste the chance to learn more.

Every fact, no matter how seemingly insignificant, had a place in the puzzle. One tiny piece could join everything else together. Or be the glue that held things in place so the entire picture could be seen.

"Amy died in childbirth, God rest her soul. She was such a beautiful, loving, gentle woman…"

For a second there, Isaac stared. The genuine grief on Duran's face shocked him. Until he reminded himself that the man was so successful because there were parts of him that were truly likeable. Authentic.

Proven by the millions he gave to children's charities every year.

And the way he doted on his daughter.

Never missing a Christmas…

"Her grandparents both passed within a year of Charlotte's birth, and Amelia had no other family," Duran said then, his demeanor returning to the hard, businesslike persona with which Isaac was most familiar. "Both of her parents were only children and were killed in a car accident when Amy was ten. So, you see, there's no way my daughter could possibly have a close biological family member. This is an attempt to get to her, convince her that her heart's desire to have family on her mother's side is coming to fruition, to worm their way in to my fortune through her."

"So why not get more from this morning's questioning?"

"When my contact called, relaying what was going on during the airport meeting, I had them let the Compton woman go. She's not going to be truthful. Which means we're going to have to let her get close enough to figure out who she's working for and what their game plan might be."

And that was where he came in. The point of the meeting became clear. "How close do you want me to let her get to Charlotte?"

"I don't want her anywhere near my daughter."

The man would have someone else dealing with the Compton woman, he translated.

"Am I to approach her if she's in our vicinity?"

Duran stared him the eye. Isaac held on with no effort at all. "I leave that to you," the boss said with a nod. "I'm trusting you with my daughter's life. And I trust you to handle this threat to it, if the occasion arises."

Isaac nodded back. Discussed a couple of minor details with

the man regarding what Charlotte was to know about the situation—nothing at all.

And then took his leave, with the man's last words of trust still ringing in his ears. If he'd heard correctly, and he had no doubts that he had, Eduardo Duran had just ordered him to kill Savannah Compton if the need arose.

Another piece of information that fit perfectly into Isaac's portfolio on the criminal.

Added to all the others that would never stand up in court.

Savannah had no idea what law enforcement had really been after in Denver. Bomb scare. Terrorist on board. Or something as simple as a suspected stowaway. What she did know was that as soon as she'd identified herself and her position within Sierra's Web, she'd become one of them.

As much as one could be from the outside looking in.

Sierra's Web had worked with the Denver FBI office. And probably the local police as well. They were known. And as soon as she'd let them know she was on vacation, heading to the ocean for some much-needed R & R, they'd let her go.

Maybe if she'd said she was working, they'd have filled her in more. As it was, she took the Denver stop as a mental note to self to get herself in check.

Just because she was going to try to see her baby sister, to ensure, if nothing else, that Nicole—using the fake name of Charlotte in the DNA database—was well and happy didn't mean that she was opening an old, very dangerous, can of worms.

If she contacted the woman personally, maybe. Attempted to speak with her, even, possibly. Which was why she didn't intend to do either of the two.

She was keeping it smart. Following the rules that had long ago been embedded into her. Being safe.

She'd overreacted. And was done with that.

She was going to San Diego knowing full well that she would absolutely never be able to tell her little sister who she was or let Nicole know where she'd come from, what had happened to their family.

But for her own peace of mind, her own broken heart, and

for her mother, too, she had to make sure that the tiny little love they'd lost had grown up healthy, happy, and was living a good life.

Just knowing, finally, that she was alive and well...

Then maybe, just maybe, she'd be ready to move forward with her own life. Five of the seven of her best friends and partners had all found love over the past couple of years. They were starting families of their own.

Even Dorian.

Yet Savannah felt no closer at all to opening her heart to more than their enduring friendship. It was like she was still caught up in post-college euphoria, unable to live more deeply, while they were all growing up without her.

And just as she was feeling her own lapse, becoming aware that she might be stagnating, possibly missing out on the best part of life, she got a DNA hit on the Family Finders website? It had to be more than just a coincidence.

More like providence—or her mother—hitting her over the head with her need to get moving into her future.

That apparently meant letting go of the past.

Seeing Nicole, knowing she was well and happy, might be the only chance she'd ever have to be able to do that.

To that end, Savannah ignored the irritating sense of foreboding, of being watched as she waited in baggage claim in San Diego for her travel bag and then loaded it into her rental car. She refused to give rein to the thought that someone was staying behind her on the road as she followed prompts from the car's mapping system to the address she'd typed in. Only watched her rearview mirror for lane changes and safe-driving protocol.

She was doing something just for her. Finally taking care of herself. The mission was a healthy one. And she was not going to let life's past occurrences steal the chance away from her.

And if, by chance, Nicole wasn't healthy and happy?

The doubt crept in. She shook her head at it, would not borrow trouble from a future that may never materialize. The present was right there. Being lived. She deserved the right to give it her all.

And when the present moment took her past the more than

ten acres of manicured lawn that bore the address she'd typed in, she slowed, took in all she could, peered anxiously for any sight of human habitation but didn't stop. She had no reason for being there.

It wasn't like one knocked on a ten-foot-high wrought-iron gate to sell something. Or schlep for charity.

But...wow.

She'd searched the address on a map site before she'd booked her flight to San Diego. The photo had shown a rural, albeit oceanfront, property with what looked like a small house behind a mass of trees.

Most definitely not the mansion in the distance that had to be worth millions.

Shaking her head in shock, she sped up as she left the property behind her, hardly able to take it all in.

Was the Family Finders entry some kind of cruel joke? Had someone hacked their system?

Had she just been fooled into thinking Nicole was actually alive and well?

Or unbelievable as it seemed...was that really Nicole's home? Had her baby sister landed in the lap of luxury? Maybe been adopted into a wealthy family?

Nicole was only twenty-five, but it was possible she'd invented something that made millions. Or married money.

Savannah drove by a few more times over the next hour, just looking. Hoping for some kind of sight of a young woman she'd instantly recognize as her sister. But she gained nothing but an increased sense of paranoia, to the point that the last time by, she was paying more attention to the car trailing behind her than to the grounds she was there to survey.

And let that fear drive her to seek out the closest hotel—a lovely beachfront property that reeked *luxury*—and get a one-bedroom suite with a balcony overlooking the ocean. On a floor high enough not to have any worries about someone breaching her space.

Savannah needed Hudson, their tech-expert partner, to do a deep dive for her, matching one of the many Charlotte Durans that had come up on her own somewhat-educated search of the name to the address she'd retrieved from the Family Finders secure match page. Hud and his team used a lot more than common search engines to ferret out information.

She couldn't call Hud. Couldn't call anyone.

This quest of hers…she was on her own.

Somewhat fitting, really, considering she was clawing her way out of a past no one knew about to find a future she couldn't see.

Chapter Three

The second Isaac finished his guard-duty shift, leaving Charlotte's safety in the very capable hands of her in-house protector, Emmajean Smith, he was out the door.

Emmajean, who slept in a room adjoining Charlotte's, was not a woman Isaac trusted with any confidences at all—she was wholly dedicated to Eduardo Duran—but he trusted her with Charlotte's life. The woman would die herself before letting any harm come to Charlotte.

And Charlotte, desperate to avoid any contact with a very determined Arnold Wagar, had claimed a migraine and retreated to her room late that afternoon. While Isaac felt a strong surge of sympathy for the young heiress where a potential forced marriage was concerned, he didn't like the idea of her spending hours at her computer doing God knew what while he had no access to find out.

Eduardo Duran had made one mandate quite clear to Isaac when he'd hired him on as personal protection director—unless the house was on fire or under attack, no male bodyguards were to have access to his daughter's personal suite while she was there.

At first, he'd thought the man had been protecting his daughter's virtue. Had found that to admire about him. He'd later figured out that the *stay away* order had come from Charlotte, as part of her agreement to remain living at home.

And with today's reveal that Charlotte owned the home, he was beginning to suspect the young woman more and more.

Eduardo Duran's daughter was not top of his mind, however, as he got in his undercover personal Range Rover and drove the short distance to La Hacienda—a five-star hotel not far from the Duran property. He'd been on the phone to his team in Washington the second he'd secured himself privately outside of Duran's office that afternoon.

Needing everything they could find on Savannah Compton.

They'd come up with surprisingly little. Other than the professional photo and bio on the Sierra's Web internet site, which Isaac had accessed himself with one quick search, they'd found almost no other information. Her address wasn't published—apparently something that Arizona law allowed in certain circumstances. None of the Sierra's Web partners, Savannah included, had any social media accounts discoverable by the FBI.

She had no police record. Not even a parking ticket.

He was the one who'd lucked into the only extremely valuable piece of information he had—the license plate of her rental car.

A simple search of the footage from the Duran estate's security cameras had shown him a new silver sedan driving slowly by the property multiple times that day. Clearly someone getting the lay of the land. The fact that it had been followed by a familiar-looking black sedan had been a pretty good clue as well. Duran's people were on her hard.

Getting the license plate off the footage had taken a quick request to the forensic lab in Washington, but his response came back with information from the rental car company, confirming the car's current renter to be Savannah Compton and, as a bonus, the name of the hotel the car had been registered at as well. He didn't ask questions on that one.

If Isaac hoped to learn anything about the Durans from the woman—perhaps gaining access to some elusive email address even, which could crack open the whole case—he had to act quickly. Duran hired the best of the best, and if he wanted the Compton woman gone, she would be.

He almost felt sorry for the expert lawyer, even if she *was* working for a scammer. As legends-long files filled with circumstantial evidence could attest, getting on Duran's bad side was most definitely not a good idea.

There was always the possibility that she didn't know that. Perhaps someone thinking they were related to the Durans through Charlotte's mother had hired her with legitimate intentions.

A second cousin, perhaps? There'd been no one biologically closer.

Could be a best friend, even. Someone who, as she aged, was thinking about the American-born-and-raised Amelia and, for her friend's sake or even her own, wanted to connect with Charlotte.

No matter the Compton woman's reason for allegedly flying to San Diego in a hunt for Charlotte Duran, Isaac had been given a very small window of what could be a huge lead. No way was he going to pass that by.

If Duran found out he was seeking out the woman he'd been told to stand down from—unless he had reason to kill her, of course—he'd handle his boss with a very quick and confident lie about some danger he'd thought the expert lawyer posed to Charlotte. And challenge Duran with a charge that he was tying his personal protection director's hands—in a way that he knew would have Duran giving him a bye on the indiscretion.

His current challenge was how to actually gain physical access to his person of interest. He was dressed in expensive but casual dark pants and a lightly striped gray button-down shirt as he parked his vehicle and walked into the lobby of the hotel.

Showing himself to her was risky. She'd recognize him if she ever actually got close enough to Charlotte to see him with her. But he had a plan there, too. He was at the hotel posing as a member of the local wealthy set—a businessman, into acquisitions, he figured. Enough like Eduardo to hopefully get her to ask questions about the area's most successful entrepreneur.

And later...he could be seen as a friend of Charlotte's. And her father's. At least that was how he intended to play it. If he did his job right, she'd never get close enough to Charlotte for an actual conversation to take place.

He'd been undercover for more than a year, bodyguard for a couple of months. What was one more character to keep track of?

The opulent, gold-plated lobby wasn't overly crowded. One glance around gave Isaac a comfortable sense of who was and wasn't there.

No Savannah Compton.

The second floor, a balcony of sorts, was open to the lobby below and was swarming with people. Happy hour was happening in the locally popular bar. He'd done his homework and intended to hang out there for a bit, have a glass of local beer, maybe avail himself of some of the freshly prepared hors d'oeuvres, while he got a real-life sense of his surroundings.

Had time to survey hotel staff and security measures.

And figure out who he could convince that he was Ms. Compton's fiancé and then charm into calling her downstairs so he could surprise her with his early return from deployment.

Still in her travel clothes, Savannah sat at a table for two in the corner of the busy open bar, sipped wine, and enjoyed being completely invisible to the throngs of people happying their way through the hour around her. She was completely alone—without being alone.

And was completely relaxed for the first time since she'd signed on to her Family Finders account to see that she had a biological match in the United States.

With her back to a brick wall, no one could be behind her, following her. She was surrounded by merriment.

And there was a very good-looking, well-dressed man riding up the escalator from the lobby. Dark hair, cut short enough but not too short, clothes that seemed made for his body, and… well…the best build she'd seen in…maybe ever. She acknowledged the thought with the caveat that she was on her second glass of wine. She wasn't going anywhere that night, except to her room. Eventually to bed.

No matter what her purpose for choosing San Diego was,

she was on vacation for the first time in years. Had left her Sierra's Web cell phone in the desk drawer of her office. Needed to "let go," as Kelly had put it.

Savannah's plan was to find a future. Enjoying a little eye candy seemed like a baby step to that end. Completely out of character, so that covered the *letting go* part.

Still, she'd have looked away, except that the man was alone and seemed more focused than ready to party. Like maybe he was meeting someone?

Curious, she watched to see who it was.

Until he disappeared behind the crowd before exiting the automated staircase and was lost from view.

Suddenly feeling lonely, Savannah thought about calling Kelly, just to check in. All her partners had her personal cell number. And all had made a pact not to contact her unless she 911'd them.

Nicole was definitely an emergency.

And the reason Savannah couldn't call any of them.

If they knew she wasn't on the cruise there'd be questions. She'd have six experts needing to know why. Ones who'd all failed to follow up with a friend in college who'd been struggling. Sweet Sierra. Who'd died in part because her friends hadn't been adamant enough about getting answers from her.

None of the partners were going to make that mistake a second time. They'd solemnly sworn the promise to each other the day they'd opened their firm.

And there was no way she could have a nationally renowned firm famous for uncovering hard-to-find answers, getting even a hint that one of them had a secret, scary past.

If someone stumbled back too far…

No.

Savannah's little trip to San Diego was going to be buried like the rest of her childhood secrets. If she was successful, maybe the "vacation" would actually be a coffin in which her past would finally be laid to rest, once and for all.

"Mind if I sit here?"

So startled out of her intense self-reverie that she sloshed wine over the side of her glass, Savannah had to do a double take when she saw the owner of the charming masculine voice. Her candy from the escalator.

Providence again?

Giving her a push out of the stagnant bubble in which she'd been living all of her life?

Or maybe even just a weirdly timed distraction to get her through a minute or two?

"This isn't a come-on, I swear," the man continued, his dark eyes seeming to wrap her in a quiet sincerity in the loudly happening room. "You just seem to be...quietly enjoying that glass of wine...and after the day I've had, I'm finding little energy to stand at the bar and make idle conversation."

Ready to smile and probably nod, Savannah's response was cut off as the man kept talking. "Not that you aren't...well... worthy of a come-on... Oh, God, you're waiting for..."

"No!" Savannah blurted before the man could dig himself into such an awkward hole that he bolted. "I'm not. And please, sit. I'd rather not look as though I'm waiting for..." She let her words trail off as his had.

And sipped from her glass as he ordered some craft beer and appetizers, feeling a smile blooming inside her as he asked her preference and included her in his order. She'd been going to get her own to take up to the room. "It's the least I can do," the man said, waving at the table as the waiter left. "Since you've taken pity on me."

He smiled. She smiled back. Without any inner voice warning her to stop. To be careful. To look behind her.

"My name's Isaac, by the way," the man said, holding out his hand. "I live close by, work in acquisitions."

She took the proffered palm, tingling at the warmth that shot through her at the contact. "I'm Savannah."

And I'm so far from any sense of home I don't know that I'll ever find my way back.

Isaac got nothing from the encounter except an unsolicited and completely unprofessional jolt to the groin. He was working, undercover, playing a part, and human.

Savannah Compton—not that she offered her last name at all

during the next hour they spent together—looked him straight in the eye, unwavering, as she'd told him that she was in San Diego on vacation. Planning to enjoy the ocean, the beach, and soak up San Diego's year-round sunshine and balmy temperatures.

She was engaging, seemingly relaxed, as though she hadn't a care in the world. And emitted a husky laugh enough times that it got to him.

In a purely male way.

When she switched from the water she'd opted for while they'd eaten back to a fresh glass of wine, he nursed his second beer—in spite of warnings to himself that one hour of her time had taken its toll on him.

It had been a long time since he'd been alone with a woman socially, who didn't know what he did for a living. One who seemed to be enjoying his company in a completely nonprofessional sense. His choice, that.

And maybe not his best one. Clearly he needed to get out more. And needed to extricate himself from the unintentional consequences of the situation he'd created.

He stayed because he couldn't get up and go away with nothing. He wasn't made that way.

And he hadn't yet figured out why he was failing. The woman appeared to be beating him at his own game. Playing a part, giving up nothing.

Did she know he worked for the Durans?

Was she somehow gleaning something about them through him?

He almost always managed to get seemingly innocuous information out of those he interviewed and have it be exactly what he'd needed from them.

The fact that she had him questioning himself intrigued him almost as much as it irked him.

Playing to his plan, he went into more detail about what he did for a living. Using a tactic of *give some to get some*. He didn't get any. Even when he point-blank asked what she did for a living.

"Right now, I'm on leave from doing anything," she told him with one of those distracting chuckles.

She told him she traveled a lot. Didn't specify that it was for the job.

He talked about college, allowed that he'd gone to the University of Michigan. And she countered with the fact that she'd made a lot of good friends in college.

She asked him nothing. Not where he'd grown up. How long he'd been in San Diego. Nothing that he could capitalize on with turnabout being fair play.

"Did you graduate?" he asked her then. He had not. He'd been at wits' end with his little sister, Mollie, seeing the trouble she'd been heading toward, and had entered the police academy instead. And then the DC police, until he'd made enough of a name for himself.

By bringing down a major dealer.

And sending his baby sister to jail for a stint, too.

Then he'd gone back for his degree in criminal justice and joined the FBI.

"I did," Savannah nodded, her words coming slowly, counter to his racing thoughts. Her brown eyes pools of pleasure, glinting with the lowered lights. Happy hour had ended. Tables were filled around them, but with couples, or parties of three and four, conversing quietly among themselves.

When the toe of her shoe lightly brushed the side of his calf, he told himself the touch was accidental.

And wished it hadn't been. Would have liked to have been able to transport himself to another world where he could have capitalized on the mistake by rubbing her back. Maybe taking her hand.

"You ever been married?" The question was not work related. In any way.

She shook her head. "No." The answer came immediately. With maybe a hint of regret?

A real reaction? One he could file as information that might fit together with something else that could come to mean something?

Had there been someone?

Could be who she was working for? An old love come back to haunt her?

"You?" she asked, her first direct question of him.

He shook his head. Looked her in the eye as he delivered a real truth that also fit his cover. "I'm married to my job."

He'd done the family thing. Had messed it up royally.

The job he got right. And to that end... "What did you study?"

She shrugged. "I bounced around."

She'd glanced at her wine. The first sign that she was hiding. Reinvigorated, feeling more like himself, Isaac asked, "What's your degree in?"

He knew the answer to that one. Waited to see if she'd tell him the truth. Or how she'd lie. Either way, she'd be telling him something useful to his professional profile of her.

"Various things."

He leaned in. Moved his hand a little closer to hers. And then, feeling slightly skanky, slid it back to his glass, taking a sip to cover the slip. "Like what?"

Savannah shook her head. Sipped her wine and covered his hand with hers. "You really want to sit here and talk about classes I took more than a decade ago?"

So he could deduce that she was in her early thirties. Something he already knew. Sierra's Web had formed shortly after they'd all graduated from college. Isaac started to sweat as he forced his mind to stay on task—and off the feel of those soft fingers on top of his hand.

He glanced up at her for a deductive assessment and got caught by those brown eyes, grabbing his as though he was some kind of lifeline. And heard himself practically groan out a solid truth. "What I really want to do right now, I can't," he told her. "Something tells me you aren't the kind of woman who hooks up for a one-night stand, and I'm not the kind of guy who takes advantage of any woman."

Not in a sexual sense.

Her gaze didn't waver. Nor did she appear the least bit embarrassed. "What if I want to be that kind of woman?" she asked him. "Just once. Maybe not a one-night stand, but a fling? You know, the fling I met on vacation?"

He couldn't help but smile. The woman had enough confidence to take a rejection and turn it into a proposition. He liked that. In any other situation, he'd have been all over it.

Until it hit him. She was working him to get to Charlotte. She knew who he was.

Was using the oldest trick in the book to get her "in."

Sex.

He'd just been played for a fool.

And while he kept the smile in place, played along with her, he made a very clear, though silent, promise to himself and to her.

It wouldn't happen again.

Chapter Four

She wasn't going to see him again. Savannah knew when she and Isaac left the bar together—parting at the escalator that would take him downstairs, across from the elevator that would take her up—that their agreement was to leave any future association up to fate. Rather than exchanging contact information, they made a choice designed to say a forever goodbye.

They'd determined in the midst of flirtatious smiles that if they were meant to have a fling, they'd run into each other again.

She almost hoped she could see him one more time. Just to thank him for being a truly decent guy. Not accepting her very out-of-character invitation, but rather choosing to be a friend. Just sitting with her through a couple of lost hours.

Almost hoped, but not quite. That impromptu break with him had been a godsend. She'd been feeling so adrift. Alone and unfound.

But the wine, the shared food, the intriguing conversation had somehow cleared her mind. Shown her the path that was awaiting her.

The trail to her freedom, her future.

And by noon the next day, she was executing the plan. She'd been on hold since she'd been seven years old, had lost her father and had her baby sister snatched out of her life. Had been wasting away in the chasm of not knowing.

But no more. The decades-long efforts and prayers she'd been putting out into the universe had borne fruit. She had a name. An address. All she needed was to see Nicole. To replace the image of the one-year-old little dark-haired baby holding her arms out to her with that of a healthy and thriving twenty-five-year-old woman doing just fine without her. Then Savannah would be free to move forward into a future that could possibly include a house she lived in with family that lived there with her.

And the damned dark ghosts that her mind kept telling her were behind her, watching her, following her would become mere cars on the road again.

Since driving by the front of a massive estate wasn't likely to give her a sister sighting, Savannah had decided to try to get her glimpse of Nicole from a vantage point that allowed her to hang around as long as she liked, without fear of being followed or noticed. One that, with the newly purchased high-end, high-tech binoculars at her side, would allow the close-up view she so desperately needed.

She waited for the skipper she'd hired to get them into a position on the ocean waters that would allow them to drop anchor with the back of Charlotte Duran's estate in full, if distant, view. Savannah breathed in ocean air from a seat on the deck of her rented boat, more relaxed than she'd been in…years.

A lot of the clarity had been gained from spending a couple of hours completely outside her real life, with a kind stranger who'd treated her like a viable dinner companion.

It was almost as though she'd been able to see herself through his eyes—and in doing so, had seen her potential. Had seen the life that was there for her to live. The life she'd been missing.

The grown-up lives her partners had all been finding.

Other than Savannah giving directional coordinates to the woman at the wheel, the two hadn't spoken. Her chauffeur was being paid to get her there and back and didn't ask questions.

Which also added to Savannah's state of inner tranquility. She didn't have to *be* anybody. Or tend to anyone, either. There were no expectations of her, no advice to give, no case studies to make, no duties for her to perform—other than to see her sister from afar. Hell, she didn't even have to make her bed. It was being done for her.

For a few short hours or days, she could just watch, wait... and breathe.

And for the first day, that was all she did. Watch. And wait. Sitting out on the ocean on her own personal cruise. Until the sun started to set and her skipper—Suzanne, she'd said her name was—advised that they needed to head back.

Savannah had talked to the young woman some. Enough to know that her father owned the marina. That she'd grown up on the water and was working at the marina while she was in college. Getting a degree she didn't want or need, simply because her father had required it before allowing her to run day cruises for hundreds of tourists at a time for a living.

A woman who knew what she wanted.

She'd studied economics while Savannah had spent hours with her binoculars, watching a small beach backed by lusciously green, perfectly manicured lawn. To the right, a gazebo with a fireplace and outdoor table and living room seating for at least twelve. To the left, closer to the house, was a large swimming pool, with plenty of cool decking and loungers, gated in black wrought iron. Leaving at least an acre of largely unadorned lawn in the middle.

For parties, Savannah imagined as she put her surveillance glasses away for the trip back. In her mind's eye she saw the empty grounds she'd been staring at filled with tables and chairs, soft lighting, a buffet table with servers making certain they kept the flies off the food. There were casually though expensively dressed people of all ages sitting at tables but also milling about. People standing with drinks in their hands as they conversed in small groups.

At one point there was a white runway in the grass—with white chairs in rows on each side of it—that led to a gilded outdoor arch. During that imagined episode her sister came down the aisle in a white dress.

In her peaceful state of mind, Savannah spent the evening up in her suite, ordering room service, got a good night's sleep, and the next day, as Suzanne zoomed them back out on the ocean, she pictured toddlers in that vast green Duran grass. Maybe twins. Girls. Running almost faster than their chubby little legs could carry them, with the soft grass cushioning one as she fell.

She and Nicole were orphans with no other relatives, who'd been robbed of the chance to be family to each other, but they could still each have biological family in their own individual lives.

As the boat slowed, nearing their anchor spot, Savannah knew that if she saw Nicole surrounded by family, she'd be able to go, to be on a plane to Florida yet that night, to spend the rest of her vacation lounging beachside on the opposite coast of the country she and Nicole shared.

Goal in mind, she watched the Duran property from afar, completely silent as Suzanne studied for the next couple of hours.

And then, heart pounding, Savannah sat up straight, frozen in place lest the binoculars giving her sight moved at all, obstructing the view. The couple—Nicole and her husband?—exited the double French doors at the back of the house together. Was Nicole really married, then? California marriage records were public, but she'd have to submit a request by mail or visit each country recorder's office to obtain access to them. Or put Hud on it.

Her stomach knotting against a swarm of internal butterflies, she scarcely allowed herself a full breath so as not to lose even a second of sight. Until the couple continued to walk—and stepped onto that luscious spread of green grass, heading right in her direction!

Half a mile away, but with her view...they'd be right in front of her.

Palms sweating, she wiped one, then the other on her beige capri pants, wobbling the binoculars as little as possible and never taking her gaze away from the slowly walking pair.

Look up! she silently implored the woman who seemed inordinately fond of the ground beneath her feet. Savannah would have thought the woman was looking for something, except that the steps were too in sync with each other, and without pause, to be giving their owners opportunity for search.

And then, one second to the next, it happened! The face lifted, eyes gazing out toward the ocean, and Savannah gasped. Those eyes...she couldn't make out the color, but the round shape...blending into a petite nose...she knew them!

Could've been looking at a photo of her mother or, around the eyes and nose, herself...

"You okay?" Suzanne's voice penetrated through a barrier of seemingly cotton-stuffed ears.

"Fine." She found her court voice. None other was forthcoming. "Just found what I was looking for."

Her voice, hearing it, the need to use it, grounded her for a second. Until the woman moving closer looked up again, and it was as though she was looking straight at Savannah. Seeing her. Meeting her gaze.

Tears flooded her eyes, and she had to blink them away. Couldn't lose one second of her time with Nicole, breathing in every aspect of the moment, knowing they were all she was ever going to have. Willing the couple to walk all the way to the beach. To stay a while.

Nothing else existed. The boat rocking gently with the waves only meant that she had to brace herself and keep the binoculars focused. No smells, no sounds registered. Just the woman, dressed in a short denim skirt and black sleeveless top, with some kind of black open footwear, coming toward her.

The couple was close enough for Savannah to notice that the man was older. Or had a receding hairline and dyed his hair gray. His skin seemed less youthfully smooth than Nicole's, and he wore wire-framed glasses.

And...were they fighting?

The man—a father-in-law maybe—reached for Nicole's hand, pulled it to the crook of his elbow and when he let go, leaving it there, she returned her appendage to her side. Was staring out toward Savannah.

As though calling out to her. Savannah heard the call, felt the pull, with such force she took a step forward.

Realized she was still on the boat.

And just a speck in the distance to her sister, if Nicole could see her at all.

But she could see…far more than she'd expected to. Disbelieving elation turned to working focus in a heartbeat as Savannah's expensive lenses showed her the sharp shake of her sister's head, followed by the male hand—from a suited body that was heavier than was meant for the shirt—reaching for her again. Grabbing Nicole's hand. More roughly.

And her sister snatching it back. The man turned to Nicole, speaking what looked to be quite sharply based on his body language, the sharp movement of his head. She was talking then. Her jaw movement left no doubt about that.

Then the man was speaking again, rubbing a hand down Nicole's long dark hair, and it was as though Savannah could feel the touch on her own matching dark strands, over her shoulder and down her side and back.

She shuddered, watching as, a second later, the man kept a hand of ownership on Nicole's body, even when the younger woman turned away.

And looked out at the ocean again.

Facing Savannah.

Who didn't need to see the way her little sister's face scrunched…the broken movement of Nicole's torso…to feel her tears.

And Savannah's fate was once again sealed by situations beyond her control.

She had no idea what came next. What she could do.

But there was no way in hell she would be catching any flights that night.

Nicole might live in surroundings that made it appear that she was thriving, but Savannah's baby sister clearly was not happy.

Nor did she look safe.

Savannah couldn't leave her like that.

Duran had ordered him to leave Charlotte alone with Wagar on the lawn. Isaac had his own job to do. And while that required his undercover persona to stay employed, he didn't follow Charlotte outside, but he did keep watch from an upstairs room in the home. A better vantage point because he could see the entire backyard at once from above, so anyone trying to get access would be immediately visible.

As Charlotte stood with her back to him, mid-lawn, having rebuffed Wagar, Isaac felt another bout of compassion for the younger woman. No matter what she might've been involved with, she'd grown up under a very powerful thumb. Without Duran, an orphan.

Meaning no one else to turn to.

Didn't forgive an adult choice to cross the line between lawful and criminal. He'd take her down when he found the proof to do so.

Her shoulders hunched, and he glanced up, feeling as though he was intruding by staring at her, and was immediately hooked by a glint out on the water. Above sea level. It was stationary. And constant. A pinprick of light seeming to point straight at him.

Cursing against the time it took him to get his digital binoculars, he had them up and focused within seconds of being back at the window.

And then, while using the camera function to click photos as quickly as he could, he stood with only his eyewear sticking through the side of the opened curtains as he stared at the woman standing on the small-range center-console boat, binoculars covering her eyes.

Savannah Compton.

Another person was on the boat with her. Female. Blonde. At the center console, reading.

A skipper. But more than that, too?

An accomplice?

Her client?

The woman who was going to pose as a member of Charlotte's dead mother's family?

Using a woman was a good move.

Made by someone who knew a lot more about Charlotte than Eduardo suspected?

Questions posed, hanging there without answers.

He needed answers.

The Compton woman, or her client, posed no immediate physical danger to the younger Duran. They needed her alive, not dead, and were so far out that without powerful lenses, the heiress wouldn't even be able to see the lawyer out on the ocean.

But the lengths the woman had gone to to spy on Charlotte did not bode well. Was she planning to approach the house by water? Risky.

Worth it for the millions she hoped to gain?

He'd arrested people who'd put themselves on death row for much less. Three zeros less.

And from there? What would the plan be? Wait for Charlotte to appear?

Had Compton been out there the day before?

After their impromptu "date" two nights before, he'd spent the next day watching out for her car on the road. Keeping Charlotte within sight at all times.

He hadn't once glanced at the ocean. Charlotte had had a closed student-only lecture, a private lunch with a women's organization at which he'd stood trying to make his tall, broad form invisible in the corner. She'd had dinner at home with her father—with Wagar as a guest.

From which she'd excused herself before dessert and retired to her suite. On Emmajean's watch.

He'd spent more than an hour resisting the urge to head back to La Hacienda's mezzanine bar, just in case. And had gone to bed, relieved that Compton hadn't made an attempt to approach Charlotte and disappointed that he hadn't seen the lawyer all day, even in the distance. He couldn't find out what he didn't know without some kind of move from her.

Which he was currently witnessing.

Down below, Charlotte walked away from Wagar, causing the man's hand on her lower left back to drop, and when the older man followed after, she turned, said something to him, and stepped out onto the fifty yards of sand that led to the water's edge.

Lenses back over his eyes, he glanced up at the boat in the distance. Saw the lawyer just as he'd left her, visually cataloguing every move Charlotte made.

It didn't take him knowing what was going on—that Wagar was determined he was going to be her husband and Charlotte was equally determined he would not be—to figure out that the wealthy twenty-five-year-old was not interested in her father's plans for her marital future.

If he was the one in the boat, he'd be forming a plan right then and there. You used the weak link, the blemish in a relationship, a bone of contention to separate powers. And Charlotte, a woman in tune with women's needs, had just shown another equally astute woman her vulnerability. The way to draw her away from her loyalty to her father.

At least long enough to get what she wanted from her. To use her and leave her feeling like a fool.

So, he had Compton's way in. Big picture. How that would translate to actual contact remained to be seen.

He snapped a couple more photos. Looked at the small screen to preview what he could.

And...wait... Lenses back up to his eyes, Isaac focused to the left of Savannah Compton's boat. Another boat, smaller. A fishing vessel. Tucked into a cove completely visible to Isaac but mostly obscured from Savannah Compton. And while there was a pole mounted on the boat with a line in the water, one of the two figures dressed in dark pants and what looked to be wetsuit tops had his own power-driven lenses. And seemed to be dividing his time between the Duran beach—Charlotte—and the larger vessel—Savannah.

Duran had made it clear he had people watching the expert lawyer. And if they were that close, that up on her movements, Isaac was going to have to be much more careful regarding his own contact with her.

He could do it.

Taking on different personas—throwing on a mustache, a wig, dyeing his hair with rinse-out color, cowboy garb with heeled boots—had become second nature to him.

While Isaac's mind began to spin with possible scenarios—starting with another happy hour that night—he stiffened as the second person in the boat reached down toward the boat's bottom.

With a quick glance to see Charlotte still on the beach, the lawyer standing at attention, her binoculars pointed in Charlotte's direction, and then back to the two men in the boat, Isaac was vetoing his disguise idea. Savannah knew him as...

No! He saw the gun rise too late. Standing alone on the third floor of the mansion, horror filling his gut, he watched the second fisherman's hand jerk with the force of the blast. Watched as Savannah Compton fell to the floor of her vessel.

And ran for Charlotte.

Chapter Five

Lying on the floor of the cabin cruiser, Savannah felt the sting in her upper arm but didn't dare move even the inch or two it would take to get a look at the sleeve covering it. Had no idea how much blood there was.

There'd been a wave, the boat had rocked, she'd been off-balance, had side-stepped, and the next thing she remembered was diving for the floor the second she'd heard the blast and staying there, frozen, as Suzanne, keeping low, had gotten the boat roaring at top speed out of the area. Driving with one hand and her eyes barely above the boat's edge.

Her arm didn't feel ripped apart, but she'd heard that gun-shot pain wasn't always immediate. She didn't feel moisture and figured that for a good thing. Surely if there was gushing, she'd know.

The entire trip back, she calculated, considered, listened intently.

And stayed rational.

Listening as Suzanne radioed from the boat that there'd been a shot fired, giving the coordinates. Hearing a return conversation minutes later, stating that police in the area were checking residences closest to the area.

By the time they'd moored the boat, an all-clear had come from the area. Only a couple who'd been out at the beach at the time of the gunfire had even heard the one shot. And both were fine.

Nicole was fine. Savannah catalogued the news.

As soon as they'd docked, she realized there was only a tiny smear of blood on her sleeve, along with a shard of the plexiglass that had hit it. It wasn't until more than an hour later, when she was back in her suite, that she became a shivering mess.

A piece of the windshield had shattered at the bullet's impact. Hitting her.

And it could have been the bullet itself. If the wave hadn't hit when it had…

She could have been killed!

At the marina, Suzanne, her father, the police had all figured the shot as coming from someone on land, aiming at something else on land. A squirrel. Snake. There'd even been a couple of leopard sightings. Deputies had been dispatched to go over the lush, treed cove area from which the bullet had come, inch by inch. Looking for the dead animal. Or signs of poaching.

Savannah had had her day's ride comped.

She'd paid anyway, leaving another day-trip's worth of pay for Suzanne. The girl had taken the whole thing in stride. Had seemed quite proud of herself for her ability to captain the boat and her fare safely to the dock, with little real damage.

She'd apparently watched Savannah on the floor, too. Had kept track of her breathing, with no sign of blood.

And had been eagerly talking to the small crowd that had gathered around her when Savannah had climbed into her car and driven back to the hotel.

But once in her room, panic hit.

With two words repeating themselves over and over.

Witness Protection. Witness Protection.

She'd broken protocol. Looking up Nicole. Coming to see her—even from a distance.

Nicole was fine, she reminded herself, pacing.

But that bullet…had it been meant for her? Not some poor rodent in the wrong place at the wrong time?

Just seemed way too coincidental that she was the only one

hit by a seemingly stray bullet at the exact time she'd been standing there spying on Nicole.

What kind of danger had she put herself in?

Once in, there was no way out. She knew that. Had been told over and over. Especially in her teens when she'd figured enough time had passed and she and her mom could start looking. When she'd been so filled with her ability to be right that she'd once tried an internet search on her own only to have her mother walk in from the kitchen and see her.

She'd heard from the witness protection marshal who'd been summoned to her home an hour later that if whoever her father had been about to blow the whistle on knew that she was going to bring up the past, that she believed Nicole was alive, she'd be living on borrowed time.

She'd never looked again.

Not until after her mother's death.

With her stomach churning and her heart pounding, she wore a path in the lush carpet from bedroom, through the double doors, past bath to living area, over to the windows lining the whole space, back again via the view. Making a circle.

Repeating the process over and over.

Thoughts reeling, one after the other. None of them coming together.

Until she stopped at the window, looked out at the ocean, and knew. If she was on borrowed time, she was. There was no taking that back.

She'd been feeling like she was being followed for the past year. Maybe now she really would be.

But Nicole was in trouble—an abusive husband or boyfriend, most likely—and Savannah couldn't die without trying to help her.

She wouldn't be able to live with herself, either in her current life or any afterlife, if she abandoned that sweet baby holding her arms out for Savannah to hold her.

She couldn't abandon Nicole.

She couldn't help her if she was dead.

So there had to be a third option.

She'd have to hire someone...and do it in a way that no

one knew the person was attached to her. Which meant she had to find out as much as she could about her sister to know how best to have a conversation with Nicole without alerting whoever had killed their father. Only then would she know who to hire.

She might've only been an expert in the field of law, but more than a decade with Sierra's Web had taught her a lot. She'd never seen herself going it alone without her partners, but she could.

And for Nicole, she would.

No way was she going to contact her best friends, who'd been her family for her entire adult life, and bring potential danger to them.

She just had to figure out what she *was* going to do. How she could stay alive long enough to help Nicole, not get her hurt— and hopefully to have her own future as well.

Staying in her suite wasn't the answer.

Leaving it didn't seem like such a good idea at the moment, either.

And yet, aside from standing there with nerves that were still jittering, she felt as though she was finally taking charge of her life. Facing it all.

Not giving in. Or giving up, either.

Rubbing her arms, she touched the small cut on her arm and, with sudden fear rendering her weak, took a step back.

Before stopping. And forcing herself forward again.

A bullet could probably plow through a cabin cruiser's windshield. But not as probably through soundproofed double-or triple-pane acrylic windows, which she suspected she was standing in front of. Hotel liabilities were legal nightmares. And the surest way for an establishment not to have to deal with them was prevention.

Which was why guests in most hotels couldn't open the windows in their rooms. Less chance of falling out. And less chance of an intruder accessing the space. Soundproofing had become a privacy issue, most particularly at luxury hotels. Guests not only wanted their own comfort not to be disturbed by other guests but also expected a level of privacy as they held their own conversations.

And liaisons.

She needed to have whatever meetings she had in her hotel room.

Good. First bullet point for her plan.

Before the second had a chance to form, the hotel phones—one on the large workspace, one in the living area, and one on the nightstand over by the bed—began to ring.

Had they found out where she was staying?

Savannah's gaze moved between the three ringing phones. Back and forth.

As she stood rooted to the floor and started to shake.

Answer.

Seated in his car at La Hacienda, Isaac listened to the phone ring two, then three times. He'd been told by Duran's head of security that the Compton woman had gone back to her hotel. At the same time the man had denied all responsibility for his team having had anything to do with the shot that had been fired at her.

Savannah's car was in the parking lot.

Happy hour had just ended. His timing was purposeful.

Isaac was there to attempt to cash in on his earlier, seemingly unplanned personal association with Savannah Compton long enough to find out what she knew about the Durans—nothing more.

But his gut still tightened when he couldn't get her on the phone. Suspecting the worst.

From everything he knew—but couldn't trace back to Duran with enough solid proof to hang him—the man's hired goons didn't generally hit and miss. An untimely ocean wave giving the smallest rock to her cruiser had been to blame. The expert lawyer had escaped one bullet headed straight at her. Chances were, she wouldn't be so lucky a second time.

Ring six. How many more would he get before the hotel's service picked up to record his message for the guest in room 11029? *Answer.*

He wasn't going to leave a message. Didn't want the recording to exist.

Holding his phone with fingers tight with tension, he glanced around one more time, just to ensure that he was alone. No eyes on him.

Duran trusted him. But he wouldn't put it past the man to have all his employees watched now and then. Just to be sure. A guy didn't get to the billionaire's stature without layers of stringent protection in place.

Just like the layers of untraceable transfers of moneys and contraband that supported the criminal's wealth. The invisible manpower for the dirty work.

Ring eight.

"Hello?"

Settling back in his seat, Isaac smiled. Getting into character. Doing it so well, he felt like a guy initiating a second meet after an enjoyable first one. "Savannah? It's Isaac..."

"Isaac?" Sinking down to the sofa, weak with relief, Savannah let herself fall back two nights to the time out of time that had given her the clarity to move forward with her life.

She wouldn't let herself be deterred from the urgent business at hand. But if a moment or two of distraction from the persistent and irritating anxiety getting in her way allowed her to proceed with the same logical thinking that had given her more than just a glimpse of her sister, then she had to take that time.

"How did you find me?" she asked, settling back with warmth flooding through her at the thought that he'd enjoyed their time together enough to try.

"You aren't going to believe this...and...well... I'd rather talk in person. I want you to be able to look into my eyes and know I'm not some creep..."

His recalcitrant tone had her smiling. Something she so very badly needed in that moment. "I find it hard to believe that I'll ever be thinking that," she said.

"So you'll meet me in the bar?"

No. She wasn't leaving her suite. Drew a blank as to any normal sounding reason as to why that was and blurted, "I just washed my hair. It takes a good hour to dry."

Not her best work.

But it sufficed.

Until he said, "You'll look like some of the other people mill-ing around down here, like you just came in from a dip in the pool. There's a party going on, spilling out onto the beach."

In another lifetime, she'd have suggested they meet there. The happy-hour crowd had worked well for them.

In another lifetime...

"You could come up here," she said, prompted by all the emo-tions she was fighting in her current lifetime. Top of the list suddenly—not being alone. Just for a few. And then, hearing herself, quickly added, "I have a suite. Bedroom door firmly closed," and got up to close said double doors—would have locked them for good measure if she could have done so from the outside.

She'd pretty much invited him the other night.

Of course, three glasses of wine had been partly responsible for the ill-advised invitation.

The man was the only nonemployee she knew in her current, very narrow present. And he'd liked her enough to find her after they'd left hanging the possibility that they'd see each other again.

She'd be lying to herself if she didn't admit that every time she'd been in the lobby the day before—and that day, too—she'd looked for him. Just in case he'd come back on the chance of seeing her again. "And I have four phones and a can of pepper spray in case I feel threatened," she added, humor in her tone as she delivered words that were also true. She kept the mul-tiple self-defense training certificates to herself.

Unless the man came up with an illegally carried gun—something that wouldn't make it past hotel security to get on the elevator—she felt pretty confident she could hold her own.

And when Isaac chuckled, sending shivers through her, and said he was on his way up, she made a run for the bath to wet her hair.

Thanking providence for saving her from herself one more time.

Isaac's steps were quick and sure, adrenaline flowing as he made his way to the access he'd just gained into what could turn out to be the unexpected flag on Duran's horizon that broke open the case. Sometimes it only took one mistake, one unsolved little problem.

And the fact that Eduardo Duran had had somebody shoot at the woman that afternoon, just half a mile from his estate, told him that she was a problem.

One that was far bigger than the older man had let on.

Which made Isaac all that more eager to find out why. Who was she representing? And why was that person such a threat to the billionaire?

Yet as he got off the elevator at her floor, adjusting his jacket over the dress pants and button-down shirt, readying himself for a professional introduction—albeit one that would only sprinkle enough particles of truth over the cover to give him the appearance of complete transparency—he slowed for a step or two.

Ostensibly to prepare, but it wasn't the speech he was about to give that had his focus. He'd enjoyed the couple of hours he'd spent with the expert attorney. Had left feeling…good. Had slept well that night. Would have liked to have left the memory alone. Something he could call up now and then when he felt a little too much…alone.

On Christmas, for instance. Those that he wasn't working.

Instead, he was about to obliterate the little screenshot of a supposedly unplanned tête-à-tête with another farce. One that wasn't going to be nearly as fun.

One that was going to wipe the smile, the look of welcome off Savannah Compton's compelling face. And replace it with…

A flash of Mollie's shocked, hurt gaze shot across his mind's eye. Followed by a couple more long-ago, but never forgotten, expressions attacking him from his little sister's eyes. A second of disbelief that settled into disgust-laced resentment. It had been fifteen years, and his little sister, his only family, hadn't spoken to him since.

While the reminder hit his gut with a familiar pang, it was well-timed, preparing him for the moments ahead. No matter how much you liked or cared for someone, no matter that feeling of connection, being on opposite sides of the law would keep you forever apart.

At least when the "you" was Isaac.

And the other side of that, when someone you trusted took information you gave freely and used it to stop you from breaking the law, you didn't hold them in high regard. When the "you" was Mollie.

But not Savannah Compton. He couldn't believe she trusted him.

Unless, in the next few minutes, she came clean with him. Told him she was there to make contact with Charlotte Duran. At which point, he would be the only one lying to keep secrets. The only one killing any semblance of trust between them.

Because he still couldn't tell her who he really was.

Either way, *vacation fling* was off the table the second he knocked on her door. A bit of regret hung over him. But his knock was firm.

And when she answered the door—with her hair so wet it appeared as though she'd really been in the process of washing it when he'd called—he didn't lean in and deliver a kiss to her cheek.

In spite of his strong inner urge to do so.

He smiled, though. Met her gaze with a long one of his own, an act, and...uncomfortably very real, too, as he allowed that much of a connection between them to continue to live.

If his plan was going to work, he needed her to trust him.

And the way he felt inside—wanting, personally, to be worthy of Savannah's trust, to continue to hold it—was one of the hurdles he was going to have to overcome to get the job done.

Hundred, thousands, maybe millions of people's lives had been negatively impacted over the years by Eduardo Duran's illegal activities. He couldn't let his own personal feelings get in the way of saving future millions from the same fate.

And while she was just flirting with a man that had nothing to do with her purpose in town for the moment—and while that increasingly irritated part of him wanted to be just a guy she met in a bar—the reality was that as soon as she heard what he'd come to say, she'd become a player in the deadly game.

Whether she told him so or not.

Savannah broke eye contact first. "Make yourself at home

while I dry my hair," she said, nodding toward the living area. "There's wine there if you want to pour a couple of glasses."

Playing his part, he took up the bottle, uncorked it. Set one filled glass on the coffee table in front of the sofa and took the other with him to look out at the darkness over the ocean, broken occasionally by the light of a ship. He heard the blow-dryer shut off but didn't turn.

Just waited.

He needed her to make the next move so he could best determine his own. Did she want to continue the flirtation?

His own "truth" could come out as a caveat to that.

At which time she'd accept the business proposal he was there to present, and the flirtation would die a natural death.

Or was she, the expert lawyer, just needing to know how he'd found her, and when he told her, she'd order him out?

In that scenario the task in front of him would be more difficult.

He heard her approach, glanced over as she stopped a foot to his right, looking out alongside him. She sipped from her glass.

He took his first sip, too. Waiting.

"So, how'd you find me? A first name, the hotel..."

Glancing at her, he gave her kudos for an expression that, while congenial, gave nothing away. Nor did her tone.

She seemed...not at all upset to have been found.

Which spoke more to the flirtation scenario, not the lawyer.

Out of time, he chose to go that route.

"I wasn't completely honest with you the other night." He started right in, his tone filled with regret that was prompted by the part he was playing but came from a place deeper inside him. The part he had to find a way to stifle once and for all.

He looked over at her, waiting for her to meet his gaze, which took a couple of long seconds. And then he said, "I do work in acquisitions, sort of," he told her. Then shrugged and added an actual fact. "I buy and sell privately, for myself. Stock, mostly. And not always successfully." A piece of information that had not been meant to escape.

What the hell?

"But my actual job...is working for the owner of one of

the world's most successful conglomeration of portfolios..."
A vague way to describe Eduardo. One that fit. Nothing about
the man's dealings were clear cut or easily understandable. He
mastered in stealth, in hiding, in making it impossible to know
exactly what he was doing.

She'd taken another sip of wine. Was facing the window
again. Seeing the sedately lit hotel grounds below, as he'd done?
The small groups of people, mostly couples, who came and went
along the softly glowing pathways that wound around and down
to the beach? Into the darkness.

He couldn't get the read on her that would help guide him.

He was just getting ready to dive in further when she said,
"And this has to do with me, how?"

Ah. Her tone had cooled.

He didn't want to lose the warmth. "I work for a man who
lives near where your boat was shot at today," he said, concern
marring his brow, urgency in his tone. "I'm a bodyguard, Savannah. And personal protection director for the household," he
added with a note of humility. "Which is a fancy way of saying
I'm the head bodyguard who is in charge of, and responsible
for, the rest of the bodyguard staff."

She'd turned slowly to face him, eyes wide, mouth open.

"The police came to the house to ask questions. I was called
in to assure the owner that everyone under our care was fine. I
asked to remain present for the remainder of the interviews so
that I could prepare my staff for any possible safety measures
we might want to put in place..." He poured on the sense that
he could serve and protect. "During the ensuing hour, we were
asked if any of us knew a Savannah Compton."

When she turned sharply toward the window, he touched her
shoulder gently. "I didn't know it was you, of course, and said
no." He explained what he had to get out there and then quickly
added, "They were asking just to make certain that no one in the
household—an estate that was within shooting distance of your
boat with a strong enough rifle—had it out for you. They were
looking for suspects. In order to keep you from further harm."

With a quick look back at him, she nodded and quickly faced

the window again, her wineglass more an ornament in her hand than a beverage she was consuming.

Because she'd switched to working mode?

Had left personal territory for professional?

Or because he'd frightened her?

Based on the frown marring her features, the tightness around her lips, he suspected the latter.

And even while that had been his goal, the idea that he might have succeeded didn't feel great.

"As they were leaving, one of the officers mentioned to me that you'd been staying at La Hacienda, had taken the boat out from there."

His words brought her glance back to him. This time she didn't turn away. She took a sip of wine.

And he knew that he was on the cusp of succeeding. That she was falling into his plan. And his faith in the idea grew. He decided to push harder. For the job. Always for the job.

But for another, very different and unfamiliar reason, too.

He cared, personally, that she stay safe.

Chapter Six

Savannah sipped wine. She controlled her breathing. Managed to maintain outward calm. But her insides were quaking.

What in the hell had she done?

She'd heard that the police were going to question nearby residents, to make certain that all was well. She'd pictured a knock on the front door, a question along the lines of *Is everything all right here?* and a quick wave goodbye.

The local police had clearly thought they were dealing with a possible illegal shooting of a rodent, a poacher, or a somewhat foolish target shooter who needed more practice.

But…putting protection staff on alert?

Thinking she was truly in imminent harm? She'd suspected, of course. And had been hell bent on getting her paranoia under control.

But what if…

She'd brought the monster out of hiding.

She couldn't stop him from gunning for her. It was too late. Like Pandora's box.

She was there. Had exposed herself to powers that be in the waters behind Nicole's house. Had her sister been told then, too? Had she answered the door to police?

After already having what had looked like a horrendous episode in the garden?

Did Nicole know she'd had a sister? Did anyone retain that kind of memory function from the age of one?

Mariah would know.

When thoughts of her child-life expert friend and partner nearly brought tears to her eyes, Savannah straightened her shoulders. She was strong.

Had always had to be.

For Nicole, she'd beat the fear. And anything else that came barreling her way.

Coming somewhat out of her fog, Savannah glanced over at her guest, realizing that he'd been silently watching her. She tried to think back to the last thing he'd said. Something about being told that the victim of the shooting had been staying at La Hacienda.

And said, "So on a hunch that Savannah was an uncommon-enough name that there wouldn't be two of them registered at La Hacienda, you took a chance, called the hotel, and asked to be connected to my room." Her lawyer mind was nowhere near working up to speed, but at least she'd woken it up.

"No, I did an internet search on the name Savannah Compton, recognized you from the photo that popped up alongside the first listing, and then called the officer who'd left her card back for identity confirmation regarding this afternoon's incident."

Right. He was in private protection but, with a good reputation, could feasibly work in cooperative conjunction with law enforcement.

Or...with a flash of jealousy another possibility occurred to her. He'd said "her" when referring to the officer. Had she been even half alive, the woman could have been taken with him. Could have emitted some sign that she'd be open to further conversation...

As Savannah had.

Which pissed her off. It wasn't like she was some needy person who couldn't get a date. And she was acting like an inexperienced girl meeting the high school quarterback.

But then, Isaac definitely had a way about him. The man oozed compassion. Charm. The fact that his body was perfectly proportioned, and he had looks that could stop an octogenarian in her tracks was like a bonus to the rest of what he brought into a room…

"From there, I vacillated," the man started to talk again when Savannah failed to respond. "I had no business contacting you, the way I'd come by the information. As soon as I was off duty, I drove over here, checked out happy hour, thinking maybe I'd run into you again…"

"I didn't go down."

Obviously, Savannah. Good one. You sound real smart now. An intelligent expert, to be sure.

He'd have read about Sierra's Web. The firm's internet presence was the only thing that came up with her photo.

"But I kept thinking…if you really were in danger… I'm trained to prevent physical bodily harm to those who could be targets…"

Her heart lurched, and she stared at him. Couldn't pull her gaze away from his deep brown-eyed silent communication.

His eyes were telling her things that it was far too soon in their relationship to say.

"I know you have a world of experts at your disposal, bodyguards on staff…"

She nodded. But didn't speak. She had to hear what else he'd been about to say. He was that compelling to her.

"I just… I'm right here, right now…off duty for the next twelve hours…and had to reach out…"

Savannah took a long sip of wine. To keep from eagerly letting down her guard, asking the man to spend the night, wrapping her arms around him, and getting lost.

"I'm on leave from the firm," she told him instead. "I needed some personal time. And since the police told me they thought the shot was someone shooting a rodent in the swampy woods there at the cove or maybe intending to do some target shooting, I haven't called anyone for help."

All true. Just minus other truths.

There were things she couldn't tell him, couldn't tell anyone, for their own safety. But she would not lie to him.

When he took her hand, she held on. Let him lead her over

to the couch. And when he set down his wineglass, she did hers as well.

Ready to get lost for a few hours. To experience the euphoria, the forgetfulness she could access. To sleep.

And wake up in the morning stronger. Better able to figure out how to go about ensuring that Nicole was all right.

Even if it meant putting herself in further harm by continuing to keep surveillance on Nicole until she could figure out a way to make certain that someone knew her younger sister might be struggling at home.

She didn't have to have direct contact. Just had to know who she could somehow alert anonymously...

Isaac hadn't spoken. Was watching her.

She liked it.

And said, "I don't know your last name."

Just didn't make good sense to spend the night with a man, even a bodyguard in good police regard, without knowing his full name.

"Forrester."

She liked that, too.

But wasn't so fond of the way his expression suddenly changed. As though he'd just then made up his mind about something.

Was he about to ditch her?

It would be a first, but why not? She'd never been shot at before, either, until that day. Nor had she ever lied to her partners before the past week.

Or even thought about, let alone been tempted to embark on, a one-night stand.

Taking both of her hands, Isaac looked her in the eye and said, "I have more I need to tell you."

Oh, God. He was married.

"I work for a wealthy man," he said.

She'd figured as much. The coast along Nicole's property was dotted with multimillion-dollar estates. And only someone with a lot of money would have a personal protection director on staff. It didn't take an expert to figure that out.

Which meant that Isaac would have already figured her for having done that particular math.

He was still frowning as he said, "Because of what he does... acquiring businesses that can't afford not to be bought out..."

A nice way of saying his employer was a corporate raider? "He's involved with hostile takeovers?" she asked.

With a raised brow and a half nod of acknowledgment, he said, "He's made some enemies. And with you having been in close vicinity to the waters his daughter sails out to on a regular basis, combined with the fact that, from a distance, the two of you share size and coloring, and with him having just completed a less than friendly takeover from someone who threatened to make him hurt..."

His voice trailed off, and she saw where he was going.

But something else entirely was making her blood race, her heart pound. Could the providence she'd thought had put her in touch with Isaac to begin with really be at work? In a much larger way?

A man known for being hostile in business. An older man refusing to take the no Nicole had been firmly and clearly stating. Her eventual tears, as though she had no way out. A daughter who resembled Savannah in build *and* coloring?

Had the man she'd seen making Nicole cry been her little sister's adopted *father*?

And even more fantastic...

Did Isaac work for Nicole?

Hardly able to breathe, she stared at the man sitting there holding her hands... Did Isaac *know* her baby sister? Swallowing back tears, finding her court face by sheer force of will or sisterly love, she waited until she could trust herself to speak with only fear evident in her voice and asked, "You think I'm in danger?"

Isaac's head tilting slightly to the side and back, almost like a nod, the way he was looking at her...

"You think I should leave town immediately." She couldn't.

And if Isaac worked for Charlotte, her chances of keeping watch over her sister without being noticed were nil...unless she told him the truth.

He was a bodyguard. He could protect himself.

In a world where crimes were traceable.

Whoever her father had been about to testify against, whoever had murdered him and then burned his corpse had had friends in high enough places that there hadn't been a single suspect in her father's murder.

Or a single clue to Nicole's disappearance.

Thoughts falling into an eerily calm place, Savannah entertained them one by one.

Women had one-night stands all the time. Just because she never had didn't mean she couldn't.

Telling anyone who she was, most particularly someone close to Nicole, could not only put that person in danger but could get her sister killed.

It took her a second to get out of the clear succession of thoughts racing through her to notice that Isaac was shaking his head.

"I think it's only fair, before I say more, that I tell you who I work for," he said. "I've seen from your firm's website a lot of the kinds of cases you've done, the wealthy people you've worked for, and I'm sure what's published there is only a smidgeon..."

She nodded. Alert. Waiting.

As though her life depended on what he would say next.

Because, in more ways than one, it did.

"It's no secret around here," Isaac said, drawing out her internal agitation almost to breaking point. She sipped her wine, praying for a hint of its calming spirit to spread through her. "Everyone sees me out and about with..."

Using a tactic that had been getting people to talk to her since college, she raised one brow as he paused. Staring him straight in the eye. No panic lurking in the conglomeration of intense emotions roiling through her.

"I work for a man named Eduardo Duran. Have you ever heard of him?"

Savannah calmed. Just...sat, all thought, no feeling. Not in that second. She'd made the right choice to come.

Frowning, she shook her head. An honest response. Which

brought sensation back. In barely containable force. While her heart pounded blood through her veins with such force she could feel it. The pounding in her chest. In her temples.

Eduardo Duran. Charlotte Duran.

Isaac, the man she'd met by chance at a hotel happy hour—and she'd definitely chosen the hotel by chance—worked for her sister's family! Worked on the estate where she'd seen Nicole that afternoon.

Arguing with her father?

Was there a woman in the picture, too? A mother? Had the couple bought Nicole as a toddler?

Had Nicole been told anything about her biological mother and sister? Was that why she'd put her DNA in the Family Finders database?

Nicole had to have been calling out to her. Needing her.

And love had carried the message.

No matter what Isaac Forrester, concerned bodyguard, advised her to do, no matter the risk to her life, there was no way she was going to disappear to protect herself.

Until she knew that Nicole was okay, she wasn't going anywhere.

Most particularly not when she finally had her in. A man in her life who had no idea she was Nicole's sister—probably didn't even know her sister's real name. A man who could tell her about Nicole, giving her a chance to make suggestions to him, a way to make a real contribution to her sister's future happiness.

A man who, in any other situation, she could be falling for.

A man she believed she could trust.

Evil had ripped Nicole out of their lives all those years ago.

But love was going to win.

Chapter Seven

The woman was far craftier than he'd given her credit for. Ignoring the pit of disappointment in his gut, Isaac watched Savannah's response to his big reveal, figuring he was going to have to change course.

If he didn't know better, he'd sit right there and believe wholeheartedly that the expert lawyer on leave to do dirty work truly had never heard of Eduardo Duran.

And if she was that good…

His job just got one hell of a lot more challenging. Damn good thing he was a seasoned faker.

"Duran's a powerful man who's made a lot of enemies. People who can't find justice through proper channels…" The words, unpracticed, flowed smoothly from the persona of a bodyguard pretending to be personally concerned for the welfare of a lovely woman in distress in whom he had interest. "From what I heard in the household security meeting we had this afternoon, Duran feels certain that whoever shot at you took you for his daughter, Charlotte."

"Household security?" Savannah's voice had just the right amount of fear to convince him she was only who she thought he believed she was. "I thought you were the boss."

And he suddenly understood the trepidation coming at him. It *was* for real. She'd had him pegged as the lead man on staff.

"I head up the personal protection detail," he told her. "But I'm under the jurisdiction of household security. Mr. Duran has a twenty-four-hour armed security detail guarding the property." He'd hoped to play things easier, but he was going to have to pour it on thick. "They call the shots where the rest of us are concerned."

He needed her to agree to his offer, once he got that far. His gut—and Duran's reaction that afternoon—were telling him that the lawyer could lead him to someone who knew more than Duran wanted them to know.

The weak link that would be the man's demise.

Isaac needed Savannah Compton alive long enough to lead him to it.

You want to protect her life regardless. The voice newly popping up inside him was an irritant. One he was going to have to shut up.

He'd give his life for another's every day of the week. But when one crossed to the wrong side of the law, as Savannah had, as he suspected Charlotte had, there were sometimes unforeseeable and unavoidable consequences that one undercover FBI agent working alone couldn't avert.

And here came the bigger news. "Household security is on high alert. And you are on the radar. Mr. Duran's head of security and closest confidant is uncomfortable with how close you were to the property. He has since learned that you bought a pair of binoculars in town yesterday morning."

He saw her throat move with the difficulty of her smile and did a quick mental check. Was he pouring it on too thick? Should he have held back?

Since when did he question himself in the middle of an operation?

Squeezing Savannah's hand, Isaac looked her in the eye. "You need to get out of town, Savannah."

She'd started shaking her head before he'd put the period on the sentence. "I can't, Isaac," she whispered, her gaze worried as she looked up at him. Holding his hand as tightly as he held hers.

As though they were evenly matched at their game.

He almost, for a second there, felt sorry for her. She had no idea who she was dealing with. In Duran. And in Isaac.

She opened her mouth as though to speak, clearly hesitated, studying him as though ascertaining whether to touch him and then, with another tight swallow, said, "I'm here…to find… someone. I'd been given information that led me to believe this person is staying on the coast, somewhere along the stretch where the Duran estate is located. I was out on the boat all day yesterday, too. Watching properties along the coastline. I…can't leave until I know they're okay."

She was good. Better than most. He was almost enjoying the parrying back and forth. Maybe he would have if innocent lives weren't at stake.

And she'd made a major mistake, too. Two of them. Duran was onto her. Had been before Isaac had ever heard of her. And on that boat that afternoon, she'd gotten too close.

Bending his head a little closer, he held her gaze and said "No one's worth losing your life over" so softly that the words didn't travel across the room.

She nodded silently. Steadily holding eye contact. As though begging him to read between the lines.

For a moment there, he second-guessed Duran's information about the lawyer's intent. She was an impressive adversary.

He took heed. Of her skill and his own emerging weakness where she was concerned. He wouldn't be caught with his pants down again.

"Who?" he asked, compassion and concern filling his voice and his expression.

When she shook her head, he relaxed a few muscles. He was beating her at their far too dangerous game.

"I want so badly to tell you, Isaac," she said. "I do." Her gaze implored him. "But I can't."

His own frown showed utmost concern. A lot of which was real.

"Why not?" He had to decipher truth from fiction and figure out what she didn't want him to know.

What she was hiding.

Or rather, *who*.

Who was paying her to be there?

Who'd hired her?

Afraid that Duran already knew, Isaac had to get Savannah to talk to him to better his chances of keeping her alive.

"Because if I tell you, I put your life at risk." The widening of his eyes was completely sincere. She'd surprised him with that one. And again, when she covered their clasped hands with her other hand, holding the bundle against her knee as though she was hugging it.

Making him far too aware of the warm flesh of her thigh beneath her lightweight pants.

Until he figured out that had to have been her intent. This woman, too beautiful, too smart for her own good, wasn't above using her sex appeal to win.

Something he'd never been called upon to do.

But would if he had to.

"I'm pretty sure that whoever shot at me today was just after me," she confided, not hiding what appeared to be very real fear in her gaze. "I've suspected someone's been following me for the past year..."

His mind scrambled to fit that in with what he knew. Tried to find the logical way it fit into what Duran had told him.

Couldn't.

Until he realized that whoever had hired her to get to Charlotte Duran probably wasn't the expert lawyer's first dark client. For all Isaac knew she'd been working dirty under the table for years. He'd had no time or ability to do any kind of deep dive on her.

Silently chiding himself for not having figured it out sooner—anyone after Duran would know to hire an experienced accomplice—he stayed silent. Keeping his gaze glued to hers. Making it as difficult as possible for her not to tell him more.

"I don't think whoever shot at me today was a poacher or target shooter. And I don't think it was someone thinking I was Duran's daughter—you said her name was Charlotte?—either."

As hard as it was for him to sit there playing the concerned new love interest who was also a bodyguard, Isaac forced himself to do it. Even rubbed the thumb of the hand she held along her leg. Encouraging her to trust him.

Trust *them*.

"And I don't think it matters whether I stay in San Diego or fly to Greece—the people after me are going to find me."

She'd played it too far. "That makes no sense," he said, working hard to keep all irritation—and disappointment—out of his tone. Making certain he remained in character.

Always playing the part.

And when she looked away from him, he called her back. "I know you and your firm have worked a lot of high-security cases, Savannah. You've got a nationally renowned firm of experts in pretty much every field around you all the time. Surely if you've been followed, one of them would have known. At the very least, you'd have reached out for someone to check, just to make sure. Your firm has partnered with law enforcement for years. You could have had access to security cameras."

When she dropped his hand, reached for her wine, he figured she'd realized she'd made a mistake. Was recalculating. Buying herself time to figure out how to recover.

They both wanted something from each other. He needed to know who she was working for and why—strongly believing she was his key to cracking the Duran case. And she wanted his access to Charlotte to use Duran's daughter to squeeze him.

For money. Or as Isaac was beginning to suspect, for something much more threatening to Eduardo Duran than cash.

Question was, who wanted what they wanted more?

"A year ago, one of our partners, one of my best friends, was kidnapped," she said, surprising him again. He took note of the tactic she'd used on him twice in one sitting. Would be better prepared the third time she tried it on him.

Showing concern again for a few seconds, he then looked away long enough to take a very small sip of wine before taking her right back into his circle of focus. "Was she…killed?"

It wasn't like the firm would have put it up on the website if she had been. The woman's photo would likely have just quietly disappeared.

Savannah's head shake relieved him. Bringing on yet another moment of warning from within him. He couldn't care.

Not until later. When the job was done and he could take his couple of days to himself to debrief.

"No," she said, her tone growing stronger as she took another sip from her half empty glass. "She was rescued a couple of days later, scared but unharmed. But ever since then... I've been...struggling with bouts of anxiety." Her gaze fluttered, meeting his, away, and then ultimately back again.

Showing...shame?

Damn. Savannah Compton had missed her calling becoming an expert attorney. Didn't matter how many high-powered cases she'd won. She was a consummate actress. Inarguably the best he'd ever met.

"I talked to Kelly about them—she's our psychiatry partner. They're normal, based on what we all went through that weekend, and something I've worked to get past. I've been telling myself, until tonight, that that's all it was. Me being paranoid. And refusing to let the fear make me believe things that aren't true."

Isaac almost sat back at that one. Talking about being convinced of untrue things while lying to the face of someone she was pretending to have a personal interest in...the woman was almost diabolical.

If there was any way she made it through current events alive and on the right side of the law, he should ask her to work for him.

Except that he could never afford to pay her. Most particularly since being the partner in a hugely successful national firm didn't seem to be compensating her to her satisfaction.

She was so good, he'd even consider that Duran had been lying to him when the crook had warned Isaac about the lawyer, except that he'd been right on target.

She'd arrived. Had clearly had eyes on Charlotte Duran. Isaac had seen those binoculars and where they'd been trained with his own eyes. And had recorded images of her spying from that boat in the event that he somehow convinced himself he'd seen wrong.

No one with legitimate interest in someone spied on them.

And Eduardo Duran might be a fiend who disgusted Isaac, but Isaac also knew, more than most, just how attuned Duran was to everything going on around him. How accurate.

He paid big for the knowledge.

It was part of the reason he'd been able to live freely when he was, internationally, a wanted man.

Isaac knew better than to disrespect the man's intel.

Savannah's glass clinked loudly as she put it down on the table, drawing his attention back to her face. Worry lines had formed, but she was still looking him in the eye as she said, "Say something."

"Who do you think is following you?"

She shook her head. "That's the part I can't talk about." The deep sorrow in her voice matched that shining from her gaze. "I wish I could, Isaac. More than you'll ever know. But I can't."

If he didn't know better, he'd think he was talking with an abused woman on the run from her abuser.

To the point that he wanted to go hunt the guy down and arrest him before he killed him himself.

She lost some of his respect for taking it that far.

"Just give me a name."

"That's just it," she said. "I don't know."

Seriously? His look of incredulity couldn't be hidden. Or faked.

And she took his hand again. He was prepared that time. Wasn't going to fall for the sex card as he listened to her say, "I know this sounds strange," she told him. "I just… I truly don't have any idea who it is. I really thought it was paranoia. Or hoped it was. Until today. Whoever it is knows I'm here. And he's after me."

Boom. As good as she was, she'd played right into his hand.

"Won't you be bringing this same danger on whoever you're here to find?"

"I hope to God not."

His impression of her acting lowered a notch. Because there was a hole in her logic. He let go of her hand to grab his wineglass. Couldn't appear too eager.

Hard to get was more what the current seconds were calling for.

"You tell me you can't tell me what's going on because you'll put me in danger, but then you tell me you don't know who's after you, and you're looking to connect with someone—who you also can't identify to me."

If she was as desperate to use him to get to Charlotte as Duran thought she was, she'd have to find a way out of that one.

She leaned in, her gaze completely serious, and fully focused on him. "I know...something. Have known for years," she said. "I don't know who. And the person I'm looking for—I have no intention of making contact. I don't want anyone to ever know I looked. I just need to...see for myself."

He got chills. She was that on target. In the space of seconds, she'd managed to climb her way out of the hole she'd dug.

"So let me help," he said, going in for his win, holding up a hand as she started to object. "I'm not saying I help you look for or find whoever you're here to see. I give you my word I won't even try to find out. Just let me help keep you safe while you go about looking."

Her chin trembled. Her eyes grew moist.

Isaac resisted an instinctive need to pull her into his arms.

"Duran's going to be watching you," Isaac told her. "Or his men are. As one on the inside, I can help you escape their notice. Say I thought I saw you across town when I know you're at the beach, that kind of thing. Not those exact details, of course, but..."

He rushed his speech purposely to let her know how badly he wanted to be there for her. To play the fool to her sexual come-ons. To seem like he was falling for the idea that there was something special to them, a *love at first sight* type of thing that had drawn them together from his supposed innocent hello the other night.

"You aren't safe here," he continued. "Duran's people know you're staying here, and as easily as I got through to you, you can bet they'd have an easier time. We'll need to move you someplace safer. And get you a different car to drive..."

When tears filled her eyes, he stopped. He couldn't help himself. He had to admire her technique.

And when a few minutes later she leaned forward, laid her forehead against his chest, and whispered an incredibly heartfelt sounding "Thank you," he kissed her hair.

Chapter Eight

Savannah liked Isaac Forrester. As in *liked* liked him. *Woman to man* liked. More than she'd been drawn to anyone in the years since her close friend, Sierra, had been murdered during college. Sierra—Sierra's Web. She and her partners had all been close with Sierra. Had fought to have her disappearance investigated. And had been the reason her murder had been solved. All of them, Sierra's friends who'd become family to her, working together.

They'd been a team ever since. And there she was, leaning on a total stranger.

Keeping secrets. All over the place.

Not calling home.

Because she was going home. Rescuing the seven-year-old girl who'd been locked in no-man's-land since the day her father had been murdered and her baby sister had been kidnapped.

She might've been fighting for her life in a very real, physical sense, but that fight wasn't what prompted her to lean on Isaac Forrester. It wasn't what drove her.

Nicole did. Needing to know that her sister was okay, being able to finally free herself of the guilt—being loved and cared for while her baby sister, who'd still been breastfeeding and needed their mother far more, who'd been completely helpless, had been in the hands of murderers—took precedence over everything else.

Including her fondness for the man who'd almost literally fallen into her lap two nights before.

Providence.

It had to be.

Not only had the man awoken the woman who'd been frozen inside her for her entire adult life, he worked for her *sister*. Or at least for the family.

Her "in" had been given to her. A sign that she was on the right track.

At the very least, a fortuitous set of events that she absolutely could not ignore.

But before she actually left her hotel room with the man who told her he had a place where he knew she'd be safer, a place no one at the Duran estate knew existed, she excused herself to the restroom. And on her phone, set her thumbs to flying over the on-screen keyboard.

Life at Sierra's Web and in court had taught her that if things seemed too good to be true, they generally were.

Except that she'd almost been killed that day. Nothing good about that.

She'd seen her sister being pressured. Unable to get away. Crying. No good there, either.

To think, even for a second, that Isaac could have had anything to do with any of that as a way to manipulate her into the hands of Nicole's kidnappers—into the hands of whoever had been determined to silence her father—well, it just didn't make sense.

He had her. He hadn't needed to manipulate her in such grand measures.

Paranoia was not going to win over good sense.

Several links popped up on her search. All ammunition to kill the enemy of fear in her mind.

She read each one.

Flushed the toilet she'd been standing by. Washed her hands.

Isaac Forrester was exactly who he said he was. With an impressive display of law enforcement endorsements. She'd recognized one of them. Sierra's Web had partnered with the sheriff on a familial child abduction case the previous year.

Looking at herself in the mirror, seeing a woman she hardly recognized with dark hair, dry again, hanging freely around her and eyes that glowed with purpose. Imagination or not, she saw more life in them than she'd ever seen before.

A product of the adrenaline flowing through her.

She was finally on the cusp of completing her life's quest.

And had a gorgeous, hard-working, impressive guy standing by her, offering to have her back as she did so.

One who'd been honest with her. He needn't have sought her out that night. Or told her the truth about what he really did for a living.

He'd chosen loyalty to her over loyalty to his career in letting her know that she was on Duran's radar, that her life was definitely in danger there. And was going to be continuing to do so, helping her escape the sights of Duran's security until she was back home.

Because it was the right thing to do. Saving lives always came before career advancement.

Which was why she had to continue to keep her decades-old secret. By speaking outside of witness protection, she could put Isaac's life in further danger.

Watching her eyes cloud, she stood there, in front of the mirror, with doubts plaguing her. Was it selfish to accept his offer of help? Would mere association with her endanger him?

If that were so, she couldn't go home, either.

Shouldn't be at the hotel, putting staff and other guests at possible risk.

Could never be around another human being...

Stop. The command came from within. Carrying a load of frustration, of determination with it. She would not entertain anxiety-induced thoughts.

She'd been honest with Isaac about the dangers. Had told him more than she'd ever told anyone about her secret mission.

It had been twenty-four years.

And whoever had killed her father had no way of knowing what a seven-year-old child had known about her father's death.

Hadn't known how precocious she'd been. What she'd figured out on her own, leading her mother and investigators to tell her the truth to prevent her from asking questions or talking to too many people and putting herself in danger.

As long as she kept that piece to herself, she'd be fine.

They'd all be fine.

She had to believe that.

And opened the bathroom door with a grateful smile on her face.

When he heard the click on the door lock, in the alcove between the suite's bedroom and living areas, Isaac quickly shoved the burner phone he'd just used into the inner jacket pocket he'd pulled it from the second Savannah had left the room.

He was back on the couch, sitting forward, elbows on his knees, hands folded when she appeared. A ready stance.

And a nonthreatening one.

"Have you had a chance to change your mind?" she asked, calm, contained as she took the seat she'd vacated next to him. Still meeting his gaze straight on.

If they weren't playacting, they'd be talking without words. Making it more challenging to get a read on her. How did the woman ooze sincerity with just a look?

He might have just taken on one of the toughest assignments of his career.

"Not at all," he told her. "To the contrary. I think you should pack. I have a place we can go to." He kept hold of her gaze even when his libido was telling him it was time to look away. His professional instincts were guiding him, and when he was working, they always took precedence. "I'm on call twenty-four seven, but I have most nights to myself. And an apartment not far from here where I usually stay…"

Her frown didn't surprise him. "You think it's wise for you to take me to your apartment?"

She'd played right into that one. "Hell no," he said and added, "I don't think it's wise for us to be seen together at all." When he saw the disappointment cross her expression, he knew he had her. And hit his end note.

The one he'd come there to play.

"When I became a bodyguard, I used some of my personal investment money to secure a small place outside the city. It's only minutes away but set in the woods, with a road that only services three other properties. It's small and old, which allowed me to afford it, but it's made completely of cement, has camouflaged surveillance cameras, and trees that keep it hidden from aerial view." He paused to take a breath but then continued right on. "In my business, you never know what you're going to be up against. I needed to know I had a place I could get to, get my charges to in the event we were under attack."

He thought he read admiration in the lawyer's eyes. Didn't allow himself, as she nodded and squeezed his hand before she went to pack, to dwell on that touch of her skin against his. Didn't matter how much he wanted to hold on. To pull her to him. To kiss her. He kept his mind firmly focused on details. The house had been designated for his use from the time he'd gone undercover. In case his cover was blown, and he had to disappear quickly. And was currently listed under the name of a deceased person in a sealed property record. But it was owned by the San Diego office of the FBI.

Was one of the bureau's safe houses.

And, as of his last phone call, was going to serve as a place for the bureau to house—and watch—a possible suspect involved with Isaac's undercover operation.

Any guilt lurking inside him for lying to Savannah about where he was taking her was somewhat appeased by the fact that he was doing everything in his power, pulling out all stops, to keep her safe.

From the danger she'd brought, and was continuing to bring, upon herself.

"A friend of mine just dropped off a car for you to drive," he told her as she rolled one bag out of the bedroom and told him she was ready. "We'll leave your rental here until morning, and then Dale, my friend, will see that it gets dropped off at the airport."

Nodding, she said, "Making it look like I left town. I like

it." And then, giving him a look that he could only describe as suggestive, told him, "You're good."

He took a step forward, his gaze on her lips…and grabbed the handle of her bag instead. "I'll take this down the emergency exit stairs. Dale's going to meet me outside the door to load the bag in the car. Five minutes after I leave, you go down the same way. He'll give you the keys. I also asked him to pick you up a new burner phone. Just in case." He handed her a napkin. "That's the address of the house and a security code for the lockbox on the door."

Her mouth fell open, and he stopped, knew he'd made a mistake, had come on too strong, too much like an agent taking a witness to a safe house, and executed a quick mental reversal. "The lives in my care depend on my ability to keep them safe," he said, his tone softening. He had to allow his gaze to dwell with hers again.

In that personal way they'd silently established.

And again felt a pang of regret in his gut.

And lower…hunger built.

Savannah's glance was long, searching, and he stood there, feeling like they were mating with their eyes, until she nodded and asked, "Will you be following me there?"

No. He was going to his small, completely sterile apartment to take a cold shower.

"Please?" Her imploring glance seemed so sincere…

Why? What was her plan? What did she expect to get out of him that night? Maybe a photo of him? Compromised? Something she could use to bribe him to give her access to Charlotte?

As the thought occurred, hit his gut soundly, Isaac saw the bigger picture. She'd known who he was the other night. Had turned on the charm.

Flirting.

Just as he'd thought. But not to get him to lead her to Charlotte. She wanted a way to *bribe* him to give her access. To better ensure her success.

Which meant that—

"Of course I'll follow," he told her, reaching out a palm to cup her face.

And to seal the devil's deal they'd just made, he bent down. And placed his lips on hers.

Savannah had been kissed before. The first time she'd had sex was on prom night her senior year in high school. She'd dated throughout college, too. Until Sierra.

There'd been a man or two while she'd been on the road for an extended period of time dealing with cases over the years. Pleasant experiences that both parties had known were going nowhere.

But as she drove the newish small blue SUV off the hotel lot, Savannah's body still tingled at the memory of that one brief touch of Isaac's lips against hers.

She hadn't completed her mission, hadn't yet said goodbye to the past to enter the road to her future. So how could the life ahead be there already?

In her experience, while the world provided a lot of good moments, there'd never been such a combination of determination and fate holding her up.

It was like Isaac had appeared ahead of schedule to show her what lay ahead, continuously calling to her, to give her the strength to get there.

Or maybe his arrival was divinely timed. Giving her something to hold on to while she let go of the past.

She wasn't building false hopes. Absolutely did not hear a possibility of wedding bells or even long-term bells ringing in her head. Didn't even want them.

But a future? One that could contain Isaac?

Her heart was opening to the idea.

His plan for her escape had worked like a charm. Easy peasy. She'd been looking over her shoulder as she drove, watching the mirrors religiously, and hadn't seen one vehicle that appeared to be on her trail.

Not even his.

But he'd called on the new phone she'd been given as she'd pulled off the lot to let her know that he'd be about five minutes behind her. He just had to make a quick stop.

For condoms?

She didn't ask.

Didn't suggest the bottle of wine she'd have liked to have, either. To share with him. They had all night, and neither of them had finished the glass he'd poured for each.

There'd be no more wine. Not now that her moments alone in a hotel room to wallow were done. She was officially on her hunt. Had a firm plan to help Nicole.

Charlotte. Her sister identified with that name. Not Nicole. Savannah was going to have to get used to it. Every time Isaac said the name, it hurt.

She couldn't let that show.

"Charlotte," she said aloud to keep herself company as she drove in a darkness lit only by the electrically charged bulbs hanging in symmetrical lines along the way. "Charlotte. Charlotte."

She didn't hate the name.

Just hated what her sister not going by Nicole stood for.

A robbed life.

Four of them. The baby girl's. Hers. Their mother's. Their father's.

They'd been a perfect, completely normal middle-class family.

She'd just made her last turn, was looking for her destination half a mile ahead, when she noticed the car that turned in behind her.

Heart pounding, she was frozen by the fear that engulfed her.

Isaac had said that after the boating incident, Eduardo Duran considered her a risk. The binoculars. She'd been spying on his property.

Isaac was in Duran's employ.

By sheer force of will, she held the moving vehicle on a straight path, kept her foot on the gas pedal steady.

The house was supposed to be just ahead. If it was, did she turn in?

Keep going? Isaac had said there were a couple or three more houses on the road. Which was it, two or three? Were they inhabited?

Did the road dead-end?

What a fool she'd been! Grabbing for the phone in her pocket, Isaac's burner phone, she let out a frustrated cry. He'd had her turn off her phone. Had said that Duran's people had top-of-the-line equipment and would be able to trace it. She'd taken out the sim card after that.

Oh, God, why hadn't she paid more attention when Hud and Glen had gone into detail about their work on cases? She'd always been so busy…had just wanted the results they'd had for her.

Hud's number wasn't programmed into the new phone.

But the burner rang. Just as the car behind her sped up, driving on the questionable shoulder of the road to come up beside her.

Her mouth opened, her throat froze. Flooring the gas, she sped ahead, holding on to the wheel with both hands, looking straight ahead. Bracing for a blast. For pain.

And heard a horn honk.

Not a gunshot.

With a quick glance around her, half thinking she might be hurt and dreaming, she saw the burner phone where she'd dropped it on the console.

It was still ringing.

And the caller ID was right there, visibly on the screen.

Isaac.

Chapter Nine

She'd gunned the gas.

Though Savannah was smiling five minutes later, profusely thanking him and seemingly at ease as she pulled her suitcase out of the back of the SUV and rolled it toward where Isaac stood at the newly opened door, he knew she'd been frightened when she hadn't recognized him behind her.

Which was why he'd called.

Yet she was playing the whole thing off as though it hadn't happened. Had pretended that she'd just missed the drive. She looked around the place with a pleasant expression on her face. Said it was cozy.

Rolled her bag into the room he suggested she take. He could hear her moving around in there, unpacking.

Because she didn't want him to know how afraid she was? Or had been?

On one hand, he didn't blame her. He'd never let fear show if it overwhelmed him while working. Or if he did, it would be his last day on the job.

On the other hand...what was she trying to hide?

As Isaac moved about the house, making sure the water was on, the refrigerator stocked as he'd been told it would be, and then securing every room to his satisfaction before walking around outside, he couldn't get Savannah's fear out of his head.

What was she so deathly afraid of?

A lawyer out to get bribe material so her client could squeeze Eduardo Duran…it just didn't track that she'd be that skittish. More likely, she'd tell her client that he'd have to find someone else to do the job.

There had to be more to the situation than he'd been told. By either Duran or Savannah.

Was she desperate for money?

That didn't make sense, either. Not with her firm's legendary success.

Or had someone she cared about needed medical treatment—another motive behind desperate actions? But that didn't fly, either. Her best friend was a medical expert with a plethora of experts working for her.

She'd said she was there to find someone. Charlotte. He already knew that.

But why?

What did her client think he could get out of the woman to hold over her father?

As soon as the question occurred to him, he was giving himself a silent verbal blasting for not having realized the possibility sooner.

She wasn't just after Charlotte in some general sense. She was after something specific.

One thing.

Savannah knew what it was. And so did Eduardo.

Which would logically conclude that Eduardo knew exactly who Savannah was working for.

And could possibly use her—force her—to help Eduardo get to her client.

He knew who she was. She'd tipped her hand with the boating maneuver. And that was why she couldn't quit. Didn't matter where she went, he'd find her.

If the man had a secret that could ruin him, he'd stop at nothing, turn the screws on every powerful person for whom he'd ever done a favor or anyone who'd ever turned a blind eye to his business dealings and could be framed to put that secret to death once and for all.

From all Isaac knew about the man, he was certain about that much.

Savannah had to know at least part of that, too. It explained her almost irrational fear. She'd mentioned it earlier—he just hadn't picked up on it as real. He'd thought she was spinning her tale when she'd talked about a paranoia that had had her in its grip for the past year.

Since her friend's kidnapping the year before.

Did her business with Eduardo have something to do with that?

Was she protecting her firm, as she'd said she was? By not telling them what was going on?

Or had the not-telling-them part been a lie? Was she there on firm business?

That didn't make sense, either. With Sierra's Web's reputation, the FBI would have stepped up in a heartbeat to help.

Was someone blackmailing *her*?

Did Charlotte know her father's secret? Savannah's part in it?

He kind of doubted that part. The woman wouldn't have been so consumed by Arnold Wagar's advances if she'd had something of a life-and-death scope on her mind.

But… Eduardo's sudden announcement of a plan to marry his daughter off to the older man… Was Wagar somehow in on things?

And Eduardo was using his daughter to buy the man off?

Bothersome questions.

He needed answers.

And had a source right there. Savannah Compton. Who was determined to stay on his good side. Which gave him some advantage.

She'd given him much greater leverage with her earlier confession, magnified by the greatly accelerated speed out there on the road.

"You're set for the night, then?" he asked her, moving toward the door as she came out of the bedroom.

She froze. Only for a second. It was all the tell he needed.

"I've only seen the bedroom. Just made the bed with the

sheets that were on top of it. Give me a second to glance around, in case I have any questions." She sounded reasonable. Capable.

Isaac admired her for it.

"You can view all of the surveillance camera footage on the television," he told her. "You'll see the icon on the screen. Passcode is already set." Ostensibly giving her access so she'd feel safe.

And reminding her that she had reason to need to keep watch on that footage.

"I know it's dark out here, but the shades are room darkening, too, so you can turn on all the lights in the place and they won't be visible from the outside."

Hating himself for playing on her fear, Isaac watched her make her way through the place, checking out the bathroom, running water in the kitchen sink, and thought about all the lives that had been shattered by Eduardo Duran over the years, the hits made at his behest, the arms and illegal drugs he trafficked. And felt his backbone stiffen.

He just had to keep his lips off her body.

When she opened the refrigerator, he said, "I had my friend stock basics. Feel free to use whatever is there. I'm assuming you aren't going to want to go out again tonight." Unfamiliar home. Remote area in unfamiliar town. With darkness adding its own edge to the unknown.

He needed her to be afraid enough to invite him to stay. To have his extended presence be her idea.

And then, while she was still peering inside the refrigerator, he reached for the door handle and asked, "All good?"

Standing there with the door open, the interior light shedding shadows on her face, she nodded. Then, with a "Hey," turned, pulled out a bottle of wine, smiling straight at him, and said, "You can stay for a few if you'd like."

And he dropped his keys onto the table by the entrance.

She had plans to use the man. Savannah wasn't proud of that fact. Not a great way to treat a once-in-a-lifetime meeting.

A part of her hoped when all was said and done, he'd understand. And be willing to forgive her. Hoped that when she returned home, she'd not only have assurance that her baby sister was thriving but that she'd go with the connection she and Isaac shared intact.

Even if only to hold on to as a wonderful memory.

Proof that providence did provide.

As she held out her wineglass for Isaac to fill from the wine he'd just opened—the same kind she'd ordered at the bar the first night they'd met—Savannah's first thoughts were not on Charlotte.

They were on Isaac. And the kiss he'd given her just before they'd left her hotel room.

He hadn't even opened his mouth, nor she hers, and yet she'd felt as though they'd just been intimate.

She was there for Charlotte. Would lose her life if she had to in her quest to ensure her sister was safe and well. Nothing had changed there.

But in those moments, with darkness outside and someone from her father's deadly past looking for her, in addition to Duran's men, she needed Isaac to take her out of her headspace long enough for her to recharge.

Except that he took a chair in the living room, not a place on the couch they could share. And had taken a sip of his wine when she'd been holding hers for a toast.

They talked about their lives, their childhoods. She'd grown up in a one-parent home with no siblings. He'd had two parents until they'd been killed in a small plane crash, leaving Isaac, at nineteen, the sole caregiver for his thirteen-year-old sister.

A woman now grown, living on the opposite side of the country, and not good about keeping in touch.

He'd delivered the facts with regret laced in understanding.

And Savannah wanted him to join her on the couch. Wanted to scoot closer to him. Not due to attraction that time, but in commiseration.

Their circumstances were vastly different, and yet they were both orphaned with only a younger sister, from whom they were estranged.

The pain in that was intense. And a normal part of life, too. You couldn't change what was out of your control. "There are some times you just have to hurt," she said softly. "You loved. Choices were made, and you're forced to live with knowing that a part of you is out there somewhere but you can't ever see her. Talk to her." She took a sip of her wine.

He'd been watching her intently, but personally so, and his eyes narrowed as she delivered the last.

She put down her glass of wine. She'd had nowhere near enough. And she was through. She hadn't said the one she'd loved had been her sister, but she'd revealed too much.

Contemplating sex with the man was one thing, pouring her heart out another entirely. And unacceptable.

"You're talking about the person you came here to see?"

The shake of her head was instinctual. And she added, "I'm not here to see anyone." She'd already told him so, back at the hotel. She had no intention of making contact.

His brows drew together, but his position remained relaxed. And far too sexy. Those open hips, the bulge visible beneath the fly of his pants now that his jacket had fallen open.

Even the gun holstered at his hip.

A gun, sexy? Had she suddenly flipped into kink, too?

More like him being in legal possession of a gun made her feel safe.

He'd taken a sip of his wine. Set the glass on the coffee table, across from her. "I know you said that, but…you're here to find someone but not to see them?" he asked. She saw the frown on his face. Knew her explanation didn't make a lot of sense on the surface. Was afraid she was losing him.

And she shrugged. A lifetime of staying safe through secrets didn't just suddenly fade because she was attracted to a man with whom she was alone.

Or one she trusted.

She'd given every single one of her partners immediate legal access to everything she owned—had already given them her heart—and even they hadn't penetrated her code of silence.

He crossed his ankle over his opposite knee, took another sip of wine. A small one. When he returned the drink to the table, the liquid had barely dropped down on his glass.

She thought about moving to the chair next to his. Touching

distance. Could tell by the smoldering look in his eyes that he was interested in her.

He'd kissed her!

So why…

"What are your plans for tomorrow?" he asked then. "I'm back on duty at nine, guarding Charlotte, and need to be able to steer security away from wherever you might be."

She didn't want to think about danger. Security. Him leaving. But couldn't pass up the door he'd just pulled wide open.

"You don't work until nine? Charlotte sleeps in?" Had he been Savannah's bodyguard, he'd have to be present by seven, which was when she left her house every morning that she was in town.

Or was at work in her hotel room while out of town on a case.

"Her nighttime bodyguard is going off shift at that time."

Which told her very little. "Every day?"

He shrugged. Leaving her to wonder if he was deliberately holding out on her or if the arrangement was permanent until it wasn't. Something that changed according to day, week, or month.

"Does she work?" she asked then—casually, she prayed. She was being polite, taking interest in his daily work. Showing some curiosity, too. Considering the young woman's wealth, it would be odd if she didn't.

And held her breath as she waited for the first real piece of news on her little sister's life. Only to receive another noncommittal lift of one shoulder. So what? Nicole worked some but not regularly?

Or was involved with charity work but didn't get paid? Based on the home she owned, it wasn't like she needed the money.

"I can't imagine…" she started and stopped, telling herself not to pour it on too thick yet buzzing with an adrenaline that had taken over her entire system. Could this be it? The conversation that would set her free?

Providence.

Isaac was watching her, engaging with her visually, holding on, as he had from the first moment he'd joined her at the bar. "Imagine what?" he asked as she took a moment to formulate questions.

"If she resembles me, that would mean she's...around my age...and...living on an estate like that... I mean, I do fine... have a nice home...but that place...and needing full-time security...a bodyguard staff... It must be tough." She chose each word carefully. Not wanting to blow the chance to do what she'd come to do but needing to maintain a sense of normal curiosity in Charlotte without seeming overly interested.

Isaac's head tilt seemed more casual than on guard as he said, "It's like anything, I imagine. You take the bad with the good."

"I just..." She kept her gaze on his, giving him honesty as she confessed, "I don't know that I could live like that. I'd think I'd feel...caged." A comment meant to segue into the tears she'd witnessed on her sister's face that afternoon.

Who better than one of the family bodyguards to be put on watch for any signs of domestic abuse?

Another shrug, one that was clearly sharper, told her to stop. Too much, too soon. As waves of disappointment crashed through her, she picked up her wineglass. Allowing herself to reassess the choice to be done with it.

And horror struck. Did Isaac already know about Charlotte's distress and was turning a blind eye to it?

The possibility hung there. She couldn't bring it in. Didn't believe it. The only way Isaac Forrester would allow a young woman to be mistreated would be if he was getting enough evidence to have her abuser taken away from her, not just warned.

He'd be in that house collecting evidence.

And clearly wasn't going to say any more about his boss's daughter at the moment.

"You don't have to stay if you don't want to." He'd been different ever since they'd moved to his house. Meeting her gaze, silently communicating his desire to be with her. But more distant, too. More reticent.

"I want to."

Three words. Spoken with feeling. They filled her body with warmth again. Reignited her desire to have him there. Reinstated her faith that they'd met for a reason.

"So why are you sitting over there, not talking, and I'm over here asking inane questions to get to know you better?" Good save. And truth, too.

"You're in my home for protection, at my invitation. I've offered to help you stay safe in any way I can. Seems wrong to take advantage of that situation."

Oh. An *old-fashioned* gorgeous hunk of man who wore a gun.

Running her tongue over her lips, more of a nervous gesture than come-on, Savannah crossed her legs as she said, "What if I want you to?"

Because she did. "No strings attached," she added.

And he stood up.

Surging with anticipation, dripping with desire, nipples hard, Savannah waited for him to finally join her on the couch. To get about the business of losing herself in the most incredible sexual encounter she'd ever imagined.

He took his holster off his belt. Set it on the coffee table. Slipped off his shoes. And then said, "I can't, Savannah. Not tonight. With everything that happened today. And tomorrow as yet unknown. I'd like to stay here on the couch, though, at least for another few hours, and then head home to bed in my apartment, alone, to get some sleep before I have to go into work. In case anyone is watching to see if I came home for the night."

She wanted so much more. And yet as she stood, still hungry for sex, she wasn't as unhappy as she'd have expected. He was going to stay.

Was watching out for her.

And that said a whole lot more to her right then than a guy who'd jump on sex just because he wanted it. No matter how sincerely offered.

Chapter Ten

No way Isaac was having sex while agents from the San Diego office were watching the house. But for some reason, when it had become obvious he wasn't going to get any information out of Savannah Compton that night, he hadn't been able to just put down his wine and walk out on her.

He could tell she'd been desperate not to be alone. He'd just known.

And so, turning on the inside camera aimed at the living area, he half lay on the couch and dozed until his watch alarm vibrated against his wrist, letting him know it was time to go.

He glanced in on Savannah only to make certain that she was there and that the covers were moving with her breathing.

He didn't let his gaze linger, didn't stare at her shoulders, bare except for one-inch silk straps, and kept his gaze firmly there and above as he left the room as silently as he'd entered.

And though he'd debated with himself, he hadn't turned off the camera before he'd left. Savannah Compton didn't seem like the type to walk naked around the living room, and he felt better about agents having an eye inside the house.

Just a precaution in case Duran's tracking abilities were impossibly brilliant. And the men the international criminal had hired found ways to land on a property invisibly and seep through walls.

All other points of entry were guarded, albeit surreptitiously. The FBI took their safe houses seriously.

Especially when they were holding potential suspects.

He drove away slowly, so as not to wake her up or draw any other attention to himself, and didn't turn on the headlights until he was a quarter of a mile down the road and passed what he knew to be a marker for a preset surveillance-tent site on the safe house property. The site was fully equipped with electrical hookup and internet connection. And when the house was in use, a tent with a couple of decent air mattresses was erected.

It didn't look like much on the outside, but the agents had everything they needed to do their jobs within. And traded off every four to six hours.

Although eager to get home to his boring little apartment, Isaac didn't even make it to the highway before his private Duran cell rang.

Dread filled his gut as he pulled the phone out of his inner jacket pocket, slowing as he drove to the side of the road. Expecting to see Emmajean's name on the screen, he came to an abrupt halt as he recognized Duran's.

Eduardo Duran had phoned that number exactly zero times in the months Isaac had been in his employ.

"Yeah," he said urgently. Thinking of Savannah. Had Duran done something to her the second he'd left the house? Was it over?

And his cover blown, too?

"Charlotte's gone."

Shock hit Isaac. Gas pedal to the floor, he flicked on the car audio system as he drove, dropping the phone into the seat. "Emmajean?" he yelled, to be heard.

And because he was pissed. Livid.

At himself. At Savannah. The distraction she'd posed. The possible part she'd played. Had she known? Was that why she'd asked him to stay the night?

"Where in the hell was Emmajean?" he demanded when no immediate response from his boss was forthcoming.

"In the bathroom." Eduardo's voice had lost some of its commanding strength. Isaac struggled to keep up. To read between lines he had and the many he didn't yet know.

"Who got Charlotte?"

"I was hoping you." Ah. The reason for the call.

And with that last statement, the man actually sounded... lost. Beaten.

It wouldn't last—Isaac knew that. Men like Duran didn't lose. Or give up.

They were captured. Or they died wealthy of natural causes.

Isaac's brain clicked into full focus. "Any sign of forced entry?" He had a job to do and was one of the best at it.

"My men are still checking. Emmajean came out of the bathroom twenty minutes ago and found her gone."

Isaac relaxed enough to take a full breath. "You're sure she's not in the house?"

"Full staff, security, household, and protection detail have been in every room, every closet. I've been calling her cell. It's not ringing here in the house, not on her charger. And she's not answering."

Didn't mean she'd been abducted.

And yet... Charlotte and her phone...the woman never let it out of reach. To the point of paranoia.

But to take her from her bed? On an estate that was armed to the hilt?

If someone was going to attempt to blackmail Eduardo Duran by taking his daughter, they'd have to be as good as or better than Duran's army.

Which meant frighteningly unpredictable.

And what better way to prove that, to break Duran, than to invade his most personal space?

Still, Isaac had to see all possibilities. "She might have left on her own."

"Her car's here."

"What about the rest of the fleet?"

"All here."

Still didn't mean she couldn't have left of her own accord. Except that unless Charlotte felt safe—as she had with her plan to hide out in a secure bathroom the other day—she never went five feet without protection detail. The need had seemed ingrained in her.

Breaking all speed limits, Isaac wasn't sure why Duran was still on the phone with him. The connection was still live.

Duran usually just clicked off when he was done with whoever he'd been talking to.

The Duran Isaac knew would be in a suit at his desk in a time of dire emergency, no matter the time of day or night, barking orders at his head of security.

Isaac was barking them at himself. Savannah Compton. Doubts hit for a second time. More solidly. Had she known the plan all along? Had keeping him with her for the night been the plan?

At the hotel or the house...either would have fit.

"Have they called the police?" he bit out, mind spinning with next possible moves.

Looking for suspects, clues he'd missed.

"It's too soon to bring them in. We need to exhaust reasonable means of finding her first." Duran's voice was small in the silence. "But I've already called in the best of the best in the private sector, and they're downstairs. You know her whereabouts and outside activities, the people who interacted with her far better than anyone else, Forrester. Get here."

The man was not himself.

Isaac almost felt sorry for him.

Eduardo Duran's daughter was gone, and he was breaking.

Isaac had found Duran's biggest weakness.

Just not soon enough.

Someone else had found her, too.

Savannah spent the early hours of the morning on the internet. Hud had set up all the partner's computers, including laptops and tablets, with complex firewalls and safety protocols so that they could travel and surf with relative anonymity. And while she couldn't control her current internet connection, she trusted Isaac.

And he'd trusted her enough that he'd left his system password on the table for her.

She'd found it within minutes of his leaving. Had heard him go. And gotten up immediately after. Until she had a chance to see the outside of the property in the daylight, to get a feel for where she was and how she might keep herself safe in the event her location was compromised while she was there alone, there was no way she'd be able to go back to sleep.

Thoughts of Charlotte had been consuming her since the second she'd awoken. The night before—the personal part, where forgetfulness with Isaac had come first—was better left in the past. She'd been scared. Not thinking clearly.

And while she was certain that she'd have immensely enjoyed a sexual encounter with Isaac Forrester, she was glad it hadn't happened. She had Isaac's attention. Was in his secret home. Which meant access to him. A chance to find out about Nicole. *Charlotte*. She couldn't blow the golden opportunity that had just landed in her lap by making it personal.

Risking a breakup.

If he was a one-and-done type of guy—and she'd offered a fling... Yeah, sex couldn't happen. She had to keep the thrill alive. The temptation.

She had to flirt.

But couldn't go all the way...

Most particularly as she took the time, used the skills Hud had taught her to do some deep diving of her own on Charlotte Duran. And found almost nothing.

No public records. No publicity photos from charity events.

No listing on popular people encyclopedia sites. And no hits using the social media hacks she'd been taught.

She'd found a university course with the name Professor Charlotte Duran as teacher, but no way to verify that it was the same woman Savannah had seen the day before. There'd been no accompanying photo. No teacher's biography.

And still, Savannah smiled. Nicole, a university professor? In women's studies? Talking about the need to be aware of cultural language in a global society? Their mom would be so proud...

Hell, Savannah was proud, and she didn't even know for sure that the two women—Professor Charlotte Duran and heiress Charlotte Duran—were one and the same.

It felt right, though. Maybe because she wanted so badly for it to be so. To know that other than the distressing personal issue she'd witnessed the day before, Nicole really was thriving. And not just financially...

The phone beside her on the table rang. Savannah jumped, the alert seeming deafening in the peaceful silence. Without touching the thing, she glanced at the screen.

Isaac.

Before eight in the morning. Four hours after he'd left her.

Calling before he went into work? The thought brought a smile, and she picked up.

"Hey, handsome..." She'd have liked the greeting to be solely powered by logical choice. Her decision to keep him on the temptation hook. The smile on her face—one he couldn't possibly see—gave lie to the wish.

"Where are you?" He didn't sound in the mood for sex. At all.

His short, staccato tone sent fear shooting through her. "At the house," she said, her focus on her surroundings, and she slowly got up from the table and moved toward the closest cement wall without window range. Shoved her back up against it. "What's going on?"

"Have you been there all morning?"

Was she being interrogated? Shaking her head against the absurdity of the thought, she said, "Yes." And as her gaze continued to take in what she could see of the house, she asked again, "What's going on, Isaac?"

"Are you alone?"

Realization dawned with enough relief to make her weak. His tension was on her behalf. "Yes. I'm fine," she assured him and tensed again immediately, too, as her mind continued to process. "You have reason to believe someone might be here with me?"

"I didn't know." Isaac's voice had softened some. "Listen, I'm sending someone out to watch the property. You'll be safe there. But I need you to promise me you won't leave. Not until I can get there."

With Isaac asking? "Of course." That had been a given. More than a decade with Sierra's Web had taught her that in a world of bad people, there would be one you could trust. And when you found that one, you worked together to combat evil.

Her life was endangered. She feared, after the previous day's gunshot, that someone to do with her father's past had found her. And she knew for certain, after Isaac's confession the day before, that Eduardo Duran's people were after her, too.

She had no choice but to gratefully accept Isaac's help.

But wasn't going to do so without further information. "As long as you tell me what's going on."

A long pause fell on the line, finally prompting her to say, "Isaac?"

"I can't go into detail, but there's been a breach in Duran security, and I just needed to make certain that it didn't have to do with someone going rogue to get to you."

The initial tension in his tone...had been concern for her.

And what did that mean, a breach in security?

"Should I be on the lookout?" she asked. "California's not an open-carry state. I don't have my gun." Didn't like the idea of being a sitting duck.

And didn't think the self-defense and knife-throwing training she'd done were going to serve her in her current situation.

"I'm guessing you're always on the lookout, but as long as you stay put, you're probably in the safest place you could be," he said, sounding more like the man she was growing to know so quickly. "My guy will be there within the next few minutes. As soon as he texts me the all-clear, I'll let you know."

"Thank you."

"Just trying to keep my promise to my vacation fling," he said then, his tone lightening considerably.

Letting her know he was no longer worried about her. Which eased her tension, too.

"What promise?" She didn't even have to work at sounding sexy for him.

"To protect you while you do what you have to do." There was no doubt of the warmth that had infused those last words.

Stumbling back to her computer, Savannah fell into her chair, her heart melting all over the table.

* * *

Darkness had long since fallen again by the time Isaac headed back out to the safe house. He'd been in touch with Savannah a couple of times, under the guise of checking in to make sure she was holding up okay, and had been receiving hourly reports from the agents watching the safe house and the living room inside it.

She'd kept the blackout curtains drawn all day.

An expected move from someone who was involved in criminal activity. And from a victim being hunted, too.

She'd made no attempts to leave—hadn't even opened the front door.

No one had slowed when passing the driveway, let alone attempted to access the property—or the expert lawyer.

But while the FBI's internet-usage access at the safe house could be somewhat monitored, Savannah's laptop had, so far, been completely unbreachable. The best tech in the FBI's San Diego office had been attempting to get in for most of the day and would continue to do so.

And if Savannah Compton had attempted to contact anyone or had been contacted by anyone, the burner phone Isaac had given her hadn't been used. They had just dumped the phone. They had a continual open trace on it, too.

He'd had her turn off her personal phone so that it couldn't be traced. Had watched her take the sim card out of it, of her own accord—reminding him that the woman was far more formidable an opponent than she appeared—but the bureau had been tracking it anyway. There'd been no activity.

She could have a third phone. Made sense that she did. One solely for the dirty job.

The woman was deceptively good. Playing the femme fatale for his sake, to lure him, and doing it so well he had to consciously stop himself from falling for her. And yet when it came to the job she was there to do, she didn't seem to miss a beat.

Even while locked up in a safe house.

She had to be communicating with her source somehow.

If not by phone, then in that firewalled computer of hers.

Which made her electronic device the number-one priority on his list of things to conquer that night.

Charlotte was still missing. Had been gone more than seventeen hours. Not something she'd have done of her own accord without at least notifying her father.

As much as Eduardo adored Charlotte, Isaac was pretty certain that Duran's daughter adored him more.

Or at least thought she did. During the months Isaac had been escorting every step she took off from Duran property, Charlotte's hero-worship of her father had been almost enviably evident.

He'd once thought his little sister looked up to him, believed in him, loved him in the same way. Having her in his life, his home, his heart had given him a lift he'd never have imagined. Her love had made him feel like Superman.

Stopping half a mile down from the safe house, he rolled down his window to speak with the agent stationed in the woods just off the road's shoulder. Heard a rendition of the same reports he'd been receiving all day.

House was quiet. Property was quiet.

No sign of the woman, other than occasional pacing to and from the living area.

Window up, Isaac touched the gas lightly, approaching the drive slowly. All signs indicated that Savannah was playing some kind of waiting game.

Forcing the rest of them to do the same.

Seventeen hours and no ransom note yet. No demands of any kind.

The good news, as Isaac had told Eduardo himself many times that day, was that Charlotte Duran's body hadn't been found. There'd been no car accidents. Duran's security had been making quiet checks all over the city. With the help, Isaac suspected, of an insider within the police department. It was reasonable to assume Charlotte was still alive. She was worth too much money for someone to just throw her away.

Taking her out of that house, getting by the levels of security had to have been a mammoth feat. One that could only have been accomplished by experts.

Not an effort one would undertake for nothing.

Turning onto the safe house property, Isaac started up the long drive, considering a revenge motive again, as he and his coworkers—FBI agents and Duran security in separate consultations—had done several times that day. Hate could consume someone to the point of doing whatever it took to avenge oneself. But just taking Charlotte from Eduardo didn't seem to fit that profile. The perp would need to twist the knife into Duran for utmost satisfaction. He'd need Duran to see him, hear him. To know from whence his pain came.

He'd need to take credit.

It was too soon for a missing person report, but there wouldn't be one in any event. Duran was choosing to conduct his own private investigation, hiring the best of the best in conjunction with his full-time security staff rather than getting police, FBI, and press involved. At least on an official level. Isaac had long suspected that the man had at least one law enforcement officer on staff under the table.

Outside of Duran's purview, the FBI agents and two agents from Isaac's team who'd flown out from Washington were searching for Charlotte. Being careful to preserve Isaac's cover.

They were too close to bringing Duran down to do anything that might blow the case.

But even with all the experienced feet on the ground, seventeen hours of collective efforts had generated absolutely nothing. Not a single viable lead.

No one even knew for sure if Charlotte had been in the house when she'd been taken. There'd been no sign of forced entry or struggle. The outdoor cameras had been blacked out, but only for a matter of minutes. No vehicle had been caught on video either in the driveway or out on the street. There hadn't even been a footprint in Duran's private beach—which was raked every night just before dark.

Isaac's theory was that they'd taken her by water. It was the only thing that made sense to him. No way had the front been breached without at least one of the half dozen security measures—including motion-sensor floodlights and a separate trigger that was turned on every night on the sprinkler system—being activated.

There were cameras at the intersections at both ends of the road that led to Duran's property. All vehicles on the loop had been investigated. And had been cleared.

Phone logs had all been checked, and Duran had also agreed to turn over all phones in his employ for physical investigation to the team of private detectives he'd hired, though Isaac strongly suspected Duran's head of security had confiscated a stash of non-registered devices before the phones had been provided.

Stopping his vehicle beside Savannah's, blocking hers from being seen upon approach, Isaac thought he saw movement, a small flash of light, from the side of one of the front windows. The dark curtain moving.

She was watching for him.

The unwelcome pleasant physical jolt that gave him kept him sitting in his car, getting his head firmly back into the case.

Charlotte was missing. Whether the young woman was truly in danger or in on some ploy with her father, whether Savannah's client was involved or not, Isaac had to give the disappearance his full focus.

The slit of light showed again from the next curtain over.

The few minutes of blackout on Duran's security cameras ate at him, too. It could have been due to a power company surge as had been reported, but the coincidence of that timing was too much for Isaac to swallow. Someone at the house had to have shut down those cameras. Causing him to think that either Duran had had his own daughter kidnapped, to keep her safe until the Compton threat had been dealt with, or someone on Duran's security staff was double-crossing him.

Both possibilities were currently on Isaac's table. The first—Duran being behind Charlotte's disappearance—didn't track with the man's obvious distress. But a guy didn't get as far as Duran had, carry the power he carried without the ability to put on a good show. To be a chameleon and play whatever part was required by the current coup.

And if his goal was to protect Charlotte, he'd most definitely hire the best of the best to find her, to make the kidnapping look legitimate.

The second possibility—that someone in Duran's employ had gone rogue—weighed more heavily upon Isaac. Maybe because being a rogue employee himself, he knew how feasible the possibility really was.

Whether the employee was connected to Savannah's client— a planted mole—or had just chosen his timing based on the shooting event the day before, Isaac couldn't say.

He'd spent a good part of the day, in between other duties, checking out every single security agent and bodyguard in Duran's employ. Finding nothing. And getting a sick feeling that he was on the right track, too, with no way to explain the sensation.

It had prompted three calls to Savannah, though. He'd made the first one half worried for her safety and half suspecting that she'd been in on Charlotte's abduction. The second two had been partially out of suspicion but more to keep her actively waiting for him.

To keep her in place until he could get there and interview her face-to-face, while allaying her fears about the supposed security breach he'd mentioned earlier.

He had to get her to go about her business as she would have from her hotel room. To feel free to leave.

So that his agents could follow her.

And then hope that she led them to whoever had Charlotte.

Or, if not that, to whatever debilitating secret she and Eduardo shared. Because Eduardo hadn't been acting himself since the minute he'd mentioned Savannah Compton to Isaac. It all had to be connected.

He sat there staring at the house, getting his head in order, and without warning, experienced again the relief he'd felt each time he'd heard her voice answer the phone that day, giving him his own confirmation—in addition to those from his agents— that she was fine. His sensations were merely an unfortunate consequence of the job. A residual from the part he was being forced to play.

Undercover agents were human. And had to learn how to

live with genuine feelings that were products of living realistically as someone else.

Learn to live with them. Not run from them.

He had to keep his eye on the final goal—putting Eduardo Duran and his multibillion-dollar illegal empire permanently out of business.

Being at the house, knowing that Savannah was right there, safe, available for him to question, Isaac suddenly wasn't as hell-bent to actually be back in her presence. It had been a long day. On only a few hours of sleep.

He'd taken on a lot of different roles during his undercover-agent career but never one that had blurred lines between reality and fiction as much as the current one was doing.

He could handle the situation. He *would* handle it. Just...

A bigger flash of light came from the front of the house. To the left of the windows. The front door had opened.

Savannah, in capri pants and a T-shirt, with her long hair loose and silky looking as it covered her breasts, stood there.

Ready to welcome him.

And, God help him, just the sight of her made Isaac hard again.

Chapter Eleven

He was back.

Savannah couldn't see enough in the darkness to tell but figured he was finishing a phone call while he sat in the drive. Was impatient to have it done.

She didn't recognize the eagerness with which she waited at the door, the pleasure it brought her to see Isaac finally getting out of his car.

She was used to living alone. Generally welcomed the rare full day she'd get at home every few months. Time to herself. Hours with no pressing responsibility. Able to move from activity to activity at her leisure. With no need for other human interaction.

But the current situation was not general to her.

And Isaac…she didn't know what he was. She just knew her spirits picked up a whole lot as he walked toward her, buttoning his jacket. Like he was getting ready to appear someplace important.

"Everything okay?" he asked as she stepped back from the door.

The question showed her how she must've looked to him. Like some lonely housewife or needy vacation fling, with so little in her life that his arrival was the day's event.

"Fine," she said. And, overall, it was. The day had proven productive. "I'm just glad you made it out."

She'd been waiting to have the one glass of wine that would help her sleep. To share it with him as they talked.

About Charlotte. Unlike the night before, she stood before him armed with a conversational plan. A way to find out what she needed to know. If she was lucky, she could be on a plane in the morning, and then, at least for a time, she could hire one of the firm's bodyguards to make certain that there was no longer anyone at her back.

Regardless of what Isaac said, it didn't make sense to her that Duran would bother with her if she just went away. And the other...the past ghosts...the same. While she was in San Diego, perhaps she posed a threat to whoever had taken Nicole. If nothing else. Maybe whoever shot at Savannah knew only about Nicole's part in the tragedy all those years ago. Someone who'd merely been a hired hand to kill her father but had found himself unexpectedly saddled with a toddler, too, and had seen her as a chance to make another buck. Or the shooter had just been the one who'd handled the human trafficking of a one-year-old child.

After a day to herself and her computer to keep her focused, she was thinking more like herself again. Logically. Not emotionally. Left brain, not right.

For the most part. Her reaction to Isaac Forrester aside.

To that end, she turned her back on the man as he came through the door. Speaking over her shoulder as she asked him, "You want a glass of wine? I waited for you."

"Sure." He didn't sound all that enthusiastic. He sounded... tired.

She reached for the opened bottle from the night before. "Did you get the security breach resolved?" She figured he must have or he wouldn't be there.

The breach must've been why he was so late visiting, too. She'd been about to make a bed on the couch for the night—to turn in early with the television showing security camera footage and a movie streaming on her computer—when he'd called to say he was on his way.

And...his coming out anyway, in spite of his long day, had put a smile inside her, to offset the doubts and distress.

It had also given her hope that any immediate danger, requiring his friend to keep a watch on Savannah's temporary lodging for him, had passed.

He'd taken the glass she handed him. Hadn't answered her question regarding the breach. Was standing there, watching her. Assessing?

Like he wasn't sure what to make of her?

She didn't think so. It was like he was taking her in. Absorbing her essence.

A ludicrous thought. She dismissed it. Wasn't going there.

She went to the couch instead. Took a seat next to the bedding she'd brought out. Left him to his chair choice from the night before.

Or not.

He sat on the couch. Not close. But there. Took a sip of wine. Laid his head back. Stared straight ahead but seemed relaxed. Or like he was in the process of becoming so.

Her heart lurched. The twelve hours he'd just been through had obviously not been easy. He needed some wind-down time. She certainly got that.

"You didn't have to drive all the way out here," she said softly, in case what he really wanted was to be home in bed. "You've had a long day and didn't get a lot of sleep last night." And, in spite of how she'd been acting around him, truthfully asserted, "I'm really fine. And can take care of myself."

Without lifting his head from the back of the couch, he turned toward her. His gaze moving over her face.

She felt like the sight pleased him. Gave him a somewhat tired, understanding smile. "I was actually about to turn in when you called." The words were meant to free him to go.

"You kicking me out?" He wasn't getting up.

"No." She'd meant to leave it at that. But added, "I was glad you called." There were things she couldn't tell him. They seemed to prompt honesty everywhere she could give it.

Something else drove her to give him the silence he seemed to need. A feeling inside that they were meant to be connected. Even if just for the moment. Like he was in her circle of people she watched out for. And she was content to sit quietly and slowly sip wine with occasional long looks but no words between them.

Several minutes later, he said, "The security breach turned out to be no more than an electrical surge from the power company."

He was staring toward the ceiling as he spoke. And she felt for him. Putting in long hours, adrenaline pumping, having the weight of lives on your shoulders, only to find that everything was just a misunderstanding. She'd been there with Sierra's Web more than once. Had engaged her entire team on just such a case—an apparent stolen will and feared lost fortune—the year before. And while there was great relief in knowing that there hadn't been criminal activity or human suffering, it was still a bit frustrating to have spent so much mental and emotional energy for nothing.

Straightening enough to turn toward her, Isaac met her gaze and said, "I apologize for holding you up here all day. I just needed to make certain…" He paused as his look seemed to grow deeper. "That it didn't have anything to do with you. I promised you protection…"

"I'm here by my own mandate, Isaac," she said softly. "I brought this on myself, fully knowing that I could be putting myself in danger. If something were to happen to me, it'd be my fault, not yours." No way could she have him taking on responsibility for choices she'd made. "You didn't even know me until a few days ago." She said the words to absolve him of any responsibility for her. To erase the possibility of him bearing guilt for what could happen in the days ahead.

But the reminder hit home, too. She was trusting a man she'd just met.

Using him for her own gain.

And falling for him, too.

Not liking herself a whole lot at that moment, she wanted to pack her bags and go. To leave the home he'd so generously opened to her.

Until she had a flash of her sister at the back of her magnificent property, standing on her private beach and falling apart because a man wouldn't leave her alone.

"I know about guilt." The words came softly from deep within her. And she turned to face him, bringing her knee up on the couch, not far from his thigh. "Sierra's Web...we named our firm after a friend we all had in college, Sierra Wendel. She'd been physically abused, but none of us knew it. I was pre-law then, volunteering as a receptionist at the law clinic, and she'd come in, wanting to find information on evidence. She'd said it was for a class, but when I asked which one, she pretended like she hadn't heard me. I figured she was just preoccupied. Didn't ask any questions. Didn't push..."

"You were working, had a duty to your employer." He said the words as though he was the lawyer, not her.

"Right, but as a friend, living in the same dorm with her, I had a feeling something wasn't quite right with her. But she was kind of an introvert. Private. So was I. And I never followed up."

She stopped. Thought about Winchester Holmes, who'd been in love with Sierra though he hadn't admitted as much to any of the partners until the previous year, and the way her dear friend had beaten himself up over the years for not asking questions.

Straightening, feeling her resolve to be there for Nicole strengthen tenfold within her, Savannah said, "Sierra was murdered as an indirect result of that abuse, and if any of us had talked, even to each other, about our concerns, if any of us had acted on them, we probably could have saved her life."

Instead, the friends had been instrumental in solving her murder.

Isaac raised a hand, opened his mouth, and Savannah gave him a sharp shake of the head. "I know," she told him. "We all did what we thought best at the time, respecting her right to the privacy she was guarding so carefully, which is why I'm telling you...my choices are mine. I'm in town for my reasons. I'm purposely not sharing the details. My choice. You aren't going to change any of that. And I can't have you feeling guilty over anything that transpires because of my presence here."

She met his gaze full on again. Speaking as much with her eyes as with words.

Life. Death. Sex. Ghosting.

Whatever happened, she'd made her bed all by herself.
And told him so.

He'd been absolved of guilt. She'd made her bed. As he saw
the pillow and blanket on the far end of the couch behind her,
remembered her saying she was about to turn in, Isaac felt the
irony of her words all the way to his bones.

She'd made her bed. And he had to lie in it. Pun intended for
his own tired brain only.

Apparently she'd been intending to sleep on the couch instead of the bedroom she'd used the previous night. Because
he'd been on the couch.

Good thing he'd used his phone to remotely turn off the inside camera when he'd pulled up to the house.

He'd made his bed, too.

He just hadn't gotten there yet.

Had been fighting his own sense of loathing at the idea of
setting in motion the grand lie he'd planned. With the goal of
getting Savannah to go about her business the next day in the
hope that she'd lead agents to secrets that could put Duran
away for life.

And if she led them to Charlotte, which he strongly suspected
she would, all the better. He wasn't completely convinced his
charge was in trouble. Though, considering Eduardo's distress,
he was leaning more in that direction.

It was likely, considering the closeness of father and daughter, that she knew the big secret, too.

Which could have put her in danger.

So he needed to get Savannah out of the house and back on
the business that had brought her to town watching the Durans
from a boat on the ocean.

He had protocols in place, agents ready to protect her if need
be. The FBI needed her alive, possibly to testify against Duran,
depending on what she knew.

But as Isaac sat there in the low light, the quiet, catching
whiffs of Savannah's light, somewhat spicy scent, he wondered
if she was struggling as hard as he was with whatever was happening between them. He wasn't imagining the heat. It wasn't

just coming from him. His was feeding off from hers. Maybe hers stayed lit by his. He was no expert on that subject.

But couldn't believe she was faking it all.

No one was that good. Not even him.

And that first night…she'd intimated that he could have come upstairs with her…and hadn't had any idea who he was.

He'd been the pursuer that night. He'd known who she was. Had been there specifically to meet her, to find out what she knew about Duran. And had come on to her for that purpose alone.

But as she'd said, she'd made her choices. Chosen the job she was on. She'd responded to his light flirting. Seemed to be enjoying their seemingly impromptu association.

As had he seemed. He'd made sure of it.

Leaning over, he laid his lips on hers. To get it done. Out of the way.

To admit that desire existed between them and wasn't going to just disappear by force of will. Or by calling off the jobs they were doing.

It was just a kiss. Meant to diffuse by taking away the mystery. The challenge. The curiosity. The sense that it couldn't happen. Was forbidden.

But when her soft lips accommodated his, he felt his body surge with heat, felt himself nearing a point where he'd hear the siren's call louder than his own determination, and he pulled slowly, regretfully back.

"Talk first," he told her. And without waiting for her response, not trusting himself to say no if she made any hint at an invitation to put talk off a little longer, he said, "Duran's security team have spent the day out looking for you. Tonight, in our final meeting, they were allowing the possibility that you'd left town. So, from that standpoint, you should be safe enough to go about your business tomorrow. I can't speak for whatever danger you might have brought with you…"

She licked her lips. Quickly, like they were dry. Not as a come-on.

That quick dart of her tongue turned him on anyway, and after a deep swallow, he kept talking. "I'd feel a whole lot better about it, though, if you'd let me run interference for you, as we'd originally planned. Letting you know where Duran's people are so you can be somewhere else, keeping my ears open to all conversations and letting you know if they're back to thinking you're still around..." Depending on what her client might say to whoever had ratted him out to Duran in the first place.

And if there was total radio silence? Did that mean her client had what he wanted?

Charlotte?

Did Savannah already know that?

Did she know if the professor was okay? Was a plan in place to make Eduardo suffer through silence before squeezing him for whatever they were after?

If so, Savannah would likely meet with Charlotte in the morning to say whatever she'd come to say, tell the secret she had to tell—assuming Charlotte didn't know it already—to be able to get a great deal of wealth out of Duran.

And if Savannah, thinking that Isaac's "friend" was no longer watching her, packed up and headed straight for the airport?

He'd have to make a quick, unscheduled trip to the terminal and find a way to convince her to stay.

More likely, if any of his stars aligned, first thing in the morning she'd lead agents to Charlotte.

Finding the missing woman was paramount in the moment. But it wouldn't be an end. Not for Isaac. He wasn't done until Duran was.

Even if it meant offering Charlotte and Savannah immunity to testify against the career criminal.

Any way Isaac looked at it, he needed more time with the expert attorney.

Had to continue growing their relationship.

And when she leaned into him, whispering a quiet thank-you before opening her mouth on his, he gave up being on duty and let the fire within burn him up.

Chapter Twelve

Savannah didn't forsake her purpose. Or her plan.

She didn't forsake herself, either. There were no promises between her and Isaac. His life was in southern California with the Durans. She was a fleeting moment there.

A vacation fling who meant enough for him to help her with her quest, without even trying to get tangled up in her private threads.

Yet passion had flamed between them. Unlike anything she'd ever felt before.

Life was too short, far too unpredictable for her to pretend she didn't feel it. Or want it.

When Isaac's tongue met hers, she welcomed the contact, shared it, giving as she took. And when he pushed her down to the couch, lying half beside, half on top of her, she wrapped her arms around him, holding him close.

There were no words. Not spoken ones. His gaze bore witness, though. With so much impact she became captivated. Staring at him as she reached a hand down to his fly, to cover the hard muscles and passion burgeoning there.

Retaining eye contact when his hand slid inside her pants and found her wetness. It pleased him. A lot. The intense darkening in his look told her as much as the hard pressure of his penis against her thigh did.

The visual communication went silent, briefly, when he pulled her shirt over her head. She shivered, with pleasure more than chill, as the air hit her skin.

And unbuttoned his shirt while he jerked the sleeves of his jacket down his arms.

The clothes fell in a pile beside the couch. Panties on suit pants. Briefs on bra. She caught a glimpse, but only one. She couldn't stop seeking out from his gaze the things they weren't saying.

Couldn't prevent herself from making visual promises that she knew she'd never be able to say. Their coming together was a blip in time, but that didn't mean she wasn't committed to it, to him, fully and completely.

For those moments, for however long they lasted, her heart was his.

When he entered her the first time and became a part of her, her soul welcomed him as a piece of itself forever. A moment, a connection that would always be with her.

And when they moved in slow, then fast, soft then harder, perfect rhythm she looked him in the eye and promised that nothing would ever mar the memory of that moment.

They came together again minutes later, with her on top, sitting on his lap.

And then, in tandem, they reached for their clothes. Handing pieces to each other as they fit and, standing, dressed side by side.

"Do you have to go right away?" she asked him when he zipped his pants and buckled his belt.

He glanced at the pillow and blanket she'd laid on the couch. "The threat from Duran might have dissipated, but while you're still on your mission, I was planning to stay here, as I did last night. Unless you'd rather I go?"

She shook her head. "I'll take the bedroom."

But instead of politely leaving the room, she plopped back down to the couch. Picked up her glass of wine. Took a slow sip and looked up at him.

The sooner she could find out what she needed to know, the

better. She had to get out of San Diego before she did something really stupid. Like fall in love.

But far more pressing, the more quickly she could help Nicole, the better off her sister would be. All day long she'd been driven by the very real fear that her sister might be physically hurt by the man Savannah had seen from the boat. Eduardo Duran? Charlotte's husband? She didn't know.

"I did some research on Charlotte Duran today," she started in right away with the plan she'd made for when she next saw Isaac. Beginning with seemingly casual conversation pertaining to something he'd shared with her about his life. The person he was being paid to protect. "She's a professor." She'd managed to confirm the fact after hours of reading write-ups of charity functions put on to raise money for women's causes. There'd been a mention, not of Charlotte directly but of Eduardo, paying tribute to his "lovely professor daughter."

And the other tidbit that had seemed to jump off her computer screen and down her throat, as she'd been eating dinner, had been Eduardo having been awarded American citizenship through the sponsorship of his daughter, whose mother had been American born.

His adopted daughter…though there'd been no mention of that distinction.

Isaac wasn't talking.

She wouldn't let herself be deterred. Not again. He expected her to continue with her plans, and there was no telling what that would bring.

"I know you probably can't talk about her, and I'm not asking you to," she said, having left the plan to draw Isaac out the night before, after its complete failure. "I just…wanted to get to know you a little better, you know, share a peek at your daily life. And…she sounds…nice."

Nonthreatening. Noninvasive—other than the fact that she'd looked up the woman. He didn't have to know some of the intricate channels she'd taken. The one that mentioned Eduardo's citizenship, in particular.

And…if she'd looked up Charlotte that day, it would mean that she hadn't already done so. That the Durans had been nothing to her until Isaac had come clean about what he really did for a living, who he worked for, and that the gunshot might have come from his employer's staff as a defense measure.

"Anyway," she continued, fear growing that with the huge unknown of the next day looming—having to be out and about to make her story of looking for someone believable—she might not get another chance.

At least not such a clean, accessible one.

He was looking at her. She'd started and stopped. She had his attention. "I...don't really know how to approach this, Isaac, and I hope so much that you take it in the way it's offered..."

Tears pricked the sides of her eyes. She couldn't let them well. No matter how sincere they were. They'd be too much, over the top, for someone she'd never met.

"I just... The other day...when I was on the boat... I didn't know it was Charlotte I was looking at," she continued, her gaze wide open to him, her tone filled with the emotion she couldn't let overpower her.

"And I saw something no one else could have seen."

He sat up then, his gaze sharp. "What?" he asked, all armed protective guard at that point. And, in a way, she fell in love with him a little bit for real, for caring about tending to her little sister so completely. Giving his all to the job.

Nicole was lucky to have him.

"There was a man there..." She was assuming he'd be aware of who was on the premises.

"Yeah."

"Her father?"

"No."

Thank God. Savannah sat a second, letting relief wash over her.

"Savannah," he said, his urgent tone calling her to point.

Embarrassed, she liked that he was so intent on watching over her sister. And had a flash of envy, too. Of wanting to be on the receiving end of his loyalty.

Until it hit her that she was. He was running interference for her so she could take care of something vitally important to her. Which meant...he cared. About her. For her. Personally.

Because she wasn't a job to him.

But Charlotte was. And after the way Isaac had stepped up for Savannah, protecting her, providing her with a safe place to stay...she believed she could trust him.

For her sister, her whole reason for being there, she had to press forward. She'd wanted to make certain that someone was aware that her sister was showing signs of being emotionally abused. Had spent the day looking for an "in," someone in Charlotte's life separate and apart from home where the suspected abuse was taking place, someone her sister would trust to help her through the situation.

Picturing the scene she'd witnessed from that boat, fear engulfed Savannah all over again. The man had been on the premises, which meant he'd obviously been someone Charlotte and her father had trusted. Someone in their circle, perhaps? Someone she'd be loath to press charges against?

Someone who'd been confident enough to continue to touch her even after she'd made it clear she hadn't wanted him to do so.

She shuddered inside. Was swamped with worry. And a quietly building rage.

Who better to tell than the man sworn to keep her sister safe?

As long as she could trust him to go against his employer if that's what it took to keep Nicole out of harm's way.

Which Isaac had proven over the past twenty-four hours. Telling her that Duran's people were on the hunt for her. Helping her stay clear of them. Giving her a place to stay. Even having a friend keep a watch on the place while he was at work.

Promising to continue to do so.

"What did you see?" he asked when she sat there, processing a closing in sense of desperation along with the rest of the overwhelming emotions hitting her one after another.

She still managed to look Isaac in the eye as she said, "The man in the yard kept trying to get close to her, touching her, even after she'd repeatedly brushed him off. He was clearly, and forcefully, refusing to accept the no she was clearly giving him."

"You got all that from a glimpse from a boat more than a quarter of a mile away?"

"I got more than a glimpse," she told him. "When I first saw them, the guy had grabbed her, and she'd jerked away. I couldn't just close my eyes to it." And then added, "And the binoculars are the strongest I could buy. I told you, I don't intend to make contact with…the reason I'm here. I just need to see…to know…" She couldn't say anymore.

Didn't trust herself, in that moment, that night, with all that had happened, not to say too much.

With her father's killer an unknown…and someone—not Duran's people, she felt sure—having taken a shot at her the day before.

"You said you saw something no one else could have," he told her. And it dawned on her, he didn't seem surprised by the scene in the yard. She wasn't telling Isaac anything he didn't already know. He'd been on duty that afternoon.

Somewhere in the yard?

Keeping an eye out from the house?

Did he know about the mistreatment? And wasn't doing anything about it?

Maybe he already had.

Maybe Charlotte had told him. Or the mysterious man had.

The way he was looking at her…as though from a distance… For the first time since they'd met, she had the sense that he wasn't all in with the moment. And she stepped up her game, giving him the rest before he started to doubt her. To think that she was crying wolf just to get his attention.

"She was crying, Isaac. She walked to the beach, her back to the house, and stood there and fell apart. Her face crumpled, like she was in agony…" As Savannah relived the moment for him, picturing it all, she felt the blood drain from her face, grew almost light-headed as it dawned on her.

That had been the last sight she'd had of her sister. Nicole's face…crushed in agony…because right then…

The shot.

At the precise moment that she'd seen more than she should have.

She *had* been followed. Someone knew what she'd been

watching. What she'd seen. And had tried to make certain she wasn't around to do or say anything about it.

Someone who was aware that she knew who Charlotte Duran really was? And didn't want her to get involved?

Someone privy to her father's murder? At the moment, it was the only thing that made sense.

Was someone trying to control Charlotte, to keep her from finding out the truth?

If Savannah really had been followed, there'd been very real cause for her paranoia. Horrifying reason to fear for her own life.

And now, to fear for Charlotte Duran's life as well.

Eduardo Duran might soon find out that what could be bought, could turn out not to be what one thought one had purchased.

What could be given could be taken away.

A lesson Savannah had learned indisputably when she'd been just seven years old.

One that had driven every minute of her life ever since.

And would drive the next one, too.

With someone from the past truly at her back…she brought them to everyone with whom she came in contact. Her silence wasn't enough to keep others safe, as her mother and the police had told her.

At least not once she'd accessed the Family Finders database.

Had they put Charlotte Duran's DNA in the database on purpose, to lure Savannah out? After Nicole's kidnapping, she and her mother had been given new identities.

Why anyone would purposely seek her out, she had no idea, but she had to cut all ties with everyone until she figured out what was going on. No one was going to die because of her.

Thoughts, possibilities tumbled through the mass of horror enveloping her. All pouring out from a part of her mind that had been frozen by that gunshot. And set free by reliving it. There, with Isaac. Where she'd felt safe.

Turning to him, she let words fall out of her. "I…actually… found what I was looking for today, Isaac. You talking about all the security cameras at the Durans' made me think about others' cameras—and the way people liked to share everything on social media...and I did a social media search and stumbled upon what I..." Weak, too weak. Embarrassingly weak. She was scrambling. Because she couldn't continue to use Isaac. Not with the love they'd made.

Not with the horrifying realization that her worst fears weren't just paranoia. That they were much more likely reality.

In the short time she'd known him, she'd grown to care about him.

She couldn't put his life in any more danger.

Because she couldn't continue to pretend with him.

What if her need to see her little sister got Nicole shot at, too?

What a fool she'd been. Thinking, after nearly a quarter of a century, she could fly into town, get a glimpse of her sister living a normal happy life, and pop back out to a life suddenly made new for herself? One wiped of the past?

"You wouldn't have traveled all this way if you hadn't already done all the social media canvassing you could possibly do."

Statement, not question. With that look that saw right inside her.

And still made her feel safe.

"The bullet hit while you were looking at Charlotte," Isaac's words came softly. "What suddenly scared you about that just now?"

The whole truth almost tumbled out. To serve *her*. Because *she* needed comfort. She'd come to make sure her sister was okay. That niggling worry as to why Nicole had been looking for family...how could she not help her sister find herself?

And then, to witness what had looked clearly like some kind of domestic abuse?

But Savannah had pursued the Family Finders notice for herself, too.

The truth hit hard. She'd been selfish.

And she had to speak the truth that was hitting her hardest.

"What if I put her in danger? Or...*you*? Just by being there?" The question had to be asked. It was lingering in the air between them.

What had she done?

Reaching out a hand, Isaac brushed the hair back from her face, his hand lingering softly at the side of her temple, as though giving her strength to hold up her head. "We've already been over this," he told her. "You've got reason to fear, Savannah—I give you that. Which is why I'm going to do all I can to protect you. But it's a stretch to think that whoever might be after you would go after everyone you look at, don't you think?"

Right. She'd lost sight of his perspective for a moment. He had no idea about the horrible secret she carried. Her connection to the Duran household.

And she was just no good at being two people at once. Or caring for someone she was keeping secrets from.

Which was the whole reason she'd concocted the cruise vacation. So she could go a period without talking to her partners without inciting their worry.

Sitting there, locking looks with Isaac, she almost blurted the truth. Almost.

"Are you ready to call it quits, then?" he asked. "On whatever your mission was here?"

Was she?

She'd told Isaac about the supposed abuse.

But what about the gunshot? Was someone going to go after Nicole next? With Savannah being the only one who could help law enforcement figure out why? The only one who knew that Charlotte Duran was really Nicole Gussman.

Just like she'd once been Sarah Gussman.

The name repeated unfamiliarly in her head. Like it was something she'd read in a family bible, not like someone she'd ever been.

She needed time to clear her head.

And then to think.

Before she made any more mistakes.

And so, mimicking one of Isaac's moves from the night before, she gave him a noncommittal shrug.

Then leaned in and kissed him. Long but not hard.

The kiss was filled with emotion. With regard for him.

And as she got up and silently left him there, stopping in the bathroom and then grabbing her computer off the table, heading into her room, and quietly locking the door—locking herself in, not him out—she let the tears fall.

She might never know for sure if Nicole was happy and well. But she was certain of one thing.

She'd just told Isaac Forrester goodbye.

Chapter Thirteen

Isaac slept well for the four hours he allowed himself. And as he quietly let himself out of the house long before dawn, having just taken a look at the closed door of Savannah's bedroom, he had a new question on his mind.

Was it possible that Savannah was being used? That she had no idea what her client really knew or held over Duran?

His gut didn't immediately dismiss the idea.

The way she'd struggled to tell him about seeing Charlotte break down while standing so no one from the house could see—those tears, Wagar's treatment of Charlotte had really hit her hard. There'd been absolutely no reason to tell him about what she'd seen.

Except that her heart had been bothered by Charlotte's distress.

As was he. He'd been standing at the window, had seen Charlotte head to the beach, had seen her standing there, and had had no idea she'd been crying. He'd figured she'd, in no uncertain terms, told Arnold Wagar that she was just not interested and to leave her alone. Had assumed she'd been standing at the beach waiting for the man to take the hint and leave.

Then the shot had been fired, and he'd forgotten all about that little family drama.

In his car, driving to his apartment in the dark, Isaac was looking at the scene with fresh perspective.

Why *had* Charlotte been crying?

And why had Savannah told him about it?

Why was she really in San Diego?

She was a lawyer, not a private investigator. Why hire her unless to make contact with someone? Offer some opportunity or impart legal advice. Maybe a make-believe business offer to the younger Duran—one she'd want to consider, but one of which her father wouldn't approve.

Something that would give someone a hold over Duran. Someone who'd held that last piece of critical information from Savannah?

Did Wagar have something to do with it all?

He'd seen the man at public functions that Duran had attended with Charlotte on and off since he'd been in San Diego. Not part of the inner circle, but definitely part of the crowd.

Isaac had figured Wagar was simply someone with money who took Duran to be exactly who he said he was. An incredibly successful businessman. He was no longer so sure of that.

Just as he couldn't let go of the idea that Savannah was perhaps more of a pawn than a mastermind.

A victim, not a suspect.

Because the woman had noticed his charge's tears? Or because she'd told him about them?

Or was it because he'd just had the most incredible sex of his life with her?

If another agent had told him that he'd had sex with a person of interest and then suddenly was considering the possibility that said person wasn't as guilty as at first thought, he'd think the man's ability to do the job had been compromised.

And maybe his had been. He didn't think so.

Yet he'd somehow failed to get access to her computer, which had been his target when he'd driven out the night before.

But even if he had been somewhat distracted by the sex, he was still too firmly in place to pull out without jeopardizing the case at the critical moment. Wasting more than a year's worth of bureau money and time. And far, far worse, making it possible for Duran to continue doing business as usual.

No way was he doing that. Blurred lines, even sex on rare occasions, were part of undercover work.

He could still get the job done. There was no doubt about that.

To that end, he reminded himself of the case against Savannah.

First and foremost was Duran's knowledge of the woman, warning Isaac to be on the lookout for any attempt the lawyer might make to get to Charlotte. And then, two days later, there she'd been spying on Isaac's charge. Didn't matter that Duran was a dirtbag Isaac didn't trust. He'd known about Savannah, knew her to be a threat, and someone who was acting above board didn't spy from boats.

He'd also verified that Savannah was not working for Sierra's Web. He'd made a quick call to her office, posing as a former client with another job for her.

Next, Savannah had said she was only there to look, not contact. So why be there at all? And she'd also told him she wasn't working for anyone. Again, then why be there?

And how had Duran known about her?

Then there was the computer. The one thing that could have led him to more truth, and before leaving him on the couch for the night, she'd quietly picked it up and taken it to bed with her.

Maybe she'd been planning to use it yet that night.

More likely, she'd been protecting its contents.

Last, she had a secret. Had admitted so during a weak moment. One that would supposedly put his life at risk if she told him about it.

How it all fit together he didn't yet know, but he could tell he was getting closer. And was wide awake, eager to forge on with the day ahead even before he hit his own shower, shaved, and then, dressed in his usual garb, strapped an extra gun to his ankle in addition to the one he'd put in the holster at his waist.

Duran had asked him to spend the day checking out every place Charlotte had gone during Isaac's tenure. Isaac had a log of every stop they'd ever made. Had told Duran so. And fully intended to do as requested. As time and opportunity allowed.

First and foremost, he was making himself available to the team of FBI agents on Savannah Compton. She knew him, so he couldn't follow closely, but he was going to be in her vicinity the second she stepped out of the FBI safe house in case he needed to swoop in with some bogus Duran news if the investigation led them in a direction that needed direct contact with her. Or to stop her from doing something. Like leaving town.

He'd also shared his log of Charlotte Duran's activities with the San Diego office, and a female agent would be posing as a friend of Charlotte's from college to trace their steps. And be able to ask questions without raising suspicions.

And the bodyguards who answered to him, with the exception of Emmajean, still had their regular duties but were fully apprised to be extra vigilant and to report to him, and to house security, the second they noticed anything suspicious.

Emmajean had been fired.

Duran's decision, not Isaac's.

Isaac's teams were in place.

He had no idea what the day was going to bring, but he knew that he was ready for it.

Or thought he was. Right up until eight in the morning when he called Savannah, and she didn't pick up. Neither the burner phone, nor her own personal number.

The one he'd told her to keep off. And had watched her take the card out of. Something she could easily have put back in.

He'd just left Charlotte's favorite coffee shop—a small mom-and-pop place by the university, where they stopped anytime she had an early morning lecture—and had called in to Chuck Knowles, the agent currently on duty at the FBI property, to see if there'd been any activity at the house yet. Then, hearing that they'd seen no sign of movement from the house, he'd called her.

Calling Chuck back, he told the more junior agent to get up to the house. To knock and then enter. And call him back.

His throat dry as he waited, Isaac sat in the vehicle owned by his undercover persona—Isaac Forrester—and felt a far more personal tug inside him. More like a younger Mike Reynolds had felt when he'd first discovered that his little sister's boyfriend was a fairly big-time drug dealer.

Mike Reynolds, the name he went by when he wasn't undercover, had no business showing any part of himself in San Diego. Most particularly not anything as intense as the tension eating away at him during the seconds that turned into minutes while he sat there, thrumming his fingers hard against the leather steering wheel.

Sex or not, he was in no way allowing Mike's personal feelings to enter Isaac's world.

The woman was probably in the shower. Hadn't heard the phone ring.

He'd caught her in the shower the morning before. She'd answered anyway. Had apologized for the extra couple of rings it had taken her to get to the phone.

For someone living a lie, pretending, Savannah Compton never missed a beat playing the part of a woman grateful to a bodyguard she'd just met, for helping her out.

An expensive silver sedan pulled into the coffee shop parking lot. Scooting down farther in the driver's seat of his own vehicle parked across the street, Isaac watched as Arnold Wagar got out and entered the shop.

If the man came out with two cups of coffee...it proved nothing.

But sure as hell made the man look more suspicious. Already holding Mike Reynolds's phone, waiting for his call back from the San Diego agent, he quickly dialed Juan Billings, one of his own agents in town from Washington, letting him know where Wagar was currently located, asking him to keep a tail on the man and telling him to keep Isaac posted.

Isaac, not Mike.

And had just hung up when his phone rang again.

"She's gone, sir."

What the hell! Sitting up so sharply he cracked his knee on the dash, Isaac swore silently at the pain and barked, "What do you mean *gone*? She drove off the lot, and you missed it?"

"No, sir. The car you loaned her is still here. Keys on the table. Same for the FBI-issued burner phone. The house looks just like it did the day we readied it for her. With the exception of the sheets on the bed. They're gone. Same with the pillow and blanket."

Isaac's gut clenched. "What about her bag?"

"Gone. Whatever she brought in with her, she took back out. Seriously, place looks like she's never been here. Even the trash is gone."

Starting his engine, Isaac pulled out into traffic. "Any sign of a struggle?" He turned, crossed three lanes.

"No. It's weird, sir. The door was locked. Curtains still drawn. Bathroom and kitchen are clean. It's like the woman removed all traces of herself and then evaporated."

Just like Charlotte Duran.

Isaac had a very sick feeling about that.

The room was dank. It smelled musty. But it had a metal door with a sturdy lock and a window high enough up that she could walk around inside without fear of getting her head blown off.

Savannah had always thought herself the scaredy cat of the bunch. Whatever bunch she was in. Growing up. In school. And most particularly, at Sierra's Web, with every one of her very brave partners seeming to tower over her in the courage department. She had every confidence in her intelligence and her ability to handle any legal problem or court battle that came her way.

Yet she'd moved through life fearing that the boogeyman could be at her back at any minute.

A fear that had turned to more of an obsession when she'd started to feel like he actually was following her. Shortly after Dorian's kidnapping.

Which, she'd confirmed the night before, had been right about the time that Charlotte Duran had first entered her DNA in the Family Finders database. Putting those two things together had only occurred to her after she'd been talking to Isaac about seeing Charlotte cry. The bullet coming when it had...

The way she'd instantly folded in on herself. The intense fear that made her feel helpless. As though she was already a victim.

Dropping her beat-up roller bag on the floor, she leaned over to let her satchel fall off her shoulder onto the one double bed and headed into the windowless bathroom to pee.

She'd suspected in the last couple of days that maybe she really had been followed, that it was possible that someone from the past had somehow known about her before she'd seen the Family Finders notice. But lying in bed the night before, aware that she might have put others in immediate danger, thinking about Dorian the year before, the way she'd felt then, and back to Sierra, too…along with the timing of that bullet…it had all just clicked.

She'd been aware of her need to watch her back since she'd been seven years old. But she hadn't been paranoid.

All the cases the firm had worked on, often putting her partners in immediate danger, hadn't brought on irrational fears.

No, actually being followed was what had made her feel as though she had someone watching her. Because they had been.

And the timing, her sense of being watched coming at the same time as Charlotte's Family Finders entry…

Someone wasn't just watching Savannah. They'd been watching Charlotte, too.

They had to have been to have known about her sister putting an entry in the database. And their knowledge of who Charlotte really was had prompted them to watch Savannah. Before the DNA match. Those results had come much more recently.

Someone had already known that Savannah was Charlotte's biological sister. Someone who also knew about Savannah's identity change.

How, she had no idea.

No one but her mother and the marshal who'd handled their case knew that Savannah Compton had once been Sarah Gussman.

Or so they'd thought.

Current facts were telling a different story.

She'd figured it all out within an hour of going to bed the night before. It was as though sex with Isaac had loosened up the tension holding her prisoner. Or it had given her the strength to believe in herself enough to allow her to see clearly.

Ironically, considering that Isaac had been the catalyst that set her free, as soon as she'd put all the facts together, as soon as she reached her conclusion, she'd known she had to get away from Isaac. From everyone. While she figured out what to do next. She'd put anyone she was with in danger, just by being with them.

Even a rideshare driver.

She'd also leave a trail. Someone they could get to who'd be forced to say what they knew.

Which was why she'd left just an hour behind Isaac the night before. After studying the televised footage from the property cameras for more than a day, she'd not only had a good grasp of the lay of the land, she'd known where all the cameras were located and how to avoid them.

From there, detailed searches on her computer had shown her the best route to move, undetected, the three miles she'd have to walk to get to the old but quaint motel that promised quiet and solitude.

The walk, while arduous, had given her a lot of time to think.

One thing was indisputable as far as she was concerned. Whoever had been watching Nicole knew that she'd had other family for Family Finders to find.

And hadn't wanted her finding them.

Only one person would likely care what Charlotte Duran discovered almost a quarter of a century later. Would care enough to have someone followed, to shoot at them. That was someone who knew that Nicole had been kidnapped.

Whether or not they knew the rest...that her father had been about to testify against someone really big, that he'd been murdered...she couldn't say.

But it seemed logical to assume so.

Which was why she'd taken the time to disinfect the safe house before she'd left. Removing every trace of her DNA from the place. She'd felt bad about the bedding. Taking it all with her. Had thrown it, with the rest of the trash, into a pond she'd seen on the cameras at the back of the property. Apologizing for having done so to any organisms living within.

Savannah wasn't suffering from paranoia due to Dorian's kidnapping. Her instincts, honed by a lifetime of hiding her true identity, had been letting her know that someone really was at her back.

Yet it turned out that she didn't fear for her life so much when she thought it was a danger to others. She feared more for theirs.

The walk in the dark had been awful—she'd cried a good bit of the way—but she'd had the strength to get it done. And done well.

Reminding herself with every step that she was exceptionally well trained. In several types of self-defense—she'd taken the kitchen knife best suited to throwing—but in ways to evade criminals, too. After more than a decade with Sierra's Web she'd heard enough to arm her well.

One of the big questions remaining was how much Eduardo Duran knew. Had the man just paid top dollar for an adoption, not knowing that Nicole had been kidnapped?

And if he knew more, how much did he know?

Just that she'd been taken?

Or had he known the man who'd killed Sarah and Nicole's father?

And if so, was that all he knew?

Still in the bathroom, she flushed. Washed her hands. Saw her face in the mirror, the dirt streaks, the brokenness staring back at her but wouldn't let herself cry again.

She'd had her time to mourn, and it was done.

Thankfully, the Sierra's Web investigative team had insisted that every expert carry safe kits with them. Including enough cash to get by for a few days. Savannah had used a little bit at a shady-looking gas station and convenience store with no surveillance cameras to pay way too much for some food and a burner phone that was likely contraband.

All the better for her purposes.

And then to prepay for a couple of nights at the motel—not that she planned to stay that long. Just seemed smart to seem as though she wasn't in any kind of hurry.

Best news, as far as she was concerned, was that she hadn't had the sense of being followed at all during her trek. By the time she'd reached the convenience store, unshowered, hair down to shadow her features, having cleaned the house, cried, and hiked for miles, her disheveled state had fit right in. She'd bet the tired and clearly stoned clerk wouldn't even be able to give an accurate description of her were anyone to stop and ask.

With that thought and one last glance in the mirror, Savannah decided to forgo the shower she'd been about to take. The disguise worked. And it didn't matter how she looked, or felt, if she was dead.

Or if someone else was because of her.

Charlotte.

The woman had been on her mind nonstop.

Worst-case scenario, in her mind, was that whoever had been watching Savannah for most of the past year, whoever was clearly currently after her, and probably Charlotte, too, was someone involved in whatever illegal dealings their father had been about to testify against.

She hadn't broken witness protection protocol by flying to San Diego or renting a boat. She'd broken it when she'd entered her DNA in family databases. She'd done so privately. Which wouldn't have put her in danger. If not for the fact that her DNA had matched that of someone who didn't know about witness protection guidelines, who'd made their profile discoverable.

Without having any idea of the danger she was putting them in, Charlotte had unknowingly exposed them both to a past that had killed their father.

Was it going to get the two of them killed, too?

If her theory was correct and someone had been watching her for nearly a year without harming her in any way, did that mean she was safe?

Another flash of the gunshot blast on the boat came to mind next.

Shaking her head as she stood on a chair to peek out the rectangular window positioned close to the ceiling, Savannah breathed through the shock of fear that rent through her.

Focused on the one thought that she couldn't let go of. Nicole. Charlotte. The agony she'd seen on her sister's face.

How much did Charlotte know?

And how much danger was she in?

Was she better off if Savannah just faded away? Neither had been in danger over the past year.

And then there was Isaac...

No. *Really.* There was *Isaac*. His car. Parking. Him getting out. Heading for the office.

Looking for her?

He'd said he would protect her. And after the hour they'd shared, naked on the couch...she should have known he wouldn't just accept her leaving without a trace.

Oh, God, what had she done?

But...she *hadn't* done a lot of it. Not if someone had been on her tail for the past year.

But that didn't mean she had to be a victim.

She had to be smart.

Isaac was back in the parking lot. Heading to his car but looking around.

Tension stiffened every muscle, every nerve in her body. He was right there. Charlotte's bodyguard. Did she tell him what she'd figured out?

If her witness protection cover was already blown, if the devil was already upon them, what would it hurt?

But if it wasn't?

He was at his car. Reaching for the door handle. Glancing back.

Was it providence again? Him being there right when she'd been looking out? Was he Charlotte's only chance?

Jumping down from the chair, Savannah turned the dead bolt. Unhooked the chain lock.

And opened the door in time to see Isaac's vehicle driving away.

Chapter Fourteen

Adrenaline pumping, Isaac pulled out into the street in front of the old motel and then pulled back in the drive as it circled the other side of the two-winged building. The desk clerk hadn't recognized the only photo Isaac had had of Savannah Compton—the one from the Sierra's Web site—and he hadn't been all that eager to talk to Isaac, either, most particularly since Isaac couldn't show Mike's badge.

But for enough cash, the man had mentioned that a disheveled-looking woman who probably matched the photo had checked in not long ago. And for another couple of twenties, had even given up the room number.

One way or another, Isaac was going to get Savannah to talk to him. Too many lives were at stake to continue playing nice.

But first, he was doing a perimeter check. And, satisfied that the couple of vehicles in the second drive weren't a threat, he drove around the block twice, too. One last check to make sure he wasn't being followed by whoever Savannah was working with.

And then drove through a somewhat questionable-looking joint for a fast-food breakfast order. Just a guy, hanging out.

The fact that he'd had such great sex with the woman only hours before she'd bolted rankled. More than it should.

He used the feeling to feed his determination to crack her.

To keep his backbone stiff as, a plastic bag in hand, he approached her door. Knocked. If he scared the crap out of her, he did. She hadn't taken her phone. Had left him no way to call ahead and make an appointment.

"Food delivery," he called. He'd bought enough for two. Would decide once he was inside if he was in a sharing mood or not.

The thought was barely complete before he heard locks click and the door flew open only long enough to pull him inside.

Taking him by surprise.

So much for pushing his way in.

How did the woman manage to continue to throw him off course?

"I don't know if it's safe for you to be here or not," she said, standing toe-to-toe with him just inside the door, her gaze wide open, her tone urgent. "I'm not sure if I'm making things worse, putting you in danger, but you're here and…" She broke off.

Glancing away from him to the bag he held.

And then down at herself.

"Talk to me, Savannah." The authoritarian demand he'd intended came out softly.

An urging, at best.

He took in every inch of her, the streaks of dirt on her face, a tear in the sleeve of a shirt he hadn't yet seen. Cotton pants that looked as though she'd slept and then crawled around in them.

No makeup.

Disheveled was an understatement. And after the way she'd run out on him without even giving him the respect of letting him know she no longer needed or wanted his hospitality, the knowledge he had of her subterfuge, how in the hell could he still find her so incredibly…desirable?

More beautiful than any woman he'd ever met.

"I figured out some things, and I'm afraid that Charlotte might be in danger." Concern oozed from her gaze as words poured out fast.

He ignored everything but the fact that hit hardest. "You know where she is?"

"You don't?" Mouth open, brows creased, she stared at him.

And then she paled. "Tell me you know where she is, Isaac." The warning in her tone came out of the blue.

Nothing he'd heard from her before.

Her true self coming out?

"She's missing." He didn't couch the words at all and wasn't sorry for the abrupt delivery.

Savannah fell down to the bed, bending over, her head to her knees for a second, and when she came back up rocked front to back. He stared at the trembling in her hands as she asked, "How long?"

If he told her the truth, she'd know he'd lied to her the night before. "Yesterday morning."

She froze then, her eyes narrowed as she stared up at him. "The breach."

He nodded, resisted the urge to sit beside her, to take her hand. "I wasn't at liberty to say anything," he told her instead. Giving her what he could of an explanation for his subterfuge, for no good reason he could think of.

With a nod that felt like a dismissal, Savannah stood. "Tell me what you know." The take-charge tone was back, and for a second, he felt like he was in court. Like he had no choice but to tell the truth, the whole truth, and nothing but the truth. Except that…he couldn't.

"I can't. But you know something. It's obvious that it's eating at you." He let the intimate tone seep into his words.

She glanced up, held his gaze for a second, as she had so many times over the past few days. And then shook her head again. "I need to know what you know first," she said.

And so he gave her something. "She disappeared without a trace. No sign of forced entry. No tire tracks. Her phone, purse, and car are all at home."

She'd stopped pacing, stood right in front of him, the dirt on her face a stark contrast to the sudden whiteness of her skin. He saw the fear in her eyes.

Knew it wasn't faked. And so he fed it.

"Her father is beside himself."

"What do the police say?" she asked then, pacing again. "The FBI?" Her back was to him as she mentioned his agency.

For a second, he considered that she knew. That his cover was blown. But nothing else gave indication of such.

Guilt was nagging at him. A never before occurrence.

"Mr. Duran doesn't want them called." He saw no harm in giving her that much. She'd be able to see for herself, soon enough, that there was nothing in the news. "He's worried that if word gets out that she's missing, unsavory characters will come out, hunting for her, putting her in even more danger. He's hired private investigators, and, of course, the entire security staff is on the case as well."

Looking up at him, she said, "Except for you."

He let her think that. It was the right move for the job. Which was why he was there.

The grateful look in eyes shadowed by worry made him want to take her in his arms. To promise that everything would be okay.

But he didn't believe it ever would be. Not for her, if she was messed up with Duran.

And not for them, either.

"Tell me what you know, Savannah, while there's still time to save her."

Her head reared back at the words, but she held his gaze and nodded, too. "You're right. And you're here. And looking for Charlotte, you're all walking into something and have a better chance if you know what you're likely up against. I'm going to have to trust that I do more good than harm by talking to you." She didn't sound happy about the choice.

He wasn't happy when she took his hand and pulled him to sit on the end of the bed with her. If she thought he was going to fall for any more of her distractions...

"Charlotte Duran is my sister."

All the turmoil raging inside Isaac just...stopped. Like he'd been put in deep freeze. Nothing happened. He just stared at her.

As thoughts tumbled all over.

Was she hallucinating?

Making some kind of sick joke?

Surely she didn't think he was so besotted with her he'd fall for something so ludicrous.

Her gaze was open, locked on his, and swarming with emotion that looked—and felt—real.

How did she do that?

"I told you I was here to look for someone. Not to make contact, but just to see that they were okay. That someone is Charlotte."

She appeared—sounded—so serious.

And was confusing an already upended situation. Wasting time he didn't have to waste. Had he fallen deeper than he'd thought? Had her siren call brought him there when he should've been out busting ground to find Charlotte Duran? As well as the proof he needed to stop her father.

Just the fact that she was making him doubt himself...

Isaac stood. Left his bag of uneaten breakfast on the dresser and headed for the door.

Savannah Compton could stay or go. She could lie and scheme and snag hearts. But not in his world. Not anymore.

He was done.

He didn't believe her.

She didn't blame him. But he couldn't go.

Isaac's hand turned the dead bolt, unhooked the chain lock, and Savannah said, "Her name was Nicole."

She stood as he slowly turned around. Reached for her computer, turned it on. Brought up the proof. Faced him, shoulders straight and head high. Uncaring that she looked so filthy. She had a story to tell.

He didn't come closer. His gaze was clearly assessing. But she had his attention.

"She was kidnapped from her daycare when she was a year old. I was seven." The words slid right out, as though they'd been there waiting for their turn.

As twenty-four years of silence shattered around her, Savannah focused on information pertinent to saving Charlotte. "Almost a year ago, Charlotte entered her DNA into Family Finders. She made her profile public, just her name and an address, so that if there was ever a match, the family member could find her. I'd tried other, much larger databases, but a client referred me to Family Finders, and I entered my information six weeks ago. And just last week was notified of the match."

She held out her laptop.

Isaac watched her as though she might sprout wings and fly away. And then took the computer, studying the screen before looking back at her, his expression stone-like.

Piercing. "I need some time to check this out."

She sat. Held up her hands.

And watched as Isaac's thumbs flew over his phone screen. Stopped as he read. And flew some more. Five minutes passed before he looked over at her again, open mouthed.

Stared was more like it.

As though seeing her for the first time.

As though he couldn't believe what he was seeing.

She waited. Feeling surreal. Her entire world had just flipped into something she didn't recognize. After twenty-four years of silence, she'd said her secret aloud. To a virtual stranger.

She hadn't obliterated.

There'd been no fanfare.

If she'd lost her mind, another calmer one had found her.

Time passed. She lost track of how much. Isaac continued to type on his phone. And then, when the silence was beginning to get to her, suddenly asked, "Why did you disappear like you did in the middle of the night?"

His softer tone reached her more than the actual words. Freeing some of the chains tightening around her chest.

"Last night, some things clicked." She started talking as though she hadn't just dropped a bomb between them, giving him the facts he needed, weeding out the things she needed to say to him. "Telling you about Charlotte crying, reliving the boat blast, feeling that fear. It's not something I've carried with me my whole life. That fear just started a year ago."

"Your partner's kidnapping," Isaac finally spoke. She couldn't tell if he was letting her know he already had that part, urging her to get on with it, or if he was joining in the theory she'd built.

"Right. But what I didn't know until last week, and didn't put together until last night, was that I didn't start to feel as though

I was being followed, didn't start noticing random different cars staying a few lengths behind me until after Charlotte put her information in that database."

She'd half feared saying the words aloud would cause them to crumble into ash. More false narrative she told herself. Like being followed at all.

Instead, they grew in stature.

Isaac approached the bed again. Sat on the corner of it, his gaze steady on her. "Wait a minute. You're saying that you think someone who knew Charlotte was kidnapped also knew you were her sister and started watching you when she started looking for you?" His words were clipped.

Hearing her theory aloud, it sounded fantastical. And sat with her in confirmation, too, as she nodded.

Close beside him, she held his gaze, needing him to talk silently with her as he had over the past few days.

Needing some real-life connection.

"I don't think Charlotte was looking for me specifically," she clarified after a long moment. "She was only a toddler. I have no idea if she even knows she was adopted. But she'd obviously been looking for family. And someone knew if I'd put my information in the database, she'd find me."

With a tilt of his head, he continued to watch her as he said, "And it's logical to assume that with all the new DNA technology, someone who'd had a family member kidnapped would definitely enter DNA into those databases."

He spoke to her point, not to the question she'd mentioned but left unasked. Did Charlotte even know she'd been adopted?

Had Isaac known?

His loyalty lay with his employer. She couldn't afford to push.

"Whoever this is who's after me, and now probably has Charlotte…it has to be someone who already knew about me because I just entered my DNA in Family Finders. But I believe now that I was really being watched all this time. Ever since Charlotte entered hers. Before, when I didn't know about Charlotte's visit to the database, I had only Dorian's kidnapping to explain the sudden change in me. But it didn't really make sense, you know? I didn't have inexplicable anxiety issues after Nicole was kidnapped. Nor when Sierra was murdered. I grieved. I got myself trained in self-defense. I walked a straight line, made conservative choices, and looked over my shoulder, always. But I was never irrationally afraid. Never saw things that weren't there."

He nodded. And more of her words found their freedom. "I'm starting to feel like myself again for the first time in months."

Isaac frowned then. Stood. Putting his hands in his pockets as he took a couple of steps, then turned back to face her.

And the look on his face, the way he was regarding her, as though only just seeing her for the first time made her want to take it all back.

Charlotte Duran was adopted.

On one hand, the news stunned him. On the other, things started to make more sense to him. Eduardo's over-protectiveness of his daughter—spurred, Isaac had long thought, by the billionaire's odd insecurities where his daughter was concerned.

A man's daughter being his weak spot was pretty standard. But Eduardo had seemed to thrive on Charlotte's adoration. And did everything he could to shine a light on it. Mentioning it in conversation every chance he got. Not just praising his daughter but drawing attention to the way she felt about him. To their bond.

A representative from Family Finders had confirmed to the FBI the DNA match between the two samples they'd received.

The birth certificate an agent in the Washington office had just emailed listed Duran as Charlotte's father. And her mother as having died in childbirth. Confirming the story he'd been told.

Birth certificates could be changed.

Falsified.

If one had enough money and knew the right people.

DNA didn't lie.

And the rest, the kidnapping…even without the confirmation upon which he was waiting…he believed Savannah.

And she was holding something back. He was certain of that, too. Didn't like it at all.

But her association with Charlotte Duran…her explanation

for her sudden appearance in San Diego...made a hell of a lot more sense than Duran's had.

Which meant that Eduardo Duran knew that Savannah was Charlotte's sister? Was that the big secret? The thing that the fearless man feared?

Charlotte wasn't biologically his.

Isaac would bet his life Charlotte didn't know that.

And the bigger news—she'd been kidnapped before.

Knowing what he did about the Duran empire, Isaac didn't struggle to believe that one at all. Or to assume that Duran had paid a lot of money to buy his daughter.

Some perp kidnapping her again made sense, too. Whoever had taken Charlotte the first time, sold her to Duran, could have taken her a second time to squeeze Duran, remind him of what he'd done, of what he had hanging over him but also to get Charlotte's DNA.

Without proof that Charlotte was Nicole, the perp couldn't blackmail Duran. It would be a scumbag's word against a respected dynasty.

They'd need Savannah's DNA, too, though. But they didn't need her alive to get it. Or to blackmail Duran. Which put her in immediate danger.

She'd told him the other night that both of her parents were gone. Her father when she'd been little and her mother when she'd been grown.

Something else made a whole lot more sense. Duran not wanting to report his daughter's disappearance to the authorities. The billionaire couldn't risk having someone ask for DNA and possibly discovering that the woman he called his daughter had been reported missing before.

A long time ago.

Agents were searching the national database for the twenty-four-year-old missing person case involving a toddler named Nicole Compton.

As he stood there in the cheap, old motel room, Isaac wasn't any closer to arresting the man he was after. He'd need more. Proof. But he finally had a road to take.

And felt an even stronger urgency to find Charlotte. He didn't believe a kidnapper would kill her. At least not until he got what he wanted from Duran. Charlotte was one person who was most definitely worth more alive than dead.

But not Savannah.

His gut gave a lurch as the thought hit him again.

When he'd thought her complicit, he'd been concerned about her safety but had figured she'd brought danger upon herself. Now that he knew the truth…

The expert lawyer had turned out to be far more fascinating, compelling than he'd thought, even the day before. She was a woman who saw a problem and took it upon herself to solve it.

One who didn't cry into her soup and wait until others helped mop her up.

And one who deserved at least a snippet of a happy ending. If he could at least give her the chance to see Nicole face-to-face. To speak to her…

His senses honed, he looked at the woman he'd been naked with the night before and saw someone entirely different.

A woman who was on his side of the law. Who had been all along.

A woman he'd purposely taken advantage of…not sexually—that had been weakness there—but by frightening her into staying at his house so he could have access to her.

He pushed the image away. Couldn't let himself off the straight and narrow.

And couldn't leave it behind, either.

Duran. The master criminal. "A profile of a highly successful criminal includes the ability to manipulate," he said aloud. "If what you say is true, I'd put money on the fact that whoever knows about you made sure that you suspected you were being followed, without providing enough proof to have you do anything about it. Different cars, behind you long enough, slowing when you slowed, turning when you turned, but then suddenly not there…"

"Yes!" Savannah stood, too. "That's exactly how it happened. Any internet search of me would have shown my vulnerability. A way to get at me. Sierra's Web and Dorian's kidnapping was all over the news at that time. And if he was watching me, he'd have seen me spending so much time in self-defense classes. I gave him the ammunition." She glanced into the food bag.

Watching her, feeling her pain, Isaac took the move as a nervous reaction more than a desire for food. A break from a situation that had to be caging her. She turned to face him, though, after taking that second or two. "That's it, Isaac. I haven't been losing my mind. But he was trying to make me feel like I was." The relief in her tone hit him hard.

He'd been pegging her for conning him when she'd been busy trying to cope with her life. There was still that "more" she wasn't telling him. His gut got that one loud and clear. The way she held his gaze so completely, until she avoided it altogether. And while he'd have to find a way to get her to confide it all, he didn't blame her for holding back.

He wasn't trustworthy. Not as Isaac Forrester. And Isaac was the only man in the room. The only life he was going to live until Eduardo Duran was behind bars.

And his adopted daughter, too, if need be.

The thought hit, as it always did. But with a force so different, Isaac took a step back. Stared at Savannah. And wondered how on earth he was going to tell her that he suspected her newfound baby sister was not only missing but was also a suspected international criminal?

As he watched her, met her gaze, the answer became clear. He wasn't.

Chapter Fifteen

The way Isaac was looking at her, as though he'd welcome her in his arms again, pulled at Savannah, but she turned away. She couldn't think of herself. Or even him.

"I have no idea who we're searching for, Isaac. There were never any suspects. And if they've already had her for over twenty-four hours..." A brand-new fear took root in her heart. Had she finally found her baby sister only to lose her again? Permanently?

"A stronger question is who was following you? I've heard nothing about any Duran detail at work in Michigan or anywhere else." Not that, in that particular case, he would have.

"Maybe the kidnapper?"

"And how would he have known exactly when Charlotte entered her information into that database?"

She didn't know. Had burst into tears while walking that morning as she'd considered the overwhelming burden her lack of information was putting on any hope of seeing Charlotte happy and then getting on with her own life.

When she shook her head, feeling helpless, Isaac said, "I have to consider that there might be a bad apple in Duran's employ. Someone with an axe to grind who somehow got close enough for Duran to have said something or to have had Charlotte's information or, at the very least, access to her computer.

Or was privy to Duran's most private documents. I don't even know where he keeps those. Nor do I think he'd keep record of something like this."

As the challenges before them—the unknowns, maybes, and suppositions—seemed to grow too high to scale, Isaac took her hand. "But what I do know is that whoever has been following you, who shot at you isn't about to stop now. So, the first thing we need to do, for sure, is to keep you hidden."

She heard what he wasn't saying. Whoever they were, they likely had Charlotte. Stood to reason Savannah would be next.

She couldn't go back to Isaac's house. Into hiding. She'd been hiding for most of her life, in one way or another. "Unless we use me to lure them out," she said, knowing she'd just made her plan of action, with or without Isaac's blessing.

The idea might have been forming under the surface, but it had just come to her in concrete thought. She didn't yet know how it would work. She'd need to go to the police. To have someone watching her so that when she lured out the hunters, even if she was hurt or killed, they'd be caught.

"I'm done being a victim, Isaac," she said when he stood there, watching her. Duran thought police involvement would put his daughter at higher risk. But what if one of Duran's own men helped her?

Dare she ask Isaac? Was it fair to do so?

So her plan wasn't fully formed.

She just knew she was the bait. And she had to try. For Nicole. And for herself.

He frowned. "To be clear, you didn't respond to Family Finders in any way?"

His question was succinct, could have been interrogation. It didn't feel that way. And she said, "Not directly. I looked up the address that populated in my private search. Just trying to get a feel for where it was. I did it in a café, just signed in as a guest. And then, when I got to town, I typed it in my phone's global positioning system for driving directions." He'd need to know about anything that could possibly be traced.

Sierra's Web had taught her that much.

"Did you tell anyone?"

She gave him an immediate shake of the head. And then said, "No one in my life—including my partners, who are family to me—knows I ever had a sister." And when she realized the statement would raise more questions, she quickly added a partial truth. "I was a kid when it all happened. My way of coping was to pretend that it hadn't. Mom moved me to another city, and I left it all behind. I felt like it could have been me, you know?"

"Your father was already gone then?" He didn't miss a beat, and so neither did she.

She looked straight at him as she nodded.

His eyes narrowed, his brow furrowed. "Have you, as an adult, ever looked back at the case? With your skills, the access Sierra's Web gives you..."

"No." She still held his gaze, but with some difficulty. He was getting dangerously close to things she couldn't say.

Her mother and the marshals had assured her, over and over, that there'd been no evidence of any link between Nicole's kidnapping and her father's upcoming testimony. Everyone was certain, based on evidence at the scene, that Nicole had been collateral damage.

They could have been wrong. Something she'd considered more than once over the years.

But as far as she was aware, she was the only person left living, other than a retired agent and a marshal someplace, who knew that her father had been about to testify the day he'd been murdered.

Nicole's disappearance, even her last name and exact details of the kidnapping, had been changed on the records as part of Savannah and her mother's entrance into witness protection.

She'd been called Natalie Willoughby in the witness protection report.

And though Savannah had asked her mother many times over the years if the authorities would be able to find them if Nicole was found, she'd always only been told *I don't know*.

As an adult she'd realized that her mother had made the very difficult decision to appear deceased in the event the authorities ever did locate Nicole. Which would have put Nicole into the foster system.

She'd turned her back on any possibility of seeing her youngest child again, of caring for her, and she'd done it for Savannah's sake. To protect her. Keep her from harm.

Which was why Savannah had to do all she could, lose her life if that was what it came to, in order to ensure Nicole's chance at health and happiness.

"Savannah?" Isaac's soft tone called her back to him.

"What?"

"I asked you why you didn't look her up."

She couldn't give him the truth. Reached for the bag of food he'd brought in. Pulled out a couple of foam cartons with lids and plastic-wrapped packets of napkins and disposable utensils. Opened a lid to see rubber-looking scrambled eggs with breakfast potatoes, a piece of questionable sausage, and a biscuit. As she was picking up the dried hard roll, the part of the answer she could give came to her, and she turned, facing him again.

"If the FBI couldn't find her, how could I?" she asked, stating the truth she'd lived with for most of her life. Until Sierra's Web had broken all kinds of records for crimes they'd solved. "And I'd been told, repeatedly, that it wouldn't be fair to her. Whether her life had gone well or not, she didn't need to know what it could have been. Unless she chose to find me." Her mouth still open on that last word, she shoved the biscuit between her teeth and bit down.

Forestalling any other dangerous tidbit that might attempt to spill out.

The woman had no idea she was dealing with an international criminal operation. Whatever deep secret she was keeping about her sister's kidnapping was personal. Isaac read the truth in her body language, the turning away and the straight glance from eyes filled with pain as she'd told him as much as she had.

Every bit of it had rung true with everything he knew about child abductions.

And the things she wasn't telling him. If he had to guess, he'd say that she'd been present during the kidnapping. Had, perhaps, been charged to keep an eye on her sister for a minute while her mother had quickly done something else.

What seemed obvious to Isaac as he sat shoveling in a cold breakfast that would have been only marginally edible when hot was that Savannah Compton blamed herself for her baby sister's kidnapping.

At the small desk in her room, they were sitting side by side on the wooden slatted bench meant to be a luggage rack, eating silently as though the questionable nourishment was actually palatable. She was staring at her food as she ate.

Clearly reliving a part of her life that no one shared.

While he contemplated what came next.

She was going out into the fray—that much was obvious. He wasn't going to be able to change her mind. Short of locking her up, he couldn't stop her.

The thought eased the guilt eating at him somewhat as the plan that had been building since she'd first revealed her connection to Charlotte solidified.

He had to use her. Savannah Compton and her shocking surprise were the world's best chance at bringing Duran to his knees.

Maybe their only chance.

She'd already brought the danger down upon herself.

But his plan would be for her own good as well. Alone, she stood no chance against the Duran empire and whoever the man was warring with. Both sides apparently after her.

With Isaac, she'd at least have a chance to stay alive. She'd have protection. His. Which she'd know about. And also that of the agents he had secretly working with him.

He was risking the case—Duran's bodyguard associating with a woman Duran was after. The fact was there in all its rawness.

If he could get to the arrest warrant with his cover intact, he'd have the win of his career.

Another truth. Not one that motivated him.

His gut was telling him Savannah Compton needed protection that he could provide and, with equal weight, it was letting him know that with Charlotte's disappearance, things were coming to a head. The Sierra's Web lawyer could very well be his last chance to get Duran before the man simply disappeared.

To set up shop elsewhere. Under another new identity. He'd had two that Isaac knew of. A third wouldn't be a stretch.

It was how his type worked. Same money, different name.

And how, international law enforcement had determined, Duran had managed to escape paying for his crimes for decades. He'd perfected the art of becoming someone else.

Isaac waited until Savannah put down the plastic fork she'd been using and pushed her container toward the wall before speaking again.

"My guess is you know more than you realize. Someone was somehow privy to Charlotte having entered her DNA with Family Finders. Someone who you might have seen in the past. Someone you might recognize, even now. What keeps bothering me is why would they manipulate you, make you doubt yourself from the moment your little sister became part of that database?"

Her gaze wasn't timid, but he could read the concern there. Mingling with shock, he thought, as she said, "I'll know him? That's what this is about? Someone thinks I know something about the kidnapping?"

She frowned then, staring at him, but the look was blank. As though she was seeing something else. And then, shaking her head, she came back to him, her gaze focused on his, and she said, "I can't pull up a picture in my head of anyone I knew twenty-four years ago. And certainly not from around the time of the kidnapping. I vaguely remember what my teacher looked like. I have memories of the neighbors but couldn't describe them to you."

As Savannah focused, showing him her professionalism, the thoroughness with which she approached every task, Isaac's tension settled a bit.

He'd come to Savannah's hotel room thinking she was a criminal. Meaning all bets were off in terms of entrapment or luring her into helping him.

Now that he believed she was innocent… Isaac and Mike weren't getting along as well. To make matters worse, he couldn't separate the two enough at the moment to know which one wanted to protect her more.

"I'd like to talk you out of putting yourself up as bait, most particularly until we have time to try to figure out who we're dealing with..." His pause was deliberate. If she agreed to hold off, he'd have to reassess his current plan to use her to draw out whoever had been following her. Had shot at her. An agent couldn't ethically engage an innocent civilian in the line of duty without her express consent to assist the FBI.

If Isaac gave her more of what he knew, which he easily could as Charlotte's bodyguard, he could talk her into cooperating.

The line he was skating had become a thread.

Savannah was shaking her head before he'd completed the thought. "My mind's made up, Isaac. No way I hide away while my little sister could be in severe jeopardy, being traumatized— for a second time in her life."

She left neither Mike nor Isaac any other choice but to get her on the plan. For her own good as much as anyone. "Then, please, let me help you," he told her, falling back into Isaac's life far too easily. "I think you're right in that you represent our best and quickest hope of finding Charlotte. I know that you'll be far safer being exposed to this creep if I've got your back. And there's more chance that we'll be able to rescue Charlotte if my team is there to help." Mike's team. Not Isaac's.

If Isaac did his job right, Duran's people weren't going to know a damned thing.

In the event of a takedown, it would be all FBI agents on deck, with Duran's people in handcuffs. At least until they could be thoroughly checked out and cleared of any wrongdoing.

And those with dirty hands would be offered the opportunity to roll on their top leader.

Savannah's gaze showed a whole lot of doubt. "Your team? Duran's people are on the lookout for me..."

He was ready for that one. "If I do my job right, they aren't going to know I've found you unless we've got Charlotte, too. At that point, your being her sister will be established, and while there will likely be a lot of emotional, and potentially criminal baggage to sort through, with no guarantee how that all plays out, you'll no longer pose a security threat."

Clearly the time to act had come. Duran was feeling heat from a source dangerous enough, bold enough to kidnap Charlotte. If Duran got too skittish, he'd pull one of his suspected disappearing acts, and Isaac would have lost his chance.

The plan was the best he had.

And was relying on a whole lot of *if*s.

Any of which could go wrong.

And get people killed.

Savannah agreed to Isaac's offer with only a moment or two of thought. Big picture, she'd be a fool not to. For herself, obviously, but more for Charlotte. What could Savannah, one lone, unarmed woman, do to rescue what could be a drugged or injured body from criminals?

He'd have a couple of buddies, bodyguards that he'd worked with in the past, at their backs.

Isaac was on the payroll of a billionaire, was the head of Duran's protection detail. And was being loyal to his employer, keeping his own counsel about the man and his business, while he did what he could, namely using Savannah, to try to find the man's daughter. Clearly he'd proven to be one of the best at what he did. He thought of things she didn't even know to consider. Field things.

When it came to the law, to making certain that the kidnappers paid for every single crime they'd committed, she'd be the one to get it done.

Isaac had been scrolling on his phone and turned it to her. "I kept a log of every place I've taken Charlotte over the past several months. My guess is no matter who's behind the kidnapping, whoever actually took her knew her patterns, is familiar with those areas. I'm assuming the current kidnapper was hired," he added as she scrolled the electronic list he'd handed to her. "But I could be wrong."

Feeling tears threaten as she read snippets from her sister's everyday life—something she'd never dared let herself hope she'd ever be privy to—Savannah forced herself to stay focused.

"I think we should start with openly, visibly visiting these areas," Isaac continued, his gaze forthright, his tone completely professional. "It's what an investigator would do if they were looking for someone. Visit the places they visit. See if anyone has heard from them. I'll get you a car to drive and be behind you at all times."

She looked up from his list, handed back his phone, her mind reeling with Charlotte's tastes. Coffee. There were a few well-known barista shops. Boutique clothing shops. And women's facilities. From shelters to high-powered charity organizations. "Sounds good," she said. Then stood, reaching into the bag she'd lugged through the woods, pulled out clean clothes and toiletries, and finished with "And please send me a copy of that log." She rattled off the number of her new burner phone as she shut herself in the bathroom just feet away from the remains of their breakfast.

Twenty minutes later, Savannah picked up her phone off the bathroom counter before presenting herself outside the closed door and was relieved to see that Isaac had done as she'd asked. His travel log had been sent to her screen.

If they got separated, she had that much to work with on her own.

She hadn't known Isaac long enough to be putting any lives in his hands. She knew that.

But sometimes, a person just had to trust.

Chapter Sixteen

Mike's people were up to speed and in place by the time Savannah exited the bathroom. Isaac took one look at her and, for that split second, wanted to call the whole thing off.

In a fresh pair of capris with a short-sleeved shirt and tennis shoes and her long dark hair pulled back, the woman looked as though she belonged on an expensive court, racket in hand, sipping lemon water in between serves.

Or in his bed.

While he was decked out for work.

Thankfully the second passed without anything of note coming from it.

As did the entire rest of the morning.

In his car, following behind Savannah in the gray rental sedan, he stayed online with her through the cars' audio systems as they started on the location log he'd sent her. They spoke only about the case and otherwise hung there on a connected line, in contact. Savannah never seemed to lose focus, even for a second, as she scoured everything in sight, anywhere they happened to be. From being aware of the vehicles behind them to the green balloon caught on an electrical wire, the lawyer proved her quick ability to mentally catalogue and recall even the smallest details.

Which made him wonder, again, about her past and the secret she was keeping from him. Had she seen the kidnapper? Did she know who they were after? Consciously or subconsciously? Had she heard anything that might help them narrow down their suspect?

They were heading toward the university where Charlotte had most recently lectured.

The place where she'd scoped out a hiding place in a women's restroom rather than be face-to-face with Arnold Wagar.

He'd had his people looking into the man Duran wanted his daughter to marry, and so far, nothing he'd learned had pointed to any kind of physical aggression in the man's past. Other than Savannah's testimony regarding the tears the man had caused Charlotte to shed.

What he found interesting, though, was that Wagar owned a portfolio of profitable, tax-paying companies, including a family-run winery that shipped expensive and very exclusive product all over the world.

Someone held in high esteem globally, with international shipping capabilities...

"I'm getting more and more uneasy about the idea of bringing in Duran's people to help when we locate Charlotte." Savannah's voice interrupted his thoughts and captured his full attention, too.

When they found Charlotte. Her goal, of course. But her course of action, making herself prey...she seemed to be gliding right over the fact that she might get found before she found.

He kept the thought to himself as he asked the more pertinent question. "Why?" Was she about to tell him more of what she knew?

A blip of doubt hit as he considered how much he'd risked taking on the woman as completely as he had.

He pushed through the unwanted blow to his confidence. He hadn't been duped. Wasn't being played.

He'd know if his cover had been blown.

Savannah was keeping an eye on him. He saw her glances in her rearview mirror. After a long pause she said, "I've been thinking about everything we've both come up with, trying to fit pieces together in a way that shows us the ones that are missing. And it seems plausible that Charlotte's father knew he'd adopted a kidnapped baby. I'm assuming it's always just been father and daughter, so maybe he wanted a girl with particular characteristics and back then it would have been harder for a single man to adopt. Or maybe he knew the kidnapper and had a reason to buy him out of trouble. Could have been a brother who'd gotten into trouble or something..."

The family-member angle wasn't one he'd considered. Duran wasn't known to have any biological family. At least not in the states. But had Charlotte found out about someone? An aunt or uncle or cousin? Someone from whom her father was estranged? Could that have been why she'd gone to Family Finders?

His mind grabbed the possibilities, finding merit rather than dismissing them outright. An estranged sibling who knew Eduardo's secret, one Charlotte had wanted to find, fit with the facts they had.

Including Charlotte's disappearance. A missing person who'd left no trace. What if Savannah hadn't been the only one who'd been sent a positive match pursuant to Charlotte's database entry? What if someone else had been notified that she'd been looking and had contacted her? A highly intelligent young woman could feasibly have planned her escape to meet up with someone she was related to, in the hopes of bringing him or her home to her father.

It sounded like something Charlotte would do.

The official version, that he'd heard from both Charlotte and her father at separate times, was that Charlotte had been born to Duran and his wife, an American woman who'd died giving birth. What he'd learned that day was that there'd been an American birth certificate and paperwork granting the child dual citizenship.

"What if the kidnapper has been in the picture for a while?" Savannah said, continuing on her own tangent. "Maybe he threatened to tell Charlotte that she was kidnapped unless he was compensated. He could have been getting paid by Mr. Duran for his silence. Charlotte could have told her father that she'd entered her DNA into the Family Finders database. Or—you'd know better than I—maybe her computer is regularly checked to make certain that no one's defrauding her, and they found record of the entry. That's why they were watching me after she'd entered the database.

"As long as I did nothing, I was no threat. But once I flew to San Diego... Maybe the kidnapper and Mr. Duran both know that I'm Charlotte's sister and are trying to get rid of me, so I don't tell Charlotte. Even if Mr. Duran didn't know at first that Charlotte had been kidnapped, when he found out, loving Charlotte as he did... It's believable that he'd buy the kidnapper's silence..."

Savannah's voice trailed off.

Isaac thought about telling her about the family angle her words had just brought to him but knew he couldn't. His assignment was for him and his agents. Savannah could only be privy to what she had to know for the sake of the case.

The fact brought a bad taste to his mouth and tension to his gut as he said, "I think you're onto something..."

Her gasp came crisp and clear over the wireless connection, followed by, "What if Mr. Duran or the kidnapper have taken Charlotte someplace—sent her on vacation out of the country even, just until they're satisfied that I've been dealt with? She might not even know people think she's missing."

He'd considered Duran as the instigator in Charlotte's absence. Still didn't feel like that one fit. "Which means you're risking your life on a wild-goose chase," he said and added, "I had a text while you were in the bathroom, letting me know that my protection team's mid-morning update from Duran security included the fact that your rental had been returned to the airport but that there'd been no sign of you heading through security to board the flight. So if you want to change your mind and go back into hiding while I sort this out..."

What in the hell was he saying?

And who was saying it? Not Isaac Forrester, that was for sure.

And not Mike Reynolds, either.

Having her exposed was their best shot at ending the case. Including removing the threat from Savannah. She'd been to San Diego once. Had sought out Charlotte. Duran wouldn't be comfortable leaving her out there anymore, a possible threat who could attack at any time.

"No way I'm giving up. If what we think is true, I'm a threat to Duran no matter where I am. I told you, Isaac, with or without you, I'm done being a victim." Savannah's words let him off the hook, with a strong note to get himself in gear, get any softness he might be harboring toward Savannah Compton off the table or get off the case.

Her tone changed, lost its energy as she added, "I'm only guessing here. And not sure I'm anywhere near the truth."

Isaac nodded. Keeping to himself the fact that he believed she was closer to finding their mark than she thought.

And that he admired her ability to get there.

What he allowed himself to celebrate was the fact that with her suspicions on Duran, as his had been all along, they were closer to being on the same page. She'd just negated the need for any lies he'd have had to tell her if they found Charlotte and she pushed him to bring in Duran's men.

Beyond that, she was just a part of the plan to complete the most important job he'd ever had. A part he was sworn to protect.

And he was just Isaac Forrester.

A fake persona.

Period.

After the conversation regarding Duran, Isaac seemed to open up to Savannah more. Like maybe he was starting to see her more as her partners did—a necessary cog in the wheel with contributions that no one else could bring to the table.

Or maybe she was just slowly starting to see herself again.

As she passed a popular gas station–convenience store chain, Isaac told her about the time Charlotte had insisted on stopping at that exact location to pump gas. She'd wanted the experience.

Keeping her gaze focused on the traffic, on her surroundings, Savannah felt her heart fill due to the real-life image of her sister that was finally forming in her mind's eye.

And a few minutes later, as she approached the university they'd been heading toward, Isaac told her about an encounter that had taken place just that week—Charlotte planning to cut her lecture to avoid someone in the audience.

He didn't say who—it would've been inappropriate for him to do so—but the way he told her...a man who wouldn't take no for an answer...she knew. The man in the yard with Nicole... making her cry...

Wait. She stiffened, shot a quick glance in the rearview mirror. Locating Isaac two cars behind her in the left lane, she said, "What if Charlotte did leave of her own accord?" Mind clear, inner vision astute, she continued, "She was willing to forgo a lecture to avoid the man. What would she be willing to do to avoid being hounded by him in her own home?"

That was it. The explanation that made sense. Charlotte knew the house, the security systems, the habits of the personnel in place to watch over everything. She'd know how to avoid all of them. How to shut down the system for the time she'd need to escape.

And would have had something in place to get her away once she was off the property undetected. Savannah had hired a boat. Charlotte, with all her wealth, could have swum and then walked before being picked up by a helicopter. Or a yacht. She could be anywhere, with anyone of her choosing. People she'd pay to stay silent.

It was an explanation Savannah could take in without losing a part of herself. Nicole hadn't been kidnapped again—she'd left of her own accord.

A silent Isaac was pulling into the university parking lot behind her. She'd get out. He'd wait in the car until she was far enough away and then carefully follow her. He'd provided them both with earpieces to stay in verbal contact.

Getting out of her car, turning on the earpiece as it connected, she walked toward the building that had housed the lecture hall and asked, "This guy who leaves her no choice but to disappear—who is he?" Her words were soft, but she issued them with definite courtroom interrogation in her tone.

Isaac's silence might have been hard for her to withstand a day or two before.

Not anymore.

She was done being manipulated by the fear her hunters had spent the last year instilling within her. She might've been cautious, but she had a mind that could untangle the most intricately weaved webs.

"Isaac?" Her gaze was moving around her surroundings, just as it had every other time they'd stopped. "Who is he?"

"I'm ten yards behind you. The door we always entered is at the left side of the building. The lecture hall will be the first door on your right once you get inside."

She veered to the left. Looking at everyone in sight. Catching no one looking back. "Who is he?" Her words were staccato.

"That's information I'm not free to divulge." There was no hint of sorrow in his tone.

His words felt like stabs. Until she reminded herself Isaac was skating a thin line, owing his loyalty to his employer—the lack of which could be a career ender for him—and...knowing Savannah.

Knowing. What else could she call the odd connection between the two of them? Virtual strangers who were somehow trusting each other with lives at stake.

Who happened to have had incredible sex less than twenty-four hours before.

"Is he on your radar as a possible suspect?" she asked then.

"Until I have someone in custody, everyone is a possible suspect." The low tone in her ear delivered his message succinctly.

She and Isaac Forrester were working together, reaching for the same goal, but they weren't a team.

And no matter how much he lit her up, he most definitely was not one of her partners.

The woman had as much energy as any good agent with whom he'd ever worked. Isaac listened in on conversations she had with people at the university, most pertinent to him being the one she held with the dean of the women's studies department.

Posing as a journalist doing a story on Charlotte Duran for an online women's publication Isaac had never heard of, Savannah had a heartfelt talk about the different cultures in which women were raised, which she managed to segue into a question about Charlotte's possible motives for being so passionate about her topic.

He didn't blame the lawyer for trying to get to know her sister in any way she could, yet time was pressing at his back. He couldn't be completely absent from Duran property for more than a day or two. Nor did he think that whoever was after Savannah was just going to give up and go home. The longer things drew out, the more desperate everyone was going to become.

The more determined.

And the less likely Duran would be to remain patient. If he didn't feel success coming his way soon regarding the threat that Savannah Compton posed to the life he'd built, the man was going to disappear right behind his daughter.

Dread weighted his gut as he considered that that had been the plan from the moment Charlotte had disappeared. Duran had already started his disappearing act. First Charlotte. And then himself…

"She cares deeply about all aspects of the female psyche, about the unique challenges all women face, regardless of race or nationality or culture, and tries to bring a sense of sisterhood into every group to whom she speaks…" The dean's voice was coming through Isaac's earpiece just as one of Duran's security guards approached the building from a parking area on the other side of the building. A third shifter, they'd never actually worked together. He knew the man by gait.

Sliding his hand to the gun holstered by his pocket underneath his suit jacket, Isaac turned, slid behind some shrubbery, and said, "Get out now. South door. Go behind the shrubs against the building, and don't move."

Without waiting for a response, he rounded the building from the opposite side and, before the guard made it to the door of the building, burst around a corner as though he'd been on the same sidewalk. With surprise all over his face and in his voice, he greeted the man. Told him he was making good progress on his day's responsibilities but had so far turned up very little. Except that Charlotte was passionate about the challenges women faced.

He kept his demeanor serious. Played the guy-to-guy, guard-to-guard card. Showed concern. And then suggested, on the down-low, that he was beginning to wonder if Charlotte Duran had left of her own accord.

When the guard responded in kind, looking Isaac in the eye, expressing his own lack of progress along with a dose of fatigue, Isaac offered to take some of the other man's assignments and was gratified when the man said he'd been specifically charged with speaking with anyone who'd shown up on Charlotte's phone records over the past week, showing them Savannah Compton's photo, and that he would get his job done.

But he thanked Isaac sincerely for the offer as Isaac barreled forward with the conversation to let the man know he'd just interviewed the dean, whom the man had been on his way to see, and had shown the photo to no avail, knowing full well that Savannah could hear the conversation.

If the guard didn't turn around, their jig could be up. Isaac would pull out all stops to prevent the guard from seeing the dean, setting off a sprinkler system or fire alarm if it came to that, but he needed Savannah prepared.

With a grateful nod, along with a comment about Isaac's reputation for thoroughness, the tired security man turned back the way he'd come. And Isaac stood watching him until he was out of sight.

They'd dodged a bullet.

And Isaac took warning, too. Isaac had been charged with looking for Charlotte. At least one member of the security staff was on another mission. Eduardo Duran wasn't going to stop looking for Savannah. He was only going to increase manpower until she was found.

Chapter Seventeen

Following Isaac's instructions completely, zigzagging her way between buildings and trees and then using his vehicle as a cover, Savannah made it back to her rental sedan. Her heart was pounding, and she was breathing heavily.

But she had completed the trek perfectly by focusing on his voice in her ear.

Adrenaline pumped through her as she started her car and pulled off the university lot. Other than her abrupt departure, claiming a sudden stomach ailment, Savannah had enjoyed her conversation with the dean. But more, she was actively engaged in saving her sister.

"We're on the right track," she said to Isaac as soon as she'd segued into traffic. "We know that Duran's men are aggressively looking for me," she said, feeling the shiver of fear the notice brought but also engaging with the sense of power it gave her. "Which means that I mean as much to them as we surmised that I did."

His grunt didn't add to her sense of accomplishment, but she didn't let him diminish her resolve, either. "I'm changing course for our next stop," she told him next, signaling a turn from the directions she'd looked up while hiding in the shrubs. He could follow or not. The fact that she was driving in front of him had been his call.

"This will work better if I have some heads-up." His tone was droll. She didn't miss the warning in the words, though. He'd probably just saved her life.

She needed him far more than he needed her.

While she wanted to be seen, to draw out the kidnapper, she'd fail if Duran's men got to her first.

"Back there, Dean Wilson was talking about Charlotte's passion, and it hit me. There were women's shelters on your log. I'm heading to the one Charlotte most recently visited—just last week. If anyone can give us any insight as to where Charlotte might hide out, I'm thinking it would be someone at the shelter. I've worked with several women's shelters, and one of the things that seems to remain true throughout the entire community of them is that shelters are a safe place for women to talk. About things they might not speak of anywhere else."

She was pulling away from the square mile surrounding the university, entering a roundabout when another vehicle entered at the same time from a perpendicular direction that should have yielded to her.

Except that it wasn't yielding. The vehicle was coming straight at her. Big. Black. Savannah gunned the gas, speeding around, heading for another exit, not slowing—though she should have, and barely escaped another car with the right of way, shooting out in the opposite direction of where she'd been heading. She heard a crunch behind her.

Cringed.

Sent up a small prayer for those involved in the crash that had been clearly meant for her. And with a shaky voice said, "Isaac?"

Fearing the worst when she didn't hear his voice reply in return.

On the phone with Chuck Knowles, rattling off a license plate number before getting out of his car to observe the wreckage he'd nearly been a part of, Isaac watched Savannah speed off into the distance.

His gut clenched tight—he knew he had to stay at the scene long enough to see who'd just tried to kill her. Someone who'd known she was at the university, who'd seen her turn onto the road leading to the roundabout and had headed her off.

One of Duran's men?

Running toward the wreckage, a three-car pileup, hearing someone say they'd called 911, he was already hearing sounds of sirens when he caught sight of a male—less than six feet tall, shaved head, white T-shirt, jeans, medium-color skin with tats on his arms—running from the scene.

To a car on the side of the road, just off the roundabout. He was in, with the blue sedan taking off before Isaac got sight of the driver. But he managed to snap a photo which, when enlarged, produced another plate number for him to call in to Chuck.

He did so as he climbed back into his own car, backed around, and sped off down the road Savannah had taken. He knew her destination, hoped she was back on the route, and, as soon as he was off with Chuck, called her back.

His jaw was clenched, his gut sick with worry as he waited for the call to connect, to hear the first ring.

He'd had to leave her to fend for herself. Had to stop and get what evidence he could before police had arrived. Car makes and models. Suspect information, if he'd had a chance to retrieve that, too. As a bodyguard he had no legal ground to stand on, but before law enforcement arrived, all bets were off. There was no law against being an overzealous concerned citizen.

Two rings. No answer.

The black SUV entering the roundabout, heading straight for Savannah. A getaway car. Or lookout. Or both.

Had a third vehicle followed her out of the roundabout?

Not immediately—he'd watched long enough to know that, but once he'd turned his attention to the plate number for Chuck...

"Isaac?" Her voice in his ear. Strong. Worried sounding.

Isaac's hand shook on the wheel as adrenaline drained from him, making way for relief. "You okay?"

"Yes."

"In your car?"

"Yes."

"Driving?" He had to know. Direct questions for direct answers. Ones she could give even if someone was listening.

"Yes."

"Alone?"

"Yes." Was that a note of warmth in her last response?

They couldn't afford warmth. Any more than he needed to be weak with relief.

"You on your way to the shelter?"

"Yes."

He knew the route. "On Randolph Road?"

"Yes."

Turning sharply, he took a turn and then another, heading toward a shortcut through an alley. "I'm on my way."

"Oh!" Her surprise was evident. And he was pretty sure he detected relief, too.

"You thought I'd abandon you?" The idea kind of pissed him off. She didn't see him as someone reliable.

And yet leaving her to fend for herself was exactly what he'd done.

"I thought you'd been hurt," she said then. "I knew you were entering the circle behind me. Heard the crash..."

Her voice trembled as her words broke off.

She'd been afraid for him. But had kept going.

As he had.

They were professionals. Focused. The only thing that mattered was the goal.

But that small tremble he'd heard in her voice...it lingered.

Savannah didn't get much from the shelter. She'd hoped, going in alone, posing as a woman Charlotte had spoken to, asking for clarification on a location Charlotte had mentioned as a place to hide out for a few days, that someone would immediately pop out an answer.

Which was why she was a lawyer, not an investigator. She'd walked into a small, empty room. Had been spoken to through what was obviously bulletproof glass via a metal speaker in the middle of it. She'd been convincing enough to get herself beyond the first locked door and into a private room with a table and two chairs. And then she'd met with a woman who was one of the shelter's volunteers. Someone who only worked two afternoons a week.

And had been told, quite clearly, that no one there would give out any information on anyone else who'd been there or worked there, ever. Most particularly not to someone who didn't have a case on file. Or who hadn't registered with them.

If she wanted to register, they could get that process started, and then she'd be able to speak with a counselor who could help her. Or if she'd rather, she could just sit for a bit, have a beverage and a snack, and when the counselor was free, she could come in to chat. But at no time did anyone give out safe locations to anyone other than someone who'd been deemed to have immediate need of one.

While Savannah was disappointed, she totally understood. Anyone could pay someone to go in and get information that would then be used to allow an abuser to get to his victim.

Which was what she told Isaac. He'd been on the lookout the entire time she'd been inside, and she'd waited for his all-clear before she'd exited the back door of the small, nondescript building and practically held her breath as she'd hurried to her car.

"You think the guy in the crash was the same one who shot at me?" she asked as soon as she was on the road again, driving to their next destination. Another shelter.

He'd said that he'd seen one man and had called in a description of him as well as a license plate number to his team. And that due to the crash, the police were involved as well.

"It's possible." His tone gave away nothing.

"Hired by Duran?" She was trying not to internalize the danger she was in or dwell on it. Doing so would be counterproductive to her possibility of survival. But she needed to understand, as best she could, what she was up against.

"In the year I've been associated with Eduardo Duran I haven't seen a single piece of evidence pointing to him ever putting out a hit on someone. Or proof that he's done anything else illegal."

She'd pretty much expected that to be the case. Isaac wouldn't be working for the man if he thought Duran was involved in criminal activity.

But her heart settled a bit anyway, for Charlotte's sake.

The getaway car had been stolen from a bowling-alley parking lot the day that Savannah had come to town. The black SUV was registered to a ninety-year-old man who'd been dead for six months. Whether it was stolen or being driven by a legal heir was yet to be determined. None of the man's relatives could be reached.

Since witnesses had all stated that the black SUV had come barreling into the circle, causing the crash, the police were designating the incident a hit-and-run crash, suspecting that the driver of the SUV had been driving under the influence.

The FBI was not involved. Isaac's call. He couldn't afford the risk of blowing his cover. They were getting close. Perps were running scared. He had to let it play out until he found proof of more than a vehicular crime.

His agents were following up, quietly, on their own.

And Isaac was finding the case more and more distasteful. And himself lacking the power that generally drove him to successfully close cases and save lives.

"Do you think someone associated with Nicole's kidnapping and Duran are working together, or do I have two separate entities gunning for me?" Savannah's voice filled the space of his vehicle so completely, he felt as though he was being washed with it.

But couldn't get clean.

"I wish I knew," he told her. "My guess would be that they'd join forces just to get you out of the picture. And then Duran goes after the kidnapper. But that's before we factor in Charlotte's disappearance. If we knew who has her, we'd have a better chance of figuring out who the enemy is and from there determine how to catch him." He heard his words too late to take them back.

He'd been talking like an agent. Like himself. Not like Isaac.

The killers weren't the only ones who were getting pushed hard enough to act in a way that could get them caught.

Isaac made note. And continued to do his job as he followed the gray sedan a few lengths in front of him. Watchful. Taking in everything he could. Gun on the seat beside him just in case he had to make a quick shot to save a life.

Worrying about snipers.

Duran's entire empire had been built with unseen, unknown, unprovable tools. Isaac had spent the past year searching for actionable proof of a ghost.

His Duran phone rang, and he glanced at the screen. He didn't recognize the number.

"Hold on," he told Savannah, tense as he cut her off from audio call and lost communication with her.

"Yeah," he barked into the air around him, more vigilant than ever at keeping watch on the woman who was not quite officially, but morally, under his protection.

"Isaac?" His system froze. And went into high-alert mode all at once. There was no mistaking the voice.

"Charlotte?"

"Yeah."

"Where are you?" He glanced behind him. To both sides. Focused on the gray sedan making a left-hand turn and drove on by. He'd take the next street. Approach the shelter from a different angle. Park a block up. Protocol.

It was stifling him.

As was his charge's lack of response.

"Charlotte." His tone carried his tension. "Are you all right?"

"Yes. Are you alone?"

"Yes. What's going on?"

"I just got a call from…someone. There's been a woman asking around about me this morning. Long dark hair, dark eyes, a little taller than me. You know anything about her?"

Breaking all speed limits, Isaac cut up a block, ran a stop sign, and turned onto the street that housed the shelter. Not taking a breath until he saw the gray sedan pulling into the driveway.

And his mind cleared to pinpoint focus as he said, "I need to know about you," he countered. "Are you alone?"

"Yes." The word meant nothing. She'd say anything she was

told to say if a gun was pointed at her head. But before he could continue the interrogation long enough to read her, she said, "I'm not going to tell you where I am. I just... I trust you, Isaac. Do you know who this woman is?"

"I need you to give me something first, Charlotte. Tell me what's going on."

Savannah had disappeared into the side door of the shelter. He had to get back to her line. To monitor...

"I shouldn't have called."

"Wait!" He couldn't lose her. She'd said she trusted him. Had reached out to him. "I do know who she is, but I can't tell you more until I know more about your current situation." Did Charlotte know about Savannah, then? Did she know she'd been kidnapped as a child? That she'd been adopted?

Though...his team still had not found verification of the missing-toddler case.

He'd seen the DNA results. Had had them verified. The two women were sisters.

"You work for my father. Your loyalty is to him."

Okay. She was at odds with Eduardo. It was something.

"He pays me to be loyal to you, not him."

"I'm someplace safe," she said then. "Using a burner phone I was given."

He believed her. For the most part.

The woman was a suspect.

He needed her to trust him. To stay in contact until he could figure out where she was and why.

And he had to get to the other line. "Did you leave of your own accord?"

"Yes."

And, a thought repeated...based on what she'd just said, she was at odds with her father?

Had he read Eduardo right? The man had no idea where his daughter was or who'd taken her?

What did Charlotte know? The question burned his gut. Almost as much as his lost contact with Savannah.

"You need to know you can trust me—I need to know I can trust you," he said then. Playing the game he had to play.

"I asked for help from one of the shelters." He'd never heard a defeatist tone come out of Charlotte's mouth. But there it was.

And it made sense. She'd just been contacted.

Right after Savannah had tried to get information from the most recent shelter Charlotte had visited.

Was she trying to tell him that Eduardo had been abusive— no. Truth hit him.

Wagar.

And her father trying to force her to marry the man.

"She's the woman who was shot at in the boat the other day," he said then, taking a huge chance, playing a hunch but needing to get Charlotte to trust him enough to get her back in his fold. "She found out I was your bodyguard and came to me to tell me what she'd seen." He risked much with his skating between truth and lie. His ability to do so well had meant the difference between life and death many times in his career. "She saw Arnold Wagar refuse to take his hands off you when you made it clear you wanted to be left alone. She said that you were in agony, crying on the beach."

He played his strongest hand right up front. Remembering what Savannah had said about the global sisterhood...

In lieu of mentioning the sisterhood about which he would not speak.

"There's something not right about Wagar. He and my dad are thick. My dad trusts him. He's pressuring me to marry him, and I won't. He gives me the creeps. Wagar's the first person to ever come between me and Dad." He heard pain in Charlotte's voice. A break from her normal confident, often pigheaded, way of handling life.

Growing more tense by the second as he watched the shelter with no sign of Savannah and no way to hear what was happening inside, he wondered if the whole Charlotte thing was little more than a spoiled young woman's temper tantrum, until she said, "I know I'm too much of a brainiac to catch all the little nuances in general conversation and I'm often off in my head and miss some of the nonverbal emotional communication that goes on around me, but I'm not wrong about Wagar."

That one sentence, telling him that Charlotte was going

through a pretty intense self-evaluation, convinced Isaac, and he sat forward. "Tell me what feels off about him."

"First, he's only been around for about a year, but Dad, who doesn't let anyone but me get really close to him, trusts him enough to want me to marry him?"

About a year. About. A. Year. The words reverberated around the car like thunder. The same time frame in which Savannah had been followed. Didn't prove a damned thing.

But it could.

"And about a month ago he said something that I don't think either of them knew I'd heard. It had to do with my penchant for computer coding. So...several years ago I wrote a proprietary program for my father. Has to do with money management. A way to have it siphon through one global location before dispersing to its various accounts so that he can, at any time, know the current value of anything he owns, but if you put a trace on it, the first stop, the global location, is invisible. We call it Glob. Anyway, I heard Arnold ask my father if he thought, after we were married, I'd do some coding for him. Like, it's not me he wants, but my computer skills. He doesn't want me. He wants to marry me so I can do for him and his businesses what I do for my dad."

All senses on alert, Isaac could feel racing in his veins as his mind became a calculating machine, and his gut told him he'd found what he'd been looking for.

He had no idea how deep Charlotte's involvement was. But she'd just told him how Duran was able to hide everything he did while still providing clearly traceable money trails. The system, Glob, was part of what had been stopping them. And clearly was much more intricate and complicated than Charlotte had just alluded to. He and his team had serious work to do. Connections to make. Major hurdles to overcome.

But he felt certain that Eduardo Duran's daughter had just told him how to find the proof he needed to take down the entire Duran empire once and for all.

Chapter Eighteen

"Della, can I speak to you for a second?"

Savannah heard the voice come from behind her as she sat on a couch, facing the middle-aged, soft-spoken, yet compellingly trustworthy domestic violence counselor who'd just been addressed.

Looking over Savannah's shoulder, the woman stood immediately and excused herself. Leaving Savannah to suspect that something not good was happening. Either in the shelter, with one of their clients, or...with her.

She hadn't planned to pose as a victim. She'd just...been one. From the second she'd walked in the door, she'd felt as though her story had to be told. Not the real one. No kidnappings, witness protection, or gunfire. No bodyguards or sisters.

But the fear engulfing her whenever she stopped focusing on Charlotte's plight, on finding her sister, had come pouring out. She didn't know who was after her or why, but she knew she was being followed. And had just barely escaped probable death in what had clearly been an intentional car crash. If the black SUV had hit her instead of traveling on to strike two other vehicles, she'd have been crushed.

After that had all fallen out of her, she'd had her plan. Had asked how one went about finding a safe house. She was afraid to go home. Afraid to leave the shelter.

Della had just been about to answer her question—Savannah had hoped for a response that could give her an excuse to bring Charlotte into the conversation, a mention of the professor's name, having been referred by her—and then, she'd been gone.

Isaac wasn't back online yet, either.

Checking her phone, she saw that their lines were still connected.

And it hit her...something had happened outside the safe house. Something to do with Isaac. Someone knew he was working with her.

With fingers trembling so much she had to press three times to get the job done, she disconnected the call. Was sick to her stomach. She'd known bringing Isaac into her sphere would put him in danger...

Savannah jumped as the door opened and then stood, turning to face whatever was to come.

Della was alone, closing the door quickly behind her, her beautiful face creased with concern.

"What happened?" she asked. She wasn't the only victim in the city, maybe not even in the shelter, but...

"We have volunteers who take turns watching footage from our security cameras anytime anyone is in the building," the woman started right in, not reclaiming her seat. As Savannah's heart pounded the woman continued, "There's a man outside—he circled the block behind us twice and then disappeared into the culvert just beyond where you parked your car."

Thank God. Almost lightheaded with relief, Savannah sank back down to the couch. Took a sip of the iced water Della had given her just after she'd arrived. "In a blue suit coat?" she asked, scrambling to find a way to explain Isaac's presence in a nonthreatening way.

If she had a protection detail, why would she need a safe house?

Della was there—sitting beside her on the couch, not across from her as she had previously—before Savannah had finished swallowing.

"No, dear. He's wearing brown pants, a darker brown short-sleeved shirt hanging loosely over the waistband, and tennis shoes. Has hair down to his shoulders and a beard. Sound like anyone you'd recognize?"

Jitters started inside her, making her legs feel as though they might start jerking of their own accord. She was trapped. A sitting duck.

She could die. Without having done a damn thing to help Charlotte.

Unless…she was getting what she wanted. Was drawing out the ghost who'd been haunting her. Was Isaac on to him?

"I don't," she said, trying to think clearly through a wave of fear.

Had they gotten to Isaac?

Did they have his phone? Had they been listening to her conversation? Had she just played into their hands?

The suspicious character had gone into a culvert by her car. Which meant they knew what she was driving. Just like the driver of the black SUV had known.

She'd wanted to be found. But the hope had been to have them apprehended before they actually hurt her, so they'd lead authorities to Charlotte. Where were Isaac's bodyguard friends who were supposed to have his back?

Tears pricked the backs of her eyes, and she straightened. She wasn't going to fall apart. She was still there. Still able to act.

She just had to think.

"Am I the only…one…here?" she asked, not able, most particularly in that moment, to call herself a victim.

Della's nod, while serious, didn't seem to hold fear. More like…determination.

"We can help you get away," she said quietly. "We have a basement with an underground bunker that leads a half mile away. It's rough. I'm guessing from the days of the underground railroad. It's the reason we bought this place. The structure was crumbling, but we've stabilized and supported it all. But it's dark, dank, and only three feet high. You'd have to climb up a ladder through a sewer to get to the street. We'd have a car parked at the sewer, so no one sees you come up. You'd climb in and be driven to a destination of your choice within a five-mile radius. The police station, or someplace else."

The police station sounded heavenly to her at the moment.

But would such a move get Charlotte killed? Duran thought so.

Isaac had seemed to agree.

If the kidnappers had Charlotte and knew that the police had Savannah, would Duran be able to save her?

Would he even try, if his own ass was on the line?

She'd said she was going to be bait. And her plan was working!

The job wasn't done, and she was still able to be out there. Trying to find someone following her before they knew she'd seen them.

And if she did?

Without Isaac how did she get them before they got her?

Or was Isaac already outside, getting them as she sat safely inside sipping water on a comfortable couch with a lovely woman who, in another world, might have been a friend.

Her mind raced as Della sat there next to her, her gaze filled with compassion while she awaited Savannah's answer.

If she was alone and saw someone on her tail, she could call Sierra's Web. Have a meeting with her partners. And let them decide if they wanted to help her or not.

She'd tried to keep harm from coming to anyone else.

But clearly it didn't matter where she went—she was a wanted woman. And eventually that would lead back to her dear friends.

Maybe, the second she was alone, she should call them anyway.

A simple desire to see her sister without poking any bears had turned into something much larger, and more dangerous, than she'd ever imagined.

And Isaac... If she'd gotten him killed...her partners had to find his murderers and make them pay.

The fact that he'd been offline didn't bode well. Even if he was on the trail of someone, he could still have his earpiece on. Would have found a second to whisper a warning to her to stay inside, if nothing else.

"I very gratefully accept your offer," she said. "With one request."

"You need money?"

She had plenty in the bag on her shoulder. Along with her computer. Had been wearing the bag every visit she'd made that day. "No. But… I thought I recognized a vehicle, parked on the next block, as I turned in here. Could you send someone to see if it's still there?"

If Isaac was okay, he'd handle a wellness check from the local police. And if he was sitting behind his steering wheel, bleeding to death…she couldn't just leave him there to die.

"Of course," Della said. "We've already called for a full perimeter check and will add the next block to it. Our volunteer called the police the second she saw the man head to the culvert. It's protocol anytime we see something suspicious in the area. The local officers are definitely our friends here." The woman was close enough to touch Savannah. Had her hands right there, where Savannah could take hold, but didn't make contact.

Staring at those hands, Savannah wanted to reach out, to avail herself of a moment to draw strength but was afraid that if she did, she'd lose her courage and ask to be rescued.

After which, even if no one else blamed her, she'd hate herself for the rest of her life.

Her baby sister had been stolen from home.

Twice.

While Savannah's life, after the loss, had been blessed. Most importantly, she'd grown up with the love of their only living parent. With their mother's love.

Something she carried within her still.

Her mom had had to turn her back on her youngest daughter, and, though she'd never spoken of it, Savannah had known it had not only broken her heart but had eaten at her for the rest of her life. Savannah had a chance to fix that hurt. To ease her mother's eternal heart.

"Do I tell you now where I want to be taken?" she asked and felt as though tension drained out of Della. As though the woman had been personally invested in her choice to accept the chance to forge ahead on her own over going back to what she knew, allowing the mistreatment for a sense of security.

"No," the woman said and then reached over and placed her

palm over Savannah's clasped hands. "It's best for you and us if we don't know. You'll tell your driver when you get in the car."

Meeting the woman's dark eyes, seeing the intelligence brimming there, the encouragement, Savannah stood.

Determined to fight, to do all she could to catch the horrible people who'd ruined her family's lives, no matter what it cost.

And to avenge the man she'd known such a short time but suspected that she already loved more than any other she'd ever meet.

He'd put his life on the line for her. Had maybe lost the battle.

She'd never have a life worthy of living unless she fought back.

Charlotte refused to let Isaac go to her. She'd agreed to have him meet her sometime later in the day, before dark, and would be calling him back with a location. Whether or not he'd end up arresting her at that time remained to be seen.

But he was getting close to successfully closing the case. The familiar sense of heady adrenaline pouring through him was evidence of that.

He hadn't decided whether he was going to take Savannah with him to meet her sister. Didn't have a clear sense of whether or not her presence would be more advantageous to the case.

Charlotte was already doubting her father's judgment where Wagar was concerned. Would meeting a biological sister help catapult the woman further from her father? Or send her closer to him? He'd see how the rest of the day went, what Savannah came up with in her conversations, who they drew out of hiding, and go from there.

Clicking back to his ongoing conversation with Savannah the second Charlotte disconnected, he listened intently. Needing to hear her voice.

Tried to convince himself that his tension at the initial second of silence was case related. That he was only bothered about the conversation he'd missed. But when no sound came on the line for the next second and the next, he looked at the phone's screen. The call had been terminated. And the jolt to his midsection was personal. As was the sudden inner push to exit the vehicle and run to the door of the house-like structure she'd entered.

The agent in him kept him in his seat while he assessed. But barely.

He'd had half of her car in sight, including the driver's-side door, the entire time he'd been on with Charlotte. Hadn't noticed any untoward activity from his view of the front and one side of the house.

And forced himself to sit and wait. Undercover work didn't proceed like clockwork. There were always unforeseen complications. You had to be able to roll with them, to change course on the fly, which he'd proven himself more than able to do.

But when another fifteen minutes passed and there'd been no movement from the house, Isaac's tension had reached breaking point. The call could have just been dropped. Cell service wasn't failproof. And Savannah would have noticed, excused herself to the restroom, and redialed. She was just that kind of detail-oriented person.

Ripping up the carpet at his feet, reaching underneath it, up behind the brake pedal, he pulled out his official creds, took the safety off his gun, re-holstered it, and, with his hand under his jacket, seemingly in his pants pocket but on the butt of his weapon, he approached the side door of the house. Rang the bell he'd seen Savannah ring.

Stood there on the stoop for a full minute with no response.

He rang a second time, turning to see a police car slowing beside his vehicle. And another, coming from the opposite direction, turning into the parking lot directly behind him, moving toward Savannah's gray sedan.

His gut sank.

If someone inside had called the police, that meant there'd been some kind of trouble. With Savannah present. Did he out himself to local law enforcement? Could he trust that they wouldn't blow his cover?

Or did he abandon Savannah? Leave her to find a way to contact him if she could? Abandoning her to likely die at the hands of Duran—or some unknown kidnapper?

Maybe both?

According to a clearly worried Charlotte, Wagar had only been in Duran's life for a year. Isaac could in no way see that as a coincidence.

But while it was just the past year that Charlotte knew about, that didn't mean there hadn't been other business between the two.

Say, twenty-four years before?

What if the men had been acquainted in a previous lifetime? Had had Charlotte in common?

Who'd called whom after all that time? Duran? When he heard about Charlotte's DNA database entry?

Or had Wagar been monitoring databases? And notified Duran?

Wagar appeared to have the upper hand.

Duran was the one who'd be paying the biggest price. To the point of marrying off his beloved daughter to the man just to keep her with him? To keep the secret intact?

Which made Wagar, what, the kidnapper?

If that was the case, why didn't Duran just have the man killed?

Wagar had to have something over Duran, something that would expose Duran's secrets in the event of Wagar's death...

Walking back toward his car, he put the safety on his pistol. Reached into his back pocket for the wallet he carried with him every day and, taking the offensive, approached the officers who'd just looked into the windows on both sides of his vehicle. "Can I help you with something, Officers?" he asked. Getting what intel he could before he even considered something so rash as to blow his cover.

He showed the officer he approached, Jayden, his identification. "I'm personal protection director for Eduardo Duran—is something going on here?"

"This your vehicle?" the second officer, rounding the hood to join Isaac and Officer Jayden, asked.

"My personal vehicle, yes," he said. "I'm here at the behest of Eduardo Duran. His daughter has expressed interest in making a sizable donation to the facility, and I'm making a routine security check as part of Duran protocol." The words poured out of him as though he'd known what he was going to say. As though they were true.

Jayden handed Isaac's ID to Williams, the second uniformed man who'd joined them, who studied it, nodded, and handed it back to Isaac, saying, "We just had a call from inside the facility. Their security cameras caught a suspicious character circling the next block..." Williams nodded toward the street behind the shelter as Jayden took over.

"He then entered the property through some shrubbery and slid down into the culvert," the younger man said, with a gesture toward the second police car, parked at an angle half-behind Savannah's vehicle.

A perp outside. Not in?

Savannah was safe?

Adrenaline spread anew as he headed toward the second police car, a rapid walk, with Jayden and Williams keeping up beside him. The plan was working?

They'd lured out whoever was after her, would have the arrest, and possibly some answers, before his meeting with Charlotte?

Not the proof he needed to take down Duran. He'd need a warrant for Duran's electronics and his best tech agents deep diving on Glob for that. Or...testimony from Charlotte Duran. But if they could expose the man's personal lies...prove that he'd hired someone to kill Savannah Compton...they could lock him up for that much while they built a criminal case that would not only get the man off the street forever but would shut down his businesses, too...

"He's gone." Another cop, thirtyish, was climbing up out of the culvert. "It's wet down there—there are footprints. Looks like he took off, followed the drainage ditch that way." She pointed to the street behind the shelter, the one the man had reportedly come from. "We'll head inside, get copies of the footage, run his likeness through facial recognition, and keep an eye out," she finished, clearly the senior officer on scene.

Isaac needed a copy of that likeness. Would call Chuck. Leave it to the agent to secure it. Run it. Keep him posted.

In the meantime... "And the woman?" he asked, nodding

toward Savannah's car. And after Jayden filled his superior in on Isaac's identity, his private security position, registration, and reason for being in the area, the senior officer, Abernathy, turned to him.

She was frowning as she asked, "You know her?"

"No," he lowered his tone, shook his head, showing her his compassion. "I saw her going in as I drove up. Long dark hair, pulled back, capris and short-sleeved shirt. The way she was looking around her... I've been waiting for her to leave before I rang the bell. But after so much time had passed, I figured maybe she was a volunteer and was just ringing the bell when your officers approached."

He was on form. Finding his confidence. Doing what he did best. Pretending to be someone he was not—to save lives.

Right up until Abernathy returned to tell him that no one that fit the brief description he'd given was inside the building. No one other than the shelter's regular volunteers were inside.

He started to push. Saw the way Abernathy's gaze narrowed and immediately backed off. Saying that he'd seen what he'd needed to see to assure Eduardo Duran that his daughter's association with the shelter would be worthwhile.

Thanked her and headed straight to his car.

Either Savannah had enlisted the shelter's help to ditch him.

Or just like Charlotte, she'd disappeared into thin air.

Calling Chuck to get copies—not just of the intruder's image, but of all the shelter's security footage from that morning, and to have someone watching Savannah's gray sedan, too—he pulled away, feeling the eyes of local police at his back.

He had to wonder...were they on Duran's payroll, too?

Was he being followed? Did Duran suspect he knew more about Charlotte's disappearance than he was saying?

Was the man having every member of his current staff watched?

Odd that after just a couple of hours of having Savannah on the road as bait, one of Duran's men had shown up at the university, right where they were at the same exact time.

And yet the security guard had seemed to trust Isaac. Turned around.

Only to have Savannah almost run off the road just a short time later.

Savannah, not him. If his cover had been blown, he'd have been the target. He had no doubts about that. Isaac was a risk to far more than just a family matter.

But that didn't mean that Duran wasn't having him—all of them—followed.

Savannah had disappeared. They had to have known where she was.

Did that mean Duran had her already? Snatching her right from under his nose?

Putting one more call into Chuck, relaying his fears, Isaac drove.

Two women missing who'd been in his care.

And he had nowhere to go.

Chapter Nineteen

Savannah didn't call her partners. Instead, she acted like she was one of them, maybe for the first time since they'd formed the firm. She put her full energy into accomplishing the task in front of her rather than just being legal counsel for those who'd always done so.

Had they all seen her lack of courage over the years? Did they consider her their weak link? No one had ever given her cause to think so. To the contrary, they all came to her for her advice, for her counsel. And always trusted and acted upon the advice she gave.

Was it possible they'd seen something in her she hadn't?

After her half-mile trek, she'd climbed up the ladder, into the back seat of the car, and told the driver to take her to a car rental place.

From there, she used her firm credit card—clearly Duran would already have someone checking anything in her name—and rented yet another sedan. Dark green.

Inside the agency, seeing a pay phone, she used it to dial Isaac's number. Just in case. But fearing that her hunters were in possession of it, that she could be playing right into their hands, she hung up before the first ring.

And didn't pick up when, minutes later, his number showed

up on her screen. What she did do was immediately turn off the location on her phone.

For once, for her mother and Charlotte, for Isaac—and for her scared little self, too—she was going to use the intelligence with which she'd been blessed and the self-defense training with which she'd armed herself and fight back. She didn't need Isaac's physical presence behind her to visit the places where Charlotte was known to have been. She had her copy of his log.

In her new car, she studied the city map she'd pulled up on the internet and memorized the way to the next location. A women's clothing boutique.

Without Isaac behind her, she had to be more vigilant than ever, but after a year of feeling like someone was following her, she'd honed her observation skills.

Which was how she'd been able to avoid the near-fatal collision that could have cost her her life that morning.

A crash that had hurt innocent people.

The thought troubled her greatly as she approached the boutique a good hour after her escape from the shelter. There were sales staff inside. Maybe even the owner. People who'd gone to work that day to earn a living. People with loved ones. Did she put them all at risk by strolling inside?

If she didn't find out everything she could about Charlotte's conversations, how would she be able to put together pieces that might point them to the ghost? If he'd been watching Savannah all those months, chances were Charlotte had been in his sights, too.

And if he was Duran, or hired by the man, chances were good that Savannah would be the only casualty. Car crash aside. Had she not acted so quickly, she would have been taken care of then.

Talking herself out of the fear that paralyzed her, she parked in front of the boutique. Waited long enough to take stock of all other vehicles in the area. Noting people who came and went. She was in a new car. With her phone's location off. Unless the shelter had burned her—and she was willing to bet her life they hadn't—she likely had a little time before anyone caught up with her.

Even if Duran had the police in his pocket.

The thought was fanciful, one based more in the debilitating fear that she'd let consume her life than in reality, but a man with that much money—and a life, a father-daughter relationship to protect—she could see him going to whatever lengths it took.

And, as a partner in Sierra's Web, knew full well how many times money swayed the minds and morals of seemingly good people. Even those sworn to uphold the law.

Particularly those.

Determining that it was safe for her to go inside, Savannah did so. And returned to her car ten minutes later with a new jumpsuit she'd purchased for her good friend, Charlotte, to surprise her for her birthday.

Savannah had learned that her sister didn't present as an uber wealthy woman. Charlotte was polite. Respectful. And, as smart as she was, was sometimes insecure about her knowledge of what was currently in fashion. Which was why she stuck to the few boutiques she trusted for any wardrobe changes.

Charlotte also hated having someone watching her every move and had once snuck out the back door of the shop to avoid her bodyguard and meet up with a woman she'd met at a shelter who'd needed some technical advice.

As Savannah watched her back, driving in zigzags to her next stop, she decided that if she saw imminent danger, she'd call the police. It was the smart thing to do.

And she let her heart talk to her, too. Even if she never met Nicole as the grown woman, Charlotte, she was getting to know her sister. And loved the person she'd become.

If she died that day, she'd do so feeling as though the last choice she'd made—to find Charlotte—had been the right one. That her life had served in the way she'd most wanted.

She'd go believing that she hadn't let her partners down. She'd proven to be worthy of the best of them.

And she'd go knowing that she'd finally found out what it felt like to fall in love, to make love with the man she'd been meant to find.

But she didn't plan to die.

As she drove and had her own back, the energy pumping through her was too strong to ignore. More powerful than fear.

Because she had one hell of a reason to live.

After twenty-four years, she'd learned how to trust herself. And to trust love to guide her, too.

Isaac's boss had given him an assignment. To visit every location he'd taken Charlotte Duran during the past three months. But that wasn't why he continued down the list he and Savannah had been using that day.

He drove to the next location because in just a matter of days he'd grown to know a woman so intimately that he knew following the list was what she would do. If she were able.

And because the plan was a good one. The tidbits Savannah had learned about Charlotte Duran during her various conversations that day were things he could use to have deeper influence on the young heiress when he met with her later.

Her passion for helping victims—if he could show her some of the reprehensible things her father had done...

Or at least get her to do a deep dive on her own invention, Glob, and let her find out for herself.

He'd promise her the best deal he could give her. Somehow over the past twenty-four hours he'd lost any passion for seeing Charlotte Duran behind bars.

He'd seen her as a suspect. Savannah had opened his mind to the person she was. A helpless toddler who'd been stolen from her family and knew only what Eduardo Duran had taught her.

One who spent her time helping women who'd been victimized.

Good deeds didn't forgive her the crimes she'd likely committed. He'd have to find out the scope of her involvement before he'd know what he could do for her, but he knew, even before he met with Charlotte, that he was committed to doing all he could for her.

Maybe he was going soft.

Maybe after he'd put Duran away, he'd think about taking the promotion that had been offered him and leave undercover work behind him.

The way the case, Savannah Compton in particular, had gotten to him, he had to consider that it was time he got out. Moved up to new challenges.

An hour after he'd left the shelter, he tried her phone again as he rounded a corner to park across from one of Charlotte's favorite restaurants. Just in case someone picked up. If he could keep them talking, he could get Chuck to get a trace on it. He'd been to the boutique which was next on their list as soon as he'd left the shelter. Then on to the exclusive salon where Charlotte got her hair done. Neither location had given him much. The boutique owner and Charlotte's hair designer, knew he was her bodyguard. He used the excuse of her having lost one of her favorite earrings and had learned that neither of the establishments had it.

If Duran was tracking his moves, he'd see that Isaac was following orders. While he waited to hear back from Charlotte.

He prayed that Savannah was alive. That he'd hear something back from Chuck that would tell him where to go, how to find her.

When his phone rang and the agent's number showed up on screen just before he exited his car to head into the dining establishment, he remembered Savannah talking about providence. And hoped to God that some worked in her favor.

Instead of the agent's call giving him any sense of direction or relief, Isaac sat there, stunned, reeling with the urgent information Chuck was giving him.

The secret Savannah had been keeping...he hadn't seen it coming.

Agents in the Washington bureau had finally found record of the disappearance of a one-year-old named Nicole who'd been taken from her daycare by her father, who'd been murdered later that same day. Except that she wasn't Nicole Compton. She'd been born Nicole Gussman.

Had been listed in the missing person database as Natalie Willoughby after her remaining family members, her mother and seven-year-old sister, had entered the witness protection program.

The seven-year-old child had been born as Sarah, but became Savannah—something similar, probably because the chances of her making a critical mistake with the name change would be lessened. Her last name had changed from Gussman to Compton.

Savannah's father, Hugh Gussman, had worked for the IRS and had been about to blow the whistle on a sizable breach he'd found in the system, a hack that had cost the government more than a million dollars.

Information that would never have been disclosed except that Savannah's mother was dead, Savannah was in danger, probably from those the program had sought to protect her from, and because of the ties to an internationally wanted criminal—Eduardo Duran.

Whether Duran had in some way been involved with the IRS hack from El Salvador or had just put in for a black-market baby and had ended up with Charlotte was something Isaac had to try to find out.

Gussman had been going to reveal all, including the source of the hack, to the FBI the day he'd been burned to death and left as a pile of ashes on a sand dune. Investigators had found a piece of skin from the bare heel he'd been digging into the sand, over and over, as he'd died a slow death, from which they'd been able to extract DNA to identify him. His shoes and socks had been found in the woods several yards away. His charred belt buckle had been discovered in the debris.

Sick at heart as he listened, aching for the young girl Savannah had been and for the incredible woman she'd become, Isaac felt his resolve to find her answers harden into a life mission. He couldn't change what Charlotte might have grown into, what she might have done as an adult working with her father, but he could end the ravaging once and for all.

In those seconds, solving the case, the job had ceased to be his motivator. He was out to get justice for Savannah. And for her mother and baby sister, too.

Bringing down Eduardo Duran was no longer a job to him. It had become personal.

Thoughts of his little sister—who was, based on his social media research, married, an elementary school teacher, and a mother of two—surfaced as he hung up the phone. He'd busted her drug-dealing boyfriend, refusing to look the other way even though it meant she'd had to do a month in juvenile detention for the drops she'd made for him. She'd been on a crash course to hell, on the verge of ruining her life, and he'd done what he'd had to do to save her.

Rather than giving the young couple the second chance they'd begged for, he'd made the bust, turned over the evidence, and cried when he'd watched her being hauled off. Maybe getting caught would have scared them straight. Maybe they'd have made good on a chance to turn their lives around. He hadn't been willing to take that chance.

Because he'd loved her that much.

Something she'd never understood.

She'd blamed him for putting the job above love and family. And had hated him ever since.

If Savannah was alive—and his gut told him to believe there was still a chance—she'd likely hate him, too, when she found out that he'd been using her all along. That the life he'd presented to her, that of bodyguard Isaac Forrester, had all been a lie.

A job.

Until that morning, he'd taken her eventual loss of trust in him as a given.

But knowing that she'd spent her entire life unable to trust anyone with her deepest secrets...and had still trusted him with one of them—Charlotte being her sister—he could hardly sit with himself knowing that she'd feel he betrayed her.

Telling himself to get it together, to get himself in gear and get back to work, he took another long study of the area around him. Giving a mental run-through of the other details Chuck had given him. Placing them firmly in the puzzle he'd been building in his mind over the past year. They'd found no trace on his phone, so if Duran was having his whereabouts checked, it wasn't through his cell. The grandson of the man who'd owned the black SUV that had caused the crash in the roundabout was wanted by local police for suspected illegal weapons charges, and surveillance footage of the man seen heading into the culvert at the shelter earlier that day had produced no matches in the bureau's facial-recognition software.

He wouldn't have pegged Duran for using low-level criminals with records. He'd pay top dollar for help that was so far
off the grid they'd be unidentifiable.

The guy at the shelter could've been one of them. So maybe
sent by Duran?

But the driver...were they looking at two groups after Savannah, as she'd first thought? Duran and whoever she'd been running from in the witness protection program for most of her life?

And then there was Wagar. Possibly the kidnapper. A third
entity who'd need her permanently silenced.

As his thoughts gelled, terror for her welled for the split second it took him to tamp them down before they prevented him
from doing what he did best.

He'd been watching a green sedan as it approached the block
where he sat. It was a newer vehicle, the same model that Savannah had rented before. When the car slid into a parking spot
in front of the small high-end family-owned restaurant, a place
that guaranteed its patrons' privacy and peace while they dined,
his senses were suddenly in perfectly tuned gear.

He saw her get out.

And at the same time, a woman who exited the attached
establishment next door, an import place that sold fine wine,
caught his attention. Held it. The bag she carried bore the
label of the store she'd just vacated, but the way she held it,
the shape...

Isaac was out of his vehicle and weaving through cars on the
road as he gave a holler, pulled his gun, and shot.

The bag flew up into the air, blood splattered, and though
he gave chase, the injured woman disappeared around a corner and was lost.

Chapter Twenty

Chest tight, Savannah was shaking as she made her way through the crowd of people forming to what turned out to be a gun on the sidewalk. She continued to shake as she pushed past them to find out where Isaac had gone.

She'd seen him. In that split second after she'd exited her car and stepped onto the sidewalk, he'd hollered, she'd ducked, heard the shot, and when she'd stood, he'd been gone.

She'd have been killed.

That gun on the sidewalk had been meant to send a bullet into her.

She'd seen the woman exit the wine shop. Had wondered if she'd bought a bottle to share with someone she loved...

She hadn't seen a killer.

The mistake had almost ended her life.

So would walking down the street unprotected, in plain view. Turning, Savannah rushed for her car. Climbed inside and drove off in the direction she thought she'd seen Isaac go. Turning into the alley a couple of doors down from the wine shop.

And saw him walking toward her, sideways, as he kept an eye on his back as well.

She stopped next to him. Had never been so glad to see anyone in her life. Felt the tears prick her eyes. But shifted into Reverse and gunned the gas as soon as he was inside.

He didn't say a word as she backed out of the alley and then took several turns in rapid succession.

Driving like a madwoman until she felt certain that she hadn't been followed. And then it all hit her and she slowed, feeling the weakness in her fingers as she loosened the death grip she'd had on the steering wheel, and glanced at Isaac.

He was studying the side mirror and then ahead of them.

And looked…just like Isaac. Strong. There.

"You found me," she said, her voice sounding unfamiliar to her and way too loud in the tension-filled car. She didn't chance another look at him.

Didn't trust herself not to cry.

"Always." The word was clipped. His response…odd. Unless he'd just been referring to every time he'd come after her in the past few days.

Her eyes firmly focused between her mirrors and the road, she asked, "You want me to take you back to your vehicle?"

"No."

"Did you get a good look at her?"

"Not good enough."

He pulled out his phone. Dialed. Said, "Chuck, I've got an update for you." And proceeded, in very succinct terms, to detail everything that had just transpired, including orders for follow-up actions to be taken. Finishing with, "She was clearly a professional. I hit her hand—not sure how bad. There was blood. I've got Savannah with me." And then, without any kind of farewell or indication of his next moves, he hung up.

Chills spread over her. Through her. Isaac, his voice, commanding and professional… Who was he?

Someone hired by the kidnappers? In the employ of whoever her father had been going to testify against?

She couldn't believe it. Was frozen inside as she continued to propel the car forward.

The man had just saved her life.

And pursued the woman who'd clearly been about to shoot her.

She couldn't afford to stop. Didn't want to give anyone a chance to catch up to her. So she drove. Turning randomly, finding a stretch of road with little traffic, she took it, heading nowhere. And when she could, she asked, "Who are you?"

"Take the next right" was his only response.

He'd saved her life.

She had little chance in a battle between them. He had a gun and, from what she'd just witnessed, was an excellent shot. She could wreck the car. Or she could do as he said.

And continued to do so silently over the next ten minutes as he watched their surroundings intently, speaking only to issue instruction.

When fear threatened to take the air out of her lungs, she reminded herself he'd saved her life. And when that quit working, she thought about the night before, when he'd let her pull his clothes off. When he'd touched her with too much gentleness to have been merely body parts seeking satisfaction.

Remembering the look on his face when she'd sat astride him and he'd spasmed inside her for the second time.

Eventually she recognized where they were. And knew where he was taking her.

Back to the house he'd provided to her after she'd been shot at.

Because she felt safer there than out on the streets that seemed to be teeming with people trying to attack her from all sides—and because if he wanted her dead, he'd have let the woman on the street kill her—she drove there of her own accord.

Signaled the next turn before he'd had a chance to instruct her. And pulled into the drive as though she'd been doing so on a regular basis.

Once in front of the house, though, she didn't turn off the car. Or look at him. She sat there with the sedan still in Drive, her hands on the wheel, staring out the windshield, and asked again, "Who are you?"

She heard him move, seemed to feel it, too, and then his gun appeared on the dash right in front of her. Another rustle and a thin leather wallet appeared there next.

"My name is Mike Reynolds. I'm an FBI special agent currently undercover as Isaac Forrester."

Whatever she'd feared he'd say, hoped he'd say—something

about Duran and his orders and Isaac choosing at the last minute not to follow them and engaging his bodyguard friends—the FBI had never, for a second, figured in.

She couldn't look at him. Didn't know him.

An FBI special agent.

Who she'd had sex with the night before. Thinking he was her sister's bodyguard.

Believing they were spiritually connected. Meant to meet. That providence had brought them together…

Embarrassed, feeling like a fool, she picked up what she assumed were his credentials. Verified she'd gotten that one right.

"I know that you were born Sarah Gussman. That your father worked for the IRS and was about to testify regarding a hack in the system that had cost the government over a million dollars. I know that you and your mother went into witness protection right after your father was murdered and Nicole was kidnapped. That her missing person report was registered under Natalie Willoughby and that your last name was changed to Compton. I know that your father's body was identified by skin from the heel he'd been digging into the sand…"

She gasped. A spike hitting her heart. She hadn't…

"You didn't know that." The words were different. Softer. Isaac's voice. When he'd been holding her the night before.

No. She shook her head. Couldn't get lost in fantasy. Her whole life had been lived with shades of fake. No more.

She had to be free.

And Charlotte? Where did she fit in?

"Let me guess—you're looking for the man my father was supposed to testify against." She wasn't proud of the sarcastic tone, even as she welcomed it. Sarcasm, any emotion at all, showed him that she'd fallen for his act.

"I am now," he told her. "Along with my original assignment."

Wait. What? "Your original assignment." There, that had been more lawyerlike. And as long as she kept her gaze glued outward, he wouldn't have even a slight chance of reading what she was choking back.

What she couldn't...wouldn't...*ever* let him know. That for a minute or two there, she'd been in love with him.

With *Isaac*.

"To find the elusive proof the United States, along with law enforcement agencies from various other countries, needs in order to arrest Eduardo Duran for theft, espionage, arms dealing, and murder—among other things."

Charlotte's father?

She'd go there. As soon as she got her head on straight.

Had the FBI been following her? Was that how he'd known how to describe to her so exactly how she'd been manipulated by fear over the past year?

Oh, God. Had it been *him*?

Tears blurred her vision. She sat up straight, took a deep breath, and held them back. And asked, "How long have you known about me? About my past?"

"Less than an hour."

The words he said, the way his voice caught, Savannah's head snapped sideways, and her gaze ran full tilt into his. Getting lost there. Burying her in the warmth she needed to survive the moments.

Finding him.

And rejecting him, too. She'd fallen for Isaac Forrester. A fake persona who'd had a job to do. Not Mike Reynolds.

She turned her attention back to the windshield—the world beyond it.

"Duran called me into his office the day you arrived in town. He told me that his intel had told him that you were in town for a rogue client, someone you'd agreed to help separately from Sierra's Web for a much larger paycheck. Your job was to convince Charlotte that she had biological family in the States, with the ultimate goal of a substantial piece of the Duran pot."

Made sense. A lawyer with supposed proof and paperwork drawn up could easily prove rights to funds, depending on what the funds were, how they'd been designated...

And it hit her...he'd known who she was the day she'd hit town. Before he'd supposedly asked to sit with her. "You... used me."

She told herself not to look at him. But did it anyway.

He didn't even attempt to deny her accusation. Looking her straight in the eye, he nodded.

It was the first thing she found about Mike Reynolds to admire. Now that the secrets were out, he was honest with her.

Even when it showed him for the... FBI agent that he was. Because she could hardly think of him as scum. He'd been doing his job.

And...he'd saved her life.

"What did you hope to gain from our...association?" *Other than sex.*

She'd given him her heart, and he...he'd used sex to get closer to her. To gain her cooperation?

"I didn't know. Multiple governments can trace activities to Duran's doorstep, but no one has ever been able to find proof that would ever stand up in court to convict him of anything. Added to that, he has friends in very high places, both here and abroad. Sending me in was our only chance to find out how he did it. To find something...anything...that we could get a conviction for, that would then give us access to warrants for everything he owns or has ever touched."

He was talking about a man Charlotte adored.

"You told me you had secrets, you were here to see someone. You were shot at. I didn't know what you knew, who you were working for, but the way Duran reacted to your presence, I knew whatever you represented to him was huge."

"So you were using me from the beginning." She had to get that one down pat. Before she could move on.

The lovemaking...the closeness...had all been on her part. Not his.

"I was." He admitted the truth aloud that time.

Her chin trembled. She could feel the tears. Refused to allow them. Didn't look at him. It was time for her to wear her big-girl panties and move forward.

Away from him. From fantasies about love and what was meant to be.

She'd come to town to make certain that her sister was well and happy.

She had not yet completed her mission.

He'd lost her. It was Mollie all over again. Except…in a way, far worse.

Mollie, as a child was to a parent, had been on loan to him, a member of his household, until she'd been old enough to claim her own life.

Savannah had felt like…more than a loan. For a moment in time, she'd made him feel complete. No matter how many times he'd assured himself he knew better than to get personally involved.

"Who knows besides me?"

The way she barely looked at him, as though she couldn't, caught at him. When, since the moment he'd approached her in the bar, they'd seemed to say so much with no words at all. He couldn't let himself get in the way. Had to stay focused on the job, period.

"That I'm undercover?" he asked, though he knew that was what she'd meant.

"Yes." Her chin jutted toward the windshield with the word. "No one."

"Who's Chuck?"

He'd known the second he'd dialed that he'd made his choice. No more lying to Savannah. He'd found her alive.

Had saved her life.

The honor or prayers answered deserved truth.

"My second-in-command here in San Diego."

She glanced his way. "You have second-in-commands elsewhere?"

"I've been undercover, full time, on different assignments for nearly a decade. I work out of the Washington, DC, bureau."

The windshield got her gaze again. He'd never have thought he'd be jealous of a piece of glass. Or grateful for it, either.

"And this house?"

"An FBI safe house."

Her lower lip jutted some as she nodded. "You've had me under surveillance since I got here."

Not a question. He answered anyway. "No. Just while you were here and I wasn't. I promised you protection."

"Must have made you mad to find out I'd slipped the noose this morning." The bitterness didn't sound natural to her. But it felt horribly real.

Life had handed the woman far more than her share of burdens to handle. But he was the one who'd made her bitter?

"You want the truth?" he shot back at her, every word personal.

She looked over at him. Held his gaze while she nodded.

And with his vow of truth pumping blood through his veins, he said, "I was terrified."

He lost her gaze. Win for the windshield. "Because you'd lost your best chance at solving your case."

"Because I was afraid I'd lost you. That they'd gotten to you."

Her head turned back toward him. "They?"

Leaning in, he gave her every piece of him he had to give in a look, with words he couldn't say. "You know as much as I do, Savannah. Or will in a minute. I know Duran is the worst kind of enemy. I believe my cover is still intact with him, but that doesn't mean he trusts me. A man like that can't fully trust anyone. I fear that Wagar might be the man who kidnapped Nicole. Giving him leverage over Duran. But that's assuming Duran knows Charlotte was kidnapped. And I'm not convinced yet that he does.

"It could be that Wagar was simply the man he used to secure his black-market adoption. Or that he's not involved at all, in the kidnapping or with Charlotte's past. What I'm certain of is that he has some kind of hold over Duran."

He stopped, took a deep breath, and barreled on. "What I also know, and found out after you entered the shelter—" he quickly stopped himself to clarify before she believed he was really made of stone, before he lost her gaze again "—is that your sister is alive."

Eyes lighting up like fireworks, she burst out with, "Charlotte's alive? You're sure? Is she okay?"

"She called me. That's why I went dark when you were in the shelter." He filled her in on his conversation with Charlotte. Gave her a rundown of his time outside the shelter. Other details that he knew and she hadn't. Pouring it all out because it was the right thing to do.

Because he trusted her with his life.

And, allowing himself to absorb a bit of her essence before he lost her eyes on him, he finished. "Charlotte gave me a major missing piece to the puzzle this afternoon. It was also one that incriminates her." He told her about Glob. And his suspicion that Duran used the coding not only to have one global pool for money that was never seen but to create an entire network of invisible money laundering that landed in accounts that the US and other countries would never have access to and then were dispersed from there.

Eyes wide, filled with alarm, Savannah continued to watch him. "You think she's involved in Duran's criminal activity?"

He had to give her the truth, no matter what it cost him. Because to not do so at that point was going to cost him more. "I'm almost certain she is."

"You're going to arrest her."

Visions of Mollie's hateful look as she'd been taken from the courtroom flashed through his head.

"If she cooperates, and depending on how deeply she's implicated, I'm hoping to offer her immunity. What I can promise you is that I'm going to do everything in my power to make her way as easy as possible. She was taken from her home, her loved ones, her safety and security when a baby needs nothing but those things. She couldn't help but cling to the man who became her entire world. We don't know what he's told her. How he's manipulated her..."

Some depth returned to Savannah's gaze. Not at all like he'd been washed with the night before. But enough of a hint that Mike felt better about himself than he had in a long time. And said, "In private, when we're alone, like now, please call me Mike."

She blinked. Nodded.

Turned away, wrapped her fingers around the steering wheel, and said, "Where to now?"

Chapter Twenty-One

Call me Mike. She didn't know Mike. She'd unknowingly played make-believe with a bodyguard named Isaac.

It might take a minute to wrap her mind around that one. A minute she didn't have to spare.

Charlotte was alive!

"We stay here and wait for Charlotte's call," Mike Reynolds answered her question—"Where to?"—a full minute after she'd asked it. He'd been watching her.

She'd ignored the opportunity to meet his eyes. To see what she read there. The connection that had seemed to give her strength…had any of it been real?

From the very first he'd been playing her.

But Charlotte was alive! Relief was palpable. Smoothing the edges of betrayal.

She'd been falling in love. He'd been doing his job.

Eduardo Duran. Her baby sister's adopted father was an international criminal. Mike Reynolds and the FBI thought Charlotte was involved, too.

She couldn't seem to get a lucid grasp on any of it. Recognized the vestiges of shock. Needed to talk to Kelly, one of her best friends, her partner, Sierra's Web's psychiatry expert, and Savannah's sounding board.

Except that…she'd been pretending with all of them from the moment they'd met.

Charlotte was alive!

"Wait," she turned to the agent, saw Isaac sitting there, doing as she'd just asked, waiting for her to continue.

And so she did.

"You said that Charlotte called you to ask about who'd been asking about her. That she'd received help from one of the shelters."

"Right. I told her that you…"

"Were the woman on the boat. Spun things around, said I sought you out because I was concerned about what I'd seen. Charlotte's tears."

His gaze didn't waver. He sought no mercy. And showed no defensiveness, either. He was who he was. Doing what he did. Same as always. Isaac. Mike. Same guy. Same job.

She saw it all there. Looked away. Wouldn't be taken in again. And heard him say, "I told her the truth I was free to give. That you're a woman who talked to me because you cared about her."

"You played her."

"Maybe." His tone, not Isaac at all and yet as compelling— maybe more so—drew her gaze. And looking her straight in the eye, he said, "It's possible I've been at this too long. Have lost sight of the distinct differences between getting what I need and being honest. I just know that untold numbers of lives are at stake—they're resting largely on my shoulders at the moment. I needed your help. You needed mine."

She swallowed. Nodded again. Then asked, "Was any of it real?"

He glanced away. And she did, too. Couldn't see his eyes as he said, "I don't know."

The nonanswer was a wake-up call to Savannah. Her love life, any future life at all wasn't of concern at the moment. Glancing back at Mike Reynolds, and Isaac, too—determining that she was going to have to live with both of them in the short go because she couldn't seem to obliterate either one of them—she saw a clear path. Put herself on it.

"I would guess that the shelter Charlotte used was the first one I visited, since they obviously knew how to reach her. I discovered, through my own escape, just how detail oriented and serious these places are about keeping their victims safe." She told him about the thoroughness of her own departure from the shelter. "We need you, the FBI, to go back to that shelter and convince them to transport Charlotte here. Maybe not you. This Chuck, or someone else—probably at least two someones. They'd need to show credentials, to let the shelter director know that Charlotte is in immediate critical danger, far more than she knows, and get her into FBI custody..."

She was talking like a big sister who'd do anything to save her younger sibling's life. But knew, as an expert lawyer, partner in a firm nationally renowned for saving lives in the most extreme of cases, that she was finally, firmly on the right path. "We get her here... Mike..." His eyes darkened as she stumbled over the name, but she pushed on. "We tell her the truth. We give her a chance to help you."

Savannah had no idea whether Charlotte was implicated in her adopted father's crimes, but she knew the truth had to come out to set Charlotte free.

Knew that there was no one better than herself to protect her sister's legal rights.

And...oddly...as she sat there, replaying in her mind what she'd said and studying the undercover FBI agent who'd played them all, she realized that she'd just entrusted her sister's future to him. He'd said he'd do whatever he could to make Charlotte's way easier.

And she believed him.

Mike called Chuck immediately. Barked out orders, named two agents from his Washington team that Chuck was to take with him to the shelter, verified that a couple of agents from the San Diego team were already on the safe house, and hung up.

There was nothing left to do but go inside. And wait.

The last time he and Savannah had been in that space together, less than twenty-four hours before, they'd had incredible sex. His best ever. And he'd had probably more than his share in his nearly thirty-eight years.

But because all he'd allowed himself to be since Mollie's disappearance from his life was the best damned cop he could be, he ushered Savannah Compton inside, checked every corner of every one of the spotless rooms, and turned the television on to security camera screens.

She set herself up at the table, computer open.

And then, with a brief glance at him that seemed to be telling him something, except that she glanced away too quickly for him to be sure, she said, "I've just sent a request to my partners for an emergency gathering on our private video-meeting software..." She paused, glancing down at her screen. "Three—no, four—of them have already responded. And there's five..."

"You're asking me to vacate." He'd been planning to walk the perimeter...

"No. I'm apologizing ahead of time for some of what you might have to sit through, but I'd like you to be present to answer any questions they might have." She was all professional, an expert lawyer.

And, God help him, sexy as hell.

She'd also just put him on notice that she was having him checked out by the best of the best. From a private firm that had been fully vetted by the FBI.

As long as her team stuck to business, he'd pass with flying colors.

"You can't take Charlotte back to Duran," Savannah said then, glancing up from her screen when he sat down perpendicular to her at the table. Close enough to touch. Which he was very careful not to do. Not even a knee bump.

Ridiculous, and wholly unlike him to even have the thought. Let alone feel regret for the loss of something he'd never really had.

And the Charlotte thing... "The longer I take to call him and let him know I have her and will be bringing her back, the more we risk someone tipping him off. He'll bolt. We could lose him forever. We have no idea how high up his power extends, who's in his pocket, which is why my team and I, along with a couple of agents in the San Diego office, are all who know about this case."

He could almost see her mind spinning and then watched as reality dawned. "You think someone at the shelter's going to tell him."

"I think it's possible. The Durans donate to all the local shelters."

"I'm assuming, then, that you have agents on him already."

"We do. But without proof, which we still do not currently have, we can't touch him. You're a lawyer. You know..."

She was nodding. Frowning. "You think it's possible that Charlotte might have to go back to get the proof."

He shrugged. He hoped not. Saw the plausibility. Knew anything was possible. And knew, too, as Savannah would, that depending on how deeply Charlotte Duran was involved, she could risk her life to take on her father, to get them the proof she needed to buy her freedom.

And was saved from any further conversation on the matter when Savannah glanced at her computer and said, "We're on."

She didn't immediately involve him. Didn't have him on screen or include him in conversations. Instead, he sat there and watched expressions chase themselves across her face as she greeted each of her six partners, calling them out by name— for his benefit, he was sure—letting them know that FBI agent Mike Reynolds was in the room.

He found it difficult to swallow over the next several minutes as he heard her telling her partners that she'd been lying to them the entire time they'd known her. In very lawyerly terms, interspersed with her own difficult swallows, she told them she had a sibling and, without pause, gave them the rest of the details of her past. The secrets she'd been forced to keep. Talking about the danger she'd recently brought upon herself. Admitting that she'd never been intending to go on a cruise but rather to see that Nicole was well and thriving. Ending with an apology for her subterfuge, along with an offer to resign from the firm if they thought it was necessary.

He heard voices then, male and female, talking over each other, and then Savannah again. "Stop." Her tone seemed to shock her partners into silence. "You guys need to talk about this among yourselves. You know I love you. You're my family. And that doesn't change either way. But we're who we are because we trust each other implicitly. If even one of you feels as though you don't really know me and can't fully trust me, then I'm stepping away. We can reconvene on the matter later. Right now, many lives are at stake and the FBI—and I—need the firm's help."

She didn't expect all her partners to forgive her. Which said to him that she wasn't going to forgive him. He'd lied for good reason. Because he'd had to. And so had she, to her partners. Witness protection as well as undercover work were only successful as long as necessary lies were told. But the lies still had consequences when it came to trust and relationship building.

She didn't believe they'd all still be able to trust her because she didn't trust him. Her message couldn't have been clearer.

And, note taken, he went to work as she turned the screen and moved over so that both of them were within camera range. The respect with which her partners treated him was noted as well. And appreciated. While they were still in the meeting, Mike got on the phone and had his people send over everything they had in the Duran file to Sierra's Web. He told them what he knew about Glob's capabilities. And tech expert Hudson Warner and financial expert Winchester Holmes were both going to work immediately, together and with their teams, to work their magic and see what they could discover without Charlotte's help.

Mike was impressed, if a bit intimidated, and more taken with Savannah Compton, too, as the meeting drew to an end. But when he'd thought they were all about to sign off, Glen Thomas, the science expert and quietest of the bunch, said, "Savannah?"

They were all staring straight into their cameras. Sitting next to the lawyer, Mike felt their pinned look strongly, though it wasn't aimed at him.

She looked right back at them. He felt her stiffen, though. "Yeah?"

"We've taken a vote, by text, and we need you to know. All these years, you've been here serving us, and we didn't look deeper. We're sorry that we didn't know. That we took you for granted and at face value. We trust you with our lives. You are one of us. Now. And forever."

Mike saw her face on the screen. Saw the love brimming from those eyes he'd somehow thought only talked to him. Saw the tears forming.

And got up and left the room. Left Savannah to her real life.

Only just starting to realize what he might have had.

And had lost.

Her team had her back. Savannah felt their support as an hour later, just after dark, she paced the living room of the small house, listening for the sound of the online-store delivery van that was being used to bring Charlotte Duran to them.

Mike had made grilled-cheese sandwiches paired with applesauce.

It had taken a while, but she'd gotten it all down. And then washed the dishes. Would have liked to shower again, to change clothes, put on fresh makeup, look her best for her and her sister's first meeting, but her things were still at the old motel.

And as much as she wanted to care about something easy, a topic as superficial as looks just didn't matter.

Hard to believe it had only been that morning that she'd unlocked the door of her clandestinely rented room. A mere twelve hours since she'd broken a twenty-four-year silence, showered, and set out to save lives. Only to find herself back where she'd been before her backbreaking trek through the woods.

Sometimes when life came full circle, it didn't look at all as you'd imagined it would.

She was about to meet her little sister face-to-face.

Was knowingly letting Charlotte walk into an FBI trap.

Because if she didn't, her little sister's life would never be safe and secure. She'd spend the rest of it dealing with the Arnold Wagars her adopted father shoved on her.

And in danger of arrest, too.

The idea was to reveal Savannah's identity to Charlotte first, to establish a place for Charlotte to belong, separate and apart from her father, before pressuring her to turn on him.

While Savannah hated that they were knowingly making

choices in order to manipulate Charlotte, she completely understood the necessity.

And fully believed that it could be the only way to save Charlotte's life.

But her heart was pumping hard with dread as much as anticipation when she heard the van drive up.

She saw Mike pause, glancing her way, as though waiting for her to join him at the door. She stepped back to the far end of the living room—as far from the front door as she could get without losing sight of it.

Standing there shivering, she heard Nicole's voice first. "Wow, Isaac, you sure know how to make a girl uneasy." The tone, while flippant, had an undercurrent of fear that struck Savannah's heart.

And reminded her of her mother, too.

She tried to draw a deep breath, but the battle against tears won out, and as she fought and blinked, her chest tightened.

Her heart pounded.

And then, with just one blink to the next—an occurrence that happened with regularity every day of her life—she saw Nicole standing there in jeans, an expensive-looking button-down shirt, and ankle boots, looking at her.

And frowning. "What's she doing here?" She shot the question over her shoulder to Mike. Isaac.

The agent glanced at Savannah, and she knew he was leaving the call up to her.

"We've got some things to tell you, Charlotte," she said, finding the name rolling off her lips with ease. Charlotte, not Nicole. Just like neither of them had been Gussman in decades. "Have a seat." She motioned to the couch and chairs across from her, waited for her little sister to take a corner of the couch before choosing the opposite corner for herself.

Leaving a chair for Mike.

The outsider.

"Stop staring at me," the younger woman said then, her tone somewhat autocratic. But Savannah was certain she heard insecurity nestled inside it. "Not only is it rude, but you're giving me the creeps."

Speaking her mind. Savannah held back a smile. And then, as the moment had fallen upon her, her lips trembled. She glanced at Mike. Needing Isaac.

Saw the look in his eye, a glint that somehow reminded her of her own strength, told her she didn't need him, and turned back to the woman with her same long dark hair, also pulled back, the same dark eyes. And Charlotte's own more uniquely oval rather than round cheeks that Savannah looked at in the mirror every morning.

And the words were there. "A year ago, you entered your DNA in the Family Finders database," she said, her tone filling with confidence as it always did in court when she knew she had an open-and-shut case.

She paused, waiting for Charlotte's nod. Just as she would have had her baby sister been on the witness stand. Only difference between court and the couch in that moment was the love brimming her heart and the overwhelming need to wrap her arms around the witness and never let go.

"I entered mine as well," she said then, slowly. Giving Charlotte time to hear, to comprehend every word. "Except that, due to something that happened in my past, I didn't make my profile discoverable."

Charlotte crossed her arms. And her legs, too. "Yeah, what's that got to do with me?"

"A week ago, I was notified of a match," she said. "Between you and me."

Charlotte's arms dropped to her sides, her legs were flat on the couch, her mouth open. When her eyes lit up, Savannah smiled, teared up, ready to open her arms and finally have them filled again with the tender body of her baby sister.

Waited for Charlotte to catch up with the bombshell she'd just had dropped on her. For her little sister to come to her. "You're, what, my aunt?" the woman asked. "My mother's sister? You look awfully young for that. Or wait, you're a cousin! I knew there had to be someone out there. Wow!" She looked at Isaac. "You knew! That's how you got the shelter to bring me here. Though, really, Isaac, all you had to do was tell me when I called." She looked back at Savannah. "Wow, this is so great."

Charlotte was babbling. Savannah had a feeling it wasn't a normal occurrence. Glancing at Mike, she read confirmation in his raised brow and head tilt.

A move that Charlotte caught. "What?" She looked between the two of them. "Isaac? Tell me what's going on."

Mike pointed to Savannah. And when Charlotte looked over, Savannah said, "I'm not your cousin. I'm your sister."

"My...*what*?" Charlotte's raised tone, the shake of her head, indicated shock. But no pleasure.

Feeling her sister's distress, and with a nod from Mike, Savannah quickly filled her sister in on the tragic details of their past. Including their father's murder. Keeping her courtroom tone and sticking to provable details, she laid it all out.

Waiting for the moment when Charlotte, who'd been looking for family, finally realized that she'd found the mother lode. The younger woman's mouth dropped open one more time. Closed. Opened again as she kept glancing from Mike to Savannah and back to Mike again.

"You're telling me I'm adopted?" The question was clearly aimed at Mike. And lacking even a hint of joy.

Savannah's heart felt the crush, but she remained, back straight, ready to give Charlotte whatever she needed. The load of information she'd just dumped onto her couldn't be helped, given the circumstances, but Charlotte didn't know that.

And deserved time to comprehend. To digest.

"She's your sister, Charlotte. I had the DNA results verified," Mike homed in on the point that he could prove right then, right there. She understood what he was doing. Was grateful he was there.

Because they all knew that if Charlotte was Savannah's biological sister, Eduardo Duran couldn't possibly be her biological father.

The younger woman shot up from the couch. Wrapping her arms around herself, she paced back and forth between Mike and Savannah and then stopped in front of Mike, stood over him, and said, "She's lying, Isaac. I don't how she's managed to convince you of this horrible falsehood. Or why she'd even want to. But her story—it's just not true. Family Finders screwed up, or she provided you with wrong DNA, but my father was not murdered. Nor was I kidnapped." She dropped to her knees in front of him, her tone as confident but softening as she said, "I know for certain that Eduardo Duran is my father. I went through a time after we came to the US, rebellious teens, whatever..." The passion with which the woman spoke—only to Mike, her back to Savannah—had Savannah holding her breath. "...I was tired of hearing any time I asked about any relatives, maternal or paternal, that they were dead. The one thing I'd wanted to do most when we came to America was see my mother's grave. To leave flowers there."

Savannah gasped. Mike looked at her. Held her gaze. But when Charlotte kept talking, without turning around, his attention returned to the younger woman. "My last straw was when he told me that the graveyard had been vandalized. That several graves were robbed. My mother's being one of them. Which meant there was no grave to visit. It was too much. I demanded right then and there that he submit to a paternity test. I needed proof he was really my father."

Savannah couldn't fight the tears that were streaming down her face. She'd quit trying. Charlotte stiffened when Savannah sniffled but still didn't turn around.

"It was the biggest fight we ever had, Isaac. But I wasn't backing down, and he submitted to the test. Which came back positive. But I wasn't going to stop there. I took hair from his bathroom sink and had it tested. I *know* he's my father."

Savannah couldn't breathe. Couldn't think. What Charlotte was saying...it couldn't possibly be right. Wide-eyed, Savannah looked at Mike, saw him staring at her, let herself sink into his gaze.

And stay there.

Chapter Twenty-Two

The blood had drained from Savannah's face. He could feel her sinking. Willed her to stay with him. They'd sort it out. Figure it out.

"How sure are you two of the validity of the samples you sent to Family Finders?" The FBI had done their own testing of the samples. He was certain of the accuracy of the results.

He was grasping. He knew that. But Savannah needed a lifeboat.

"I work with one of the nation's leading forensic scientists." He hardly recognized the deadpan tone in Savannah's voice. Kept hold of her gaze.

Charlotte wasn't going anywhere. The job would get done.

"He wore gloves as he extracted hair from my skull and then carefully packaged it. And did a buccal swab as well."

"I went to a lab at the university. Did both as well. And had them sealed before I personally sent them off. I was present, with eyes on the samples, the entire time."

So unless Family Finders or the mail service had switched samples and one of the sisters had a different sister—which was unbelievable at best—the two were sisters.

Savannah wasn't fully with him yet. He wasn't sure she ever would be. She needed support from loved ones. Her partners.

If what Charlotte had said about the paternity testing...

His adrenaline started to flow and, knowing what he had to do, that he had to work quickly, get the sting over with so that he could be a friend to Savannah, he broke eye contact with her to look at Charlotte.

"I'm not Isaac Forrester," he said, succinctly. "My name is Mike Reynolds, I'm with the FBI, and this house is surrounded." As Charlotte's face paled and she sank to her butt on the floor, staring at him open mouthed yet again, he proceeded to tell her why he was in San Diego, working at her home, guarding her. And was ready, every second, to grab her if she tried to run.

Whether she didn't try because she knew she wouldn't make it far, didn't want to be shot at, or because she simply couldn't, he didn't know.

He didn't hold back describing her father's crimes, stretching back twenty-five years—that they knew of. The timing hit him. He stopped. Quietly finished with, "But we're certain that he was busy building his empire long before that. No one has been able to determine what country he was born in, where he started out, but we will…"

Unless they just had.

On his phone, he dialed his Washington office. Had them do a deep dive on Hugh Gussman, his gaze shooting between both sisters as he did so.

And then, taking it upon himself, he dialed Sierra's Web. Had had the number programmed into his phone from the moment he'd been told about Savannah Compton.

Hudson Warner answered, and while Mike sat with two statue-like women, both looking as though they might be sick, both avoiding looking at the other, he made his request for the Gussman deep dive a second time.

And then listened as Hudson Warner told him a thing or two. Hung up. And looked at Charlotte. The time had come. "I don't know how much you know about Eduardo Duran's money laundering," he said, all business. "And until I have the full scope, I can't offer you anything concrete, but considering the egregious circumstances, I'm prepared to try for full immunity. But only if you cooperate right now. We need to get a warrant to arrest the man before he's certain that we're onto him."

"I'll call him," Charlotte said, her voice cracking. "I'll tell him what I did, how I got away. Tell him that Arnold makes my skin crawl and that I'll come home only if he promises me that I won't have to marry the man. He'll wait for me. Which will buy you some time."

Mike didn't even glance in Savannah's direction. He couldn't. Not then. Keeping his eyes fully on Charlotte, he nodded. And waited while she made the call. She hadn't said she'd cooperate with the rest. But she'd given him a show of faith.

When the call was done, he looked at Savannah, who was staring at the back of Charlotte's head as she nearly whispered, "I can show you your mother's grave…"

Charlotte turned slowly. Mike couldn't see her expression. But he saw the trembling in her shoulders as, on her knees, with her arms reaching out in front of her, she moved over to meet Savannah, who'd fallen to the floor to catch her.

No words were spoken. The two women clung tighter than anything Mike had ever seen. Both were crying what were clearly a lifetime of unshed tears.

Moisture pricked his eyes, too. But the emotion was vicarious only.

Wasn't personal.

He couldn't possibly be jealous of two women who'd been robbed of the chance to grow up together.

Mike Reynolds had closed his case. Within an hour of Charlotte working together online with Hudson Warner's team, giving them full access to Glob's coding, the original programming she'd written to provide her father with a single location to store all his money intake, they'd been able to have enough proof to get an arrest warrant for Eduardo Duran.

Savannah had been given a chance to see the man face-to-face. She'd seen photos, had heard the facts about his multiple surgeries for a supposed deviated septum that had resulted in a new nose and occipital bones, and had no desire to look at the man eye to eye.

She'd heard that he'd begged to see her.

But he'd lost that right the day he'd faked his own death, just as he'd fabricated his intention to blow the whistle on whoever had been stealing from the government. He'd been the one pilfering money, double the amount the government had known about. He'd known he'd been about to be caught and had gone to his boss, pretending that he'd just discovered an intricate hack in the system and had offered to testify in exchange for protection for himself and his family.

He claimed that the government moved up his date to testify and that was why he'd only had the chance to take Charlotte.

Savannah believed differently. He hadn't taken her or her mother because he hadn't been certain of their cooperation. Her mother, at the very least, would have figured out that something had been grossly wrong when they'd have had to leave the country. Witness protection didn't stretch that far. And Charlotte... sweet little baby Charlotte...she hadn't known any better.

But in the end, she'd known enough.

To stop the man.

Put him behind bars.

And to be able to prove that she hadn't had any part in their father's illegal empire. She'd written Glob when she'd been a bored, off-the-charts intelligent teenager with no friends. Hugh, who'd started out a regular guy, also with an above-average intelligence quotient, had been so bored with his IRS cubicle and daily grind that he'd found ways to make enough money on the side to quit his job. At first, he'd just dabbled for fun. For something to do. But when he'd seen how he could manipulate the tax system databases, he'd been hooked. Addicted.

And the addiction had been driving him ever since. As Kelly had said on numerous occasions, as they'd worked on various cases over the years, it was a sad truth that sometimes it was more of a challenge to be bad than to be good. Which was why prisons oftentimes had inmates who measured with above-average intelligence.

Arnold Wagar had been a kid then. Barely an adult. Nobody Hugh had known. But he was wealthy. More so even than Duran. Came from a well-respected family. His father had been a Salvadoran dignitary in the US at one point. And when Charlotte had told her father that she'd entered her DNA into that database, Duran had known that he could be exposed at any time. He'd simply wanted Charlotte married, with a prenup that gave her half of her husband's wealth were he to divorce her, to secure her future in the event that the worst happened. In exchange, Wagar not only got a beautiful young wife with excellent skills he could use, but he got a sizable chunk of Duran's legitimate business dealings as well.

Charlotte had relayed a lot of the personal facts to Savannah. She'd gone home the night she'd met Savannah at the FBI safe house, as promised, had insisted on doing so, and had been present when, at two that morning, their father had been arrested.

She'd said she needed the closure.

Savannah wasn't sure they were ever going to have that. Not completely. But they had each other, which was more than either of them had ever dreamed possible.

Most of Eduardo's assets had been frozen. The property was up for sale. Charlotte had had a sizable savings of her own, earned from her lectures and a couple of the computer programs she'd written and sold.

But she didn't seem to care all that much about money. Most certainly wasn't driven by it as their father had been.

She'd moved to Phoenix, into Savannah's sizable home in a gated community, and was helping out at Sierra's Web as a private contractor until she figured out what she wanted to do with the rest of her life.

Kelly had cautioned Savannah that it would take time, a lot of it, for Charlotte to be anywhere near healed. Her entire life, every memory she'd had, had been built on lies.

But a month after Duran's arrest, Charlotte was already singing when she made coffee in the morning. And talking about applying for a professorship in women's studies at Arizona State University. She'd been offered a job at Harvard but wanted to stay close to Savannah.

A choice that Savannah wholly embraced.

Other than necessary separations during working hours—Savannah had chosen not to travel for a while—she was with Charlotte. They'd even slept in the same bed a night or two, when Charlotte's demons had been getting the better of her in the dark and she'd come to Savannah's door asking if she could stay, just for a few hours.

Savannah had her own internal struggles to get through and was working on them with Kelly, unofficially, and with one of the experts on Kelly's team, officially, too. But she was coming from a much easier starting point. She was the lucky one, having had the honor of being raised and loved by their mother. Only a small portion of her life had been a lie.

The lies she'd told all her life...that was one of the things she was working through.

Along with the whole Isaac thing. She'd left San Diego without telling him goodbye. How did you offer a farewell to someone who hadn't been real? But her heart continued to ache.

She'd wake up in the middle of the night with a vision of his eyes sharp in her brain. She couldn't make herself believe that the connection between two souls hadn't been real.

And so, though she barely acknowledged the fact to herself, she waited for him to contact her. He knew her name and where she worked. If he ever wanted to find her, he could.

For all she knew, he was already off on another undercover case somewhere. Living a new pretend life, among other criminals. Having sex with another suspect.

At least, that was all she knew until one Sunday afternoon, while she and Charlotte were lying on rafts in their backyard pool and her little sister said, "Mike gave up undercover work and took a promotion they'd been offering him for years." Just dropped the words into the middle of their peace. Casually. As though she'd mentioned the dove in a nearby tree.

Mike. Charlotte didn't seem to have a problem seeing Isaac Forrester and Mike Reynolds as the same man. But then, her sister hadn't slept with him.

Mike. Isaac. Whatever.

He'd given up undercover work. Because he'd lost his professional perspective with Savannah? The possibility sat there in her mind. Taunting her.

"He has a sister, you know." Charlotte dropped another bomb into the air just as Savannah had started to relax again.

"No, I didn't know," she said, trying to sound as though she was half asleep. Hoping Charlotte would take the hint and let her wallow her way out of the frame of mind she'd sunk into. Her little sister seemed truly fond of the man who'd guarded her for several months. It was one of the few good memories Charlotte had carried with her to Phoenix. At least that she talked about.

Savannah's job was to welcome the conversation.

"Her name's Mollie," Charlotte said. Whether her sister of such high intelligence had missed the hint or, more likely, had simply chosen to ignore it, Savannah didn't know. But the wondering gave her a place to focus her thoughts.

"Their parents were killed when Mike was barely out of high school. She was still a kid. He raised her."

He'd raised his little sister on his own? Right out of high school? She didn't want to care.

"Yeah, but then she fell for this bad boy. Truly bad. He was dealing drugs at their high school. Mike was a cop then, and he busted them. Sent the guy to prison, and his sister ended up in juvie for a month."

"He told you all this?"

"Some of it."

"When?"

"The night that dragged on to the next day when Eduardo was arrested."

Charlotte and Mike had spent hours at the San Diego bureau. While Savannah had been helping a Duran housekeeper pack up the list of things her sister had said she wanted immediately and then checking Savannah and Charlotte into a hotel by the airport.

"Anyway, Mike figured he was saving his sister's life. Tough love. All of that. She hated him for not loving her enough, trusting her enough to give her a second chance before busting her."

"I'm guessing he'd already warned her to stay away from the guy. And the stuff," Savannah said, eyes wide open as she drifted over to the deep end of the pool.

"Yeah, knowing him, I think that's probably a given. Anyway, they haven't spoken in years. She's married now. Has a couple of kids."

"He told you that, too?"

"Nah, I looked her up. And… I wrote to her."

Sitting straight up, Savannah upended herself, falling back first into the water, and came up sputtering. Holding on to her raft, she looked at her sister. "You what?"

"I wrote to her. Told her who I was. Told her about us. And how Mike had risked his career to bring us together. And how even though he'd have had to turn me in if I'd been involved in Eduardo's dealings, you were both there for me."

Savannah stared. "And?"

"She wrote back. We're kind of pen pals now."

Whoa. What in the hell was going on. Pen pals? With Mike's sister?

"Does he know?"

"He does." The voice…male…came from behind her. Swinging away from her raft to verify that her eyes weren't playing tricks on her, Savannah went under again.

Considered staying there. For all of a second.

She wasn't a quitter. Never had been.

Shooting up, she looked to the cool decking around the pool. And saw Mike Reynolds, in swim trunks, drop a towel next to hers, just as Charlotte, still on her raft, leaned over and grabbed her arm, dragging Savannah out of the deep water. When Savannah's feet were on the bottom of the pool, Charlotte rolled off her raft, leaning in to whisper, "You love him."

She shook her head. "I only knew him for a few days," she whispered back, imploring her sister to tell her she'd just imagined what she'd seen. To tell her that she hadn't set her up.

And praying that she had.

"I knew I loved you an hour after I met you," Charlotte whispered then. "Love is funny that way. It doesn't care about our rules, our understandings, our logic. It just lives. And spreads. And is ready, whenever we are, to bloom inside us and gift us with its bounty."

With that, Charlotte made a small, graceful dive that took her into a glide to the side of the pool. She passed Mike, grabbed her towel, and was gone before Savannah had the wherewithal to go with her.

"You coming out, or should I come in?" His tone was teasing. The look in his eyes as his gaze connected with hers was anything but. She read pain. Sorrow.

Need.

When her body flared in response, she figured she was better to stay covered by water rather than stepping up to him in her very brief bikini.

"You can come in."

That was it. He was allowed in her pool. Nothing more.

She watched as he walked down the steps, the journey so excruciatingly slow she couldn't help but notice every muscle, every cluster of dark hair...and the enlargement in his groin area. All of which she'd seen before.

She stood firm, waiting for him to make his move so she could reject him.

She'd been home a month. He could have called.

Or texted and asked her out for a drink rather than sabotaging her at home.

He came into the water slowly, walking in deeper.

God, he looked good.

So good.

Too good.

The water was up to his belly button. She was glad for the respite. Honestly glad. She had to think.

To exist in reality all the way.

She didn't quite meet his gaze as she said, "Charlotte told me you took a promotion."

"Did she also tell you it's in the Phoenix bureau?"

Ahhh. So her little sister had been...the thought stopped. She wanted so badly to yell at the man standing before her, absorbing her with his gaze. Telling her things she'd needed to hear.

For maybe her whole life.

Everything had always been so complicated. The secrets she'd had to keep. The lies she'd had to tell. Or risk lives.

Kind of like him. His duplicity had had one motivation. To save lives. Like Mollie's.

"I take it she didn't tell you," Mike said, taking a step closer to her. She could step back. Thought about it. Didn't move.

And then he was right there, a couple of inches of water between them, still looking at her. Compelling her to look back.

"You asked me if any of it was real," he said to her, his gaze glistening and pointed.

And she waited. She needed truth. Not pretense.

He nodded. Then said, "The things that mattered—the fact that you showed me a part of life I'd never seen before, a part I wanted, the fact that I couldn't do my job if it meant not protecting you, the fact that I've never, ever had such mind-blowing sex before...those were all real. As is how excruciating these last four weeks have been without you."

"You could have called." She'd tried for levity laced with sarcasm. Her words came out as a needy whisper.

"I needed to get my life in order, to figure out who, and what, I had to offer first."

Tears filled her eyes as she asked, "So who and what do you have to offer?" She was crying—and smiling, too.

"I'm offering dinner," he said. "A real date. Tonight. And then, another one. And another."

"And if I said that, after only those few days together, I think I'm in love with you?"

His eyes glistened as he slid his arms around her and murmured against her neck, "I'd say, thank God."

He kissed her then. Desperately. Without air. And then gasping, more softly. With stomachs pressing together, skin to skin, he lifted his head. Met her gaze and said, without words, everything she'd ever need to hear.

"I love you," the words were like icing on the cake. She saw his lips move. Put her fingers over them.

"Just don't ever quit looking at me like that," she whispered. "It's all the *I love you* I'll ever need."

He kept his eyes trained on her as he lowered his head, breaking the connection only when their lips joined again.

And she let herself fly. Really fly. For the first time since she'd been seven years old. She was young again. Older than the sky. She was a daughter. A sister.

She was a woman.

And had finally found the security that had set her free.

The love that had been with her from the beginning. A love that didn't care about rules or understandings. That didn't answer to logic. It just lived. And spread. And was always ready to be accepted.

To live through anyone who would let it. Anyone.

Instead of living in fear, Savannah was going to spend the rest of her days spreading the greatest truth in the world.

Love, not logic, conquers all.

* * * * *

Find Her
Katherine Garbera

MILLS & BOON

Katherine Garbera is a *USA TODAY* bestselling author of more than one hundred novels, which have been translated into over two dozen languages and sold millions of copies worldwide. She is the mother of two incredibly creative and snarky grown children. Katherine enjoys drinking champagne, reading, walking and traveling with her husband. She lives in Kent, UK, where she is working on her next novel. Visit her on the web at www.katherinegarbera.com.

Books by Katherine Garbera

Harlequin Romantic Suspense

Price Security

Bodyguard Most Wanted
Safe in Her Bodyguard's Arms
Christmas Bodyguard
Find Her

Visit the Author Profile page
at millsandboon.com.au for more titles.

Dear Reader,

Price Security has grown so much from my initial idea of writing a billionaire's bodyguard. Honestly, it's been so much fun to explore all of the people who work for Price Security. Lee Oscar's not a bodyguard per se, but more of a security operative who is most comfortable sitting behind her bank of computers watching over everyone and gathering intel.

So I knew she needed to be pushed out of her safe zone and into the real world. What starts out as a favor to a friend drags her into the undercover operation of Aaron Quentin, Xander's hot brother, who Lee has been ignoring since they first crossed paths in Miami. But there is no ignoring him when he spots her at a club he's just been placed in, and to protect them both, they fake being a couple.

Being undercover and trying to find a missing girl is enough stress for anyone, but fighting her attraction to Aaron makes it even more challenging for Lee.

Aaron is happiest when he's undercover and pretending to be someone else. He's responsible for an accident that left one of his brothers paralyzed. So he's careful...very careful. Until suddenly he's Lee's pretend man, and he knows deep down he wants that to be real.

I loved writing this story. These two characters were so much fun to explore. Thanks for picking up this book!

Happy reading,

Katherine

To Ryan and Rachel, who are just starting their
life together. I hope it's full of love, laughter
and happiness.

Love, Aunt Kathy

Acknowledgments

I'm so lucky to be a writer and get to spend every
day at my desk living in story worlds that I create.
Thank you, reader, for allowing me that.

Also thank you to Joss Wood and Tina Maria Clark.
I do writing sprints with them every day, which keeps
me on track and gives me a place to just chat on my
breaks about the world and writing.

Chapter One

Lee Oscar didn't do regrets. She might have had a different life if her best friend, Hannah Johnson, hadn't gone missing two weeks before they graduated from high school. If she spent too much time dwelling on those mistakes, then she went down a rabbit hole that led to pain and destructive tendencies.

However, Boyd Chiseck was one of those people who *did* regrets. Hannah's disappearance when they'd all been seventeen had forged that in both of them. After living through that, Lee had learned there was no one who could keep her safe except herself. And had decided from that point on to arm herself with skills, both lethal and technical, to fight evil in this modern age.

She spotted him right away. He was just under six foot and had broad shoulders, but the years had softened his shape, giving him a bit of a dad bod even though he'd never had children. Boyd kept his brown locks trimmed short, but he still had a full head of hair even though he was in his forties. Her attention shifting to his face, she took in his neatly trimmed beard and preppy clothing. Today he was adorned in neat dark jeans that he'd probably pressed and a Ralph Lauren polo shirt.

His eyes were brown, not really remarkable except that he always had an intensity and sadness about him. The two were inexplicably twined, and whenever Lee sat across from him, she almost felt the weight of those emotions.

For Boyd, he'd gone into protection mode. Trained as a teacher while Lee had been going through training for an elite intelligence agency based in the US. Both of them determined to help people when they hadn't been able to save their good friend Hannah.

So when he called out of the blue asking her to meet him for coffee… Well, her first emotion wasn't excitement or nostalgia for catching up with an old acquaintance. Because Boyd would forever be tied to that one moment that had shaped her into the woman she was today.

At forty-two, she might have fooled herself into believing that what had transpired twenty-five years earlier would always stay firmly in her rearview, but as she walked into Zara's Brew, she knew that wasn't the case. There was never going to be a time when she and Boyd met up that Lee didn't remember Hannah Johnson and wish she'd done things differently.

But a seventeen-year-old's worldview was a lot different than a grown woman's.

He waved when he saw her and she moved through the café to take a seat at the booth that he'd selected. He had no way of knowing that she'd watched a shoot-out take place in that very booth six months earlier when her coworker and friend Kenji Wada and his fiancée, Daphne Amana, had been ambushed while the international rights lawyer had been trying to get evidence in a case she'd been working on.

No regrets, the voice in her head said dryly.

But, in reality, there always were. She'd been monitoring all the cameras and wasn't sure how she'd missed the sniper that had set up on the far side of the parking lot.

"Hiya. I ordered you an Americano with three sugars," Boyd said after he'd stood to give her a hug. "Told them to bring it when you got here."

"Thanks. Been here awhile?"

"Not really. You know me…thirty minutes early always feels late," he replied.

That hadn't always been the case, but she understood why it had become his habit. "I do. So you mentioned you needed some help."

"No small talk?" he murmured dryly. His dark brown hair had grayed over the years, and he was still in shape but not as muscled as he'd been when he played on their high school football team.

"How's the family?" she asked, a tinge of heat rising to her cheeks. "Sorry. I pretty much spend all of my time at my desk with monitors around me and only talk to the team when giving recon info or issuing a warning or order."

"Fair enough," Boyd said. "Parents are good. Dad finally retired and Mom is trying to push for that move to Arizona. We'll see what happens."

"And Daniella?"

"Good... I hear she's good," he muttered.

Lee lifted both eyebrows.

"She left about six months ago. I see her at work but we're separated," he told her with a shrug. "Mom suggested maybe marriage isn't for me."

"Wow. Sorry about that," Lee said. Daniella had been his third wife.

"Me too. She said I can't let go of the past."

Lee nodded. This wasn't news. She and Boyd both knew that he couldn't. That he would always blame himself for staying late at the gym to hang with the guys instead of going to meet Hannah. He'd always wonder if had he been there for his girlfriend she might not have been taken and would still be alive today. Lee wondered the same thing but about herself. If she'd left the computer lab with Hannah and gone to wait for Boyd with her instead of trying to get the program language for the algorithm she'd been working on to track grades and prove that her English teacher graded down on girls...

She reached over and squeezed his hand. There wasn't really anything she could say that would make him feel better. Or herself, for that matter. "So..."

The barista dropped off Lee's drink and then Boyd leaned closer. "One of my students hasn't shown up to class for the last three days. She has a rough home life and I'm not sure what happened. She might have run away. I called the number on file for her mom but haven't received an answer."

Lee wasn't exactly surprised by this. Boyd had come to her before when he thought things were odd with a student. "Name."

"Isabell Montez, but she goes by Izzie."

She pulled out her smartphone and started making notes on the notepad. Boyd gave her a physical description and Air-Dropped Izzie's yearbook photo to her. "I went to the cops and they said they'd do a wellness visit to her home," he added. "But I haven't heard back from them."

"Did you go by the house?"

He nodded. "I did. There's no sign of anyone there. I think the cops will probably just write it off, but my gut says there's more here."

Because of what they'd both been through, his gut was always going to say that, Lee realized. "Okay. I'll check into it. Does she have socials?"

He shrugged. "No clue. That's not really my thing."

Why did that not surprise her? Boyd wasn't exactly the Facebook type. "Fair enough. I'll check into this and get back to you when I hear something," Lee said.

He flashed a quick grin. "Which *is* your thing."

"What do you mean?"

"Just that you only come out from behind your computer when there's a crime to solve and then you go back."

She shrugged, not really able to argue with that.

They'd already exhausted the small talk, so she took a quick sip of her sweet, dark brew and then nodded at her old friend and got up, ready to start digging into Izzie Montez to find out where she'd gone.

A new puzzle to solve and hopefully a girl that could be saved. Van would say she'd joined Price Security to rescue people. Hell, everyone on the team had done that. But this time because Boyd was involved, the need to get this right and find that girl was stronger than it had been in a while.

Aaron Quentin liked life undercover. He didn't need a therapist to tell him that he used his work to hide from life. He knew that. However, over the last year, he'd started to get closer to his youngest brother, Xander, which was making him reevaluate some things.

He was British but worked for the DEA on their large criminal-gangs task force. Aaron had originally come to work for the DEA when he'd been on holiday in Miami. He'd been at loose ends, making money fighting in some underground clubs, when a fellow fighter had introduced him to his backers who were part of an East Coast drug syndicate.

Aaron had realized he was at another crossroad, and for the first time in his twenty-eight years, he'd decided to do the smart thing and not screw up again. He'd used a contact he had from his time in the SAS to get a meeting with a local DEA agent, and that had been it. Now ten years later, he was almost feeling like the work he'd done taking down two large criminal networks almost made up for the angry, tough youth he'd once been.

The accident was something he'd never be able to forgive himself for, and his family would never fully be healed. But looking at forty gave him a different perspective. Seeing Xander settled with his fiancée, Obie Keller, and working in private security was also helping. Also, having his brother back in his life… Well, it was making Aaron see his life through a different lens.

There was always that question of how long he could be effective undercover. He'd come out to the West Coast because after a high-profile bust in Miami, he felt he was getting too well-known.

Or at least that's what he *told* himself. The other reason, which he wasn't ready to delve into, was to be closer to Xander. The two of them, along with his future sister-in-law, had all gone home for Christmas. It had been…eye-opening to realize how much he'd missed the family, and after a long chat with Tony, he was starting to see himself in a different light.

Of course, it wasn't as easy as it always seemed on TV shows or in movies. The truth was, violence was where he was most comfortable—or had been. That's why undercover work suited him. He had no issues being a tough guy, or fitting in with the criminal element.

They were his people. He understood what it was like to

grow up in a crowd of testosterone and always fight to be the alpha. He was the third of four brothers who'd grown up wild.

He and Xander were the youngest and their older brothers never pulled punches. He'd learned to be resilient and to survive by example. Fighting to be the top dog was all he'd known until a rugby game where his second-oldest brother was left paralyzed after a tackle by Aaron.

He'd blamed himself. Hell, they all had in different ways. Could Tony and Abe, the older two, have stopped antagonizing him and Xander? Couldn't he and Xander have just walked away? Sure, but that wasn't the Quentin MO.

Aaron blew out a breath. All this wading through the past was making his skin feel too tight and itchy, had him wishing he could just down a bottle of whiskey to forget. But he hated being drunk and how that thin veneer that he called control would often slip away and he'd wind up in a fight—because he *always* did—and then would most likely add to his list of regrets.

As much as he'd told himself he was in LA because of Xander, he knew there was another reason. Lee Oscar.

She was the tech genius at Price Security. Hot as hell…as much as he didn't do romance because of his job and basic lack of good relationship skills. Still, he couldn't shake her from his thoughts.

She wasn't his usual type of woman, which didn't mean crap to his libido. Apparently faded tight jeans and T-shirts that skimmed her curves were what he was attracted to.

"Mate, what are you doing here?"

Aaron glanced over his left shoulder to see Xander striding toward him. His brother was just coming off a job—Price had let Aaron know and also let him into the building. He'd been waiting in what served as a guest lobby on the fourth floor.

"Hoping for some hang time. Obie called."

Xander rubbed the back of his neck as he dropped his duffel on the floor at his feet. Aaron walked over and hugged his brother. Not for a moment embarrassed by the emotion that swamped him. He'd been alone for too long.

"Yeah? I can hang. Gotta shower though, and Kenji and I have a *Halo* match."

Price Security was so much more than a workplace. Giovanni "Van" Price had created a family out of the loners he'd hired as first-rate bodyguards and security consultants, something that Aaron had seen firsthand in Miami.

For a moment, he was jealous of the found family that Xander had here. But then shoved that down. He was slowly trying to rebuild the brotherly bond that he'd ripped the hell out of when they'd been in their early twenties. "Cool."

"Great. Let's go up to my place. You in town for work?"

"Yeah. I start on Monday. Trying to lie low. Was going to hole up in a hotel but then... Obie."

"You didn't have to wait for her to call. You can always crash at my place," Xander said.

Aaron shrugged. He still wasn't used to this either. He'd made himself into a lone wolf after his pack had disintegrated. Convinced himself that he liked it better that way. But recently he was beginning to rethink it.

Starting to want to see Xander and his family more often. And wondering if maybe there was a different life out there for him.

When they got on the elevator, Lee Oscar was on there. Their eyes met and she lifted one eyebrow when his gaze lingered too long. Lee was about five-five and fit. She had long brown hair that she habitually wore pulled back in a ponytail and was whip-smart.

He'd talked to her in Miami after she and the rest of the Price Security team had helped him wrap a delicate case he'd been working. He'd noticed her as a woman the very first moment he met her. He leaned against the wall of the elevator, crossing his legs at the ankle as he watched her, trying to figure out what was different about her.

"Hey, babe, how's life treating you?" he asked. Noticing his brother shaking his head. But Xander hadn't been there in Miami when they'd done shots of tequila, and for a moment in the hot moonlight, something had passed between the two of them.

"Fine. You, babe?" she asked.

He noted Xander trying to hide a smile but ignored his brother.

"Same. Just starting a new gig."

"Are you staying here?" she asked him, not Xander.

"Do you want me to?" he asked. If she ever gave him the hint of an opening, he'd jump at it. But with Lee, it was like he had no game. None. Other women usually took one look at him and it was game on. But not Lee.

"Not really," she said.

"Ouch."

"Sorry. It's just your job is high-risk and it would mean extra security measures in place and that's more work for me."

"I don't want to cause that," he said. "Plus I'm undercover, and this building is a bit too high vis for my MO."

"Another case like Miami?" she asked.

"Something," he said. He couldn't divulge the details and didn't want to. His life worked because of the compartments he kept.

"Be safe," she said as she exited on her floor.

"You too, babe."

She paused, glancing back over her shoulder. "It's Lee, not babe."

He gave her a slow smile and arched one eyebrow at her. "Noted, Lee."

"Mate, seriously?"

"Seriously."

"She's not a casual-type woman," Xander said. "She's like a sister to me, so watch yourself."

"She's got her own back," Aaron said. He wondered if he should apologize to his brother but wouldn't have an idea where to begin. It was probably better he wasn't staying here.

Lee had his attention and it was clear that Xander wasn't down with that. But still he couldn't stop thinking about her... Something seemed different.

She looked worried. He hadn't seen her that way before.

Isabell Montez wasn't that hard to find. She had the regular socials and had been pretty active until about ten days ago. Thanks to Isabell's feed, Lee was able to pull together different photos and start running them through a facial recognition program that she had helped develop back when she'd been working for the government. She attended San Pedro High School, which of course Lee had been aware of since that was where Boyd worked. The program had been improved in the last fifteen years, and Lee had kept up with updates for herself and the government.

She thought about Boyd as she ran the search. That boy had never been the same after high school. She got it—she hadn't either—but it seemed to Lee that Boyd had been trapped in those four years. The good *and* the bad.

She couldn't get far enough away from her past. It was ironic that when she retired and started working with Van that she'd ended up only an hour away on the 5 from where she'd started her journey. Her grandpa had died a few years ago and Lee never went back to Ojai. She didn't want to. The past for her tended to stay there.

She was too busy doing her job and keeping her clients and the staff at Price Security safe. In a way, she was the opposite of Boyd. Having had that one lapse in judgment, she'd focused on never letting it happen again. Her old classmate, on the other hand, felt as if he were trying to fix what happened to Hannah. That if by being vigilant he could bring her back. But that wasn't ever going to happen.

Even though they'd never found her body, which of course made things more complicated. Like, maybe she was still alive. Though the years Lee had spent working in human trafficking made her doubt that. She'd looked for Hannah over the years. Had even used some software to age her old pictures and run them through every facial recognition program and came up with a few likenesses.

But they'd never panned out.

She stood and stretched as the program kept running, when the door behind her opened. Her office was a bank of computer screens and then, behind her, a big conference table that the team used when it was time to have a confab or for Van to hand out assignments.

She glanced over her shoulder to see her boss walking toward her. Van Price was a big-muscled bald man with intense green eyes that warmed when he laughed. He wasn't tall, just presented himself in a way that made everyone take a step back. When Lee had first met the security guru almost twenty years ago, she'd been intimidated until they'd been paired on an undercover assignment and she realized that the tough exterior hid a softy with a heart of gold.

She was one of a handful of people who knew that fact, which she also knew was intentional. Van was lethal, never hesitating to do what was necessary to keep his clients and his staff—or *family* as he called them—safe.

"How was old home week?"

She shook her head. "Painful. Boyd has another missing kid."

"*Another* one?"

"Yeah, every five years or so, he calls me about a kid he thinks has been taken," Lee said. Her mind naturally identified patterns, and even if they might be coincidences, she hadn't been able to ignore the fact that it was every five years since Hannah's disappearance that Boyd reached out.

"Was the kid taken?" Van asked.

"Not sure yet. I mean, the police definitely checked out her house after he called, and found nothing. The family was gone, so it could be they are just in the wind. But her socials went quiet too, which isn't normal for that age," Lee admitted. "So… what brings you by?"

"Just checking on one of my favorite girls," Van said, with that slow smile of his.

"Just checking in, huh?" She narrowed her eyes at him. "What do you need?" she asked, knowing Van never did anything without a reason.

"Kaitlyn Leo from the CIA reached out again asking for Kenji and Daphne's help. I thought we had an agreement. Can you look around and make sure they aren't active again?"

By "look around," he meant hack into the CIA's servers and check on the agent status. "Kenji would tell you."

"I know he would, but there is always a chance that Leo would go behind his back," Van grumbled. "We've both known that to happen."

They had. After they'd retired from the government, Kenji

and Daphne had been asked to do favors, which both of them had agreed to, but then their status had been changed to active until they notified their bosses that they were definitely inactive.

"I'll let you know what I find. Aaron's here, by the way. I bumped into him in the elevator." She was still buzzing slightly from the interaction with him. He got her that way. That insolent way he leaned casually against the wall of the elevator and then checked her out in a manner that was anything but casual. Mixed Signals should have been his name.

There was a quiet intelligence to him that drew her, but then he opened his mouth and came on like someone who spent too much time in a bar. Which should have made it easier for her to ignore him completely.

But it didn't.

"Yeah, I gave him access. He's working in LA and needs a safe place for his downtime."

"Cool. A heads-up would have been nice," Lee said. Since she kept the building secure, she liked to know when they had someone new on the premises. Especially someone like Aaron Quentin who was usually deep undercover with drug cartels.

"He just arrived a little while ago," Van pointed out. "You sure you're okay?"

She knew she was touchy. It was Boyd and of course Hannah and this young girl, who'd looked funny and happy in her social media photos, who was now missing. Her mind could easily supply all the scenarios where she might be and how they could find her. It made her edgy.

She just shrugged.

Van put his hand on her shoulder and squeezed.

They both knew that there was nothing to be said. That world—the murky crime-filled one—continued to thrive no matter what they did and nothing would change that.

Lee's best hope was to find Izzie before too much more time passed.

Chapter Two

You only come out from behind your computer when there's a crime to solve...

Boyd's words sat in the back of her mind as she moved her fingers over the keyboard. It wasn't like her job had forced her to this position of observing everyone and everything. She'd had a rough upbringing and had learned early on to keep quiet and stay out of the way.

School had reinforced those behaviors, and four years in college and her recruitment by a secret government agency had finished the transition for her. She'd always been more comfortable observing and analyzing.

It was easier to make the tough calls when she wasn't in the field or interacting one-on-one with the person whose life was in her hands. But for some reason, tonight it didn't feel the way it usually had. Maybe it was the fact that Luna had gotten married and moved out of the tower.

Luna Urban-DeVere habitually wore her hair back in a tight ponytail. She had high cheekbones and a pert nose. Her eyes were worried when she met Lee's stare. Luna had been a solid hang, where they'd sort of sat in the same room and read together. Some people might not get that kind of friendship but for Lee... Luna was one of her besties, even if the other woman might not realize it.

Rubbing the back of her neck, she got up and walked to the kitchenette that was part of her setup at Price Security. She had a nice apartment across the hall but spent all of her time here in front of her computer monitors, accessing information and monitoring the team. Luckily she didn't need a lot of sleep—a solid six hours was all it took for her to feel refreshed, so she was ideally suited to be *overwatch* for Price Security.

The guys called her that sometimes. Well, Xander did because he'd been in the military. Rick dubbed her "chief" because he'd been a cop and then a DEA agent. He was used to a chain of command. Van was definitely the commissioner role.

Lee was sort of the glue that held everything together. She monitored everyone when they were in the field, relayed information as it came in, to different cases. No one asked her to do it 24-7, but it had sort of become her habit. At some point, she'd stopped dating and leaving the tower...like Boyd had mentioned, unless someone needed her.

She'd sort of lost herself in her work. It was safer when she was in the tower. Something she didn't allow herself to unpack.

She shook off whatever emotion was responsible for her melancholy as she made herself a cup of coffee and added a splash of skim milk. Grimacing as she did so. She liked coffee, even this version of her old favorite that she'd had to change as she got older.

She was resisting switching to decaf, even though the doctor wanted her to in order to cut back because of her acid reflux. She'd already given up sugar and cream to stop the spread of her hips, so it felt insulting that her body was now demanding she quit caffeine too.

Her computer pinged, which meant it had a hit, and she hurried back to her desk and sat.

She scanned the monitor she had running a search for Isabell's EID, embedded identity document. Basically it was a way to track the teenager's device without relying on the phone number. Since Isabell's phone wasn't responding to any calls and the girl had disappeared into thin air, Lee had thought to start this trace.

And she saw now it had pulled back a location that wasn't

too far from here. Over in West Hollywood, in close proximity to Zara's Brew where Lee had met up with Boyd. She opened a map and tracked the location, switching to street view and noticing it was a club called Mistral's. It didn't look like a club for teens. So what had Isabell been doing there? How did an establishment that had hits on the internet from a teenager tagging the place not appear in any database?

Then she remembered that Van had asked her to make sure Price Security didn't show up on any map or internet tool for locations. Someone had also made sure that Mistral's wasn't on the map.

And the last ping of Isabell's phone was from there. She pulled up the file that Boyd had given her and searched for the cop's name who'd taken the report from him. It was someone she didn't know. She knew it wasn't Detective Miller's case, but she knew her pretty well from a couple of other cases.

Lee put in a call to Miller and then sat back in her chair. Looking again at the geotag on the social media posts, she used other sites around Mistral's to find the coordinates and then came up with a position.

One that she would check out tomorrow.

It was 4:00 a.m., just about time for her to head to bed. Lee left the other algorithms running and went across the hall to her apartment. Van had insisted she decorate it, so she'd bought some floor samples for a living and dining area and then a bed for the bedroom.

Lee had never really felt like any place was home. She had always carried it inside of herself. Plus, she also knew better than most that nice furniture didn't mean safety. So this sort of used stuff suited her.

She walked into her bedroom. Showering before hitting the hay was her habit, as was putting on her sleep headphones after climbing between the sheets. Bar sounds might not be anyone else's soothing sound, but it had always been for her. As a child, she knew she was safe sleeping in a backroom behind the bar with Grandpa working. Closing her eyes now, she could almost smell beer and cigarettes as she drifted off.

But what about Isabell, she wondered? Did that girl have

any safety? From what Boyd had told her, the teen's home life wasn't great. But then that could be said of so many kids, and many, like her, had survived and didn't end up disappearing. So what had happened to this girl?

Tomorrow she'd start to unravel it. There wasn't a puzzle she couldn't solve given enough time. The team were all on relatively routine assignments, so Lee had time for this. She'd never shirk her duties, but Van always considered this type of job one that kept her skills fresh.

He'd had worse gigs, no denying that. Currently Aaron felt like he was inhabiting some sort of English version of what living in California was. He had a van that was on the beach and had been told to carry a surfboard. Except he couldn't surf and looked like a knob walking around with a board under his arm.

His boss wanted him to blend in, but he figured being a poser wasn't the right guy for this gang.

The Cachorros had been operating up and down the West Coast for more than a decade. Aaron had worked for the DEA for about the same amount of time. He'd primarily been based in Florida since that was where he'd shown up. But after he'd taken down a large crime network, his cover had been blown. His boss suggested it might be time for Aaron to get out of undercover work, but he wasn't ready for that yet.

So here he was, working his way up another crime cartel to get to the top. The street dealers were different in Cali than in Florida, but the same could be said of the differences between South London and Florida. Aaron was good at adapting and changing to meet the needs of any situation. He'd brought a lot of cash, made some big buys and started making waves when he'd first gotten into town a week ago.

He'd also found a mole from the Chacals, another crime organization, named Chico del Torro, and used him to move his way up. Chico was in charge of this seaside operation. Mainly overseeing sales on this stretch of the beach. There was a club at the end of the pier that was also owned by the gang and where Aaron had been hanging at night, trying to learn more about the organization.

To say that the Cachorros didn't really trust him was an understatement. And everyone was watching their backs around him. But that was fine with him. He was good at fighting and being a guy, so he knew how to bond over blood and beer. That was sort of his specialist skill. He could drink any of these Yanks under the table but he knew how to appear as if he'd had too much.

Like many of the people within large crime organizations, he didn't use the products they sold. Something that Aaron was grateful that he'd never been tempted into. Probably because he was one big rage machine underneath what he'd been told was a charming smile. He had known better than to add drugs to the mix.

"Boss wants to see you," Carmen said. "He's upstairs."

"Uh-oh. Am I in trouble?" he asked her, stealing some peanuts from the bar cups she was filling up.

She shrugged, tossing her long brown hair over her shoulder. "Do you *think* you are?"

"Sure hope not," he said with a wink before taking the stairs up to the office two at a time.

The boss was Jako Lourdes. He'd been the one who'd promoted him from street selling to running bags. The file that Aaron had read on him hadn't really matched the man he'd met. From the intel that the DEA had, he'd thought that Jako was just this big Pacific Islander who spent his time lazing around on the beach and surfing in between deals.

But in truth, he'd been implicated in a few hits on rival gang members. Though nothing had stuck. And the photos hadn't exactly been up-to-date. Something that Aaron had rectified. Jako owned several establishments in the small beach town of San Clemente. Most legit. Including one where the guy taught fire dancing and his sister taught hula.

So far, Aaron hadn't been able to figure out what the school was used for, but given that every other business Jako owned was doing something illegal, Aaron knew he was missing something.

He rapped on the door at the top of the stairs.

"Come in."

He entered the room and Jako was sitting on his desk, looking at his phone. Two of his closest were already there, both sprawled out on the leather couch. The room wasn't anything special. Faded wallpaper on the back wall that had been whitewashed and then had some basic graffiti of the gang's symbol.

"Quinn, my man. How's things?"

He always went by the name Quinn when he was working undercover. "Good. I think they're good. Completed the run and drop," he said.

"Yeah, heard that. You're efficient," Jako said.

"Try to be." Aaron was bigger than Jako and Roman, but not Steve, so if this went sideways, he figured he could take two of them but he wasn't getting out of here easily. Also mentally going over the last few days, he couldn't see where he'd have fucked up enough to warrant a beatdown.

"You are. I need you at another location. My bosses heard about the solid you did for me and they want to see what else you got."

Not what he was expecting. "Where am I going?"

"Los Angeles. That operation always needs new blood. The cops make our guys every few weeks and arrest them."

"I'm going back on the street?" Aaron asked.

"No. A club. Mistral's. We need you overseeing the operation. Someone got sloppy," Jako said.

Depending on how mucked up things were, Aaron wasn't sure whether he'd be able to clean this up. But he had worked in a nightclub in South Beach for four years, so at least a club was more his thing than surf shack on the sand. "I'll need to grab my stuff but can be ready to go in an hour." There wasn't anything keeping him in Cali except his brother...and Lee. Though it had been days since he'd seen her in the elevator, he was still replaying their interaction, wishing he'd been different but not sure how.

"Good," Jako said. "Make me proud."

"I will."

Aaron left the meeting knowing he couldn't risk checking in with his partner, Denis. He also suspected that this reassignment was more than what Jako had said. His bosses clearly wanted to be reassured about the kind of man they were getting in Aaron. This would be good for Jako, if he delivered. As for him? Well, it was getting him one step deeper into the organization, which was exactly what he needed.

Running algorithms on her computer was one avenue to explore, but Lee knew she also had to do some legwork. Which she was currently embroiled in. Sitting in the conference room, she had a map spread out on the table along with the records she'd managed to get from a contact that showed the different cell phone towers that had been pinged by Isabell's phone.

Stopping for a moment, she looked down at the girl. She had long, curly hair that hung past her shoulders, her face was long and square, and her eyebrows on the thicker side, but Lee knew that was the trend nowadays. Her expression was solemn yet there was an air of maturity to her that belied her age. But... she was still a baby.

The picture that Lee was starting to put together of Isabell showed someone who was making choices that might have put her in danger. She had a meeting with Detective Miller later that day. She was going to introduce her to the man who was working Isabell Montez's case, Detective Monroe. It would be good to get some insight.

That said, cops were busy and this girl wasn't a top priority. And the fact that it was her teacher and not her parents who'd reported her missing was odd... Lee checked her watch. If she left now she could swing by the last known address.

The door to the conference room opened and Lee glanced up to see Luna coming in.

"Hey, girl."

"Hey. Van said you're working a side case. Thought I'd see if you needed to bounce ideas off someone," Luna said, coming over and putting a skinny decaf latte in front of her.

"Thanks. Actually, you fancy going on a field trip with me?"

"Sure. I'm between gigs for another week," she replied. "Where are we going?"

"I'll catch you up in the car," Lee said, grabbing her bag and her keys, keeping her coffee in the other hand.

"This the missing girl?" Luna asked, holding up the photo.

"Yes. Isabell Montez. She hasn't been to school in ten days," Lee told her bestie as they took the elevator down to the garage and they headed to her black Dodge Charger. The entire team at Price Security drove them. They'd been special ordered with bulletproof glass and reinforced bodies. Not that she was anticipating trouble, but the car was fast and easily maneuverable. Something she appreciated in LA traffic.

"Ten days. That could be a lifetime," Luna said. "What did the cops say?"

Lee started the car after they got in and put on her sunglasses as she exited the parking garage onto Spring Street. She headed toward the Boyle Heights area where Isabell and her family had lived. "They looked into it, but the last known address looks like it's been abandoned, and when they questioned the neighbors, no one had seen them or heard anything." She huffed out a breath. "So they are playing wait and see."

"I hope they aren't waiting for a body," Luna muttered.

"I don't think so. They are overworked and the only one who's concerned about the girl is her teacher. They have feelers out with next of kin and are trying to track down her parents."

"Have you found them?" the other woman asked.

"Not yet. The cops put a bolo out for their car, but so far, nothing. I've also run the license and make through my visual recognition program, checking cameras at traffic lights and ATMs and anything, really, but again nothing," Lee said. "Which I don't like."

"I don't like it either. Cars usually get a hit. We heading to the kid's house?" Luna asked.

"Yeah. Just want to look around and see what's there. The cops went and knocked on the door and looked in the windows and didn't see any signs of foul play, according to the report I read."

Luna arched a brow. "How'd you get the report?"

"I asked Detective Miller if she could help me out. And she did. It's public record so it's not like it's illegal," Lee said.

"Yeah, I know. I figured you just backdoored yourself into their files," Luna said with a laugh.

"Uh, no. Van doesn't want me doing that anymore. Kenji's boss from the CIA poking around last December made him wary of drawing any unwanted attention from the government. So... I'm trying. But, as you know, I am used to just getting what I want by any means..."

It wasn't that she couldn't appreciate that there were laws and they were meant to be followed. It was simply that when it came to criminal activity, the law was usually an afterthought. So she didn't like to hamper her own investigations by following rules that the bad guys were probably breaking.

"So. What are we looking for?" Luna asked when Lee pulled up in front of Isabell's house and turned off the car.

"I'm not sure. But *something*. That girl looks years too old to be sixteen. Something was happening here and...there are always signs," Lee said, remembering her own childhood.

Obviously she had no real idea if she was projecting her fractured parental relationship onto that picture of Isabell, or if the girl actually was in a hostile home situation. She just felt that by coming here and looking around she might get a better idea.

"Fair enough. Are we breaking in?" Luna asked.

"No, but if any of the doors or windows are open..." Lee trailed off.

Luna just nodded, and from the corner of her eye, Lee could see a slight smirk on her face as they both walked toward the house. Boyle Heights was an older neighborhood. Each of the yards had an overgrown lawn and the worn-out homes showed all of their years. And it was eerily quiet. No one was outside and there weren't a lot of cars on the street either. Lee shrugged. It was the middle of the workweek and workday. So that wasn't much of a red flag.

Luna moved to check the side yard and Lee was glad she had her friend with her. She'd missed working with Luna since her friend had quietly married billionaire Nicholas DeVere last February.

Lee moved up to the front of the house and paused. The front door had been kicked in and hung off its hinges. Definitely not the state it had been in when the cops had visited the first time.

She knew she had to call it in to the police.

"Uh, that doesn't look like no sign of foul play," Luna murmured.

"Yeah, exactly. You report it while I go poke around."

"Go on. But as soon as they say don't go inside, I'm going to mention my friend is in there and when they tell me to, I'll call you out," Luna said.

"That works for me."

She used her foot to open the door, pulling her weapon, not sure what might be waiting inside.

Chapter Three

Aaron and his partner, Denis, had been working for six months before they even hit the ground here in LA. It wasn't easy to find a way into a gang from the outside. Their boss wasn't even sure it was worth the effort and had warned them this might be a long-term gig.

Which suited Aaron. He liked disappearing into anyone who wasn't Aaron Quentin. He'd been working in San Clemente for a minor player before he'd finally had a chance to work his way into Jako's crew. The Cachorros squad was tight and didn't trust easily. Aaron had expected that and played it cool. Focusing on his position as a bagman for the organization.

Doing his runs, Aaron had noticed another member of the crew who was working for the rival Chacals gang. Which he'd used to earn Jako's trust and move up in the ranks. He wanted to be in charge of an operation so he could get access to the lieutenants. Aaron's investigation had led him and Denis to a shadowy figure who was known by one name. *Perses.* Jako hadn't mentioned him, but a member of one of the other gangs had one night when the dude had been drunk out of his mind.

Finally they had a lead. He'd been working low-level organizations up and down the coast of California for months trying to find the one that would lead them to the person they were after. Their intel thus far led them to believe that drugs were just part of a bigger international operation. Aaron's boss at the DEA told him that there were other agents from an FBI task force also looking into Perses.

Steve had gotten Aaron to LA and then told him to meet him at a club called Mistral's later in the evening around seven. In the meantime, Aaron had gone back to his apartment—the one that the DEA had set him up in for his cover—and done some computer work. The rival gang member had worked for the Chacals and they ran their operation out of the Boyle Heights neighborhood of LA. He had trailed Chico to a drop house on Euclid before reporting back to Jako.

Jayne, his boss at the DEA, wanted him and his partner, Denis, to go and hit the place on Euclid and see if they could find any further evidence of that rival gang's operation.

Before heading out to meet up with his partner in West Hollywood, he checked the place one more time to ensure he had everything set up for tonight. This was his first step into the bigger world of the Cachorros gang. He wasn't going to screw it up.

He made sure he had his badge on a chain around his neck and tucked into his T-shirt and then walked out of his apartment. He kept his gun in the locked glove box of his van. He and Denis had comms, so as soon as he was in the vehicle, Aaron let him know he was on his way.

They were going to rendezvous at the house just in case Aaron had a tail. He'd have an excuse if Steve was following—he could say he was checking on the place where he'd last seen Chico make his drop.

He drove through traffic, focused on the job ahead, when he noticed a black Dodge Charger. Not really the kind of car that stuck out but he recognized it as one of the vehicles his brother drove for Price Security.

He drove past, checking to see if it was Xander, but saw a woman behind the wheel. Lee Oscar…he thought. He'd flirted with her hard the first time they'd met and she'd shut him down.

Fair enough.

Not everyone was into him, he knew, but he'd been intrigued by her. Hyperintelligent, quick-witted and never missing a beat. Not to mention the fact that Lee was an attractive woman. So was it any wonder that he'd been turned on by her? But at the same time, he wasn't just one big hormone. She'd said no and he respected that.

Didn't mean he'd been able to stop thinking about her. He was pretty sure she hadn't noticed him driving by, which was a good thing. He was on the job and really shouldn't be thinking about her curvy hips in those worn jeans she favored. Or the way she tipped her head to the side when he pushed too hard trying to charm her.

Everything about her just fascinated him, which was for another time. He signaled and got off the freeway, driving into an older, rundown neighborhood. The roads were quiet and he dumped the van in a park that had a swing set and merry-go-round. Two of the swings were fine but the third hung on one chain. He walked across the playground and noticed Denis waiting for him.

"Dude."

"The boss has SWAT standing by in case we uncover a money-counting operation. They want to shut this down," his partner said.

"Got it," Aaron replied.

They moved in together, crossing the park before stopping at the second house on the block. It had a chain-link fence around the yard but the gate was open. There was music playing as they approached and two guys sat on the front porch in lawn chairs.

"Hey, uh, is Chico here?" Aaron asked.

That got their attention. They both sat up straighter and Aaron noticed one of the men pulling his gun up from his side.

"That's far enough," the other man said.

Lee entered the house and paused in the doorway. She heard Luna making the call, which meant that she had to be quick. The cops were right to tell her not to disturb the scene and she wasn't going to touch anything; she just wanted to see where Isabell had lived. Get an idea of the girl she was looking for. The living room smelled of old pizza and had been turned over, probably by whoever had broken in. Looking around, she noticed the cushions were off the couch and everything had been dumped.

Lee moved quickly down the hall past the kitchen. There was a bedroom on the right that was pretty nondescript and had been treated the same as the living room. Then another one, also containing a queen-size bed, with drawers dumped on the floor and an en suite bathroom. The last room on the left was smaller than the other two and had a single bed pushed under the window. The dresser drawers were open, but there were no clothes on the floor. In fact, it seemed like none of the furniture had anything in it.

This had to be Isabell's room. Had they already gotten rid of her stuff? Perhaps the parents had been hiding from the cops when they stopped by. It seemed odd to Lee that one room would be empty. Well, *this* room in particular, considering that Boyd was concerned about the girl.

Scanning the place further, she saw there was a poster on the wall of BTS, a K-pop band, and small desk that wouldn't have been out of place in Lee's own bedroom when she'd been a teenager. Someone had written on the surface in Sharpie.

Lee put on some medical gloves she'd brought with her before she ran her finger over the words. "This is just a phase." Then looked in the desk drawers, which were all opened. She tried to pull the top one out farther—it was stuck on its track—and when she did a Polaroid picture fell onto the base.

Isabell…but a very different, more mature-looking girl. She had on makeup and wore a choker around her neck. She was smiling at whoever was taking the photo, and it looked like maybe a bar in the background. Quickly, as she heard Luna calling her name, she took a photo of the Polaroid with her phone so she could reference it with the other pictures she'd found online.

"Coming."

She looked around, snapping photos of the writing on the desk and then took a quick peek into the closet. There was a jacket toward the back. A zippered army-green one that had a bunch of pockets with different patches sewn on it. She captured an image of it and then put her hand in the pocket, feeling around. She found a vape and some receipts, but they just had totals and not a retailer's name printed on them. She fanned them out on the desk and took a photo as Luna called for her again.

"Two minutes!"

"I'm almost done," Lee yelled back as she returned the stuff to the pockets and then turned, catching her foot on the bottom slider of the closet, which made her stumble. Before getting back on her feet, she glanced under the bed, remembering her own childhood home and the one place where she'd hidden stuff from her parents. Under the box spring of her bed. She lifted it up and found a file folder and, at the same moment, heard sirens. She wanted to look in that folder, but there was no time. She sprinted out of the house and slid next to Luna as the first cop car rounded the corner and pulled up behind the Dodge.

Luna turned and lifted one eyebrow at her. Lee knew she was asking if she'd found anything. She nodded.

The officers came up to the porch and asked them to step back to the sidewalk. Both women did. A second car arrived with two investigators. They came over to talk to her and Luna.

"Ladies. I'm Detective Monroe. What were you doing here?"

"I'm Lee Oscar and this is Luna Urban-DeVere. We're from Price Security and we've been hired to find a teenager who was living here," she said.

"Miller mentioned you were interested in the Montez girl. The place was like this when you got here?"

"Yes, sir," Luna said. "Clearly it's been vandalized. We called it in and waited as instructed."

"But if the girl's MIA, why did you come out *here*?" Monroe prodded.

"Wanted to see if the parents or the kid were back. It's been ten days since she stopped going to school. Something might have changed."

"Evidently it did," Monroe said, taking in the sorry state of the home.

"Yes. I'm not sure what this means. Maybe the entire family is in danger," Lee said. Though, based on what she'd seen, it was obvious that Isabell hadn't been living in this house for a while. Had she run away?

She blew out a frustrated breath. This fishing expedition had turned up more questions than answers.

"That's one of the things we will be investigating. I want you both to give a statement as to what you saw when you arrived. Can you come by the precinct later and do that?"

"Yes, of course," Lee said. Knowing from his tone that Monroe was dismissing them. "Any chance I can wait around and take a look inside?"

"No."

Well, okay then.

"We can talk when you stop by later. But this is an open investigation now, and I don't want anyone getting in the way," Monroe said sternly.

"Fair enough. We'll see you then," Luna murmured, taking Lee's arm and leading her back to the Charger.

Aaron launched himself the six feet toward the porch as he heard Denis doing the same. He knocked the gun from the guy's hand but was off balance. The momentum carried him forward and he rolled as he hit the ground, coming to his feet as the guy he'd rammed out of the chair followed suit.

He was a big, muscled man, and as soon as Aaron was on his feet, he took a punch to the throat, which hurt like a bitch. Retaliating, he struck his opponent hard with a front kick, catching him in the nose. Blood spurted on the other guy's face, hitting Aaron. But he ignored it as he followed the blow with a punch to the gut that sent the perp back against the front wall of the house, where his head hit on the brick before he slowly sank down to the ground.

Aaron was on him in an instant, rolling him to his stomach and wresting his hands behind his back to cuff him. He read the gunman his Miranda rights, glancing up to see Denis finishing up with the second guy.

"Front muscle down," Aaron barked into their comms, letting their reinforcements know that it was safe to approach. "Is the team in position?"

"We are. Go on your command," Harris responded.

Aaron glanced over at his partner, who nodded. They both drew their weapons before Aaron said, "Go!" and then kicked in the door. The house was dark with blacked-out windows and women in their underwear working money-counting machines.

There were two guards at the front of the room and two at the back. Denis and Aaron each moved to take down the guards.

The fight was as quick and short as the one outside. Aaron used another kick combo that had the guards down and cuffed in seconds. The women who were working the machines didn't stop what they were doing until the power was cut and the machines turned off. Then they looked up before huddling closer together.

Aaron's boss took control of the scene, ensuring that the armed men and the women were escorted into vans for transport down to the police station. While that was all taking place, Aaron and Denis headed back to their vehicles. But as they got close, Aaron noticed a low-riding Dodge that he recognized but wasn't one of Price Security's.

"That's one of Jako's crew," Aaron muttered under his breath.

His colleague dropped back as Aaron tucked his badge under his shirt and kept his head down, walking a bit faster as if he was trying to distance himself from Denis.

Steve pulled up next to him. "What the hell are you doing over here?"

"This was where I tailed Chico, figured I'd make sure no one else was doing double duty. What are *you* doing here?" Aaron asked Steve.

"Same," the man said.

Which immediately made Aaron wonder if Steve had been running with both gangs. He decided to alert his boss and have him start tailing Steve to find out what was going on there.

"You get into it with them?"

"Yeah. Then the cops arrived and I beat it," Aaron said.

The gang member narrowed his eyes at him. "Cops? What kind?"

"I didn't stick around to find out. Are you going back to San Clemente?"

"Yeah. Figured I'd do a drive-by to where you said you saw Chico before I did," Steve said.

Again something about that was making the back of Aaron's neck itch. He nodded toward the other man before walking to his van as Steve pulled away. Denis had stopped at a bench in the park and looked like he was taking pills or something. But Aaron just got in his vehicle and started it up. They both had wireless comm devices that they wore in their ears.

"I'm heading toward the freeway, will double back and meet you at the station. Ask Jayne to tail that car. I'm not sure what he's doing in a rival gang's neighborhood."

"Will do. Let me know if you need an assist in losing him," Denis said.

"I won't."

"It's okay to ask for help," his partner reminded him.

"Yeah." He tapped his earpiece to mute it and continued driving toward the freeway, noticing that Steve was taking the same route. He signaled at Del Taco and pulled in. Steve just kept driving as Aaron got in the drive-through lane. His throat still ached from that punch he took. He ordered a Coke, which was sweeter in the US than in the UK, and then took his time leaving the parking lot. He headed back toward the freeway, looking for Steve's vehicle and saw it waiting in the McDonald's parking lot.

The guy was definitely up to something. But what?

Aaron drove past him, but when he pulled up at the traffic light, he saw Steve move into traffic behind him.

Great.

The light changed and he started to move again. He tapped his mic to unmute it. "I might have to go back to the apartment so my cover won't be blown."

"Go ahead. I'll see you soon."

Aaron got on the freeway, heading back toward his apartment in the Echo Lake area of Los Angeles. Steve took off as soon as they were on the freeway, and Aaron stayed in the slow lane, doing the speed limit. The gangster slowed down when Aaron got to his exit, no doubt making sure he got off where he'd said he was going. Once back at his place, he showered and changed before heading back to the police station to meet up with Denis.

It was late afternoon by the time he arrived, and he parked his van a few blocks away, walking the rest. He liked to have some distance between his cover role and his real-life one. It was easy to let the lines blur unless he kept them carefully drawn. When he got closer, he noticed another black Dodge Charger and glanced at the plates. Same one as earlier.

Lee was at the station.

Which really didn't concern him, but he stepped up his pace a little, hoping for a glimpse of the lady he couldn't seem to stop thinking about.

Chapter Four

Detective Monroe waved her over after she and Luna had given their statements. Luna had to leave to get back to Nick—they were hosting an event that night at Madness, the club her husband owned. Lee hugged her friend goodbye before heading to speak to Monroe. Given the workload she knew he had, she understood that the detective couldn't prioritize looking for Isabell over other cases that involved an obvious crime. After all, although the teenager was missing from school, there was no body and no one other than her teacher had reported her gone.

"Thanks for talking to me."

"No problem. Miller called over yesterday to ask me to speak to you about the Montez girl. We really don't have much to go on. The break-in at her last known address is something, but it doesn't mean a crime was committed. The parents work for WINgate, who has them listed for a month-long vacation. The B&E at their place might just have been opportunity."

She got that. "Or could the family have split because they owed someone money?"

"We don't know yet. I don't like how clean the girl's room was, but I don't know who else was living there. I have a deputy talking to the neighbors. But that neighborhood, no one notices anything, you know?" Monroe said.

She got it. She'd grown up in a suburb just like it. Everyone kept their heads down and minded their own business. "Did you find anything I could use to try to locate Isabell?"

He crossed his arms over his chest. "Not really. We dusted for prints at the house and I'm expediting reaching the next of kin to try to find out where the family is."

"That's good. So at least you'll know who was living there," Lee said. "And speaking of Isabell's relatives…" She pulled out her phone and opened a document. "I have her parents' names and have also compiled a list of Isabell's extended family. There's a maternal aunt in Cleveland and a cousin in Dallas. Want a copy?"

"Sure," he said, giving her his email address, and she forwarded the report to him. "Miller mentioned you were good with computers and tech. I'd say to focus your search there. If you find anything, bring it to me," Monroe said.

"Will do. And you'll do the same?"

He nodded tersely. "Oh, and one more thing…"

"Yeah?" she asked.

"I don't want to see you at another crime scene."

She took that as her signal to leave and got to her feet, heading down to give her fingerprints so they'd have them in case hers showed up at the crime scene. Which they shouldn't, since she'd been careful when she'd been in the house.

"Lee."

Turning, she came face-to-face with Aaron Quentin. Despite herself, she couldn't help the way her pulse sped up. "Wh-what are you doing here?"

"Paperwork," he said. "Thought I saw you on the freeway earlier."

"Did you?"

He shook his head. "Lame. I have no game with you."

She laughed at the way he said that. "Because you try too hard."

"Is that it?" he asked, that British accent of his teasing her senses.

"Yes. Just chill out and stop trying to be a stud."

"I *am* a stud."

He was. No denying that Aaron was in top shape. Even

though he was dressed in a T-shirt and jeans, the cotton fabric, while not tight, hugged his biceps. His jeans were the same, formfitting against thighs that were the shape of tree trunks. His eyes were blue and always seemed to be sparking with mischief. She let her gaze slide down his face to the square jaw that was clean-shaven and then she noticed a bruise forming at his throat.

"You okay?"

"Yeah. Rough day at the office."

"At least you didn't get arrested…or did you?" she asked, referencing when he'd called his brother for an assist after landing in jail in Miami.

"Not yet." He winked. "Actually, I was *making* an arrest."

"So you're not undercover right now?"

"I am. But I still have to do other parts of my job," he said. "It's not all working my way up the Cachorros."

"Maybe you can tell me about it sometime…"

"Yeah?" he asked, putting his arm on the wall behind her head and leaning in. "I'll tell you anything you want to know."

She smiled again. "Keep Mr. Hey Baby in check. I like you better that way."

"I'm just hearing you like me. So what are you doing here?"

"Tracking down a missing girl. Her last known address had a break-in, and Luna and I discovered it and called it in."

His eyes gleamed with interest. "Over in the Boyle Heights neighborhood?"

"Yeah, how'd you know?"

"Clocked you on the freeway heading that way and this police station is the nearest. You find the girl?"

"No, just a roughed-up house. No evidence of blood or a fight, and signs point to the girl leaving before the house had been tossed," Lee answered.

"That's a tough neighborhood. You think she ran away?" Aaron asked.

"No clue. Her teacher reported her missing, and her folks are gone, too, on an extended vacation…"

"Seems pretty straightforward. Like they cut bait and ran," Aaron said.

It did. She knew that the evidence was all pointing to that

exact scenario, but that didn't sit right with Lee. Was she looking too hard for a crime that wasn't there? This was precisely
why she usually stayed at Price Tower working the tech end of
investigations.

But she couldn't rule out something dangerous happening to
Isabell. Her gut, which had never let her down before, was telling her there was more here than she'd seen. She headed down
to give her fingerprints.

When she got to her car, Aaron was leaning against the hood,
waiting for her. She shook her head. *This man.* In Miami, when
she'd first met him, they'd drank too much tequila and she'd
contemplated making a bad decision. But in the end, the fact
that he was the brother of a man she considered a brother…
Well, she'd gone to bed alone.

But now he was in LA, hanging around and looking just like
the distraction that she really needed.

"Can I help you?"

"Yeah. I need some tech help," he said.

Oh. She tried to tamp down her disappointment. Well, she
had told him repeatedly that she wasn't interested in anything
with him, so why should she feel let down now? But then again,
he'd been flirting hard in the station and she had a little bit
hoped… What? That he was going to ignore her earlier rebuffs?
That was outdated early 2000s thinking and that twenty-year-
old had matured.

Or so she'd thought.

"No problem. Want to follow me back to Price Tower?"

"Actually, I was hoping you could come to my apartment,"
he told her.

His apartment… It was for work, she reminded herself. But
what did it say about her that immediately her body went hot
and she was thinking about doing something reckless with him?
Glancing down at her watch, she had an hour or so she could
kill. "I can do that. What kind of problem is it?"

"I'll tell you when we're at my place. It's my cover apartment,
so probably best if you look like someone I picked up when we
get there," he said. "That work for you?"

"What do you have in mind?"

His piercing blue eyes locked on hers. "Just hand-holding, maybe a kiss…"

"Maybe?"

"You said no in Miami," he reminded her gruffly.

"I did. But maybe I've changed my mind," she demurred. Seeing that sad bedroom left behind by Isabell reminded her of where she'd come from and the glorious life she'd promised herself. Somehow during her twenties and thirties, work had taken over and she was still that same lonesome girl, just in a better living situation and with a better family, albeit a found one, around her.

"Which is it? Maybe? Or yes, you have?" he asked, straightening from leaning against the hood of her car to take one step toward her.

Though that one move didn't really lessen the gap between them, she knew it was his way of showing her he was interested too. Like she hadn't picked that up from all the times he'd tried his cheesy lines on her.

Biting her lip, she took a step toward *him*, wishing she'd picked up some sort of decent interpersonal skills over the course of her life that would help her seem seductive and, well, not like herself. "Yes."

He lifted both eyebrows and crossed his arms over his chest, smiling down at her. "Good. Very good."

Rolling her eyes, she wondered if this impulse was going to bite her in the butt, but she wasn't interested in changing her mind. It had been a long day…actually, a long year…maybe even decade. And she was tired of always staying safe.

But it wasn't physical danger she kept herself safe from, it was the internal injuries. Like caring too much for the wrong person, getting too involved in a case, those kinds of things that had made Lee start to feel like she was all alone in the world. And not really, truly engaged in anything.

Aaron closed the rest of the distance between them, and put his hand on her waist, leaning closer to her. "So kissing…?"

"Yes."

Before she could second-guess herself, he was lowering his

head toward hers, blocking out the afternoon sun. The warmth of his breath brushed over her lips before the gentle touch of his mouth against hers. Her heart stuttered in her chest and she stood there, realizing how out of her depth she was with Aaron.

But then she shook herself. She wasn't. He was just a guy. A hot, *British* guy she wanted and had decided she was going to have. She shoved the scared teenager she'd been back into the box where she usually stayed.

Grabbing his shoulders, she shifted closer and then pushed her hand into the hair at the back of his head as she deepened the kiss. His mouth opened against hers, his tongue brushing against hers.

He tasted of coffee and mints…and something else. Something that she was pretty sure was just Aaron. His hands slid down her hips as he pulled her more fully against him. She felt his erection growing against her lower belly.

He lifted his head and their eyes met. She wasn't sure what he was looking for in her expression, but it was hard to hide the fact that she wanted him. That this lust had sprung between them and caught them both off guard.

It would be easy to say it was the frustration of the day or anything else, but the truth was she liked Aaron. She liked his big, hot, muscly body, his devilish smile, his eyes, which always looked like he was up to no good… And when that intense blue gaze was laser-focused on *her*, like it was right now…?

She was a goner.

Aaron reached out and stroked a hand through her hair. "I don't think this is going to be a hard charade to pull off."

"Me either. But I'm not playing a part," she whispered, because honesty was one thing she never compromised on.

"Yeah?" he asked.

She shook her head.

"I'm deep undercover, Lee," he said in a low, gravelly voice.

"I know. So we'll just keep it casual for now. I can't… I'm not good at keeping real life and a pretend scenario separate."

"Fair enough. Want me to get someone else to help with the tech? Xander's pretty good."

She didn't. She completely understood where Aaron was

coming from and the fact that he'd told her straight-up instead of just going along with what she wanted meant a lot. "He'll just come and ask me."

Aaron laughed. "He's been helping me out when I need it, or was it you?"

"Me. He brings your stuff to me and I tell him how to do it."

"That dog."

"Yup. So I'll meet you at your apartment later?"

He nodded and with one final look her way, turned and went to his van.

Lee needed time to think. Some people would head to the beach, but for her it was always a walk around the Echo Park neighborhood in East-Central LA. There was a nice path around Silver Lake and one of her favorite taco trucks tended to park there. The neighborhood had become trendier in the last few years, but as far as she was concerned, it would always be the place that Grandpa had taken her for Swan Boat rides on Sunday mornings.

That girl she'd been… It was hard not to confuse Isabell with that youngster. Lee acknowledged she was seeing an abusive home for Isabell simply because that had been the reason Lee had wanted to run away. However, she'd never done it.

Hadn't had the courage. Lee had tried to improve the situation by going to the cops and filing a report. Calling them when her dad hit her hard enough to bruise her ribs and asking to be moved to a halfway house. Her grandpa had stepped in and taken her to live with him.

Lee had always relied on herself but she'd never wanted to be alone. She still didn't. Her family at Price Security were tight and everything she did was to keep them all safe.

It was the one thing she hadn't been able to do for her best friend, Hannah.

One of the few regrets she carried with herself.

Looking through the clues around Isabell's disappearance, it struck her that there weren't many at all. She got why the cops had put the case in the same category as other missing kids.

There wasn't anything remarkable about it. Sad as that was to think and say, finding Isabell wasn't going to be easy.

It was even harder now that her parents weren't at their place. And had gone missing just like their daughter. Who were they? she wondered. Had they been like her parents and didn't give a shit about their daughter?

Or was it more complicated than that? Life was busy for everyone. It was part of the reason why Lee had never allowed herself to settle into a permanent relationship with anyone. It was hard to keep a bond strong with herself and anyone who didn't work for Price. That was where her focus always was.

Aaron was sort of an extension of her affection for Xander. Yeah, right. There was so much heat when she looked or thought about him that she'd made the decision to steer clear of him back in Miami.

Of course that was much easier when he was acting like he was *People*'s Sexiest Man Alive. Hell, he was too sexy for *People*. The last few years their selection had just been kind of meh.

Shaking her head, she got out of her car, tipping her head back to enjoy the Southern California sunshine. People were going about their regular lives, walking dogs, herding kids and going for runs. It should have made her feel lighter, but it didn't. There was no shaking Isabell Montez from her mind.

That teenager, who should be doing the same thing. Going to high school and hanging out with friends and hating one of her classes. Instead she was…where? Lee wished there was some way she could get in touch with that age group. But it had been years since she'd graduated and none of her friends had kids.

Boyd was the only one she knew with any connection to high school and she wasn't about to go back and talk to him again. Not right now. Seeing him just muddied everything as far as Lee was concerned.

She walked for about thirty minutes, clearing her head. The thing that had always served her was gathering information. That was what she needed to do. She'd start with the photo she'd taken from Isabell's desk; once she identified where it was taken then she'd have her next step.

Pulling out her phone, she looked down at the yearbook photo

of the brown-haired girl with her face slightly rounded, probably still from baby fat, and those guileless eyes. What had
happened to change her look into the girl in the instant photo?

That was what Lee had to unravel.

Her phone rang. Glancing at the screen, she saw it was Xander.

"What's up, X?"

"Aaron said you were helping him out. Thanks for that,"
Xander said in his slightly aristocratic British accent. He was
a big guy who was normally pretty quiet. Wickedly smart and
lethally strong, he was one of the best assets on their team.

"No problem. I'm giving him the family discount."

"Good. I owe you."

"You don't owe me. Aaron does," she retorted.

"Ha. You might be right."

Xander hung up as Lee got back in her car. Assisting Aaron
wasn't really a big deal. Kissing him… That was something else
entirely. Friend-zoning him was a little bit for her own sanity
since he was so hot and so aware of his charm. But also she
didn't want to make things awkward between her and Xander.

The people at Price Security meant more to her than anything
else. So if things got too heated or complicated with Aaron,
well, that wasn't a risk she was willing to take. No matter how
much she wanted to know what his mouth felt like on the rest
of her body.

The traffic was intense, giving her more time to think before she headed toward Aaron's apartment to finish setting up
the tech he needed her help with. The distraction from thinking about Isabell would be good. Lee always did better when
she turned her attention in another direction and gave her sub-
conscious time to work on the problem.

Chapter Five

Sitting at the dining table in his apartment, Aaron was determined to keep things professional with Lee. But the smell of her perfume, the air around them and each breath he took reminded him of how enticing this woman was.

She glanced over at him. "Is this making sense? Van constantly reminds me to keep it simple."

"Sort of," he said. Realizing he had to start paying attention to what she was saying instead of how her fingers looked moving on the keys. Her voice was sort of husky for a woman, but when she talked it was all business, which was totally turning him on.

He needed to get his body under control, because as he'd told her earlier, there was no place for this kind of relationship in his life at the moment. He had to continue doing his job investigating the Chacals as well as continuing his infiltration with the Cachorros. His partner and his boss were counting on him being the Aaron they knew. The guy who got his man and finished jobs.

"What's confusing?" she asked, turning to him.

You. You are confusing. "Why did you change your mind outside the police station? For months, whenever I run into you, you've been shutting me down."

She shrugged and he realized that she was hiding something too. Which wasn't a surprise. Everyone hid something. *Everyone.*

"I wish I could point to a reason and say it, but it was just sunny and you looked hot as usual and for once I just wanted to be the woman who said yes and took what she wanted."

He got that. He wanted her to take him. If they surrendered to their attraction, he'd give her everything he had. But it would have to end at being a hookup. Which wasn't wise for the two of them because she was tight with his brother, and unless Aaron wanted to walk away from Xander again, he was going to be bumping into Lee for the rest of his life.

"I'm undercover," he reminded her.

"I know. I did some undercover work when I was with the government. I get where you are coming from. It's hard to have a real life when the assignment has to be the priority." She sighed. "Just wish I didn't feel like this."

"Me too. But I've had a bit of time to think things over, and while I'm not saying no to exploring whatever this is between us, it's complicated."

"I get it. I don't want to be responsible for anything happening in your case," she said. "So…maybe we should just focus on business?" She pointed toward the screen. "What was confusing about what I showed you?"

"I'm not sure… I was distracted," he admitted gruffly. "Show me again please. I'll pay attention."

She looked like she was going to say something else but just bit her lower lip and then turned back to his laptop. He groaned to himself, trying not to focus on her mouth. "These are the cell towers that operate around the city, and the tracker that your partner put on Steve's car will ping it as he drives around. So right now, it is hitting one here."

Aaron stood up and leaned over her shoulder, putting his hand on the table next to the laptop. Looked like Steve was still in LA, despite the fact that he'd been heading south on the 5 the last time Aaron had seen him. "Can you get an exact location?"

"The nearest we can get is the tower and then we'd have to have a visual. But it seems like he's in this area. You could do a drive-by," she suggested.

"Good idea. Okay, so when he moves is there a way I can get a notification?" Aaron asked. Taking out his phone, he planned to text Denis and give him the area that Lee had identified. It was smack in the center of a neutral zone where neither of the gangs had sole territory.

Lee's fingers were moving on the keyboard and she glanced over at him. "Want the texts to go to you?"

"Can you send them to me and my partner?"

"Sure. Just give me the numbers. What do you want the notification to say?"

"Get fifty percent off pizzas if you order by 5:00 p.m.," he said. He and Denis used variations of food offers when they needed to get in touch with each other. "Will it send a location too?"

"It can, but given that you probably don't want to give too much away, I can make it so you log on to this site and get the update," she told him.

"Thanks, that works," Aaron said, walking over to the kitchen to call Denis and update his partner.

When he finished, he saw that Lee was gathering up her stuff and getting ready to go. Which he knew was for the best. She'd helped him, she turned him on and they'd both decided now wasn't the right time.

For the first time ever, he regretted his job. He regretted that he'd made the choice to be a loner. He regretted that he was going to miss out on knowing her better. Because he was smart enough to know that Lee wasn't going to ever open herself up to him like this again.

"I guess this is goodbye."

"Yeah. But if you need help with this Steve guy let me know. I can keep an eye on him from the tower for you as well."

"Nah, I know you're busy," he said, plus it would be easier for him if he limited his contact with her. After the accident that had paralyzed his older brother, Aaron had vowed to never hurt anyone again.

It hadn't been an easy vow to keep and he'd done a good job at trying to destroy himself before he finally found the strength to acknowledge what he'd done and forgive himself. But today was the first time when he was almost tempted to ignore it.

To pretend he could have Lee and keep her safe. Physically, he knew he could, but emotionally…that was a different story. For him and for her.

She seemed to get him like no one else ever had and that scared him.

Aaron Quentin, who prided himself on being the biggest, baddest mofo in the room, was scared of what Lee could make him feel.

"How's it going?" Van asked in that gravelly voice of his when he walked into Lee's office later that afternoon.

"With the missing girl?"

"Yeah," he said as he turned a chair around at the conference table and sat down.

"Dead ends mostly. Her house was tossed, but to me, it looked like she'd cleared out before that happened. Her room was practically empty. Just found these two receipts in a left-behind jacket and this Polaroid," Lee said, tapping a key to open her evidence file so Van could get a look.

Her boss had always been a top investigator when they'd worked together for the government. She needed a second pair of eyes. And Van was the perfect man for the job. She'd taken some photos of the house as well, and she sat back in her chair while he took his time looking through them.

She'd spent the drive back to Price Tower pushing Aaron firmly out of her mind. There was something between them, but the two of them had jobs and being distracted could cost someone their life. That was something she wasn't willing to do.

"I've got a geotag on a club in West Hollywood on Isabell's phone, but Detective Monroe said that the phone was registered to the family, not just the girl. He's not going to investigate further unless they find a body or the family so he can question them."

"Well, time is money and the police force is stretched thin." Van scrutinized the items in the folder. "This receipt looks like it's from a food truck... Let me look around. It's familiar, so I might have grabbed lunch at it."

"Thanks. The instant photo and this one from her cloud account appear to have been taken in the same place. But she looks drastically different in both," Lee told him.

Van leaned in and switched between the two photos that Lee had directed him to. As he clicked between them, Lee watched Isabell's face go from a girl's to a woman's. It made her wonder if the high schooler had made a choice to leave and make her own way in the world. She'd be a runaway, but this other life might be better than what she had at home.

Lee was pretty sure it must be given that the girl had left and her parents hadn't reported her missing.

"Yeah, I think they are the same. You know where this place is?" Van asked.

"The geotag is that club I mentioned. Mistral's. Might go and check it out," she said.

"Good idea. If you find something and need backup, holler. I'm going to talk to a potential client tonight. Do you think you'd be able to do a two-week gig?" Van asked.

"Yeah. This is a side investigation," she said.

"But it's important too. I've been thinking of bringing on some more staff," Van added.

"I don't think we need it," she said with a shrug. But she suspected that was just her not wanting the team to change.

"Haven't made up my mind yet. We do have your new security team for the corporate client, which is a good revenue stream," her boss reminded her.

It was his subtle way of pointing out that things were already in flux. New team members would be added eventually. Lee knew from the past that waiting wasn't going to make it any easier for her to adjust to having unfamiliar people around. "I'm just being a hermit, I guess."

Van laughed. "But on the other hand, we got a good thing here."

"We do. But it's already changing. X is splitting his time between work and Florida to be with Obie. Luna's living at Nick's place."

"Yeah, but at least she's close and so is Kenji," he said. "Our profile is growing and I'm not sure I want to take on bigger clients, but there are some jobs I'm not sure I want to pass up either. I need your buy-in. We started this together."

They *had* started it together. Both of them pissed at their government bosses, who'd missed the fact that Cate O'Dell had been a double agent, and tired of seeing innocent people paying for big decisions that left collateral damage.

"We did, but you've always been the leader," Lee pointed out.

"And you the behind-the-scenes wizard who makes everything happen," Van said.

"Sometimes. You needed systems and that's where I shine. If we add more team members, would you bring them to the tower?" she asked. "We might need a second location."

"Or just leave that out of the employment contract," Van suggested. "I'm not sure what I'll find. We won't be hiring just *anyone*. It's important to get people who think like we do."

"I agree." For a moment, Aaron's face drifted through her mind. He was like-minded but not suited for bodyguard work. Maybe that was why she'd been afraid to take a chance on him that night in Miami. She knew that he was too much like her. Today had confirmed it.

They were both always going to put others first. Put *the job* first. They had to. She couldn't give in to lust or love or anything that would put innocent lives in jeopardy.

And she knew she was an all-or-nothing kind of woman. So when Aaron had told her he was the same, it hadn't really been a surprise. He was sort of the masculine version of herself. She knew better than anyone what that cost.

The fact that Mistral's was in West Hollywood wasn't surprising for Lee. She'd wanted to come during the day to scope the place out but hadn't been able to get free. And as she'd told Van earlier, this was her side gig. He had been contacted by a big corporate client who was thinking of hiring them for their internal security. Which was basically a new thing that Van was trying out, thanks to her suggestion.

She and Xander had worked together to write a proposal for

a passive security system that would be monitored by a program that Lee had written. If they got this gig, Van would in fact have to follow through on his plan to hire a small staff that would work out of the client's building and report to her. From the moment they'd started Price Security, Lee hadn't exactly been in her element. She wasn't a bodyguard, though she was a sharpshooter, and was trained in hand-to-hand combat.

She knew that Van was doing this for her, to give her a chance to shine the way she'd helped him in the beginning, and she truly appreciated it. He'd even had her do the presentation, which she hadn't really liked, but everyone said she'd done good.

Getting changed back into her jeans and T-shirt with a flannel shirt over it had been the first thing she'd done after the meeting. And then, of course, she'd made sure the team were all set before heading out.

Once she left Wilshire and drove toward Mistral's, she wondered if she should have brought backup. But she was just going to ask a few questions to try to find the spot that Isabell had been in when she'd taken her selfie. Lee figured she'd be good.

She pulled into the parking lot and noticed that the club was at the end of a strip mall and most of the other shop fronts were dark and closed for the night. It was just about seven, so that made sense. She parked her car and, looking around, noticed that the club was a bit more upmarket than she'd expected.

Sitting in her car, she waited. She took a few pictures with the camera on her phone. A few minutes later, she got out and walked up to the club. It wasn't exactly empty but it wasn't crowded either. However, she knew she was early for the club crowd, and as she peered inside through the window, she didn't see any teenagers inside.

Or what *appeared* to be teenagers. Detective Miller had sent over the report that the officer had filed, and Mistral's had been ruled out as a location because they hadn't been able to verify that Isabell had been the sole user of her phone.

But in any case, Lee was here to see if the selfie had been taken in the club. To be accurate, she started at the far end of the mall, checking out the interiors of the shops, which wasn't too difficult as most had security lights on. She moved down the retail stores, getting to a coffee shop that was still open. She went in and the barista behind the counter informed her they were closed.

"No problem. Can I use the bathroom?"

"Okay," the barista said in an annoyed tone. "Just make it quick."

Lee made her way toward the facilities at the back and looked at Isabell's photo again. She was still trying to remotely crack the phone. Maybe then she'd be able to find other photos and where they were taken. She wanted to find something in the same time frame as the one the girl had posted.

The walls in the coffee shop didn't match the background, so she crossed this place off the list. She thanked the barista as she made her way out.

Her gut had said it was the nightclub, and now that was the only location left. Tucking her phone into her pocket, she strode back toward Mistral's. They didn't open until nine and Lee rapped on the door, which was opened by a bouncer.

"Sorry. Um… I'm looking for a job," she said.

He eyed her up and down. "Not sure you're qualified."

"Trust me, I am," she assured him.

"Flo is the one hiring. Go around the back. She might not let you in," the bouncer warned.

Of course, since in her casual T-shirt and jeans, she obviously didn't look like the ideal candidate. Lee debated leaving and coming back later, dressed for the club. But figured she'd give this a go first.

She walked around the side and immediately noticed that the brick wall in the background of Isabell's photo was very similar to the bricks here. She pulled her phone out and took a quick photo, not stopping as she kept going to the back door.

It opened outward toward her as she stepped up to it, knocking her back, and a strong hand grabbed her arm, steadying her. She glanced up into ice-blue eyes, her own going wide as she recognized Aaron.

He turned, pressing her between the building and his hard, muscular body. "What the hell are you doing here?"

"I'm here for information," she hissed.

"Fuck. I'm new here. You need to go."

Lee didn't have time to come up with a plan. She needed to get inside and didn't want to screw things up for Aaron. But she wasn't leaving. Since he was pressed against her, she just cupped his butt and said loudly, "You're the one who called me, babe."

"Quinn, this your chick?" someone asked.

He looked at her and could almost see him thinking things through.

"Yeah," she said, turning and tucking herself against his side.

Lee wasn't sure what being Aaron's chick involved or how she was going to get out of this, but for right now, it seemed to be her best way into the club.

Aaron tipped her head back up toward his and looked down hard into her eyes. She guessed this wasn't what he needed at the moment, but she wasn't going to let the chance to find Isabell slip away.

Chapter Six

Well, hell. That was all that Aaron was thinking as he dragged Lee into the club and into the office he'd just been given.

Steve left them alone, but Aaron hadn't swept the office yet, so he didn't know if it was safe. He wasn't happy with Lee. She was screwing up his job and wasn't she the computer geek? She should be at Price Tower and not at Mistral's, where he was on the trail of a drug kingpin.

Minor point, but she wasn't hot enough to be his undercover chick. Normally if he was paired with a partner undercover, it was a woman who had all eyes on her. Lee wasn't that. Sure, she was hot as hell and he hadn't been able to stop thinking about that kiss she'd dropped on him that had left him hard and wanting, but she wore jeans and a tee, neither were formfitting, and that flannel she threw on made her look like a biker babe from the '90s.

She didn't seem too happy with him either, but tough. He wasn't about to let her dictate whatever the hell this was.

Wait… Was Xander okay? Was she here because something had happened to his brother?

"I told you I'd see you at home," he growled as soon as they were in the nondescript office at the top of the stairs, over the bar. There was some music playing that could be heard through the floor, but it wasn't loud enough to mask their voices.

"Yeah, well, something came up that couldn't wait," she said carefully. Then mouthed, "I'm sorry."

"Is X okay?" he asked. He and his younger brother had just started talking again and the last thing Aaron wanted was for anything to happen to him.

"What? Yeah, he's fine. Sorry, it's, um, something else."

Which told him shit. "This *something else* couldn't wait? Jako wants me to impress these guys," Aaron said. Not that he expected she'd know who Jako was.

She bit her lower lip and nodded her head.

"I'll get you some other clothes if you're staying. I really have to prove myself here."

He pulled her close to him, dropping his head to whisper in her ear. "What are you doing here?"

"I'm looking for a girl who disappeared," she whispered back, wrapping her arms around his shoulders and shifting her body closer to his. "I'm guessing we're not alone."

He couldn't help but notice that Lee fit into his frame perfectly, her head at the same level as his shoulder. "I haven't had a chance to confirm."

"Okay. Sorry for this. Didn't know you'd be here. Could I look around and see if my girl was here?" she asked.

"No. Can't risk it," he said.

The door to the office opened and Steve walked in with another man. He was the same height as Aaron but brawnier, and it was hard to tell if it was muscle or girth. Cocking his head to the side, he waited.

"You Quinn?"

Aaron nodded.

"Hector Ramos. I run this district. Who's that?"

Steve stepped forward and spoke before Aaron could. "His old lady. Bouncer said she's looking for work."

Aaron squeezed Lee's waist, hoping she'd get the message to keep her mouth shut. This was a complication he didn't need. Part of his success undercover was keeping things simple and uncomplicated. Nothing about the situation with Lee was simple.

"What do you do?" Ramos asked.

"I tend bar. Sorry for these clothes. I wasn't sure if Quinn was going to be able to get me a gig," she explained.

The other man looked her up and down, frowning with disapproval. "You got anything else to wear?"

"Yeah, of course."

"As long as Quinn is here, you can tend bar," he said.

"Thanks—"

"Quinn and I need to talk, so you go get changed and report to Flo," Ramos told her. "Steve will intro you."

Aaron felt his cover getting more out of his control. His partner wasn't going to be happy to hear about this. But at this point, Lee was now his woman and she was going to be working here.

She turned to Aaron, reached up and pulled his head toward hers. "I'm sorry," she repeated softly.

He was too, because she was stuck until he figured out how to get her out of this. He drew her closer, his hand on her ass, and kissed her hard. She pulled back and then followed Steve out of the office. Aaron crossed his arms over his chest and turned to Ramos.

"Jako mentioned this place needed a firm hand."

"It does. We run two operations out of here and the cops are checking up all the time. We can't afford sloppy management, and I don't do second chances," Ramos informed him. "You have two weeks to get this place in order."

"What's happening in two weeks?"

"That's your deadline, Quinn. Don't disappoint me. I've got two people who will be checking in with you and making drops. You let them know if anyone isn't pulling their weight. Even your woman. Don't let her take you down."

Quinn nodded. "Who are they?"

"Jorge and Diana. They'll stop by tonight to introduce themselves. Jako told you this place is different, right?"

"Yeah. Came straight from San Clemente. I've got some smarter clothes in my van," he said.

"Okay, then go get cleaned up and get ready for opening," Ramos said. "I'm sticking around tonight."

Great. But Aaron just nodded. "Be nice getting to know you."

Ramos just dismissed him. Aaron left the office and went down the stairs to find Lee getting shown the bar area. "Flo?"

"Yes."

"We have to go and get ready for opening. Can you show her the rest later?" he asked.

"Sure thing."

Lee walked to his side in that long, sexy stride of hers. If this entire mission hadn't just gone FUBAR then he might appreciate the way she was blending in. *Might.* But that was something he was going to have to appreciate later.

She followed him out the back and to his van. Once they were inside, she started to talk but he shook his head. "Not until we are out of here."

Instead of driving to the apartment Jako had offered him, he headed to a safe house that the DEA had set up for him. It was a crappy apartment off West Hollywood. Lee stayed quiet, following him up the stairs to the first-floor apartment. Once she was inside and he'd closed the door behind him, he shook his head.

"What the actual hell?"

"Sorry," she said again. But really, at this point, so much of her recon mission had gotten away from her that she had no idea what to do next. "Like I said, I'm looking for a girl."

"And you think she was at Mistral's?"

"Yes. I tracked a photo she posted, but she's underage so… I'm not sure how she got in. Also the cops aren't certain if she shared the phone with someone else in her household, so I need to identify the background and the location to confirm she's been there."

"I really don't want you at the club. I'm just setting myself up with the gang," he said. "We can't take too long to confab. My partner should be here in a minute with a pizza so I can pass him the new setup info."

"How can I help?"

"You have to go back with me. So, what's your size and we'll get you a dress to wear behind the bar," he said.

"Clothes are really that big of a deal?"

"In the club they are. Also I'm sort of a player."

She arched a brow. *"Sort of?"*

He shook his head. "Yeah. Size?"

"Twelve and I have big hips," she said.

"They look okay to me," he said, letting his eyes drift down her body, sending the information to Denis, his partner.

"Is this a Price thing?"

"No, it's a favor for a friend," she said.

"That explains the lack of coordination. Normally you guys are top-notch."

Lee felt that. He was right—she should have made a solid plan. Part of it was she just wanted answers so she could close off the loop with Boyd and stop letting in those memories that he'd stirred up. The other part was that she was feeling the loss of Hannah and it made her want to do all the things she hadn't done for her friend.

"We are. I won't make this worse for you," she promised.

"We'll see. Ramos is going to be watching the club and the employees. So, as it turns out, we're going to have to ride out this couple thing after all. Can you do it?" he asked.

She wasn't entirely confident she could. She had her job at Price and she wasn't exactly great at relationships. "I have to talk to Van."

"Fine. Go ahead and do that. My contact is here."

Aaron left the apartment and Lee sank down on the couch, noticing it was very similar to the one in her apartment. She put her head in her hands for a minute and then took a deep breath.

This was an opportunity to really see what was going on at Mistral's, from the inside. But she was going to have to get clearance from Van. But even if she did, could she pull this off? It had been a long time since she'd been undercover. The last time had been with Van and Cate...and Cate had betrayed them. Van had changed while they'd been undercover, and she knew that it was difficult for anyone, herself included, to keep reality straight when you were living a lie 24-7.

She hit his number and he answered on the first ring.

"Lee," he said, his voice that warm, deep tone that made her smile. "How's my favorite girl?"

"Not sure she's going to be your fave for long. I was doing

some legwork on my missing-girl case and crashed into Aaron's undercover op. I'm now his girlfriend and will be working at the bar..."

She heard the squeak of his chair as he leaned back in it and knew him well enough to know he was probably weighing all the options. "For how long?"

"I don't know. I can still work during the day," she said. "But I'll need my stuff brought to Aaron's apartment. He's talking to his partner. I'm not sure what the op will entail and if they will even clear me to stay."

"So the situation is fluid. You think the Montez girl was at the club?"

"Not one hundred, but everything is pointing that way."

"Keep me posted. I'll support you however I can," Van told her.

"Thanks."

Disconnecting the call, she leaned back against the couch and stared up at the ceiling. Her mind going a million miles a minute. *I can do this*, she kept telling herself. But at what cost?

Aaron walked back in with a duffel bag in one hand and a pizza box in the other. He tossed the box on the table. "Food and small comms devices in there. Clothes in here. What did Van say?"

"To keep him posted. I'm going to have to figure out how to work and do this," she said. "*If* I'm cleared to stay."

"Denis is checking with our boss. I don't think they'll like it, but you have undercover training and were an operative, so they'll probably clear it. However, they'll want me to get you out as quickly as I can."

"That works for me. I just need a quick look around and then we can orchestrate a big fight tonight," she said. "I'll storm out and that will be the end of it."

"Not tonight. I am meeting two lieutenants. I could use your eyes. You might pick up something I miss," he said.

"Okay. You got it. Different gangs?"

"We're not sure. Ramos said different operations, so it might be money houses and drug drops. I can't be certain. I was sent here because I helped clean house at Jako's."

"They are expecting you to do that again?"

"Yes, and I intend to." He crossed his arms over his chest and drilled his blue gaze into hers. "But, before we go any further, there's something you need to know…"

"What's that?"

"I'm not a super-nice guy undercover," he warned.

She shrugged. "I've been underground. I know nothing's real," she said.

"And yet *everything* is. You know that you can't fake anything. Be honest about everything in the lie so it seems more real."

Which wasn't an easy thing to do. She had always prided herself on her practicality, but she knew that being undercover made the world seem very different.

Aaron had to be at his office in the morning to talk to his boss. There was a lot of explaining he needed to do, and he got that. As upset as he was at seeing Lee, he knew the blame was solidly on him for putting her in this situation.

Reuniting with Xander meant that he had more connections in the US than he'd had before. Aaron had been uniquely suited to his undercover role because he was estranged from his family until now. Was he now more of a liability than an asset? He mulled it over as he changed in the living room while Lee used the bedroom to get ready.

Putting on a dress shirt that molded to his muscled arms, and then a pair of dark blue pants and a matching vest, he knew he looked sharp. He took a minute to make sure his hair was curling the way it was meant to and then decided to leave the stubble on his jaw because it made him look just the slightest bit like he was trying too hard.

One of the first things he'd learned about being undercover was that most of the time people saw what they wanted to. If he came off as someone who was willing to do anything to work his way up in the organization, then everyone would treat him that way.

Aaron sat down to put on his shoes. They were dress oxfords that had a knife in the tip of one toe. He'd had them specially made after watching *Kingsman*. He liked the idea of a hidden blade and had used it, well, zero times, but there was also a chance he might get to.

He also had a small flesh-colored device that he put behind his ear, which would record all of his conversations. It was activated by sound, so he couldn't turn it on or off. His clothes were made of the latest-technology cloth and were bulletproof. But his boss had wryly admitted probably more bullet *resistant*, so best not to get shot at.

After bending down to put a small handgun in the ankle holster he wore, he secured the large diamond in his left ear. Then stood as Lee opened the bedroom door and came out.

She wore a tank-style dress made out of the same bulletproof material as his clothes. It hugged her curvy frame, and until this moment, he had no idea how fit she was. Her hips, which she'd warned him were ample, were actually *perfect*, and his palms tingled thinking about grabbing hold of them. In her jeans he hadn't realized how hot she was. Which he really needed to forget because he was working.

It didn't matter that the scoop neck of the dress showed her full breasts off or that her waist was tiny and that all he could think about was sweeping her into his arms and kissing her soundly.

But they were supposed to be acting like an ordinary couple. He had to be able to touch her and not react. And right now that wasn't possible. Maybe he should have gone and gotten laid instead of visiting with his brother before starting this job. Then maybe Lee wouldn't be hitting all of his buttons and making it impossible for him to think about anything other than taking her to bed.

She arched both eyebrows at him. "You look like someone's version of a pimp."

"Ha. I like to dress nice and it's sort of my rep. You look good."

"Thanks. I hate clothes like this because I feel so exposed."

She kept one arm over her waist and he realized how different this was from her normal attire. "We can get you something else."

"No. They'll be expecting me in something like this, and it will make it easier for me to remember this is all pretend."

She had a point. "Speaking of that, you were good earlier with the close touches. If you get in a jam, you come and grab me."

She nodded. He walked over to her, pushing her silky brown hair aside, and put the small gadget, just like his, behind her ear. "This is a listening device. Just speak and backup will raid the place and get you out."

"Won't that set you back?"

"Your safety is more important. We can always rebuild. I'm new to this area so won't be connected to any raids, but you..." He shot her a stern look. "Don't mess around if you feel you're in danger."

"I won't. I didn't bring a weapon because I was just doing recon but—"

"That's fine. I don't want you armed. But once we see the setup, there might be a chance to put one behind the bar. Just in case you need it."

She nodded silently, waiting for him to continue.

"As you know from Ramos, I'm called Quinn. That's it— just one name. I came from London and work in the Hollywood scene. And as for how I rose up the ranks... I saw something that wasn't right in Jako's organization and alerted him to a mole from another gang, which he took care of." He cleared his throat. "They know your first name is Lee. I'd stick with something hard to trace like Smith or Jones for a family name if you're pushed. But normally, that's not an issue."

"Okay. Quinn. Got it." She pursed her lips. "And what about us? How'd I end up as your old lady?"

He didn't miss a beat. "We've been working together since I got to LA. You were tending bar at a club where I was employed, we hooked up and have been a team since."

"Love it." She smirked. "Tomorrow I'll build an online presence for us and get some IDs. Are we staying here?"

"We'll be here at night, but you can go back to Price Tower during the day," he told her. "The situation is fluid until I figure out what's going on at Mistral's and you get what you need for your missing girl."

Chapter Seven

Aaron's partner was going to be nearby, and Lee suspected that Van wasn't too far away either. She'd tapped into the feed that the DEA device had and sent a signal back to her computer at Price Tower. Then she sent a text with the link to Van.

He'd just thumbed-up the message.

Lee was the first to admit that things weren't the best. But whenever she was forced back into her adolescence with Boyd and Hannah, they never were. The past wasn't a place she wanted to be, so she shook the memories off and turned to Aaron, watching the streetlights illuminate his face as he drove.

He and Xander had similar features, but there was something different about Aaron. A rougher edge than Xander had. Probably because of working undercover, she supposed. "In case it comes up, when did you get to LA? And also…where in the UK are you from?"

He gave a sort of nod and she watched as his accent and body language started to change. Watching him shift into Quinn was interesting.

"Six months ago, babe. I am originally from East London but had been living and working in North London—Finchley," he said. "We met my first night here. It was instant connection and you couldn't resist my charm."

She arched one eyebrow at him but realized he couldn't see

her. "You *thought* I couldn't, but you did have charisma, and even though I saw through your practiced moves, I let you buy me a drink at the end of the night."

He turned to look over at her. "I liked that you saw through me, and even though I needed to get myself established, you and I hooked up."

"Am I aware you deal drugs?" she asked.

"All you know is that I do something that involves me moving around and being out of our apartment all day and night. You were working at a different bar… The specifics are up to you," he said.

Lee pulled her smartphone out of her pocket. "Let me set that up in case they check."

She sent a quick text to Nicholas DeVere, billionaire business and nightclub owner and also the husband of her bestie Luna. He was down to have his staff vouch for her. "Done. We met at Madness, and I was working as a bartender there. I left because they banned you."

"Good. That works. I guess they were suspicious of what I was doing," Aaron said.

"Definitely." She shot him a worried look. "I don't want Nick caught up in this," she said.

"Me either," he said as he pulled into a parking spot at the strip mall. "I'm not sure what we're going into. It's nothing I can't handle, but like I said, if you get scared just say the word and the DEA will raid—"

"I'm not going to get scared. You know I've worked undercover before," she said.

"But you got out," he said pointedly.

"I did," she admitted. "It's not my favorite gig, but I want to find this girl. And the cops aren't going to start looking unless they have some evidence that she was somewhere she wasn't supposed to be."

"Fair enough." Abruptly he shifted around, his hand on her face, his eyes more serious than she'd ever seen them. "Stay safe."

"I will. You too," she murmured.

He parked his van off to the side, and after they got out, she pulled the ponytail from her hair and shook her head, feeling the weight of her long hair fall around her shoulders. It was June in LA, so the heat of the day had sort of disappeared, but it wasn't chilly. It had been years since she'd worn heels but that first step shifted something inside of her.

Her hips sort of fell into a different rhythm as she stretched her stride to keep up with Aaron. He stopped and watched her walking, shaking his head and letting out a wolf whistle. He put his hand on her butt and leaned in, kissing her but also whispering against her mouth.

"Last chance to walk away," he said.

She nipped his lower lip. "Stop trying to make me leave."

He straightened and turned, keeping his hand on the small of her back as they approached the club. The bouncer nodded at them as they strode past the queue of people waiting, dropping the rope and letting them in.

Her stomach was a riot of butterflies and as much as she'd reassured Aaron she was ready for this, she knew that she wasn't. She'd been at her desk for more than a decade. Fieldwork required a lot more than just knowledge and nerves. It required her to really reach deep and be someone she hadn't been in a long time.

A woman she wasn't sure she liked but one that she knew she had to be if she was going to find Isabell.

She headed to the bar and Aaron just nodded at her as he headed toward the stairs and whatever it was he was going to do. Flo gave her a welcome look.

"We're slammed, hon. Get to work and I'll show you the rest of the setup when we have a lull."

Lee started taking orders and there was a moment where her memories of Grandpa's place flooded back. He wasn't just her comfort at night when she couldn't sleep. He'd taught her how to tend bar, make drinks and observe people. He'd been the biggest influence on the woman she was today, and she knew she'd done him a disservice by trying to leave all of that behind.

"Do we ID?" she asked, noticing some customers who looked questionable.

"We do early in the night but stop around ten," Flo said.

"Cool."

This was the first chink in the no-minors policy she'd seen. And the time stamp on Isabell's photos had been 11:30 p.m. She tucked that information away and started taking orders and making drinks. Flo handled the register since Lee hadn't been trained, but making drinks was pretty easy.

As the night went on, she noticed a number of customers disappearing down the hall toward the bathroom and then coming back with a different energy. Another tidbit she filed away.

Ramos was still in the office and there were two other dudes with him when Aaron walked in. They didn't have the polish of what he expected from the two people that Ramos had mentioned earlier.

One of them had gang tats around his neck. Aaron hadn't been on the West Coast long enough to ID them, but he was pretty sure he'd seen them in the dossier he'd been given when he landed. The guy also had the word *pain* tattooed on his knuckles.

"Quinn, these two will report to you. Pain and Panic work Mistral's and two more clubs in the area. They'll pick up from you at the beginning of the night and pay out at the end."

"Pain and Panic?"

"Yeah, we liked Hercules as kids and it sort of suits us," Panic said.

Aaron watched as a safe built into one wall was opened and the men were given their take for the night. Both of them left a few minutes later and the safe was closed. Ramos gave him the combination to the lock and told him that his second-in-command, Jorge, would come by every morning at nine to collect the money.

There were a few more housekeeping things. Mainly that he was the one responsible for the take at Mistral's, and if there were any discrepancies, Aaron would be responsible for sorting them out before Jorge came by for the money.

"Jorge will give you more info on that when he gets here. Diana has been running out of the club for the last three months. Her operation is different and you don't do anything but make sure that the room down the hall is kept locked. Her people move in and out throughout the night, and they do their pickup at noon," Ramos told him.

"What are they picking up?"

"You don't need to know. Flo cleans the room after they leave," Ramos said. "You just make sure that door stays locked and no one goes in or out. Got it?"

"Got it," Aaron replied, spreading his hands out. "Do I stay up here or down on the floor?"

"Normally you'd be downstairs. You're in charge of Mistral's, so keep your eye out for plants and make sure no one makes trouble. We don't need the cops called for drunk and disorderly."

Aaron cracked his knuckles. "I can take care of anything that comes up."

"That's what I like to hear," Ramos said. "Jako speaks highly of you."

Aaron nodded. He wasn't sure how to respond to that. "That's good of him."

"It is. He's also put his neck out for you."

There was a knock at the door before Ramos could say anything else. He called out for them to enter. A man walked in first who was definitely Ramos's second-in-command. He wore the wealth he'd made off the streets like a big, gaudy badge. Thick gold chains wound around his neck and a diamond as big as Aaron's pinky glimmered in his ear. His head was shaved, and when he smiled, he flashed a gold tooth. He greeted Ramos like a brother and then turned to look Aaron over.

From the looks of it, this guy was a fighter and used to being the alpha, something that Aaron always saw as a challenge. It was probably why he'd been so good at working his way up organizations when he was undercover. That Quentin boy in him wasn't going to settle for second place, even when he was undercover.

"Jorge, this is Quinn. He's going to be running Mistral's," Ramos said.

Jorge held his hand out, and when Aaron took it, the other man squeezed hard. He returned the favor, not letting up until

Jorge sort of grunted and let go. "You won't deal with me unless there's a problem."

"Then, I hope that won't happen," Aaron retorted.

"Agreed. Diana here yet?"

"No. She should be," Ramos answered. "Want a drink?"

"Tequila on the rocks," Jorge said.

Ramos looked over at Aaron and he just nodded. "Same."

Retrieving his phone, Ramos called down and placed the order just as the door opened and a woman walked in. She was tall, dressed all in black and had gorgeous red hair that hung around her shoulders. She wore a similar-style dress to the one Lee had put on. But that was where the similarity ended.

This woman carried herself as if she were on a runway. She commanded attention and knew it. All eyes were on her and he had the feeling that was exactly what she wanted.

"Diana."

"Ramos. This the new guy?"

"Quinn," Aaron said, going over to her.

She gave him a shrewd glance, her gaze moving over his body and then coming back to meet his eyes. The way she searched his face, Aaron knew she was probing to see if he was what he said.

He just held that stare and then gave her a slight smile. "Like what you see?"

"A Brit?"

"Yes," he replied, lifting both his eyebrows. "Do you like my accent?"

"It'll do and so will you for now," she said. "Were you told to stay out of my way?"

Aaron nodded. Still not sure what it was she was in charge of. There was a knock at the door and he heard Lee's voice saying "drinks."

Ramos nodded at him to go and get them. He went to open the door and took the tray from her. Making sure she didn't enter the room. He had a feeling that Ramos didn't want her in here, and whatever was going on, it felt tenser than it had when only he and Jorge had been there.

The redhead was beautiful, but there was something dangerous about her. Whereas with Jorge he'd felt that stir of fighting to be alpha, Diana was something else and Aaron wasn't sure what yet.

One thing he knew for sure—he wanted Lee as far away from this as he could get her. Something he was pretty damned sure she wouldn't agree to.

Aaron took the drinks from her, and Lee glanced over his shoulder as she started to turn away, but did a double take when she recognized the woman. She tried to turn back, but Aaron put his hand on her hip and pushed her toward the stairs, stepping back into the room and closing the door firmly.

Lee stopped on the stairs, trying to process what she'd just seen. *Cate O'Dell.* The woman who'd betrayed her and Van on their last mission for the government and nearly cost Van his life and his reputation.

Lee couldn't believe she was here. Maybe she'd been mistaken. She had to be careful because Cate would recognize her. Nerves roiling through her, she hurried back down the stairs. Could she be jumping to a conclusion here? Well, until she saw the woman again, she couldn't be sure.

She went back behind the bar but kept her eye on the stairs. There was only one way down, so Cate would have to take them.

She mixed drinks and joked with customers, but she couldn't concentrate. Cate shouldn't be here. She'd been revealed to be a top lieutenant in an international crime syndicate that Lee knew still operated. But Cate had been rumored to have been killed at the Mexican border nearly four years ago.

"You can take a break if you want," Flo said.

"Thanks."

Lee grabbed her bag and went down the hall toward the bathroom. She took her phone out, pretending to use the camera to check her makeup but really checked out Isabell's selfie. Then Lee lifted her phone and took a photo of herself with the wall behind her.

She'd analyze it later. She turned to walk away from the bathroom since the line wasn't moving and she'd got what she'd come down there for. But she halted when she noticed someone coming down the stairs. It wasn't the red-haired woman but, instead, a big man who noticed her watching him and flashed her a big grin. She smiled back before heading behind the bar. Her heart was racing and she really wasn't sure she could remember anything.

But the familiar sounds and smells of the bar comforted her as they always had. Making Jägerbombs for a group of college-age kids was what she needed to start feeling normal again.

She could almost convince herself that she'd imagined Cate. That was probably the case. She forced herself to concentrate on tending bar and not let her anxiety get the better of her.

She was pouring shots of tequila for a group a little while later when she noticed movement out of the corner of her eye. Aaron came down and the woman was behind him. Lee kept her head lowered so that her hair fell forward to block her own features but she could still watch.

As the redhead said something to Aaron, Lee got a good look at her and the blood in her veins went cold.

Cate O'Dell was definitely alive.

"Whoa, we don't overpour!" Flo reprimanded.

"Sorry." Lee lifted the bottle and then took a deep breath. "I'll pay for that."

"You will. Don't let it happen again."

Hands shaking, she put the bottle back on the shelf and then turned, but Cate was gone. Aaron was working the club, moving through the customers, and Lee turned to face the rear of the bar. What was she going to do?

Van was wrecked after Cate had betrayed them. Like, broken in a way she'd never seen him before. Which meant she wasn't going to be able to take this back to the team. She was going to have to handle this herself.

Immediately she started to concoct a plan to distance herself from Price until she could take Cate down. Get that traitor locked up where she couldn't hurt Van again.

Because that woman had been Van's Achilles' heel. The one weakness in a man who seemingly had none.

Fitting that her boss's weakness should be in play at the same time that hers was. She was here trying to make up for losing

Hannah, on a mission to find and save Isabell for Boyd, who had also lost Hannah.

It wasn't going to bring their friend back, or make either of them feel better, but they both had to keep doing this. Had to keep trying to watch out for the innocent. Now she had a second goal.

Keep Van safe.

He'd rebuilt his life and his career with Price Security. He was respected again and Lee knew that her friend was stronger because of everything he'd survived. Lee had always believed she was too, but there was a part of her that wondered if she truly was.

Her body's reaction to seeing Cate told her there was still unresolved issues from the past. She might like to say she was a no-regrets kind of woman but deep down she knew the truth.

She *had* regrets.

Trusting Cate, letting her in and believing that she could have a genuine friendship with someone while undercover had been a mistake. She'd missed things she should have seen because she'd started to believe the lie they were living.

It was doubly important she didn't do that this time around. Didn't allow herself to see Aaron as anything other than a coworker. No matter how powerfully drawn they were to one another or how much she saw the humor under his flirty facade. She had to keep her guard up. She had to remember that Aaron was simply playing a role.

That what they were feeling wasn't *real*.

And besides…she had cast herself into his undercover mission. He had made it clear that he didn't want her there and he'd do what he had to in order to shut down the drug operation running out of this club.

He wasn't her friend and he wasn't someone she could lean on. Even if she wanted to.

Bottom line? She was in this on her own. Finding Isabell was still her main focus, but now bringing down Cate and ensuring that Van never found out she was alive was her second.

Chapter Eight

Lee was pissed at herself for getting distracted by this bomb-shell over Cate O'Dell. Aaron was on the floor, and she thought she'd seen Denis a few minutes ago but he looked more like a party dude than he had earlier in the day.

Flo was watching her, so Lee knew she needed to get her shit together. Cate wasn't a bit player. Whatever was going on in Mistral's...if she was here, then this was big. Her mind was racing as she made a tray of shots to take to the VIP booth in the back.

Was Van in danger? Was *she*? Why was Cate back in LA after having been reported deceased? Lee really hated this role she'd been forced into, because she wanted to be at her computer. Fingers moving over the keyboard so she could confirm once and for all that the woman she'd glimpsed was from Lee's own past and not just another ghost who was dogging her.

Hannah's ghost had been there since the moment she'd taken that damned meeting with Boyd. The past had been stirred up and nothing she did, no matter how many programs she wrote or algorithms she created, was going to give her an answer that would put it to bed forever.

She knew that.

Aaron glanced over at her and lifted both eyebrows, but she just gave him a tight smile. That was all the reassurance that she could muster for him at the moment. She was dealing with her own stuff and it was taking all she had to stay in the role.

She *had* to. Aaron's life depended on it. If she went after Cate, she could blow his cover. The chances of the other woman recognizing her were high, Lee knew that. She was no closer to finding Isabell and this gamble to try to discover if the club played a part in her disappearance hadn't paid off so far.

Cate was part of La Fortunata crime family. Though no one in the government had been aware of it at the time, she'd hidden her connection during her recruitment and training. She'd been a plant from the beginning. And Lee and Van had teamed up with her, thinking she was like them. Someone who had wanted to change the world.

Idealistic and young, they'd bonded into a tight threesome who worked their way through assignments and racked up praise and wins. Wins had been so important to Lee back in the day. That might have been part of the reason she'd kept quiet when she realized that Van and Cate were having an affair.

Even though every bit of training they'd had warned them not to get involved during undercover work. Except Lee had thought the bosses must be wrong because that relationship had been leading them deeper and deeper into the underbelly of one of the largest crime syndicates in the world.

Until it wasn't.

"Hey, your man's watching you. Take the shots to the VIP room, see what he wants and then get back here," Flo said, breaking into her thoughts.

Lee nodded. Taking the tray, she slowly made her way through the throngs of people dancing and hooking up in the club. It was hot in here and Lee shook her head as she skimmed the crowd. The woman was gone. She wasn't going to see anyone else from her past in this room. She knew that.

But it felt like every instinct she had was overstimulated, and now she wasn't sure of herself. The bouncer for the VIP section let her pass and she took the shots to a table of twenty-somethings that had been splashing cash all night. They had a group of women with them now and Lee searched their faces, looking for Isabell, but the girl wasn't there.

So even if the hallway leading to the bathroom was where she'd been, there was no sign of her at this table. She served the shots and then walked out of the VIP section. But Aaron was waiting for her, taking her wrist and turning her so she was pinned between him and the wall.

His move blocked her from the room and he kept a distance between their bodies. "You okay?" he whispered.

"Yeah. Sorry for trying to get in earlier. I thought the woman looked familiar."

"We can discuss it later." His blue gaze captured hers. "Do I need to get you out?"

"How?"

"Like you said earlier. We orchestrate a big fight and you're gone," he said.

She thought about it. But that would be taking the easy way out. Plus, if her instincts were correct and that woman was in fact Cate, Lee wanted to stay close to her to find out what she was up to. It was just that she'd been reported and confirmed deceased. Lee always trusted her gut, and right now, it was saying that Cate O'Dell was not dead. "I'm good."

Aaron lifted his hand and touched her face. "Would she recognize you?"

"I don't know," she said honestly. She'd changed a lot from the woman she'd been at twenty. Her hair had darkened over the decades and Lee's body had become rounder and more *adult*, for lack of a better word.

Aaron took a deep breath. "We'll let this ride for now."

"Yeah," she said.

"Back to work then," he ordered, turning and smacking her ass as she walked away.

It wasn't a move she would have expected from Aaron, but she guessed this was more *Quinn*. Van always said, when working undercover, to keep the parts of yourself that were at your core but to create another version. Lee had sucked at it back then, and given how she was feeling tonight, was pretty sure that hadn't changed.

What she wanted was to have never come to this club. Then she wouldn't be Aaron's pretend lover, she wouldn't have seen

Cate and…she wouldn't be closer to finding Isabell. Because one of the things that La Fortunata crime syndicate ran was a very lucrative and prolific human trafficking network.

Lee found herself hoping that Isabell was a runaway in a bad situation, and not a victim of La Fortunata, because if they had her, it was going to take more than research and knowledge to set her free.

The rest of the evening was uneventful, and when it was time to go, Lee followed him back to his apartment since she'd left her car at Mistral's earlier. Aaron was worried about the unknowns on this mission. Denis had followed a group out of the club and was still tracking down that lead. Aaron debated telling his partner that Lee might have a connection to the woman. But they hadn't had a debrief yet and so much information was still in flux.

He parked the van and then waited for Lee to get out of her Dodge. The day had been hard for her and it was written all over her lovely face. He had to find a way to get her out of this undercover gig. No matter that she was smart and capable and had worked undercover for the government, this wasn't an easy job and not everyone thrived in it the way Aaron did.

He also was distracted by her. Tonight he should have been working the club and figuring out who the regulars were. He was concerned about the Chacals because it was clear there was something more going on with the rival gang. But then he'd seen Lee looking—*lost* wasn't the right word but something pretty damned close—and he'd had to check on her.

She came up next to him now, putting her arm around his hips as they walked up to his apartment. She smelled of booze and the club and when she dropped her arm as he unlocked the apartment and opened the door, she smacked him on the butt as she walked in.

He had to smile because he'd suspected that she'd be offended by his ass tap earlier. But he hadn't been able to resist. He'd determined to keep a physical distance between them, and while he'd worked undercover with another female operative as a "couple" in the past and kept it strictly platonic, this was Lee and he wanted her.

Badly.

"Guess you're not a fan of that," he quipped as he closed the door behind him.

His apartment had been set up with silent alarms and he knew no one had been in there since they'd left.

"No. But I get that Quinn is."

He grinned. "Yeah. I have to be sort of smarmy as Quinn." He undid his tie and the buttons on his vest. Then, shrugging out of the vest, he hung it on the back of a chair. He leaned against the breakfast bar, watching as Lee took off her shoes before sitting down.

"Catch me up on your investigation. Do you think the girl was at Mistral's?" he asked. Work was the only thing he was going to think about tonight. Not how long her legs looked under that slip dress she wore or how, when she had her hair down, she looked softer, *sexier* than she had before.

"Actually, I think she might have been. Not that that is going to help me find her," Lee said, standing back up and coming over to him with a photo that she'd pulled up on her phone. "This is the one I snapped in the hall leading to the bathroom at the club." She swiped to a second image. "And if you compare it to the brick wall from this Polaroid I found in what I assume to be her bedroom…it's the same." She sighed. "Of course, right now, I know it's circumstantial and not solid."

He took her phone and their fingers brushed, sending a tingle up his arm. Which he ignored, concentrating on the photos on her phone instead.

The background did look similar, and he studied the girl's face but couldn't recall seeing anyone who looked like her tonight. "I'll keep my eye out for her."

"Thanks. What about your investigation? Any new developments?" she asked.

He turned toward her. "We're not done with you yet. The woman. Who is she?"

"Well, first off she's supposed to be dead." Lee sighed. "But before we get into it…do you have anything to drink?"

"A couple of Coronas and water," he said. "Sorry, just got back here."

"Corona would be nice," she said.

"Go sit down and I'll grab them."

She went to the couch, curling her leg underneath and sitting in the corner against the armrest. Rubbing the back of her neck, she rotated her head and then tipped it back for a moment. He opened the beers and walked over, handing her one before sitting down in the armchair across from her.

"So she's *supposed* to be dead...?"

This was knowledge he needed so he could figure out what to do with Lee. Already his mission had changed because of her appearance, and now she might be putting his investigation at risk. He and Denis had done months of work before he'd come out here and gone undercover. That was something he wasn't going to sacrifice.

Not even for her.

"Yeah. So she looks like Cate O'Dell, but she had other names and aliases. She was part of La Fortunata crime syndicate. She used an assumed name to get into the FBI where she worked with myself and Van."

"What happened?"

"She betrayed us. Almost got us killed and then escaped before she could be arrested. I've kept tabs on her but, four years ago, got word she'd been killed in Mexico."

Aaron took a sip of his beer, draining half of it in one long gulp. He couldn't help noticing that Lee just held her bottle, rolling it between her palms and switching it from hand to hand but not drinking.

"And tonight?" he asked. He felt like he was interrogating a subject. Lee was hiding something, giving just bare-bones answers to every question he asked. He couldn't allow secrets in this apartment; this part of the relationship had to be real and honest.

"I don't know. She looks like Cate and everything inside of me is telling me it's her. But I need proof." She blew out a breath. "I want to get back to Price Tower and start searching security footage to confirm that she's still alive," she said.

"Okay. Do that and let me know the minute you find anything." He turned to her and muttered, "But fair warning—we've danced around La Fortunata crime family for years and they are a tough nut to crack. My boss figures they are made up of different smaller groups and so getting to the top is almost impossible," Aaron said.

"I will. If it is in fact Cate... I don't want Van to know. She almost killed him," Lee said.

"If it is, then this entire op just leveled up."

Lee was tired *and* wired and wanted to be at her computer, but she also didn't really want to leave Aaron. He was pulling information from her with an innate skill that she wouldn't have expected from him. Which was definitely her bad. She'd just seen the muscles, those blue eyes and his charming smile and figured he didn't have a subtle bone in his body, but she was starting to see more.

She wondered if his bosses at the DEA were aware of it but figured they had to be. That was probably why they were taking him from the East Coast to the West Coast instead of pulling him out of undercover work. He had been good at changing to fit his environment as well, which should have made her a little bit wary of him. But instead it just intrigued her and made her want him more.

There was so much to unpack on this case, and if she could give the DEA a lead to La Fortunata, then she knew that Aaron would take it. But he might have to burn her to do it. Being a liability to him and creating risk to him and Denis wasn't something Lee wanted, but she knew the possibility was there.

"I'll pull what I have and send it to you," she said. "Okay, your turn now. How's your op?"

"Interesting. I was a bagman in San Clemente, but up here, they have me overseeing drops and just making sure what comes in stays in. Might have something that could help with your missing girl."

She leaned toward him, intrigued. "How so?"

"Well, the redheaded woman, whose name is 'Diana,' has a room that is kept locked and that no one is allowed in except at 10:00 a.m. to clean it. Sounds to me like human trafficking, which I'll be including in my report to my boss. That means that FBI will probably be getting involved."

"And I'll duck out if that's the case but still keep trying to find Isabell. Actually, that makes sense if the woman is Cate. Human trafficking was what we had been investigating when she burned us and left us for dead."

"Do you have a contact still at the agency?"

"I do," she admitted. Not that she wanted to reach out, but she would. "Want me to see what they know?"

"Yes. Are you working tomorrow at Mistral's?" he asked.

"Yeah. The next three nights. Eight to two."

"I'll be at the club in the morning to see who comes in and out," he said. "I'm meant to watch the pickups and make sure nothing goes wrong. Denis will be doing surveillance, so if you want to get a less conspicuous car, maybe you can follow them when they leave."

"Will Diana be back to do the pickup?" Lee asked.

"Doubtful. If it's people then they'll be moved in a van or larger truck. Denis is going to follow the drug money, and until we get in touch with the FBI task force, the human trafficking won't be tracked."

"Yeah, I can do it." She rolled the beer bottle between her hands again. Tonight she'd felt wild and not in control, but tomorrow she would be. Well, later today, since it was nearly 3:00 a.m. She still had work to do back at Price Tower for her day job and this investigation.

"I need to head home if I'm going to get started on this," she said.

"That's fine. Be back here by 8:00 a.m. Can I ask you a personal question?"

"Yes."

"Why ask for the beer?"

"Oh… I thought it would make you more at ease," she said. She didn't drink very often for a number of reasons. It would be easy to point to her addicted parents and use that as an excuse, but the truth was she had drunk a lot in college and hated how out of control it made her feel. It had warped her senses and made it hard to remember what was real.

"I'm always chill," he said.

She lifted both eyebrows. "I thought we had honesty in this room."

He laughed and reached over to take the beer she'd put on the coffee table. He took a swallow and then sort of nodded. "Fair enough. I'm not always chill, but I don't need a drink to put me at ease."

She could see that about him. He was very good at controlling himself and letting others see just what he wanted them to see. There were a few glimpses of the man she'd kissed, the man she'd drunk tequila with in Miami. That man tempted her and would be a welcome break from the tension riding her harder than any case had since Cate O'Dell had betrayed her.

She saw a competent agent in this apartment, someone who was more intelligent than she had guessed, and savvy at knowing how the gang he was infiltrating worked.

"Just seemed like an icebreaker, and in case you haven't noticed it yet, I'm awkward when I'm not behind my keyboard."

"You're not awkward at all," he said. "Or at least not around me."

He leaned forward as he finished her beer and put the bottle back on the table. "I think that's my signal to tell you good night."

She almost asked why, but she knew. The tension between them was palpable. It had been a long day and falling into his arms and into his bed would be a nice stress reliever, if it wouldn't create more problems. She stood up and got her belongings from earlier and just nodded at him.

"Good night."

Chapter Nine

It felt like it had been months since she'd been back at her place, instead of just a day. The map she'd spread out on the table still sat there as well as a note from Van that just had a smiley face on it.

What was she going to do? He'd been in here telling her to make sure the CIA understood that Kenji wasn't available for any work and yet Lee was going to have to make contact with their old boss at the FBI and the human trafficking unit. She rubbed her neck as she stood in the middle of the room. She had a lot to do before 8:00 a.m. and honestly was wrecked. It had been a long day; she was going to try to get a solid four hours before she had to be back to trail the woman who she believed to be Cate.

She checked her computers for results and they still had nothing. This missing girl had opened a breach to her past that Lee didn't want to deal with. There had never been anything tying Hannah's disappearance to human trafficking; in fact, there had been nothing in all these years. Just that one kid who'd seen her get into a gray Jeep Cherokee and that was it. Nothing ever again.

No body, no ransom notes, no sign of the girl that had been her best friend. Her stomach ached at the thought of Isabell Montez having the same fate. And a part of her knew she was reaching when she tried to tie Isabell to human trafficking. But it was an explanation.

She'd meant to go to bed, but instead grabbed a Red Bull from the fridge and pulled up a program that analyzed backgrounds in photos to identify the location. Specifically, those two photos. The one she'd taken tonight and the one of the Polaroid that Isabell had taken were scanned in. She took a sip of the Red Bull and grimaced, not really liking the taste, and realized that it wasn't working anyway.

She was exhausted and no amount of caffeine was going to help.

Yawning, she glanced down at her phone and saw it was already 5:00 a.m. She had a lot of work left to do here and wasn't going to be able to get back to Aaron in two hours, no matter how much she wanted to. Leaning forward, she put her head on her desk. Never had she felt this out of control. Facts and information were power and she always made sure she had them both at her fingertips.

But this time her facts were leading her to the past and she wasn't sure if it was just what she wanted to find or actual truth in the information.

There was a knock on the office door before it opened and Rick Stone walked in. The former DEA agent worked for Price Security. He gave off a big, soft puppy-dog kind of vibe. His thick blond hair was tousled as always and he had on jeans and a button-down. "Hey. Van mentioned you were pulling an all-nighter and might need a hand."

Van once again was two steps ahead of her. Which she appreciated as always. Trusting in others had always been hard for her, but with her friend, he just was there. All the time.

"Are you free today?"

"Until four this afternoon, when I'm working. What do you need?"

Was she really going to send him in her place? She didn't want to but didn't have much choice in the matter. "I'm meant to meet Aaron Quentin and his partner, Denis, to do some surveillance. Could you take it?"

"Sure. What's the situation?"

She quickly filled him in, and since Rick was former DEA, he had contacts in the local office and sent a text getting approval from Denis and Aaron to take her place. She kept the fact that the woman might be someone from her and Van's past quiet.

"If you can get clear photos of all the players, I'd appreciate that," she said.

"I'll do my best. So, how did you stumble into this?" Rick asked. "I thought you were looking for a missing girl."

"I am. She was at that club and I'm trying to prove it so I can get the detective assigned to her case to really start looking for her," Lee explained. "My gut is telling me that she's in danger, but so far, the evidence isn't showing much. Her home was broken into and tossed, but it seemed as if the girl left before that."

"So were they searching for the parents or the girl?" Rick furrowed his brow. "Who brought the trouble to the house?"

Her colleague's questions were good ones that Lee knew she had to find answers to. "Not sure. How do I find out?"

"I'd start with arrests. Do you know the parents' names? Why haven't the cops checked with them?"

"They did. They've been gone, and no one has seen them or their car. It's like they disappeared into thin air," Lee said. Just like Hannah. Except that no one just disappeared without a reason. She had to start compiling a better picture of who Isabell Montez was.

Which meant she was going to have to go back to Boyd and maybe to the high school he taught at to ask about her.

"Well, in that case, start with what you know and go from there."

"Will do. Thanks, Rick, for the advice…and for helping me out," she said. "There's Fanta in the fridge if you want some."

"Appreciate it. I haven't had breakfast yet. I'll grab one and head over to Mistral's. They said the FBI is sending over someone too from human trafficking," he mentioned as he walked to the fridge. "I'll get as much as I can from them."

"I'm going to reach out to my contact at the FBI as well," Lee told him. "If the girl was taken then this changes things."

"It does. And it definitely raises the question about what really happened to the rest of her family," Rick said.

"I'm going to try to narrow that down today. I need a few hours of sleep first though…"

"That's what Van thought. You sleep and do your magic with the computer and I'll report back," Rick said, waving as he strode out the door.

Aaron had talked to Rick Stone in Miami when his brother had helped him out taking down the La Familia Sanchez crime gang. The former DEA agent was quiet but efficient and easy to get along with. In a way, he reminded Aaron of Denis. The two men were sitting in their respective cars on opposite sides of the parking lot, both of them seeming to be asleep in their vehicles.

He walked into the club, his hair still a little wet from the shower. Sleep was always a luxury when he was on an op but Lee was making it even harder to crash. All he'd been able to think about was her in the bed next to him.

It was quiet but smelled of booze as he walked through. He closed the door behind him and heard the voices at the top of the stairs. The money was all in a safe in the office that Ramos had given him. Aaron now had the code, but no one else did.

Last night before he left, he'd stored the bags of money in there. He knew that a shipment of "goods" was meant to arrive after lunch at a location that Aaron hadn't been informed of. And he was pretty sure that Ramos was checking to make sure he wasn't a snitch. Seeing Steve yesterday made Aaron edgy. He didn't know what was going on, and after all the research he and Denis had done before getting here, it seemed there was still a lot they didn't know.

Jorge was waiting at the top of the stairs with another man Aaron didn't recognize. They both straightened from the wall when Aaron walked up.

"Was about to call Ramos."

"Why?" Aaron asked.

"Thought you'd skipped out with the money," Jorge said.

"No. Just not a morning man." Before unlocking the door and going into the office, Aaron gestured toward the other dude. "Who's this?"

"Palmer. Somedays it might just be him or me. We're the only two authorized to make a pickup for Ramos. You don't give the bags to anyone else, got it?" Jorge commanded.

"Yeah," Aaron said, nodding for emphasis. He went to the safe, opening it and taking out the bags that he'd put in there the night before. Jorge and Palmer took them and put them into backpacks before they both left.

Aaron was glad to see them go, and as soon as they were out the door, he signaled Denis that they were on the move. He heard the door to the other room open, then close about two minutes later. He'd been champing at the bit to see what was happening in there but knew that he had to bide his time because Diana looked like she wasn't messing around with her operation. Aaron counted footsteps for about forty-five seconds and guessed there were under ten people walking down the stairs. But definitely more than one. As soon as it was quiet, he went into the hall and picked the lock on the room.

It should be empty, but he wasn't taking any chances, so when he carefully turned the handle, he had his weapon in his right hand as he opened the door quickly and scanned the room. It was vacant and dirty. There was a bucket that had been used as a toilet. It smelled of sweat, blood and urine.

Making him gag. That potent cocktail of rage and revulsion went through him. This wasn't court-admissible evidence, but Aaron saw all he needed in order to know what this room was being used for. It sickened him and made him determined to put an end to the human trafficking going through this club.

Aaron double-checked the hallway before quickly documenting the room with the camera on his phone and then making sure to lock the door as he left. He tucked his weapon in the small of his back as he heard someone coming back up the stairs. He moved to his office doorway, which he'd left opened, and stepped out as a man he didn't recognize come into view.

"Who the hell are you?" the guy barked, pulling a SIG Sauer from his pocket.

"Quinn. Ramos brought me in to run this place," Aaron said smoothly. "And you?"

"Javier. I work for Diana. You stay out of the hallway until I knock on your door from now on. Got it?"

Quinn nodded. "No one mentioned that."

"I just did," Javier snapped. "Ramos knows better than to mess with Diana."

So the redhead was higher up than Ramos in the organization. Aaron just shrugged. "Fine by me."

He wasn't sure if he could get any more information from Javier, but figured it was worth a try. "So Ramos works for her?"

"He works for Perses."

A shot of adrenaline pumped through his veins. *Perses.* The shadowy head of the crime syndicate they were trying to bring down. He hadn't realized how close he'd been to the top when he got moved here to Mistral's. But it made sense. Syndicates with lots of employees were harder to control. But this way you had a few top lieutenants and one big, shadowy boss man.

"Cool," Aaron said, going back into his office and closing the door. He wasn't sure what Javier was returning to the room for, but he hoped to find out soon. Meanwhile, Rick was meant to follow the van, and he texted Denis and Rick to see where each of the men were.

Heading west. Best guess Port of Los Angeles.

Aaron told Rick to keep him posted. Then his phone pinged with a message from Denis indicating that his guy was going toward the coast but more toward Malibu. So both men were moving.

Aaron knew he was done for the morning at Mistral's and left. He thought of going to his office, but he wanted to see what Steve had been up to and he also wanted to check with Lee. She was part of his current mission, but he knew that didn't justify him heading to Price Tower.

He ditched the van he drove as Quinn for a nondescript rental at his apartment, in case Ramos was having him followed, and then headed downtown to his office. He needed to update his boss on the room in the club and figure out how they were going to work that into the current operation.

Lee felt more rested when she woke up at eleven. She showered and packed a small bag to take to the apartment Aaron was using for his cover. Her old boss from the FBI had been in touch and Lee knew it was time to bring Van up to speed. She'd used the app to check in on Aaron's location. His warning for her to stay safe lingered in her mind. His role was much more dangerous and she wished she'd felt confident enough to ask the same of him.

She messaged Brody Hammond back and he told her to come into the field office for an update. Then she went to find Van. He was in his office, which was on the same floor as hers, and she saw him sitting behind his desk reading something on his computer when she walked in.

"Morning," he said.

"Morning. Thanks for sending Rick."

"No problem." He shot her a look. "Hammond just messaged me."

"I'm here to explain," Lee said.

He gestured to the guest chair in front of his desk. Sitting down in it, she wondered where to begin.

"So?"

She started talking, catching him up on everything that had happened the day before, from inadvertently getting pulled into Aaron's op to discovering the room at the top of the stairs. "I reached out to Hammond because I have the feeling we're dealing with human trafficking. And you know he's in charge of the task force."

"I do. Are you going to liaise with him on this?" Van asked.

"I'm not sure. He wants me to stop by the field office and have a debrief. I'm not sure if Isabell Montez fell into this or if she's separate from it," Lee said.

"What *do* you know?"

"She was at the club. My eyes told me it was the same place but the computer verified it," Lee told him. "I was going to take this to the cops, but with that locked room and the other signs pointing to some kind of trafficking, I think that Hammond would be better hands for it."

Van leaned back in his chair, crossing his massive arms over his chest. "I agree. And as much as I don't want you to get sucked back into that life, it seems like you are already."

"Yeah." She hesitated. "But that's not all…"

He raised an eyebrow at her. She took a deep breath. She'd pretty much decided she wasn't going to mention Cate to him. But sitting in his office across from him now, she knew she *had* to. There was no justification to keep quiet about it. *If* she was still alive and in LA, then Van needed to know.

"I saw someone last night who looked like Cate."

The air seemed to leave the room, and though Van didn't change position, she could tell he had tensed his body. He lifted one hand and rubbed it over his bald head before he leaned forward.

"*Looked* like or was?"

Lee shrugged and shook her head. "I can't confirm it, but I did get a good look at her…" She swallowed hard. "And a locked room, a missing girl and a woman who is her doppelgänger. I didn't want to wait to tell you. Plus, as we speak, Rick is trailing the van that definitely has young people in it."

"Okay, well, let's deal in facts. Keep Cate between you and me for now. I'll come with you to see Hammond," Van said.

"I can handle this," Lee protested.

"I know you can, but if it is Cate, then the fact that a girl was taken that your friend knew links this to us. After Hammond, I want you to go talk to Boyd again and find out more about the girl's family connections."

"This is *my* case," she said.

"Sorry. Didn't mean to overstep." Van stared at her, and despite what he said, she knew deep down he wanted to take over. Had sort of guessed he would from the moment Cate's name came up. But that didn't mean she was going to just sit back and let him. "I was already planning to go and see Boyd again. I will continue to do that."

"I trust that you will. And, yeah, it *is* your op, Lee. But I want in. I'm not letting you face alone whatever she's bringing to us."

"I'm not positive—"

"You are or you wouldn't have come in here to talk to me or reached out to Hammond," Van said calmly. He wasn't asking her to confirm; he knew her that well.

"Yeah, I am. I mean, I have no proof, just my gut and that brief glimpse. I could be wrong."

"You usually aren't," Van said. "I'll drive to Hammond. Have Rick report to us there."

She nodded. "We're also looped in with the DEA."

"Okay, I assume Hammond's not going to object to sharing intel?" Van murmured.

"Too bad if he does. We're independent now and this case isn't his."

Her friend just gave her that slow smile of his that brimmed with pride. "That's right."

Lee knew that Van's first instinct was to protect his family, and that meant her, Rick and Aaron, because Aaron was Xander's brother. But he also knew that his family was strong and needed to stand on their own and handle this.

She wasn't sure what Hammond was going to say or what he'd tell them to do. But unless she actually was ordered to stop trying to find Isabell Montez, she was going to find the girl and hopefully take down Cate O'Dell in the process.

Chapter Ten

The meeting with Aaron's boss made a few things clearer. The FBI Human Trafficking Task Force wanted to send in their own people, which Jayne had pushed back on. Jayne reminded him of Lee in a way. They were both ultra-efficient, smart and used to taking care of themselves. Too many new people were going to disrupt the operation and could jeopardize all the work they'd done to get Aaron in place.

"The woman, Lee Oscar, used to be an agent for them and they are going to use her, I believe. We should know more later," Jayne told him. "Denis has checked in and the location for the drop is at a house in Bel Air. We've got agents who will be watching it starting later today. While there, he got a ping about Steve... Want to tell me about that?"

Aaron rubbed the back of his neck and nodded. "Yeah. Lee set up a tracking app to show us his location. I think I mentioned it in my report. Denis put a small tracker on his car, and now when he moves, we are getting hits off cell phone towers as he goes past them."

"Good. He's the one who was in rival gang territory?"

"That's him. Did Denis say if he was back in Boyle Heights?"

"No, he's still on the Old Mission Trail," his boss said. "We should know more when he gets back. Rick Stone checked in as well. The van he was following got off before the port and he's watching the house where the people were moved. I passed that info on to Hammond, who will be taking over that surveillance for us."

"And keeping us in the loop?"

"Definitely. If Lee declines to work with the FBI again, then we'll have to have you end that relationship and bring in someone from their team." Jayne sighed. "Not ideal, but that's where we are at the moment. Let's hope she agrees to working with the FBI. How did she get involved to begin with?"

"She's looking for a missing teenager. The trail took her to Mistral's." Aaron cleared his throat, contemplating how much to say. "We know each other through my brother, just one of those things."

"Once she clocked you, you made a play to keep her quiet."

His boss knew what it was like being undercover and how every element had to be managed, even the unexpected. Though it had been Lee's idea for them to pretend to be a couple so she could get inside the club, he wasn't going to tell that to his boss. He nodded at Jayne. Lee was part of the op now and his feelings on the matter weren't going to be an issue. Had he ever felt this way about a woman before? No, of course not. But was he going to fuck up his mission? Hell no.

Aaron was *still* in control of the op, and he knew that he was going to have to step up his role in the organization quicker than planned once the FBI got involved.

"Ramos reports to Perses," he added. "So I'm going to try to take someone else down in the gang and move up to get closer. I want to do that as soon as I can. But I need to get a feel for everyone in and out of the club. Jorge is definitely tight with Ramos, but there might be a chink I can use to pry them apart. There are two lower-level punks that I could also use if needed."

"Sounds like you have everything under control."

"Or as close to it as I can," Aaron said with a laugh. "You know how it is undercover."

"Yes, I do. Every day is a new problem to solve. I guess that's why you like it and I miss it."

Aaron rubbed the back of his neck again, feeling the tension that had settled there as soon as Lee had become involved. Another variable in this entire thing that was adding to his uncertainty. Everything he'd thought he knew about Lee had changed. He'd barely scraped the surface of who she really was.

"Oh, hey, as a heads-up, there is a little complication," he said.

Jayne's face went completely blank, a frown furrowing her brow. "Bad?"

Taking a deep breath, he crossed his arms over his chest and tried to give off a nonchalant and totally not-worried vibe. "Lee thought she recognized a woman last night who was part of La Fortunata crime syndicate. Cate O'Dell. She's known to the FBI, and Lee mentioned that everyone believed O'Dell to be dead."

Turning back to her computer, Jayne's fingers started moving over her keyboard and she leaned back, motioning for Aaron to come around the back of her desk. The woman on the screen did resemble Diana. But it was hard to tell from the somewhat grainy, long-distance photo if they were the same person.

"That her?"

"Maybe. I could talk to a sketch artist or we can try to install some cameras, but there are people in and out of the club all the time," Aaron said.

"I'll get a second team on surveillance to watch for her. Do you think she'll come back again or was she there to meet you last night?"

"I think it was to meet me and approve me. Ramos is not her boss, and he said they were in charge of different operations, but he seemed wary of her," he replied.

"Interesting. She might be the big fish who can lead us to Perses."

"Exactly. I'll keep my eye for her and try to get closer to her if she shows up again. The guy who works for Perses is tough, but I could take him. I could start something with him and try to get in with her," Aaron suggested.

"We'll see." Jayne rubbed her chin, contemplating. "But first, we need to find out what Lee Oscar is going to do before we move this forward."

A part of Aaron hoped she turned the FBI down and walked away from him and this situation. He wanted her safe, but then part of what drew him to her was the fact that she wouldn't stop until there was justice. But he was pretty sure she wouldn't. Or, at least, the woman he thought he was starting to know wouldn't.

The FBI field office was in one of those government buildings that had been built in the '70s and really didn't stand out. Lee had wanted to take her Dodge but remembered what Aaron had said about it being a flashy car. So she'd used a Toyota Prius that they kept in the garage. She missed the power of the Charger, but until she knew how big this missing-girl case had gotten, she wasn't taking any chances.

Van was with her since he insisted on coming along. He was in the passenger seat because he hated driving the Toyota. He'd been quiet on the way over, but that wasn't too unusual. Still, a part of her wondered if he was still processing the fact that Cate might be alive.

They were taken to a small meeting room and Hammond joined them a few minutes later.

"Price, didn't think I'd see you," Hammond said as he entered and held his hand out to Van first, and then to her, to shake.

"Thanks for coming down here, Oscar."

Hammond was in his fifties and fit. He looked like he'd been born in LA. His hair was thick and perfectly styled; his teeth were probably caps they were so white and straight, and his clothing was always fashionable and trendy. Lee knew that was just the image he wanted to project. He'd grown up back East and worked his way up the ranks in DC.

"Wasn't sure I had much choice," she said as they all sat down.

"There's always another option. But in this case it will be easier for all involved if you agree to work with us temporarily."

What? That wasn't what she'd been expecting. Van seemed to go still next to her as well. "I'll continue to work for Price but liaise with you and your team."

"That might work," Hammond said. "Right now, the DEA agent in charge, Jayne Montrose, doesn't want anyone new to interfere with her op. She said you are already known to the operative and to the gang they are infiltrating."

Hammond's statement was leading and Lee wasn't sure that he knew about her involvement and how much she could say without giving away Aaron's cover. "I…"

"Let me make this easier. We know about Quentin and his partner and that you are pretending to be his girlfriend to find…" He glanced down at the notes he had in front of him. "Isabell Montez."

Good that he already had that intel. "The cops aren't putting much effort into finding her and it looks like she might have run away, but I didn't want to leave any loose ends. There is a photo of the girl at Mistral's, which I confirmed last night. Now with the human trafficking, I'm not sure that she ran off. Her last known address was broken into and ransacked. Not sure if that ties with this in any way."

"We don't know either," Hammond said. "What is the address? I'll have our people look into it and see if there is any connection to this operation you stumbled into."

"I think Agent Quentin was surprised by the holding room for people in the club. Though it's noisy at night and no one is there during the day, so it is sort of ideal for a stash house."

"It is. We were working another location on the Old Mission Trail. I believe Rick Stone—he works for you, Price, right?—is there now."

"He does work for us. He checked in from a location where the people were moved to," Van confirmed. "Was it known to you?"

"We suspected it might be a location they were using. We think this is a branch of La Fortunata. They operate the way they used to," Hammond said.

Lee glanced over at Van. He gave her a small nod.

"I thought I saw Cate O'Dell last night. I only got a glimpse of her. I believe she's using the name Diana and is somehow connected to the gang that Aaron is investigating," Lee said.

"O'Dell was reported deceased," Hammond said. "Are you sure?"

"I'm not unsure." Because that was the truth at this moment. She couldn't rule that woman out as Cate and until she did no one was going to be safe. Cate was ruthless and would do anything to please her father, who they suspected was the shadowy head of La Fortunata known only as Perses.

"Then, I'm going to have to do the hard sell to keep you on this operation, Oscar. You know Cate better than anyone but Price. If she's involved, then we know we are close to the top of the organization and we could take it down for good."

If only it would be as easy as he was making it sound. "I'll report to you each day and keep you in the loop, but I'm not working for you."

Hammond looked like he was going to put up a fight, but Van leaned forward. "You owe us. You used her and me without any compunction, setting us up with O'Dell to see how far her deception would go and how far she'd take us. Lee will work with you but not *for* you, and when this is over you don't contact us again," Van said.

Hammond leaned back in his chair, swiveling it from side to side. "I'll have to check with my boss. I'll see what I can do."

He got up and left the room. She turned to Van. "Thanks for having my back."

"You know I always do."

Aaron wasn't surprised that Lee had agreed to continue working with him on this operation. He was relieved not to have to try to bring someone else in, because that would have been difficult, but he would have managed it. Also he just wanted to keep working with Lee.

The attraction between them lent a believability to the charade of them being lovers, which would be harder to get Ramos to buy with a new woman at this point, because he really wanted Lee. There was a tension between them that he knew couldn't really be faked.

"The FBI briefed her on what they have and you know everything we have. Meet with her back at the apartment. In fact, after today I want you to be full time on the gang. It feels like everything is going to break sooner than we expected. Denis will be a regular at the club and you can pass info to him via Lee," Jayne said. "Push to get close to Ramos and his boss. We need to get the proof of the connection to Perses."

"Got it. I'll send reports each day. I think that with the hours at the club, the reports are going to be short," Aaron said.

"That works," Jayne said.

Aaron left a few minutes later and realized that, once he walked out of the building, he wasn't going to be Aaron Quentin for a while. It was time to shed that man and to wholly become Quinn. He left his car at the office and took the bus back to his apartment. As usual, his attention was on high alert, watching the passengers around him from behind his sunglasses. He didn't think he'd been followed earlier or now. But he wasn't taking any chances. He had to walk three blocks from where he got off the bus to his apartment in Echo Lake, and when he got there, he spotted Lee sitting outside the apartment with her back against the door. His breath caught in his chest as it always did when he saw her.

This was getting…out of hand. He'd never been a man ruled by lust, but with her… She was always in his mind. Right now, that was a danger to both of them.

She had her laptop open and her fingers were moving over the keyboard. She looked up when she heard him on the stairs. She closed the computer and stood up.

"Hey. Forgot to get a key from you," she said.

"Yeah, we'll fix that today," he murmured, noticing she had a duffel bag and a large computer bag with her. He knew she was here to stay for the duration of the operation as well.

As soon as they were inside, he leaned against the door, watching her stand sort of awkwardly in the middle of the living/dining room area.

"You're working with the FBI now?"

"Sort of. Still working for Price, just reporting to my old boss. They wanted me back on staff, but that was a no-go. Your boss okay with this?" she asked.

"She kind of had no choice. But yeah. I'm glad you said yes."

"I wasn't going to say no. I still don't know what happened to Isabell, and there is a chance that she's been moved through the club. I want to find her and put a stop to the human trafficking operation."

"Do you have any idea why they are taking teens from this area?"

"The FBI doesn't know, but then they didn't know about the connection to your drug gang. My theory is that it might be to pay debts. Could that be a thing? I mean the way the Montez house was turned over, it was clear they were looking for something," Lee said.

Aaron walked farther into the room as she put her computer bag on the floor next to the table and set down her laptop. "That house was in Boyle Heights?"

"Yes. Which reminds me I need to follow up on the fingerprints from Detective Monroe."

"We were at a house in the same neighborhood, making a bust that same day. It's interesting because there is a rival gang who operates there, but they had infiltrated the Cachorros and I was able to use that to move up the ranks."

"That is interesting... Use that information how?"

"I burned the other gang member," Aaron said.

"Burned?"

"Ratted him out so I could gain trust," he explained.

"What happened to him?" Lee asked.

Aaron wasn't sure how much Lee understood of working undercover in criminal gangs. "They made an example of him and dropped his body back at his old gang's hangout."

"Did you know they'd do that?"

"I did. We might need to do something violent at the club. You going to be okay with that?"

She didn't answer him, but he saw on her face that she wasn't going to be. "I'm trying to protect people, babe. Sometimes that means picking an innocent life over one that has been corrupting innocents. If you can't handle it, you should back out now. I'll look for your girl."

Lee pursed her lips and shook her head. "No, I get it. I forgot about that side of being undercover. We're mainly a bodyguard service... We protect, and though sometimes that means firing a shot, I'm in the office watching over everyone. It's just been a long time for me."

"It's okay. This life, it's not for everyone. No one is going to think less of you if you say no and go back to Price Tower," he said. He would be disappointed because he wanted to spend more time with her, and not just because of the job, but he didn't want her to have to do anything that made her uncomfortable.

"I would think less of *myself.* Isabell might have been traded for her parents' debts, and I can't just walk away from that or from people who would take a child that way."

He got it. "Good. I'll try to keep you away from that."

"You don't have to," she said. "You don't have to protect me."

"But I want to," he ground out. Even though he knew he should have kept that sentiment to himself. It was the truth and she deserved that and so much more from him.

Chapter Eleven

Protect her. It wasn't a sentiment that she'd ever heard from anyone else. Maybe her grandpa had made her feel safe... No *maybe* about it, the old man had kept her safe. But he'd been the only one. She'd learned to fend for herself at a young age and had never forgotten those lessons.

"Thanks. But I got me," she said, sitting down at the table. Aaron dropped into the chair next to her.

"I know. I've seen you rolling with whatever is thrown your way," he told her gruffly. "I'm the same."

"Oh, I know that, but you do it in a different way. I'm in a corner trying to get as much information as I can to figure out how to get the upper hand, while you're in the center of it dancing around and changing to suit the environment. Why do you do that?" she asked.

He rubbed the back of his neck. The question was personal. *Too personal?* Maybe, but she wanted to know. There was no denying that part of the reason she was here with Aaron was the man himself. In fact, she wouldn't have gotten this close to Cate or working with her old task force again without him.

She also wouldn't be closer to piecing together a theory on what happened to Isabell Montez. It wasn't lost on Lee that the more days that passed, the less likely it was that they were going to get that girl back alive. She needed to be here to save her. And knew that her hero complex was as strong as Aaron's.

But she was also here *for* him.

She wanted him, and the time apart hadn't lessened those feelings. At this moment, everything felt out of control, including herself, and the one solid in the maelstrom was Aaron.

"I don't know," he said with a shrug and then turned back to facing the table, his hands steepled together.

"I thought you said there would be no lies when we were undercover. That lying increased our chances of failure."

He let out a long, hard breath. "Do you want to do this? I'm not a man for half measures, Lee. If I start opening up to you, then I'm going to have you in my bed and we both said that wasn't a good idea."

"Don't I get a say?" she asked.

"Of course you do. But we both know you won't say no," he muttered. Then crossed his arms over his chest as he used his feet to turn the chair he was sitting on toward her. "Would you?"

She chewed her lower lip. *No lies.* She should have guessed that he would push back. Aaron was a predator. He was always going to go after any weakness, but that was tempered with that need to protect. She wanted to know what had made this complex man the way he was.

His brother Xander also had this solid core of protectiveness and remoteness. What happened in their upbringing to shape them this way?

"Do you know much about the Quentins?" he asked.

She shrugged, flashing him a coy look. "Some. I mean, I know you're all big, British, stubborn and trustworthy."

"Thanks for that. *Stubborn* though? Isn't that a bit of projecting?" he asked, his mouth lifting on one side in a slight smile.

"Perhaps. So…"

"We are all close in age—all four of us—and we grew up like a pack. Fighting each other to be the dominant, protecting each other from anyone outside who threatened. It was a rough-and-tumble childhood where my mom did her best but we were a lot."

"Sounds interesting," she murmured, unable to fathom the

kind of childhood he was describing. She'd always been alone. Even at Grandpa's bar, she'd been by herself in the back, staying out of sight. She'd always known how to be quiet and keep out of the way.

"Probably sounds nuts to you, but the truth is we are all alphas, so we fight everyone and everywhere. It made my life difficult until…"

He trailed off and shook his head. "I had to leave the family and it was a wake-up call. I couldn't be the alpha out in the world without getting into a lot of scuffles and ending up in jail. So I took a few classes at a community college in Florida and started to get into law enforcement. It gave me some discipline that I didn't realize I had been lacking. The rest is history, as you Yanks say."

A glossed-over version of who he was, but it gave her some insight into him. "Every time you say 'Yank,' it reminds me of some Southern folks who'd strongly state they are *not* a Yankee."

"Yeah, there were a few folks in Florida who didn't appreciate being called that," he chuckled. "What about you? Why are you in the corner gathering intel?"

Hmm. What to tell him? Her past was so typical, she thought. So many kids grew up in a bad family situation, and while that didn't make it right, she'd never wanted that to be what defined her. "Dad with a temper, mom with a drinking problem. I learned if I was quiet and stayed out of the way, things went better for me. So I was sort of training for my job in childhood." She glanced over at him. "I guess you were too. Learning to fight and protect your pack. But undercover, you're alone. How does that feel?" she asked. Feeling pretty proud of herself that she'd answered his question and then turned the spotlight back on him.

Because the last thing she wanted to do was to talk about her past or her childhood. That one bit she'd shared was enough. Gave him a picture and he could draw in the rest, because she wasn't one for rehashing.

"Nice try, babe."

She furrowed her brow. "Huh?"

"I see what you're doing. And it's not going to work. I told you I'm used to being the alpha, and I do that with my strength. And you are used to being the alpha too, but you do it with your mind. And there was a time when you'd get me talking about myself without returning the favor. But you haven't really told me anything yet."

"I doubt there was ever a time when you talked about yourself. You play it close to the vest," she said.

"Just like you."

She'd opened up the past and now he wanted to know more about her. Trusting her with his back wasn't as difficult as it would be with a stranger. Her relationship with Xander made her sort of a known quantity. Plus she'd stood by his brother more than once.

That was great and all, but he needed to know what made her tick. What were her weaknesses and when was she going to crumble? Everyone crumbled at some point, and it was important to know what would trigger her. He knew his own triggers and Denis's—both of them had worked together for long enough to realize when the other one needed a break before they shattered.

But Lee wasn't like him or anyone else he'd worked with before. How she'd handle everything in the club and the investigation, he wasn't sure. Last night she'd been solid, but he saw her try to push her way in when he'd been with Ramos. She'd backed down, but there might come a time when she wouldn't.

She was looking for a missing teen and he had to wonder why. This clearly wasn't a Price Security gig, and she'd given little away on that front. "Why are you looking for this girl?"

"A friend asked—"

"I'm going to stop you there. You already told me that, but I want to know *why you*? Why did the friend come to you? You work for a bodyguard firm."

She sort of went white and looked down at her laptop screen. It was open, but the screen was black and had gone to sleep while they were talking. He saw her fingers flex and he knew she wanted to start typing on the keyboard and disappear into the web of information that she was weaving. But he wasn't going to let her.

This could be her crucial weakness and he needed to know it.

"Uh… Boyd and I went to high school together. My best friend was his girlfriend, and she disappeared one day after school. It's definitely the reason I wanted to join the FBI and get on the human trafficking task force. After I retired, Boyd still gets in touch when he notices things with his students. He's a high school chemistry teacher."

There was more here beneath the surface than he was picking up on. He knew that and pushed it into the back of his mind to analyze later. "Are you trying to save the friend you couldn't?"

"Are you trying to save the brother you injured?" she countered.

That froze him in his tracks. He wasn't aware she knew about Tony and what had happened. Aaron's rough rugby tackle on an uneven field in the mud. Tony's head had hit the ground hard, and a rock that no one had noticed damaged his spinal cord, leaving his brother paralyzed from the waist down.

She'd done it again. Turned things back on him to keep from revealing too much. There was a time when Aaron would have walked away, but he and Xander had been talking and he'd talked to Tony as well. Things were getting better there. "I'm not hamstrung by my past anymore. But you still are."

She shrugged and looked away. "I'm not sure what any of this matters. You don't need to know about my childhood."

"Actually, I do. You are part of my team now. I can't keep you safe if I don't know what is going to break you."

"Nothing's going to 'break' me. I'm strong and can take way more than anything this crime syndicate is going to dish out," she said.

"I don't know that. I've never seen you under pressure and past the point of exhaustion. Living two lives and moving an investigation forward inch by impossibly slow inch. So I'm going to prod and probe until I know all of your secrets."

She chewed her lip again and then shook her head. "I can't talk about it. It's all tied up in guilt and drive and ambition. I'm a loner because that's easier for me."

"You're not a loner at Price. You're a big part of that team," Aaron pointed out, tucking that other fact away.

"I'm in the tower. I'm watching and directing them. I make them keep in touch at all times. I don't let anyone out of my sight. That's my weakness. When I can't find someone I sort of get frantic. I have to know where the people I care about are."

"So you don't lose them. This girl... You want to find her for your friend so he doesn't lose someone else."

She was a protector, like him. The incident that shaped her happened about the same age as his had. That type of thing had a way of leaving a mark on the soul. One that wasn't going to go away.

"So you go frantic, how?" he asked.

"I get information. Find the weakness in someone else and I attack. I do whatever I can to get them back. And while I don't know Isabell, Boyd did, and he thinks she's worth saving, so I'm going to gather every bit of information I can find and I'm going to find her."

Or her body, but he didn't say that out loud.

"Okay. I learned that it took more than strength to be strong after Tony's accident. It was a tough lesson to learn and took me years to recognize, but that's where I am." A muscle ticked in his jaw. "My temper is my weakness. If I get pushed too hard and too long, I snap and then I'm a danger to everyone." He turned toward her, pinning his gaze on hers. "Denis's weakness is a bit like yours. He has to know where all the players are. He'll put himself in danger to find me if I miss a check-in. He'll do the same for you, so never miss one."

"I won't," she said. "Am I part of the team now?"

He nodded.

Aaron was still tense from that moment she'd asked about his brother Tony, which had been a dick move. But when she felt attacked, she always came out swinging. No matter that she understood what he was doing.

She should apologize but wasn't really sure how to go about it. "So who is on your team?"

A distraction from what she truly wanted to do, which was

just go over to him, climb on his lap and put her arms around him. But a hug wasn't going to take away the sting of her words. Information had always seemed more dangerous than physical strength to Lee. It gave her a bonus hit point in the game of life against most people who were content to take the news at face value and bump along the path of their lives.

Not her. She'd always been digging deeper and pulling out little tidbits that she tucked away to use as ammo when she was backed into a corner.

"Denis and my boss, Jayne. Rick is also going to be part of it. Price agreed to let him work with us on this. He's got good instincts."

"Rick's the best. I wasn't seeing the drug connection to Isabell's disappearance at first," Lee admitted. "If you give me their cell numbers, I can add them to a tracking app that I use so I can keep tabs on them."

"I will," he said, standing up and starting to move away from her.

"Where are you going?"

"We have some downtime before we have to get to the club, and I want to pinpoint the houses that Jayne mentioned to see if I can find a pattern."

"I can help with that," she offered.

"I'm sure you can, but I need some alone time."

He left the main living area of the apartment, and a few minutes later, she heard the shower come on in the bathroom. It was hard to wait for him to be done. The guilt she felt over hitting him with that accident wouldn't let her just sit still. She waited a good ten minutes—surely that was enough time for him to get dressed—before she got up and went to the bedroom.

She knocked on the door.

"Yes."

He didn't open it or invite her to enter. Leaning her head against the wood door, she closed her eyes.

"I'm sorry."

He didn't say anything. She knew he had to have heard her, and a moment later, the door opened, almost catching her off guard. He stood there, wearing a towel wrapped around his hips. His big, muscled torso was bare and she wasn't going to lie. She couldn't take her eyes off him.

He had those big biceps that she found attractive and a long scar that ran from his left shoulder down toward his nipple. She shamelessly continued to drink in the sight of him. He had a light dusting of hair on his chest, which grew narrower as her gaze dropped down and saw where it disappeared into the towel.

He put one arm up on the doorjamb and stood there, letting her look at him. God, when was she going to stop making mistakes with this man?

Probably never.

Realizing she was still staring at his chest, she closed her eyes and took a deep breath.

"I shouldn't have brought your brother into things earlier. I was feeling pushed into a corner and just used the only ammunition I had that I thought would make you back down," she admitted. "I'm sorry."

She kept her eyes closed because if she opened them again and saw his bare chest and the bed right behind him, she might do something impulsive. No *might* about it, she thought. She was definitely going to—

His finger brushed over her cheek and then pushed a strand of hair behind her ear. "I'm sorry too."

"Sorry? For what?"

"For cornering you. You're too good at revealing nothing of yourself and I want to know more."

"For the mission," she whispered, still not opening her eyes because she was afraid if she did, he'd stop touching her.

"No," he said.

His forehead rested against hers and the softness of his exhalation brushed over her mouth, making her lips tingle. She did open her eyes then. Her heart beat faster, seeing him so close. Their eyes met and she realized she was holding her breath, waiting for…something. For him to make the next move?

The truth was, she wasn't certain what exactly she was waiting for, but she wasn't sure of herself with him. Which was so unlike her.

But she was *done* waiting.

She lifted her hand and cupped his jaw. He'd shaved, so the skin was so smooth she couldn't help running her finger over it. Then she tipped her head to the side, leaned up and kissed him.

A real first kiss. Not one for show but one that they both wanted. One that was just for the two of them. His lips were firm and he kissed her back. His mouth opening slowly as she sucked his bottom lip into her mouth. He tasted good and minty.

His hand stayed gently against the side of her neck and she kept her hand on his jaw. That was it. They were barely touching, but she felt flayed bare to her soul. The need for Aaron was so strong inside of her that she was on fire.

He lifted his head and their eyes met. Watching her, he was waiting to see what she would do next. She splayed her hand in the center of his chest and just stood there, her heart in her throat, conveying with her touch that she was all-in. The next thing she knew, his arm went around her waist and he lifted her off her feet, pulling her into that big, strong body of his. She wrapped her legs around his hips and her arms around his shoulders and kissed him again.

Knowing that this was the only place she wanted to be right now. The only place that felt right, and for the first time since her grandpa had died…the only place where she felt safe.

Chapter Twelve

All his life, he'd been strong and unbreakable. No one understood better than him what a fairy tale that belief had been. He'd thought of his brothers, the Quentin boys, as unbeatable as well. But one rough tackle had shown him the lie of that and he'd never been the same since.

Not once.

That Lee had known that was his weakness and had gone straight for it to even the playing field told him how much she hated being vulnerable. It was odd to look down into her face and admit to himself just how much alike they were. There was no comfort in it.

Her apology… That was the one thing he'd never been able to figure out how to do. Of course he knew he just had to say the words *I'm sorry*, but they never came. Not once.

Then she had kissed him, turned him on with her apology and her kiss. She had a rocking body that he had been noticing the last few times they met. Something about dealing with Xander and that entire situation meant the first time she'd just been one of the Price Security team and not a woman. Even when they'd been doing shots and flirting, it had been more of a blowing-off-steam thing in South Florida. Now…this was anything but. This was a need-to-have-Lee-in-his-arms thing. He hadn't noticed how thick her eyebrows were or how, up close, those brown eyes of hers actually had flecks of green and gold in them.

She had pretty eyes.

"Aaron?"

Just his name, but as a question. Why was he hesitating? That had to be what she wanted to know. But she'd been up-front with him in the past. She hadn't wanted to have sex with him back in South Beach because she liked him.

"Do you still like me?" he gritted out. Because he *really* liked her. She was in the middle of an operation and part of his cover now, so that complicated things. *Ya think?*

But she was so close that he could smell that subtle floral fragrance that he only associated with her each time he took a breath. So close that the heat of her body was making him hotter and harder than he'd been in a long time. So close that complications were melting away and a more primal instinct was taking over.

"Yes," she murmured. "Do you?"

He turned and felt the towel he'd knotted around his hips slip. It fell to the floor as he shifted and walked with her to the bed. "What do you think?"

His hard-on was pressed against her and she had shifted as he was walking, tightening her legs around his hips. Her hands were in his hair and he knew that if he was going to stop, it would have to be now.

"Do you want this?" he rasped. "We're still undercover, still living a lie."

"Yes."

Just one word but so damned confident and sure that his cock jumped, and he knew this wasn't going to be one of those take-him-a-while-to-get-going sessions. He had been wanting her for too long, yearning for her more and more since he'd seen her at the police station...

He set her on her feet, his hands going to the waistband of her jeans. He undid them, hearing the button pop in the quiet room, and then she brushed his hands aside, twisting her hips and pushing her jeans and underwear down her legs.

She still had her shoes on, so she had to lean down to toe

them off. As she did so, he felt the warmth of her breath against his naked legs and couldn't help running his hands over her back and down to her butt as she bent toward him.

"You have a fine ass," he said.

Which made her laugh. "Thanks."

Lee stood up slowly and then put her hands on the hem of her shirt, but he stopped her. He wanted to undress her, not just watch her strip for him. He pulled the shirt up and over her head. Once it was off, he looked down at her body with her small belly and curvy hips. Her breasts were full, her skin sort of olive-toned. He reached behind her with one hand to undo her bra, but her hand found his cock, fisting him, and he forgot about everything but the pleasure of her touch.

God, that felt good. As she stroked him, he rocked his hips into her touch. She squeezed him as she went up his length, running her finger around the rim at the tip and then moving back down. He shook when he felt her mouth on the base of his neck, sucking his skin.

It took more concentration than he wanted to admit to get her bra undone before peeling it away from her breasts.

Aaron cupped her breasts in his palms, rubbing her tight reddish-brown nipples with his thumbs. She arched her back and returned the favor by stroking him faster. He was close to coming and hadn't felt like this since he'd been in his twenties. He took her hand from him and gently pushed her until she fell back on the bed.

Her hair spread out around her head, her legs fell open and his breath caught in his chest. He'd had sex fairly regularly over the last few years, but it had been a lifetime since he'd made love to a woman that he liked and cared about.

He didn't want to rush this. He didn't want to ruin this by coming too fast or not being what she needed. But he *did* know that once he and Lee hooked up, nothing was going to be the same again. He put his knee on the bed and leaned over her. Wanted to take his time with her but also to take her as fast as he could so that she would finally be his.

Well, be his for as long as he could hold her. If there was one thing that Aaron Quentin knew, it was that nothing lasted forever and that he needed to savor every moment, which was exactly what he intended to do with Lee.

There was no use in pretending that she wasn't going to keep falling for Aaron while they worked together. So why deny herself this? Lee had no idea what the world would be like for them when they finished this operation, but she knew that she'd regret it if she didn't give everything of herself to him while they were together.

Coming to apologize had been hard. Admitting she wasn't her best self always was, but she'd known she had to acknowledge her shortcomings and was glad she had. Aaron reminded her so much of how she could have been if not for Van and the team at Price Security. A loner. But now that he was slowly moving up her body, she couldn't really think about anything except the aching emptiness between her legs and how much she needed him inside of her.

He had lean hips but strong, muscled legs. Everything about this man was better than she'd expected. He had lifted her easily into his arms, and that was no small feat given she was a big girl. But he'd done it without much strain. There was something about that that had really touched her in a way she hadn't expected.

She reached between them as he sucked her nipple into his mouth and found his erection. His hips canted forward and she stroked him. Then couldn't help rubbing the tip of his cock against her clit. That felt so good as his mouth was sucking on her. Her hips writhed against him and she realized she was going to come if she kept touching herself with his dick.

His dick.

She let go of him. "Aaron."

He lifted his head, and her nipple tightened even more from the coolness in the room.

"Do you have a condom? I'm on the pill, but I don't like to take chances with pregnancy or STDs… I know, such sexy talk—"

He put his hand over her mouth, smiling down at her. "It's sexy to know you care about yourself. I do. Give me a second."

He got off the bed and she watched the fluidity of his movements as he walked to the bathroom and returned a moment
later, putting the condom on as he came back to her. Her heart
beat faster at the sight of him. How natural he was in his own
body and with her. She appreciated that.

"Where was I?" he asked as he knelt between her legs again.

She pointed to her breast but then opened her arms and legs.
"But I don't need more teasing. I want you inside of me."

A guttural sound came from him as he fell on her. His mouth
found hers and his hips shifted until she felt the tip of him at
the entrance of her body. She opened her thighs wider and
lifted her hips as she wrapped her legs around him. His tongue
pushed deep into her mouth, rubbing over hers, and she sucked
on his in return. Then, lifting her hips, she found herself pushing down with her heels on the small of his back, but still he
didn't enter her.

His mouth just moved on hers, his tongue plunging deeper.
And as she arched her back, he shifted his chest against her,
the hair on his chest rubbing against her already hardened nipples, making her moan deep in her throat and try harder to get
him inside of her.

One hand moved down the side of her body and she felt his
finger on her clit, rubbing and tapping against it. He lifted his
head and growled, "Come for me and I'll take you."

It wasn't that hard to come. His chest against her breasts,
his hand on her center...that teasing tip of his dick inside of
her. She pulled his head back to hers and sucked hard on his
tongue, arching her hips against each movement of his hand
until she felt everything in her body tightening and cresting as
stars danced between her eyes and she came hard.

He didn't need her to tell him; he just made that deep groan
again and thrust all the way inside of her. He held himself there,
deep in her, as her body continued spasming, now around his
cock. She opened her eyes and saw he was watching her. He put
his forehead against hers as he started to drive into her again
and again. Going deeper and deeper every time, until she felt
her orgasm building again. She used her heels on his back to
urge him to keep going, and he did until she cried out his name.

He pushed one hand under their bodies and grabbed her butt, lifting her up into his thrusts and driving harder and faster and deeper. Until she heard him bellow out too, and felt his cock got bigger inside of her, but he kept on thrusting. Until he came.

She wrapped her arms around him as he rested his head against her shoulder. Lee kept her legs around his hips, holding him to her, as her hand tenderly moved over his back as he came back to himself. This man that she was realistic enough to know she wasn't going to hold forever was hers. He was hers *for now* and that was all that mattered.

She knew that she would do whatever she had to in order to keep him safe. That her circle of family had grown larger, and she didn't allow herself to sit in the thought, but she knew that Aaron was more than family. More than a lover or even a potential boyfriend. He was the man that she could care more deeply about than anyone else.

And that frightened her. She hadn't let anything frighten her this much since Hannah had disappeared.

Aaron didn't want to move. But he also didn't want to acknowledge the emotions that she stirred in him. Life was easier when he was focused on the job and not on people or his connection to them.

He knew it was fucked-up that he didn't know how to emote except physically. Lee wouldn't know that this was him pretty much telling her how he felt. But he did. And it shook him.

She was stroking his back and he shifted his weight so that he rested on his hip, off her, and let her touch him. There had been so few gentle touches like this in his life. Maybe his mom before he'd tackled Tony, but after that, Aaron hadn't felt worthy of being comforted. He wasn't sure he still was, but for right now none of that mattered. He just lay in her arms, breathing in that floral scent that was hers and taking comfort from that warm, feminine body beneath his.

Except it wasn't just a feminine body. It was Lee. He was very aware of who he was here with and how much he wanted to keep her in his arms for longer than they had. But he knew his alarm was going to go off in a few minutes, and he had to go on a call with his boss to update her on his progress.

"I can feel you shifting into work mode," she murmured.

He lifted his head, their eyes met and he wished... Well, not that he was a different man because as messed up as he was inside, he didn't want to be anyone else but Aaron Quentin. But he wished they'd met at another time, under different circumstances. However, when was he going to meet a woman like Lee Oscar *except* when he was undercover?

All either of them did was work.

That was a truth he would do well not to forget.

"Yeah. Sorry about that."

"No, it's cool. I'll get a shower and then I can help you with linking the houses," she said, then chewed her lower lip between her teeth. "Are we good now?"

He had to smile at the way she'd asked it. "We're better than good. Sorry I got my—"

She put her long, cool fingers against his mouth. "You don't owe me an apology."

"Well, you're getting it," he muttered, shifting on top of her again and rolling until their positions were reversed. She put her arms on his chest and lifted her head up to look down on him.

The long curtain of her hair fell around them, brushing his chest and tickling against his neck, and he closed his eyes as he felt himself stir. Getting turned on by her. But at thirty-eight, he knew the chances of him going again were, well, not realistic. But he wanted to.

"Thanks, then," she said.

His alarm started going off before he could say anything else. Sitting up, he shifted her to the bed next to him, then went to the dresser where he'd left his phone and turned off the alarm. "I've got a call in five."

She got up too and came over, wrapping her arms around him from the back and hugging him. She kissed the middle of his back and then walked into the bathroom. He followed her because he had to deal with the condom and wash up and finish getting ready.

She acted so natural as she grabbed a towel and got in the

shower. Going over to the sink to brush his teeth and wash up, he realized he was surprised by that. But then knew he shouldn't be. Lee wasn't going to do a whole postmortem on having sex with him during an undercover operation. She didn't need to. They'd both said everything that needed to be said earlier.

Now they were in uncharted territory; whatever happened next would be new. To them both. He wanted to believe that in some way this would be okay, but that was never the case when he was undercover. Hell, the last time, he'd been working in a coffee shop and ended up putting his boss, Obie Keller, in danger in the swamp. It had only been the fact that he'd reached out to his brother that had saved her.

This time Aaron knew he was going to have to protect Lee. She was the kind of woman who would take risks and put herself in danger to make sure the operation was a success. He understood how important it was to her to find the missing girl and catch the people responsible for taking her, if that was the case. He exhaled roughly, shoving a comb through his hair. There was still so much work to do and his concentration should be focused on that.

Not on Lee showering behind him. Or the fact that he wanted to take her back to bed, pretend that this apartment was anywhere but in Los Angeles. He wanted a life with her. He'd never let himself need anyone. Never. So these emotions swirling around inside him scared him more than anything he'd ever faced undercover.

And that made him hurry through washing up and getting away from her.

But there was no life with Lee or anyone else. Not for him. He wasn't being dramatic. That was the truth. He kept his balance by living undercover. By protecting people who would never know what he did.

He'd tried getting close to someone once, ten years ago, and it had been a disaster.

His life had crashed and burned, and he hadn't allowed himself to get personal since then.

He went into the bedroom to get dressed, thinking that he wanted to believe he'd changed since then, but the truth was there hadn't been anyone he'd allowed himself to care for in that decade. He hadn't even gone home or talked to his brothers.

Not until he had reached out to Xander, and nothing had been the same since then.

Nothing.

Chapter Thirteen

When Lee got out of the shower, she noticed that Aaron had brought her duffel bag into the bedroom and left it on the bed. She left her hair to dry naturally and put on a pair of faded jeans and a short-sleeved T-shirt.

Strangely she wasn't overanalyzing what had happened with Aaron. She knew at some point it was going to hit her, but for now, it seemed like she was cool with it. Or as chill as she *could* be, starting an affair while working undercover for the FBI again. But it was harder than she'd thought it would be.

That woman she'd been back when she was employed by the FBI was so different from the one she was now. Sometimes it felt like she hadn't changed a bit, but this afternoon had shown her just how much she had.

Even so, she had to be careful that she didn't let this thing with Aaron get in the way of the job. The more days that went by without finding Isabell Montez, the more worried she was for the girl.

Heading into the living room, she saw Aaron was on a video call with his boss, Jayne, and his partner, Denis. She also recognized a familiar figure in the background, fellow Price Security employee Rick Stone.

Aaron turned when she walked out and gave her a half smile. "We need your help tracking some addresses. Rick and Denis each went to different locations, but Rick said you noticed they were on the Old Mission Trail or as it is also known the Camino Real."

Lee moved to her keyboard and felt a sense of calm come over her. Yeah, this was what she needed. Nothing got her back to her center like working on a problem on her computer. "Did you enter them in the database, Rick?"

"Yeah. It pinged a pattern, but you know me and technology. I tried to tap it, but then it got messed up. Can you look at it?" he asked.

"Of course," she said, accessing Rick's files remotely and pulling up the geotags he'd put in for the location he'd visited, plus the one Denis had. There was a third address in there as well. "What's the other place?"

"That's a known drop house where weighing and packaging takes place. Also we can add the house in Boyle Heights for money counting. Mistral's as a..." He trailed off, not entirely sure, but it seemed like everything was in close proximity to Mistral's. "Is it central?" Aaron asked, coming to lean over her as her fingers moved on the keyboard, putting in the coordinates for each of them. It wasn't exactly on the Old Mission Trail, but it was pretty close, and all of the locations circled around Boyle Heights.

"It seems like this is the area they are operating in," she said, pointing to her screen.

"Share it to the video call," Aaron told her.

Nodding, she connected wirelessly to his device and shared her screen. While the others were looking at it, she added labels to each area.

"Could you add in where Steve has been traveling?" Denis asked. "I think that we might be seeing two gangs covering the same territory."

She pulled up the algorithm she'd written for him and Aaron to use and loaded those coordinates into the map. There was a small bit of overlap in Boyle Heights, but then Steve was handling things more toward the coast and San Clemente, also a stop on the Old Mission Trail.

"What's in this overlapping area?" Aaron asked. "It's hard

to tell if Steve's working just for the Cachorros or if he's also a player for the Chacals."

"Or is he independent, reporting to someone else?" Rick murmured. "La Fortunata syndicate runs deep and has connections to almost everyone. Is there a chance Steve is more direct to them—not really part of either of the two gangs?"

"He was near the house where you saw the teens taken," Lee confirmed. Thinking that possibly that meant Steve was working for La Fortunata. "But why is he playing at being part of the other gangs if that's the case?"

"We don't have a name or photo for Perses," Denis reminded them.

Aaron looked over at her. "Do you have one of Steve?"

He and Denis both went to their devices, as did Rick, all three men trying to go through the surveillance footage they'd taken. "Send it all to me. I can collate and pull out individual faces."

"Great," Rick said, sending his first.

"How quick will it be?" Aaron asked.

"Not that fast, unfortunately," she replied. "It takes time to run their faces through the databases I have access to so we can identify them. Then you can tell us what name you know these guys by," Lee said.

Denis kept studying the map. Then a moment later, the door opened and Lee noticed her former boss from the FBI and Aaron's boss enter the room. She guessed that their display was up on a big screen because both of them moved closer to it.

"This is where the teens are?" Hammond asked.

"That's where the van stopped and I saw them transferred inside. Not sure if they are still there. I left after the van did and followed it," Rick confirmed.

"Where did it go?" Hammond asked him.

"Toward the Port of Los Angeles," he said. "They turned into this residential area and it was harder to tail them, but my guess is to one of these houses."

Rick leaned forward to touch the screen. "I can't see where you are tapping," Lee told him. "Give me the map coordinates and I'll put a circle on the area."

He gave them to her and she indicated them.

Then she sat back to look at the track. They now had a pretty large circle that the gang was operating in. "We need to get into that house. I can't get a warrant without more than this. Any chance you can get into it, Aaron?"

He went still and Lee turned, watching as a calm came over him. It was almost as if she could hear the wheels turning in his mind.

"I'd have to start something and take down Jorge, but yeah, I could do it," Aaron said.

Taking down Jorge wasn't going to be easy. He was well positioned and Aaron was going to have to do it in front of Ramos. Who knew when Ramos would be back? Unless he went after Javier. There would be more opportunity and it would interrupt the flow, maybe give the team some time to put a tracker on the van they'd used. Right now, they didn't know if the teens were being moved every day or what.

"There's another player I can try for. But we are going to have to establish a pattern before I can do that. I'll keep my eye open for an opportunity," Aaron said.

"Good. I trust you. Denis is going to be at Mistral's tonight and Rick will be at the parking lot in the morning, watching," Jayne said.

"Lee, I need you looking out for teens being brought into the club," Hammond added. "Is there a chance you could set up some cameras in the hallways and at the back doors?"

Aaron realized that this joint operation meant he was no longer in charge of his own op. "She can watch, but the cameras are going to have to wait. I need to get a better feel for who's in and who's out of the place."

Hammond didn't like that and shook his head. "Without eyes—"

"Aaron's in charge in the club. We'll wait for your direction," Jayne interjected.

He smiled, glad to know his boss had his back, but Aaron had always suspected she would. "I will find a place. Just need time to see what's happening. Last night was different with me meeting the other players."

"Fair enough. I'm planting an agent at the coffee shop... Zara's Brew," Hammond said. "Also, I've gotten permission to put cameras on the streetlamps around the strip mall and the coffee shop. We'll keep an eye on what's going on outside until we can get eyes inside there."

"Give me access to the cameras so that I can flag it against the footage I'm already running through facial recognition," Lee said.

Hammond nodded. "You have total access to all the information we have. Did the missing girl you are tracking have a connection to any of the shops in the mall?"

Lee accessed her photo library via the cloud on her computer and clicked on the receipt. Then opened a second window to look at the shops in the mall. Looking over her shoulder, Aaron noticed the receipt was from an old till, the kind that was typical of secondhand or charity shops.

She painstakingly went through each store, finally getting to Frankie's Vintage Fashions. Zooming in on the shop, she hovered over the mannequins in the windows wearing secondhand clothes. Aaron could tell from the excited look on her face that she might have discovered something.

"There's a place that could be a potential lead. Frankie's," she told the team. "I have a receipt I found in the pocket of a jacket at Isabell's house. I'll check it out tomorrow."

"I'll send some undercover agents in too," Hammond said.

"No. There's too many new people," Aaron told him. "That's a sign that La Fortunata syndicate will recognize. Let the three of us do it. Rick's just sleeping in his car, but Lee can go in and say she needs some new clothes for this gig. She's new but known to the gang," he said. "Your coffee-shop person is the only new person I want there."

Before Hammond had a chance to argue further, Aaron went on to say, "We spent a long time setting this up, Hammond. We're finally close to catching La Fortunata and I think they might be part of your people smuggling ring as well."

"We believe they are pulling the strings behind the operation. We've only uncovered small players so far, and they don't have the funds to move the teens around the way they have been. Which means these kids stay gone," Jayne said.

"How many teens are missing?" Denis asked.

"Dozens in this area. Usually from the same school district or neighborhood," Hammond said.

"That explains why the cops are so blasé about looking for Isabell. What about the families?" Lee asked. "Are they usually gone?"

"Some are. We are getting about fifty percent reporting from teachers and the other reports from parents," Hammond replied. "The cops direct all of the cases to us to investigate."

"Do you think there is someone in the schools involved?" Lee asked.

Hammond raised his eyebrows as if to say he wasn't sure. "I've got two subs at the schools to see what they can find. But right now, we're not entirely certain. Your girl is from the same high school as several kids who disappeared."

When the meeting broke up he pulled Lee to the side.

"What's up?"

"I don't like those numbers," she said to him quietly. "Why didn't Boyd mention the other kids?"

"Sounds like he's hiding something," Aaron said.

Lee gave him a hard look. "I've known him since high school."

"So?"

"Forget it."

She turned to leave and he stopped her with his hand on her shoulder. "Sorry. I don't trust anyone."

"Anyone?"

"Well, you," he said, leaning in close. "Sometimes Xander and Denis."

"Me?"

"Don't make me repeat it," he said. "Call your friend and talk to him."

"I'm planning on it."

Aaron needed to be at the club before Lee and they'd decided to ride over together. She'd done her hair and makeup and put on the same dress as the night before. She was going to go into the vintage-clothing place while he went to the club. They hadn't had any time alone, really, until now when they were in the car heading back to Mistral's.

"You okay?" Aaron asked her as they were driving. She seemed distracted and that wasn't what he was used to from her.

"Yeah, why?"

"You don't seem to be all here," he said. "If you need a night off, I can make an excuse. You've had a rough day."

"No, I'm good to work. I'm not distracted per se, but the connection between the school and these kids isn't one I was expecting," she admitted.

Her friend worked at the school. "Did you get a chance to call your friend? Do you think he knows more than they said?"

"Not really sure. It is interesting that he came to me with this girl after so many other kids have gone missing there," she said. "Hard not to think the worst."

"How so?"

She really didn't want to say it out loud, because then it would be real. Kind of like when she'd recognized Cate and tried to convince herself that possibly it couldn't be her. She didn't want to think the worst of Boyd. He was all she had left of Hannah... But Aaron was right there. Supportive and waiting. "What if he's working for the bad guys and maybe Isabell got away, so Boyd asks me to track her down?" she said hoarsely.

He put his free hand on her thigh, squeezing it to comfort her. "It's not out of the realm of possibility. Depends on how much her parents owe or took from them. But he could just be a concerned teacher too," Aaron told her.

Her lips quirked. "Playing devil's advocate?"

"Just learned through experience that you can't rule out common decency." No one was all good or all bad. Even if her friend was involved, he might genuinely care for the Montez girl and want to keep her safe. Working undercover showed him all the time the varying degrees that people were willing to go to. Everyone cared for someone. "So what are you going to do?"

"About Boyd?"

He nodded.

"Not sure yet. I'm going to go to the school and check up on her friends. I'd already planned to do that. But I'll check on him too. Hammond will pull the class schedules for the kids who have disappeared. Maybe there will be a pattern."

There was *always* a pattern. Aaron knew half of his success came from spotting the connections and making the right ones. However, there were spontaneous coincidences as well, which could be misconstrued as patterns. He'd gone down the wrong path more than once. That was part of undercover work. No one was perfect.

"I'm happy to help if you need me to," he offered. "You're not working this on your own. I'll ask around and see what I can find out about the school dealers."

"Thanks. I'm worried about how much time has passed. If she's being held, then there's a chance we're not getting her back unless we can get into that house. Which even Hammond knows is a long shot. That's why he was so keen on your boss pressing you to get moved there." She shot him a warning look. "You can't trust Hammond... I mean, not with yourself. He'll always put the mission first. He's single-minded when it comes to stopping trafficking and he'll throw you under the bus to do it."

Aaron wanted to ask her more about that but wasn't sure if the timing was right. But in the end, he couldn't hold off. "You worked for him, right?"

"Yeah. What do you want to know?" she asked.

"What happened, but I'm not sure we have time before we get to Mistral's," he admitted.

"I'm not sure I want to tell you."

"Fair enough. But it's tied to the woman you thought was Cate?"

"It is. If she is in fact Cate, she's dangerous. We suspect she is the daughter of the head of La Fortunata syndicate, raised separately from Perses and brought up with no connections so she could infiltrate the FBI and become a mole. She gave them the entire operation that we used to have." Lee blew out a breath. "She didn't just burn me and Van, she shook Hammond to the core. He wants her."

"You and Van do too," he said quietly.

"We do. I hope you never have to experience it, Aaron, but when someone betrays your cover it feels *personal*. I don't know how I couldn't see past the role Cate was playing. It made me second-guess myself for a long time," she admitted.

He squeezed her thigh as he turned into the parking lot of the strip mall where Mistral's was. "It's in our nature to trust people we have a bond with. That's why working undercover is so successful. Everyone is looking for another person who sees the world the way they do."

She put her hand on his and rubbed his knuckles where he had a thick scar from cutting his hand when he'd punched a window as a sixteen-year-old boy. It had bled like a mother and hurt like a bitch, but he hadn't flinched or reacted to it. Just took it like a man. Which was the dumbest sentiment he'd ever heard. How did that prove anything except that he was stupid?

He shook his head. "We all make mistakes."

"We do, but mine and Hammond's cost lives. I can't do that again," she said. "This scar looks old."

"It is." He didn't want to talk about it so he kept the focus on her. "You *won't* do it again," he said.

"How can you be so certain when I'm not?" she asked as he pulled into a parking space and turned off the car.

"You're not a woman to make the same mistake twice. That's why you're tracking down this girl and that's why you're going to investigate your friend. You don't trust easily and you're not afraid to change your opinion of someone. A lot of people are."

"You're not."

"No, but then I tend to see the worst in everyone, so when I change my opinion, it's because they've proven they aren't a piece of shit," he said. "Not a great way to live your life."

Chapter Fourteen

Frankie's wasn't that busy when she walked through the door. Like most of the retailers that operated here she was sure they did a really brisk business earlier in the day.

"We're closing in thirty minutes. There's a fitting room in the back," the lady behind the register announced when she saw Lee.

"Thanks, I won't be that long. I work over at Mistral's and need a few more dresses," she said. "Can you point me to some? I'm a size twelve, not sure if you have a lot of those."

"We've got a pretty good stock," the woman replied as she came around the counter. "Though I'm not sure they'll suit you for Mistral's."

"Have you been in there? I'm Lee, by the way."

"Candace. A few times. My boyfriend, Pete, is a bouncer there," she said. "You might know him."

"Yeah, we've met. The first day when I was trying to get a job and he mentioned my wardrobe needed an upgrade."

Candace winced. "That's not like him."

"To be fair, I was in jeans and a flannel shirt," she said wryly. *"Girl."*

"I know. But they are comfy." Lee giggled, finding herself slipping into her undercover role. "Have you met my man, Quinn? He's just started running the club."

"No, but I might try to stop by later after I close up here," Candace said. "Here's the rack. Take your time."

Lee flipped through the clothes on the rack, looking for a similar dress and instead finding something that she loved for herself. Not for the undercover gig. It was a fit and flare–style dress, which was always flattering on her curvy body type. She took it off the rail and noticed it had a sweetheart neckline. It was made of a deep sapphire velvet. So not for the bar, but she wanted it and a quick look at the price tag told her it was within her budget.

She found a few more dresses that would work for Mistral's and then went to try them on. The velvet had no give and the size twelve was from probably the '40s, so not as roomy as the same size today. But she was able to get the side zipper up, and when she turned to examine herself in the mirror…she saw a different version of herself. In this dress, she'd look right on Aaron's arm when he was dressed in those skinny suits he favored. Maybe out for a nice dinner…except that seemed like a dream.

Not when they were undercover and everything was so up in the air. Who knew if they'd even be able to go on a date after this operation was over? She knew he might be sent to another location to infiltrate another gang. Another worry was that she was part of his cover, like he'd told her. And the cover always came first when working this kind of operation.

She was still getting the dress though. When she looked in the mirror and saw herself…she liked what she saw. This wasn't a version of Lee that she had ever allowed herself to be.

Only one of the slip dresses worked; the other one clung to her hips and she struggled to get it back off. She heard the door open, and this time, Candace greeted the person who entered.

"There's a customer in the changing room," Candace said.

Lee hurried to get back into her own clothes and used the camera on her phone to try to see who Candace was talking to. A tall redheaded woman with her back to the dressing rooms. *Was it Cate?*

Lee swallowed hard. Unsure if she should go out there to find out. If it was Cate, and she recognized Lee, then Aaron was in danger. And she might put the entire operation in jeopardy.

Candace's face as she looked up at the woman's was tense, and she nodded a few times before reaching under the counter and handing something to her. The redhead took it and put it in her bag before walking out of the shop. Lee put her phone away and then left the dressing room area.

She noticed Candace was slightly paler than before but smiled at Lee when she saw her. "Find anything? Oh, that blue dress is divine!"

"It is and I'm taking it even if I only wear it at home. I'm also getting this dress," she said, holding it up before laying both garments she was going to purchase on the counter. "Was there someone else in the shop?"

"Just a regular who checks to see if I get any Prada stilettos in a size six. She comes in pretty much every week," Candace replied.

"Do you get a lot of luxury brands and high-end customers?" she asked casually. All the while thinking about Isabell, who was definitely not buying high-end. But Lee didn't have a receipt yet so she couldn't pinpoint this vintage shop as the place the missing girl had been.

"No, definitely not. I mean, you've looked at the racks. I get a lot of old vintage stuff more than Prada or Dior. My clientele consists mostly of a lot of teens and gals in their early twenties who have a good eye for clothes and are watching their budget."

"That makes sense," Lee said. Candace rang up the dresses while Lee toyed with showing her a picture of Isabell. But right now, she couldn't rule out that Candace was part of the operation.

The redhead had definitely picked something up from her. But what?

Candace put the dresses in a brown bag stamped with the Frankie's logo and handed her a receipt. One glance confirmed that it matched the one that Lee had found in the jacket at Isabell's house.

A zing of satisfaction went through her. She was getting

somewhere with the case. Her gut had told her she was in the right place and now she had a connection.

"Thanks. Stop by the bar if you're in Mistral's later," Lee said, taking her bag and walking out of the shop. She used the spare set of keys that Aaron had given her to unlock the van and put her dresses in it. While she was there, she leaned against the side and texted an update to the team about the receipt and the redhead.

Pain and Panic were sitting at the bar when Aaron walked in. Both looked up from the drinks they were nursing, clocked him and then went back to their conversation. The bagmen would know all the houses. Which was why Aaron liked being one of them. But it was going to take time to earn enough of Ramos's trust to get that job. And these two were a team. He wasn't going to knock one of them out and take his place.

Or *was* he?

"Dudes. How's it going?"

"Not bad. You settling in?" Panic replied.

Aaron grinned. "Trying to. I like Mistral's."

"Everyone likes the club, and you haven't even been here on a Friday night. That's when things are another level," Pain told him. "Not that we get to enjoy it."

Pain reached behind the bar and hit the tap, filling up his glass, and tipped his head toward Aaron, who nodded yes, he'd have one. The other man went around the bar and filled up a glass for him.

"It's not always all work and no play. Sometimes we do get to kick back and have some fun," Panic said, handing a draft beer to him. "It's alright."

"Yeah. Maybe we can swap for a night down the road so you can hang here," Aaron suggested to Pain.

"Doubt that Jorge will allow that. We're part of his crew from way back," the man said. "Who do you know here?"

"Jako. You met him?"

"Yeah, he's alright," Panic replied. "You with his crew for a while?"

"Some time. Helped him with a problem and now we're tight," Aaron said.

The door opened again, and this time, Jorge strode in and nodded to Pain and Panic, who got up and went to follow their boss. The other man didn't acknowledge Aaron at all. Aaron left his beer on the bar and went upstairs to the office. The door was closed and he opened it with the key Ramos had given him earlier.

Though Aaron knew he wasn't the only one with access to this place. He guessed there had to be five or six keys to this door. However, the code to the safe was known only to himself and Ramos. So at least that was a bit more secure.

He sat down at the desk, realizing that he was going to have to start hanging with the rest of the gang. Getting to know them better. But that meant taking Lee with him and it would cut into the amount of time they had to go look into other leads.

Knowing Lee could hold her own in any situation didn't mean he wasn't still worried for her safety. Their cover was holding, but only a fool wouldn't know that it was tenuous at best. There were so many little things that could trigger suspicion. Sometimes it wasn't anything real. These guys were over-the-top paranoid.

His phone pinged. He glanced down to see the generic notification that he and Denis used, which meant that someone in their operation group had sent a text. Leaning back in his chair, he put his feet up on the desk and then used his passcode to unlock the message.

He was pleased with what he read. Apparently, Lee had spotted a redhead in Frankie's and verified the receipt her missing girl had was from the vintage shop. She also told him there was a connection between the shop girl and his bouncer.

Aaron closed his phone and got up. Time to meet the staff and start putting his stamp on the club. He went downstairs as more of the bar staff and bouncers were arriving.

"Gather up," he commanded.

Jorge was gone as were Pain and Panic. But Flo and Lee were there. Along with the bouncers whose names he hadn't learned and mentally was calling Tweedle Dee and Tweedle Dum. Plus, there was a staff guy and the VIP bouncer as well as the wait-resses. All in total, ten people including himself.

"I'm Quinn. I've met some of you but not everyone. Tell me your name and what you do," he said.

"I'm Flo, I run the bar. Along with your woman, I have two other bartenders that work on the weekends, Marshall and Tyler. They take a few of the weeknights as well."

Aaron tipped his head toward the burly bouncer. He stepped forward.

"Name's Brian... I'm in charge of security." He pointed to three men standing near him. "That's Pete and Dan and Jack. We rotate between the front doors and VIP. On the weekends, I bring in three other guys who also spell us during the week."

"Jessie. I'm the head VIP hostess. This is Dana and that's Laurel. We have four more girls who come in on Fridays and Saturdays."

"Nice to meet you all," Aaron said, briefly making eye contact with each of the staff members. "For now things will oper-ate as they have been, but if I see something that I think could run more smoothly, I'll mention it. If you have any problems, bring them to me."

Everyone either nodded or rolled their eyes and then dis-persed to go finish getting ready before the doors opened. He noticed that Lee was back behind the bar, prepping glasses and her station. He headed over to the bar, leaning on it. "You find a dress?"

"Yeah. Found two actually. And met Candace, who is with Pete."

Aaron glanced over at the muscled man who stood inside the door, checking his phone. He'd start with Pete. It was going to take a bit to get everyone comfortable with him, but it was crucial he get to know all the players. He rubbed the back of his neck and then felt Lee's hand on his as she leaned over the bar and kissed him.

It distracted him from his own thoughts and he appreci-ated it. He would find a way to move up the ranks, he always did. An opportunity would present itself and then he'd use it to his advantage.

"Later, babe."

"Later," she said.

As he walked away he was aware that Flo watched his every move.

Flo kept her busy up until the time the doors opened. Lee had been hoping to find a moment to get a better layout of the entire club. She wanted to design some passive security features that they could use to monitor what was happening inside. But it seemed to her that there was always someone either observing her or asking her to do something for them.

"I'm going to be off tomorrow night and Marshall will be here. He tends to run late, so make sure you're here early," the woman said when they had a lull at the bar.

"Yeah, I will be. Quinn and I drive over together."

"How long you two been an item?" Flo asked curiously.

"About six months," she said.

Flo furrowed her brow. *"About?"*

"Yeah, he counts it from the first time we hooked up, and I count it from the first time we had coffee and I decided it would be more than a one-night stand," Lee explained.

Flo smiled. "Guys always think hooking up is a relationship."

Did Aaron? Hell, it was definitely more than a one-night stand, right? It had been for her. She'd learned early on that she couldn't control anyone else's emotions, only her own. "Yeah, can't argue with that. You with anyone?"

"Not now. This job is very demanding and I have a lot of responsibility here. So I have to take calls when I'm off, and it's a lot."

"Wow. Really?" she murmured. "My grandpa owned a bar and he was always fishing when he wasn't working."

"Every place is different. But I knew what I was getting into when I took this job."

Which told Lee nothing. "Will I have to be that available when I'm off the clock?"

"Girl, you already are. You're with the new boss and he's going to be pretty much living out of this place," Flo said.

"Do you do other stuff around here besides overseeing the bar?" Lee asked, being as subtle as she could.

"I do. I've worked with Ramos for a long time." Flo gave her a pointed look. "You'll probably be involved as soon as Ramos gets to know you."

Lee took that in. It seemed to her that everyone who worked here was part of the criminal gang as well. The last time she'd been undercover, she'd been in the command center watching over Van and Cate. But this time she was in the mix and it felt odd. Like she was out of control.

The rest of the night went by quickly and though she watched the doors she didn't see any teens in the club or going up the stairs. Aaron was the life of the party, circulating through the dance floor and mingling with all of the people in the VIP section.

When the club closed, Flo reminded her she'd be out tomorrow, then showed her how to make the deposit to take to the bank at the end of the night. "Marshall should pick up the bank for the register on his way in. When I'm back, we can work on getting you set up to do it too. Have a good evening."

"You too," she said with a bright smile.

Aaron was busy talking to Brian so Lee decided to check out the bathrooms and the hallway again. From her spot behind the bar, she hadn't seen anyone bringing money or drugs in or out of the club. She knew she was missing something.

But what?

Taking her time as she sauntered into the ladies room, she noticed that one of the stalls was out of order. Scanning the walls of the bathroom, she didn't see an obvious camera in there, but there was a mirror over the sink and she had no idea what was behind it. To be on the safe side, she turned on the hot water faucet until it steamed and started to cover the mirror. Then she went to the stall next to the out-of-order one, climbing up on the toilet to peer over the top. The "faulty" toilet looked fine and there was a crack in the brick wall next to it.

Glancing at the door to make sure she was still alone, she got down on the floor to crawl under the locked door and then stood up. She ran her hand along the crack and felt air stirring behind it.

Was this the outside wall? Mentally she reviewed the lay-out of the club. She was pretty sure this wall would be under the stairs that went up to the office and the locked room. But it was a *brick* wall. She didn't see any hinges to indicate a door.

She pushed on the wall and it budged. Not easily. So she pushed again and it moved a few more inches. The entire section of cracked brick moving as one. One more shove and a gap opened, big enough for her to stick her head through.

It was dark, smelling of dirt and a little bit like the club and bathroom. Then she heard the bathroom door open and froze.

Her heart racing in her chest, she waited with bated breath.

"Lee?"

Aaron. Thank God.

"Yeah. Sorry, won't be a moment," she said in case he wasn't alone.

"It's just me," he assured her, coming toward the stall where she was.

She unlocked the stall and opened the door. The water was still running at the sink, providing a fair amount of steam.

Aaron put his fingers to his lips, cautioning her not to speak, and she gestured to the opening she'd created.

He put his hands on her waist and shifted her to the side so he could look into the opening. Turning back, he whispered. "I'm not sure if this place is wired."

"Me either. I don't know how to close this," she whispered back.

He shoved on the wall again and it opened all the way. They noticed that it was a short hallway but couldn't see where it led. Aaron motioned for her to stay behind him as he used the flashlight on his phone to light the area up.

There was a door at the other end, but no one in the hall. He moved farther into it and Lee started to follow, but when he stepped over the threshold, the bricks shifted and started to move back into place.

"Wait here."

Chapter Fifteen

Aaron was aware of Lee watching as he moved farther down the hallway. There was a door at the end that had one of those bar handles, and he pushed it open and saw the main parking lot, which was almost empty except for his van and two other vehicles. There was no light above the door and it was pretty much dark, but he wasn't sure if he could be observed or not.

He hadn't noticed the door and would have liked to observe it from the outside but still wanted to finish checking out the hallway. There had to be stairs if there was an exit leading out back, because there was no way into the club from the hallway.

He went back, letting the door close behind him, and only then turned the flashlight on his phone back on.

"Where does that lead?" Lee asked him quietly when he approached.

"Parking lot," he said, shining the light on the wall until he found cement-block stairs, which were narrow and not lit. "I'm going upstairs. Go back out in the club and wait for me."

"What if you need backup?"

"I'll be fine. Everyone's gone, but I'm not sure if someone will come back. I need you to watch the club. So far, at least five people seem to come and go at will from here," Aaron said, coming back to her. "I'll be fine. Don't forget to call for help if you get into trouble."

"I'll be okay," she promised, then touched his face. "Don't do anything rash."

"I won't."

Watching her go, he waited until she stepped back into the bathroom stall and the bricks slowly slid closed. Could this entrance have been the one originally used to bring teens in? He wasn't sure yet. He knew that Lee would figure it out. That was her strong suit, he'd realized over the last few days. Give her a puzzle and she'd come at it from every different angle until she solved it.

He turned back to the stairs, not using his flashlight as he went up, because he wasn't sure what he'd find at the top. There was another door with a bar handle. Aaron took a deep breath, mentally ready for a fight when he opened it. He didn't have a weapon, but at his size, he didn't need one to deal with whatever he found on the other side.

He pushed the door but it was locked.

His adrenaline still pumping, he considered what to do next. He had kicked in a few doors in his time, but that would leave damage, which would alert Ramos and his people that someone had broken in. So that was a no-go. Then he remembered he had his keys, with a pickpocketing tool that he thought should enable him to open the door.

Squatting down so he was eye level with the handle, he propped his phone on his thigh, with the light angled so it shone on the lock. Then he started working. It took him longer than he wanted to admit until he heard the click and the lock opened.

Voilà.

He switched off the flashlight again and pocketed his keys and phone. Then, rolling his head from side to side, he cracked his knuckles and exhaled deeply before opening the door. When he stepped through it, he realized he was in the locked room.

There were four teens on the floor, all with their hands and feet tied together. They didn't even look up when he entered and he realized they were drugged. One of them sort of noticed him, but then their gaze dropped back to the floor. There wasn't anyone else in the room.

Fuck. Just fuck. Having suspicions, hearing that Cate O'Dell had been linked to human trafficking and seeing the evidence with his own eyes made him sick. He was on his knees next to one of the kids before he could stop himself.

Aaron couldn't free them without raising suspicion, so instead, he took photos of each of them and then took his tracking-and-communication device off his neck and put it on the girl at the end behind her long hair.

"I've transferred my device to one of four teens that are bound and drugged in the room at the top of the stairs at the club." Denis was monitoring his comms and Aaron wanted his partner to know that he'd left the device behind. He might not be able to get the kids out tonight, but he was damned sure going to track down where they were being moved to.

With his visual confirmation that it was teens being trafficked, the joint task force would be able to take action.

He left the room. Relocked the bar handle before going downstairs and exiting into the parking lot. He carefully made his way back to the bar entrance of the club. Then texted Lee to let him in. She didn't answer, which he suspected meant she wasn't alone.

Fuck.

He got to the door and had to pick the lock again. Which was slightly quicker this time. He let himself into the area behind the bar and took a moment to listen and try to identify who might be in there with her.

"You still have connections at Madness?"

Aaron thought it might be Ramos, and he was surprised because the dude said he wouldn't be back. Also was he looking for Aaron? If so, what had Lee said to cover for him?

"I know one of the other bartenders, but we aren't close," Lee said.

"Do you think you could *get* close?" Ramos asked brusquely.

"I can try. On my day off, I'll see if she wants to meet up for coffee," Lee said. "Aaron should be done moving those tanks around for me. Let me go check."

Before she came around the corner, Aaron walked out. "Tanks changed. Ramos, you need me?"

"I do. Let's go upstairs," Ramos said.

"I'll wait in the van," Lee told Aaron.

He just nodded at her. She gave him a worried look; now that he'd given his communication device to the teens, there was no backup if things went wrong. He squeezed her butt for reassurance on the way by.

After Lee left the club, he and Ramos went up to the office. Aaron wondered if there was a silent alarm on one of the doors that they had opened and if his cover might have been blown.

From the moment she'd come out of the bathroom and seen Ramos standing at the bar, Lee had been on edge. She had no time to warn Aaron. Denis was listening, but he would only send in help when and if she asked for it. Which right now she didn't know if she would.

"Where's Quinn?" Ramos asked.

"I asked him to change the tanks for me. Trying to prep for tomorrow. Flo's off and she mentioned Marshall tends to run late," Lee said.

"You're Quinn's woman," he said.

"Yeah, came over when Quinn did. I used to work at Madness," she said, using the cover story they'd already established. She'd okayed it with Luna and Nick, so she felt safe mentioning it to Ramos.

"How long did you work there?" he asked.

"Almost a year."

"Why'd you leave?"

"Quinn said he'd be running Mistral's and we thought it would be nice to work together," she told him. Not sure if that was what Ramos wanted to hear or not. He was a big man with a buzz cut and tattoo sleeves on both arms. She noted he had something written in Spanish on his neck, but Lee didn't recognize the word.

He watched her but gave nothing away. At this moment, she had no idea if he was toying with her or just feeling her out.

"You still have any contacts there?" he asked.

She told him that she had a friend that she wasn't close to, figuring she'd use Luna if she needed to. Then he asked her to try to get closer.

She guessed he wanted a connection in that club. Nick ran a tight ship, so there wasn't a chance for Ramos or his gang selling in there. Aaron came back, and he and Ramos went upstairs. She left and went back to the van, very nervous for Aaron.

When she got into the vehicle, she jumped out of her skin when Denis said quietly, "I'm here. Just get on your phone and act normal."

She shifted her hair forward, so if anyone was watching from the side, they wouldn't see her talking. "I'll try. Ramos took Aaron upstairs."

"Yeah, I heard. There are four teens in the locked room. Aaron left his device with them. So far, there hasn't been any noise in the room. But I have the team back at the office monitoring it. We are going to track them when they are moved tomorrow. Might be the same house that Rick followed them to yesterday. Not sure."

Lee was horrified but not surprised. As soon as she'd glimpsed Cate O'Dell, she'd known in her gut that kids were in danger. The information would be helpful as much as she wished she'd been wrong. She opened the app she'd created on her phone to double-check the device was still sending a signal so she would be able to monitor the movements. It took her a few minutes, but she'd already connected wirelessly to both her and Aaron's device, so she would be able to listen back and search for anything she missed while working.

"I've got it here. I'll monitor as well," she said. "Did you see Ramos enter?"

"Yes. He went in about a minute before you came out of the bathroom. He drove up in a Chrysler 300 SRT8 and his driver is still sitting in the car. Not sure if there is anyone else in the vehicle."

"When did you get in the van?" she asked.

"After I left the club. There wasn't anyone watching."

Good to know that he had gotten in undetected, but that brought another question to mind. "Where's your car?"

"Jessie came and got it earlier so I could stick around."

"Who's Jessie?" Lee was very aware that she was asking questions to keep the conversation going so she didn't have to dwell on Aaron by himself with no listening device in the club with a very dangerous man.

"My girlfriend."

She nodded and then looked back down at the phone. She saw the pictures that Aaron had sent of the four teens. They looked so young sitting against the wall. It almost seemed as if they were sleeping, but she knew they were drugged. Two of them had cuts on their face and necks. And one had a bloodied lip.

Safe to say, they hadn't gone willingly.

"I'll run the kids' faces and see if I can identify them," she told Denis.

"Thanks. That'd be great. I'm giving Aaron five more minutes and then I'm going in."

"I'll go too. Just need a weapon," she said. Relieved to hear that Denis wasn't going to just leave Aaron in there alone.

"Aaron's should be in the glove box. Use the key to open it."

She nodded. Denis was tapping something on his phone and Lee got to work putting the teens' pictures into her database. It started searching and kicked back Snapchat accounts on all of them. She traced it back further and got names, then felt sick when she realized they all attended local high schools, one of them San Pedro High. Boyd's school. Isabell's school. What was going on there?

Tomorrow she was going to pay Boyd a visit and get some answers.

"We've got the go-ahead to go back inside. I'll follow behind you. I need you to be sort of whiny, like it's getting late and you want to go home. Take this hoodie of Aaron's and put the weapon in the pocket. Depending on what you find, use the opportunity to get close to Aaron and give him the weapon and then dive for cover."

Hearing what Denis wanted of her made her hands shake as she unlocked the glove box and took out the weapon. She put it in her pocket and then took a deep breath and closed her eyes. Trying to get her head to the place it needed to be to do this.

She was nervous and scared, not for herself but for Aaron. He'd been up there with Ramos a long time, and she had no idea what she and Denis were going to encounter.

"How will you get out?"

"Side door when you open yours. Ramos's car doesn't have a view of it. I'll stick to the shadows as best I can," he replied.

"Let me go in and I'll call you if we need you," Lee said. "No use giving you away if we don't have to."

"Okay. But if I don't hear Aaron's voice when you get to him, I'm coming in."

Ramos didn't say anything until he was seated behind the desk. He leaned back in the chair and rubbed his chin. Just making Aaron wait.

He lounged against the door and crossed his legs casually to let Ramos know he wasn't scared. But, in reality, he was tense and ready for a fight. Had been ready for one since he'd found Lee in the bathroom with that opened brick wall behind her.

This gang was dangerous, more so than they had guessed when he'd been set up to infiltrate and try to get the identity of Perses. He was also angry and wanted someone to pay for those kids who had been bound and drugged.

"Jorge said you were palling up to Pain and Panic."

Aaron shot Ramos a look. "They work for me."

"*You* work for me. They work for Jorge. Leave them alone."

"What's the big deal?" he asked. Not sure why Jorge was worried unless one of them was a weak link.

"He doesn't like anyone messing with his boys," Ramos bit out. "I'm telling you to leave them be."

"Sure. Was just being friendly. I'm new and don't really know who I can trust," he said.

"That seems to be going around. Jorge doesn't want you poaching his boys, got it?"

"I don't have a team other than the club," he said.

"The club is all you need. You stick with the club and keep everything running smoothly and we'll be okay."

Aaron shrugged and nodded. He had no issue with that for now.

"I want to get a toehold into Madness," Ramos informed him, switching gears. "Encourage your woman to use her connections there."

"No problem. I'll get her on it." Aaron knew Quinn would be the kind of man who'd make his girlfriend do what he wanted. Aaron not so much. But this was the business of living undercover. He had to play that part. Be someone that he knew wasn't true to himself.

Usually it didn't bother him, but this time, he wasn't sure. It was starting to wear on him in a way that it hadn't before. "That all?"

"No," the other man answered. "I heard you had some problems with Javier."

"Not really. Just walked out into the hallway after I thought it was empty and he was there."

"Watch yourself," Ramos warned. "Anyway, how did you think the club was tonight?"

"Not bad. One altercation, which Pete handled. I was hoping to wade in, but he didn't need me."

"You a fighter?"

Aaron shrugged. "Only if I have to."

"And you often have to?"

"Not all the time. I don't look for trouble, but if it finds me, then I'm happy to oblige," Aaron replied. Knowing that wasn't a lie. That part of Quinn was totally him. He had no problem when things got physical. He liked to test his strength and a part of him was always ready to prove he was the alpha.

"Babe! I'm tired. Where are you?" Lee's voice came up the stairs.

Ramos raised both eyebrows at him, then tilted his head to the door. "Remember what I said."

Aaron nodded, opening the door and heading down the stairs as Lee was coming up. She had his hoodie on over her dress, and as soon as he got close, she pressed the pocket of the hoodie with a weapon against him.

"I told you to wait in the van," he snapped. "You're embarrassing me in front of my boss."

"It's cold and I'm tired," she said in a sort of whiny tone that he'd never heard her use before.

"Believe me, babe. I'll warm you up when we get home."

"Are we leaving now?"

"Yeah. But next time stay in the van," he said harshly.

Ramos had come out and was at the top of the stairs. Aaron wasn't about to get physical with Lee, but he did take her wrist in his hand and sort of drag her behind him down the rest of the stairs and out of the club.

He noticed Ramos's car, and the driver was behind the wheel looking down on his phone as they walked by.

When he got to the van, he opened the passenger door and lifted her up onto the seat before slamming the door and walking around. Acting like he was angry. Anyone watching would definitely buy it.

He got behind the wheel and shoved his keys into the ignition, turning the van on and driving away.

"Sorry."

"Don't be. I'm glad you came in. But I had to be Quinn. I didn't hurt you, did I?"

"No. You didn't," she assured him. "Denis and I were afraid you were in trouble. He's in the back of the van by the way."

"Denis, did you get the message about the teens?"

"Yes. It's been relayed. The FBI and control agreed to leave the kids where they are for now. Tomorrow after they are delivered, wherever it is they are going, they'll access the area and plan a raid," Denis told him. "Jayne is pissed, by the way, that you took off your device. That's your backup."

"They were drugged and tied up, Denis. I had no choice."

"I know. I would have done the same. She's suggested you carry an additional tracking device from now on."

"Sure. Whatever. It's been a long night and I am spoiling for a fight," Aaron muttered. "Sorry for being an ass."

"You weren't," Denis said.

"Want me to drop you somewhere?"

"Jessie is meeting me at the gas station near your apartment. I'll walk over when you go in," he said.

They got back to the apartment. Aaron knew the other man would wait until they were gone before getting out. He went up the stairs to the apartment, aware of Lee walking quietly next to him. She hadn't said much since they'd gotten back to the van.

He wondered if she didn't like what she'd seen of him tonight.

She had to know that undercover personas were just amped-up versions of traits that were already inside. He didn't like that part of himself, but he knew it was there and worked hard to control it.

He wished she'd never seen it.

Chapter Sixteen

Neither of them said much once they were in the apartment. Lee was still processing the change in Aaron. It made her uncomfortable to be around him. But she knew that was *Quinn*, not Aaron. He kept running his hands through his hair and finally put his hands on his hips as he turned to her.

"I'm sorry. I had to do that. Ramos was expecting it," he said.

"I know that. Don't ever compromise doing what you have to while you're undercover. I get that. It was just unnerving to see the anger on your face when you looked at me." He'd scared her. She never allowed herself to dwell on the fact that he was so much bigger and stronger than she was. And while she didn't see herself as a victim, his strength gave him an advantage that she was never going to match.

"I would never hurt you, Lee," he rasped. "I need to know you trust me."

She hesitated. More than anything, she wanted to but, honestly, wasn't as sure about him as she'd been earlier in the day. It was almost as if she'd been in some sort of dream state of what this undercover gig would entail. Sleeping with Aaron... She had no regrets about that. She'd wanted and needed him with a fiery intensity that took her breath away. But leaving herself vulnerable to this complex man...? Well, she had second thoughts now.

"You don't."

She took a deep breath, wondering how to put it into words. "I trust you to do what you have to in order to take down Ramos and get to the head of La Fortunata syndicate. And I know you'll do it."

He closed the distance between them but stopped when there was a few inches left. "Of course I will. That's my job. But what about you and me?"

"Like you said, the lines blur. Aaron and Quinn are very different men and I'm still Lee in both situations—"

"Put a barrier up. That's how I do it. I take what people want to see, and that's my persona in the club." A muscle ticked in his jaw. "Can you do that? Get that Lee and Quinn might be toxic as a couple because they are in a bad situation but Aaron and Lee aren't?"

It seemed important to him that she see the distinction. Part of her did. She knew that Aaron and Lee worked and played well together. But she hadn't thought of putting up a barrier in her mind when she was in the club. Could she do that? Would it make a difference?

"Lee, love, please see that," he ground out.

She met his blue gaze and wavered for a moment before asking, "Why is this so important to you?"

"I don't want to be the monster I used to be. I need to know that you can see something else in me," he said, his voice low and harsh.

One small step closed the gap between them and she wrapped her arms around his middle, resting her head on his chest. "You are *not* a monster."

His arms went around her and his hand ran up and down her back. He held her to him but didn't say anything else. She hoped he believed her. Because as scared as she'd been by the change in him at the club, as more time passed, she was starting to see the differences in his behaviors.

"I just wasn't ready for any of that tonight," she admitted. "The last time I was undercover, I was in a van the entire time, monitoring everyone and everything."

"You're doing great. It was a lot tonight. I wasn't prepared to see those kids in that room. I knew what they were using it for, but that... It was a lot."

She squeezed him tight and stepped away. "It was. I have managed to identify them. They all go to local high schools, one of them the same one as Isabell did. I'm going to go visit Boyd tomorrow and push for some more information."

"Good idea. I was planning to see if Jorge will let me ride along with him tomorrow. Trying to build trust."

"That's fine. I'll be safe at the high school and you need to move up quickly. I don't imagine Hammond is going to wait to get the plan in place once he sees those photos. He wants the head of the organization, but he can't let those kids be used to get them."

He lifted a brow. "Do you really believe that?"

"I do. That's why he does that job. Depending on what I find at the school, I'm sure he's going to have an agent or asset who works for him set up there and let them get taken. He'll find another way in, once we know for sure what is going on."

Lee knew her old boss. The loss of those young kids when Cate turned on them all those years ago still haunted him like it did her and Van. No one was going to sacrifice those teens to get Perses. Not if they could help it.

"If Jorge says no, then Denis and I will tail him, but I'd like to get inside and see what the setup is like at these different houses," Aaron said.

They both went to their laptops and did a little bit of work checking in with their bosses and sending updates to the entire team. Lee was happy to see that Van was on assignment, so he'd be distracted from Cate still being alive. She'd always been good at watching his back and knew that she still was.

Aaron cracked his knuckles and then closed his laptop. "You want me to sleep on the couch?"

She looked over at him. *Did* she? "No. Do you want to?"

"Definitely not, but I don't want to push you either. Like you said, tonight wasn't what you expected and you might need time."

"Do you need time?" she asked.

"No, I need comfort. It always leaves me feeling gross and

dirty when I have to really get into my undercover role, and those kids…"

She understood that. She felt the same way. Like everything good in the world had been sullied. She took his hand and got to her feet, leading him into the bedroom.

The night had been long and hard. A part of Aaron wanted to just find a way to get Lee out of this world and far from the gritty place that he lived in. The place that he'd made his own.

He wasn't even sure touching her was okay. He felt dirty by association, but when she pushed him down on the bed, falling down on top of him with her arms and legs on either side of him, he put his arms around her and held her close.

Burying his head in her neck, the scent of her shampoo strong in his nostrils, he closed his eyes and, for a moment, just held her. Lee had seen the same seamy side of life, and somehow there was still something good in her. There was a part of Aaron that was no longer sure he had that.

How could he be with this woman if all of that was gone?

"What are you doing?"

"Holding you. Keeping you safe," she said.

He tipped his head back so that he could meet her gaze. "Do I need to be safe?"

"We all do," she said. "It's really hard when you realize you can't protect everyone."

"A lesson we've both learned," he said.

His hands slipped down her back to cup her butt. She rested her forehead against his. "We have."

It was really hard to stay trapped in his own morose feelings when Lee was on top of him. Her breasts pillowed against his chest, her thighs on either side of his hips and her mouth so close that he would barely have to lift his head up to kiss her.

He wanted to kiss her.

"I'm not that guy that threw you in the van," he said. Feeling he had to clear that up before he kissed her.

"If you were I wouldn't be on top of you right now," she answered.

"Why are you?"

She closed her eyes. "I told you I'm not good at pretending. I like you. You're hurting and I want to comfort you."

"So, pity sex."

"Never." She got to her feet. "I'm hurting too. I need to feel like there is something good in the world."

She was looking at him. "I'm not good."

"You're not bad. You do the right thing in your own way. No matter the cost. And don't deny that you're paying the price from seeing those kids."

He scrubbed his hand over his face. He was. He definitely was. "I can't get them out of my head."

"Do you want to?" she asked. "Van needs to keep those images to hang on to his anger and determination."

"Your boss?"

"Yeah. He relives his worst moments again and again. Says it's his focus. I can't do that. That weakens me and makes me crumble."

"What do you do?"

"*Halo* with the boys sometimes. Manicures with Luna."

He put his arms behind his head, raising one eyebrow at her.

"We paint our own nails and drink wine and talk," she said.

"I use a punching bag normally, but nothing about this op is normal."

"No it's not," she said. It wasn't like she was just figuring this out. She slowly got undressed, not in a stripper, sexy way, just took her clothes off.

Aaron sat up and was naked before she was. He took her wrist in his hand, pulling her with him back to the bed. "I can't promise this is going to be the best sex we've ever had."

"I just need to feel close to you and know that we both are okay," she said.

They fell on the bed together. He rolled until she was under him. His mouth was on hers as she parted her thighs. He slipped into her with one long thrust, filling her completely.

He stayed there for a moment, not moving. Then he tore his mouth from hers, burying his face in her neck, whispering dark words of need and longing against her as he drove into her again and again.

* * *

She thought she wouldn't orgasm, that this was for him. But then there it was. Just out of nowhere. She arched her back and dug her heels into the bed to try to take him deeper as she cried out his name. He kept thrusting a few more times before he emptied himself inside of her.

He didn't say a word. She rolled to his side, keeping them joined together. He pressed her head to his chest, stroking the back of her hair.

"Lee."

Just her name. But the way he said it had her breath catching in her throat. There was so much emotion—need, longing, caring. She hugged him back, kissing his chest, telling him without words she felt the same.

Aaron got to the club just before Jorge the following morning. He'd dressed for a run in jeans and the hoodie that Lee had worn last night. And had his weapon tucked into a holster he wore at the small of his back.

"Mate, you mind if I tag along today?" Aaron asked when the other man came into the office upstairs.

"Why?"

"Just give us a chance to get to know each other. I'm used to being with a crew I know," he said, trying to reinforce the things that Ramos had mentioned the night before.

Jorge shook his head. "Nah, we're good. You steer clear of Pain and Panic too."

"Yeah, but why? We're all on the same team now. Unless you're hiding something," Aaron said. It sure felt that way. One of the things that he was always slow to remember when he was undercover was the fact that he wasn't the only one concealing stuff.

Jorge definitely had something he didn't want Ramos or anyone else to know about.

"You threatening me?"

Aaron put his hands up. "No, man, just calling it like I see it. The big boss might see it the same way."

"Not unless you say something. I just don't like strangers."

Jorge moved farther into the room, going to the safe in the wall as if the conversation was over. But Aaron wasn't backing down. "I don't either, so I'm riding along today."

Jorge turned to him. Frustration but also something else on his face. Fear? Maybe. Unease? Definitely. What the hell was going on here?

"Why? This isn't your job."

Good point. "Like I said, so we get to know each other."

"I don't want to know you. You're not riding with me, Quinn. If you push this I'm calling Ramos."

"You run to him all the time," Aaron taunted, realizing he was pushing the other man because he was itching for a fight. He needed to get rid of the anger and guilt and frustration that had been eating at him since he'd gone up those back stairs the night before.

Jorge turned and swung, clocking Aaron in the jaw and snapping his head back. But he'd taken harder hits. He retaliated, with a one-two punch, socking Jorge in the face and the gut before spinning away.

The other man came after him and they traded hits for a good five minutes before Jorge realized that Aaron wasn't going down and shook his head.

"You crazy, dude? You won't know where the houses are if you take me out," Jorge snarled.

"I don't give a damn about that."

"You just wanted a fight," Jorge said with a smile, and then he nodded a few times. "Fine. You can ride along today."

Aaron nodded back as he wiped his nose with the sleeve of his hoodie. Jorge did the same. They were both covered with bruises and blood from broken noses. Aaron realized that he'd needed more than the physical release of a fight with someone who was his equal. He'd needed to let Quinn out in a way that wouldn't scare Lee.

He'd said he wouldn't let her compromise the operation, but he wasn't sure about that now. Being this guy gave him a safe place to let out all the rage that was always bottled inside of him. But around her, he didn't dare risk it. Not just because he didn't want her to see him that way. But because it was hard to put that monster back in the cage. With Jorge, they'd created a bond.

He'd wager Jorge had grown up fighting the same way that Aaron had.

Neither man said much as Jorge emptied the safe after Aaron entered the combination. Aaron followed him down the stairs and out to the parking lot. He put on his sunglasses and didn't bother checking to see if Denis was in the parking lot; he was sure that his partner was.

He also knew that Rick was nearby with an FBI agent, and they'd tail the teens when they were moved. He took a deep breath as he stepped outside. "It's going to be a good day."

Jorge laughed. "Ya think?"

"Started with a fight," Aaron said with a shrug.

"Yeah, I guess."

Jorge led them to a black Camaro SS and they both got in. He tapped the screen with the built-in GPS after he put the money he'd taken from the safe into the glove box and locked it. "You can ride along, but you stay in the car at the first stop. They are really touchy about who comes and goes there."

"They?"

He didn't respond, just said, "Even Ramos isn't welcome. If anyone comes up to the car while I'm inside, keep your head down. You don't see anything. Got it?"

Aaron nodded. His gamble had paid off. Wherever they were going, it had to be someone high up in the Cachorros organization.

He and Jorge chatted as they drove toward Bel Air. Which fit with some of the locations they'd found Steve driving to. "Are you the only one who delivers here?"

"Nah, all the districts have someone. But it's just one person. No days off," Jorge said.

"You like that?"

The man shrugged as he turned the corner. "Yeah. This job is my life. My crew is my family. I'm good."

That was something he'd seen mirrored time and again when he went undercover. A lot of the thugs had no family and had found one in the gangs. They were fiercely loyal because the gang members were the only ones who had made them feel seen. In a way, that might be why Aaron felt so at home in gangs. He was seen not as one of four brothers or as the dangerous adrenaline junkie. But as himself.

His *true* self.

Which he'd fought so hard last night. He never wanted Lee to realize that Quinn was who Aaron was at his core, and Aaron was the mask he wore to try to seem more civilized than he ever thought he would be.

Waiting in the high school parking lot for Boyd brought back so many memories. Though, back in the day, Lee had walked to school and would have been sitting outside in the hall waiting for the doors to open.

The school was in the center of a busy commercial area with a burger joint across the street that looked like an old drive-in/diner.

Boyd pulled in on his motorcycle after students had started to arrive and took off his helmet, stowing it in the compartment under the seat.

Several students waved at him as they headed into the main school building. She got out of her car and headed over toward him.

"Boyd."

He turned, surprised to see her. "Lee. Is everything— Come to my classroom so we can talk."

He didn't say anything else, just directed her through the campus and into the main building and up to the second floor. There was a student waiting for him and he slowed down when he saw her.

"Give me a minute," he told Lee.

"Sure."

She leaned against the wall, watching him as he went to talk to the girl. Lee didn't even pretend she wasn't listening in on the conversation. There were too many connections to this school for her not to be suspicious of everyone who worked there.

"Hey, Mr. Chiseck. I didn't get the homework last night and

wondered if you'd have time today to help me with it," the student said.

"Yeah, I have time after second lunch. Does that work for you?" he asked.

"Perfect. I'll see you then."

Once the girl walked away, Boyd opened his door and Lee followed him into his classroom. That seemed like a normal student/teacher interaction. Somehow that reassured her. But then again, she didn't know what was normal for Boyd. They only saw each other every five or so years when he asked her to look into a missing kid.

"Did you find her?" Boyd asked.

"Not yet."

"Then, why are you here?" he clipped out. "I don't have a lot of time before class starts."

Lee shook her head. "You didn't tell me there were other students who've gone missing from this school, Boyd."

"I didn't think it mattered. They aren't my students."

"It *does* matter," Lee insisted. "You only care about your students?"

Shoulders tensing, Boyd turned and strode to his desk at the front of the classroom. "It's not the way you're making it sound. Isabell started changing in the weeks leading up to her disappearance. I have no idea about the other kids. I think one of the other students… The principal told us his family had moved."

Lee didn't know about that, but it made sense. "Have any of them come back to school?"

"No. Lee, this is what I'm worried about. Something is going on here," Boyd muttered.

Yeah, something was… But how involved was her friend?

"Why didn't you mention that other student earlier?"

"I wasn't sure you needed to know or that it was relevant to Isabell," he said.

Her friend was contradicting himself. "What's going on here, Boyd? Don't tell me any more lies."

He shoved his hands in his hair and turned away from her. "I don't know. That's the *truth*. When the first kid went missing, all of the teachers were concerned and we spoke to the principal, who brought in the cops. They assured us they'd do everything to find him, but he often skipped school and wasn't the best student."

"So everyone assumed he dropped out?"

"Something like that," he answered. "But the next one was a girl. Honor student from a good family. They were furious and went to the commissioner and two days later her body was found by the side of the road."

That was horrifying. An image of Isabell dead on the side of the road flashed through Lee's mind. Her heart thundered in her ears as sweat formed on her chest. She needed to find Isabell. Now. She wondered if he even knew about the girl that Aaron had identified last night. It hadn't been long enough for her family to report her missing.

"The next boy is the one who moved, Harry. So when Isabell didn't show up to class and her friends hadn't heard from her… I was afraid to go to the principal or the cops. I knew you'd find her."

"Do you think the principal is involved?" she asked.

"Who knows? All I've got to go on is that two boys are still missing and a girl showed up dead after her parents made a big deal out of finding her. I don't want Isabell to be the same."

She could understand that. Sort of. "You should have come with all of this at the beginning. Again, why didn't you?"

"I was afraid you'd say no." He scrubbed a hand across his face and released a rough breath. "A missing girl is one thing, but missing teens and something going on at my high school… that's a *big* ask."

She narrowed her eyes at him. "Is that the *only* reason?"

"What are you asking me?"

"Do you have anything else that you aren't telling me?" she prodded.

Boyd shook his head. "Daniella was the teacher of the first boy. We had a big fight at home about it because I said some unkind things. She got pissed at me for being insensitive and left."

Interesting. "Did you tell her about Isabell?"

"She knew and said 'that's karma, asshole.' She's not wrong. All students should matter, not just the ones who show up every day clean and ready for class. I know that Sam—that's the boy—he had a rough home life. I shouldn't have been so judgy about him."

Boyd seemed contrite, but was it all an act? She honestly wasn't sure. "I need all the names of the kids and their addresses. Could you get them for me?"

"Yes. Do you want to talk to Daniella?"

"Why would I?" she asked.

"She sees all the kids because she teaches PE and they all come through her door. She might be able to find a connection," Boyd replied. "I didn't see one with Isabell, but you might."

"In that case, then yes, I would like to talk to her."

"I'll set it up." He met her eyes. "Lee, I'm sorry I didn't tell you about the other missing kids. I was hoping there was no connection and you'd track down Isabell's family and she'd be fine."

Of course he was. Didn't everyone who lost someone hope that they'd just show back up? That their worry was misplaced? But with so many kids going missing from one school, something else had to be going on.

Lee was determined to get to the bottom of it.

Chapter Seventeen

Boyd's estranged wife Daniella reminded Lee fiercely of Hannah. It was obvious she must have run track-and-field in high school. Healthy-looking and fit, she had her long blond hair pulled back in a ponytail and her skin was naturally tanned. It was clear she didn't want to talk to anyone associated with Boyd, which made Lee wonder what had happened between them.

"Thanks for meeting with me," Lee said to the woman as she met her in her office inside the gym. "I'm investigating the disappearance of Isabell Montez, and Boyd mentioned you taught all the kids who've disappeared. I'm looking for a connection between them."

"Yes, they were all students in my gym class. As far as I can tell, there is no connection. I mean, they didn't hang together and their parents run in different circles," Danielle replied. "So I think the only thing these kids have in common is that they've all gone missing."

"And the principal, is he connected?"

Daniella shrugged. "He wasn't concerned when I first raised the issue and then I'm sure Boyd told you about Grace."

"The honor student?" Lee asked.

She nodded. "After that, we've all kept quiet hoping that... I don't know. It's hard to explain to someone who's not a teacher, but I'm invested in these kids. So when I see one missing or sick or clearly in a shitty home environment, I want to help." She blew out a breath. "But the law limits what I can do."

"I think that's why Boyd reached out to me," Lee said.

"Yeah, probably. Also, he knew Isabell. I asked him to contact you sooner, but he wouldn't."

This was news to her, but she worked to keep her expression neutral. "I wonder why not?"

"He hates your connection to Hannah and yet that's the only way he can still feel her... It's complicated with him." Daniella sighed. "But after Grace's body was found and we were all freaking out, I guess something changed in him and he told me he was going to reach out."

"Tell me what you observed of Isabell, if you don't mind."

"She was bookish and not really into running but loved soccer," Daniella began. "I think one of the boy bands she follows likes the sport and that's why she was fixated on it." Her lips quirked. "That age is so interesting, like right now, I have a bunch of kids asking me football questions so they understand the game when they watch it because Taylor Swift is going to games."

"Do you think Isabell was trying to be like someone else?" Lee asked curiously.

"In what way?"

"Well, her yearbook photo is nothing like this one I found in her room," Lee said, showing the two photos to the teacher.

"Wow, never saw her like that at school. She usually kept to herself, participated if I made her, but that was about it. I didn't see her hanging out with any of the other groups of kids. And I pulled her records—I'm sure Boyd did as well—she was a good student. You might try to talk to Tess Long, her English teacher. That was where Isabell's grades were the highest."

"Thanks for chatting."

"I just want her found. I want all of them found. And not the way Grace was. I want them home and safe and full of teenage drama and angst. That's all they should be worried about," she said.

"I agree." Lee reached into her pocket, took out a Price Security business card and held it out to Daniella. "If you remember anything else, please don't hesitate to reach out."

"I will." She took the card. "I really hope you find Isabell."

After saying goodbye to Daniella, she texted her update to the team. Aaron had his notifications silenced, which Lee knew probably meant he'd been able to go on the run with Jorge. Not that it was surprising that he'd managed to pull that off. Aaron was very good at his job…something that she knew she'd do well to remember.

Tess Long didn't have time to chat but did jot her a note that said, according to her, Isabell's home life wasn't difficult and she'd never talked about running away.

Lee sort of groaned when she read it because she was no closer to figuring out where the teen had gone. That room of hers had been picked clean, so it was possible that she lit out on her own before whatever trouble her parents were in came to find them.

It might be two separate incidents. She needed to get to her computer and start inputting everything and searching for patterns—

She was jolted from her thoughts when she noticed the tracker on her phone indicated that Aaron wasn't moving. Looking it up on the map, she saw it had stopped transmitting thirty minutes earlier.

She called Denis to see if he knew what was going on with Aaron.

"He's on a bag run and went to a new location. I had to drop back and am now in a waiting pattern. How'd you make out at the school?"

"No link between the missing kids, but when they made a fuss over one kid, her body showed up two days later. Not sure if that's coincidence or something else. Trying to dig deeper. I'll keep working on that. Let me know if you need me for anything," she said.

They hung up. Looking back at the pictures of Isabell, she studied them closely again. Both of those girls looked like they were trying to prove something. In neither photo did she seem to be a victim, which made Lee hopeful for her chances of survival. Unless the girl pissed someone off and then she was probably already dead.

But how would she have gotten trafficked? Those kids that Aaron had photographed last night weren't easy to identify. But she had a list and only one of them was from San Pedro High School. Hammond was ready to raid the house after his task force member identified it, but he was also waiting to see what else they could find. He wouldn't let those kids be taken any farther, but he was going to wait as long as he could to get the most out of the raid.

Same as Aaron, she guessed. It was all they could do. They weren't going to be any closer to shutting down whoever was going after these kids until they had a lot more information.

Aaron wished there wasn't a part of him that really loved this kind of day. He'd had a fight, and that always seemed to set him back to normal. There was no pissing contest with him and Jorge; they were both big guys used to being in charge and they both recognized that in the other.

But he also wasn't part of the pack, and that was apparent when Jorge told him to wait in the car. That wasn't something that Aaron was going to do. Even if he wasn't undercover. He got out as soon as the man went inside of the large mansion that they'd pulled up to.

The fact that the property was landscaped and had a large twelve-foot privacy fence and gated entrance was already setting off alarm bells for Aaron. He was close to someone. Maybe even Perses, whom they'd been working overtime to identify.

The mansion was a large modern structure. There was a bridge that they'd driven over, and he noticed that there were wading pools that resembled a moat surrounding the entire complex.

The house itself was all painted concrete and glass. There was a large blown-glass sculpture in the yard that looked like a cyclone.

Perses was known as the god of destruction, and the cyclone seemed to fit that. His skin prickled in excitement. Was this the home of the shadow head of La Fortunata crime syndicate? The one who'd eluded government agencies for so long?

He wasn't sure what kind of security there was at the place but assumed they had cameras and that his moves were being watched. He lounged against the car for a few more minutes, looking around the property like he was bored, before heading toward the house. Scoping out his best point of entry, he wandered down a lush tropical path that led to the side of the mansion. He noticed a patio off what appeared to be the kitchen.

Aaron hesitated. Once he entered the house, everything would change. He didn't pull out his weapon, which didn't worry him too much, but still he was going into an unknown situation. His blood started pumping heavier in his veins.

"I'm entering the house," he said under his breath for Denis, who Aaron knew was listening and had his back. There were two people in the kitchen, clearly staff who didn't even look up when he entered. He took a minute to scan the room, making a mental note of the layout in case he needed it later.

Aaron spotted a butcher block holding kitchen knives near the stovetop but ignored them as he had a switchblade in his pocket. He moved into the hallway and looked left and right. It was empty. He took a deep breath as he stood there and listened, trying to figure out where he should go.

Then he made his move. Stepping quietly into a large foyer, he stopped briefly to observe a rotating statue of another Greek Titan—or rather that was what Aaron assumed based on his knowledge that Perses was the man he was here to meet. The closer he looked at the statue, the more he realized it was a three-sided statue of the same woman. *Hecate?* He was struggling to remember his Greek mythology, but that made sense given that Lee thought Cate/Diana was Perses's daughter. She was depicted as she usually was, clad in a long robe, holding burning torches and standing back-to-back. But the rotating statue revealed that one of them was holding a sword in each hand and the other held a lead on a large ferocious-looking dog that lay at her feet.

His team had thought Perses had taken the name to create

fear in those he led, but he was starting to wonder if the family were of Greek descent.

Not the usual drug kingpin in the US. But if they were trafficking internationally, perhaps a former shipping magnate? All questions that Aaron knew he'd have to wait to answer.

Hearing footsteps on the stairs toward the right made him move in that direction. He waited behind some sort of marble plinth that was taller than he was. Watching to see who came down. The first man was tall, older, with a square jaw and a full gray mustache. His hair was salt-and-pepper and full, falling neatly to his shoulders. He wore a white linen suit and loafers, and he moved like someone who was used to power and control.

Behind him was Diana, dressed in a full white pantsuit, her red hair swept up in an elegant chignon. As she walked down the stairs, Aaron couldn't help noticing the resemblance between the two of them. Her eyes were set the same as the man's and there was something about the bone structure of her face that made him believe they were related.

Aaron stepped around the plinth when they got to the bottom of the steps. "Hello."

The man looked over at him, acknowledging him with disdain. "What are you doing in here?"

"Sorry, mate. I'm riding with Jorge to get a feel for the operation and needed the toilet," he said.

"This is Ramos's new man at Mistral's," Diana murmured, coming over to him. "Quinn. He's been on the job two days."

"Do you want to keep your job?" the man asked.

"I hope to."

"Then next time, wait in the car as you were told," he snapped. He gestured to the corner where an armed, muscled man, dressed all in black, appeared. "Take him to the bathroom and then escort him back to the car."

Following the bodyguard, Aaron was tempted to walk slowly, but he could tell that Diana and the gray-haired man weren't going to be discussing anything while he was around. Which made him wonder where Jorge was. He'd been inside for a long time.

The bathroom was neat and large for a downstairs loo. Aaron

took his time opening the cabinets, and knowing it was a long shot, placed a listening device under the mirror and notified Denis that he'd done that. He also provided a description of the gentleman he'd encountered, hoping that a sketch artist would be able to utilize it.

He was back at the car a few minutes later and Jorge was waiting for him. "Dude, I told you to stay the hell in the car."

"I had to take a leak," Aaron said, shrugging.

"Next time, hold it. The big man doesn't like anyone in his place."

He got into the passenger side while Jorge climbed behind the wheel. "Who's he?"

"The head honcho. He's in town for a few days for a big shipment and you don't want him to know who you are."

"Too late," Aaron said dryly.

"You better hope he forgets about you. He's not someone's radar you want to be on. Ramos is already feeling the pinch of that collar."

"Do you know his name?"

Jorge shook his head. "No one does. I'm not even allowed to look at him," he admitted.

"I see." Aaron now had a clearer picture of why no one ever gave up the Perses guy's name or likeness. There were few people who had that information and fewer still who would be willing to talk about it. He couldn't help but feel like he'd made a big breakthrough today.

Jorge didn't say much as they made the rest of the journey, eventually taking him back to the club before they parted ways. Jayne had messaged him saying they were having a meeting of the joint task force and Aaron knew it was time to get some new information.

The conversation with Daniella sent her back to find Boyd again. She wondered if he might know more about Isabell's disappearance than he realized. Waiting in the hall until his class ended, she was strongly reminded of her own high school days.

It was easy to remember standing by her locker between classes, while Hannah was chatting with her about Boyd and their dreams for the future. They had been one of those couples who'd started dating in ninth grade and seemed to be really in love.

Lee had never really been much of a believer in love. Her parents hadn't been the best role models. And her grandpa had a girlfriend, but they definitely weren't in love. She hadn't seen any good examples of it until, well, Luna had fallen head over heels for Nick, she thought.

Luna and Lee had immediately recognized another survivor in each other and their friendship had been quick and solid. So watching her friend fall in love hadn't been easy. Love made people vulnerable. The one thing that Lee had always struggled to let herself be. She wasn't saying that she wasn't starting to get the feels for Aaron or that they weren't deep. Just that…she wasn't really ready for wherever they might lead.

But Hannah and Boyd had been ready and never got the chance to see if they could make it outside high school. Well, she assumed that was the case, because Boyd had no staying power in his relationships. But how much of that was due to the fact that his first love had disappeared all those years ago?

The doors opened on the classrooms and the kids started pouring out. Boyd noticed her outside and gestured for her to come in.

"How'd it go with Daniella?"

"Goodish. She did know all the kids, and like you mentioned, they don't really seem to have any connection," Lee said. "But I was thinking there might be something that I'm missing."

He scrunched his forehead. "Like what?"

"I found this Polaroid photo of Isabell in her room at her house and I can't place it. It looks similar to a geotagged photo that was definitely taken at a club called Mistral's, but this Polaroid isn't from there," she explained.

"How do you know that?"

"I got a job there and have been looking around to see if it was," Lee said. "Do you recognize the location?"

She handed her phone over to Boyd and he leaned forward. His hair sort of shifted and she noticed the all-star quarterback's hair was thinning. The decades since high school were there on both of them, but not visible unless you really looked. She thought about the fine lines around her own eyes, which Van called laugh lines but Lee was pretty sure were stress lines from late nights staring at the computer screen.

She noticed an odd look on Boyd's face and realized when she'd handed him her phone the photos had shifted and there was a photo of her and Hannah visible. She reached over his shoulder to swipe, but he stopped her.

"She was so pretty…"

"And trusting," Lee murmured. She'd always thought that Hannah had been trying to help someone who meant her harm. That was the only thing that truly made sense for her best friend to just disappear.

"Yeah, she was. So where's the photo of Isabell?"

Lee pulled it up and Boyd studied it. She couldn't read anything on his face and she knew in her gut it was another dead end. Frustrated that she couldn't get a solid lead when it felt like she had a lot of pieces of the puzzle. But something was eluding her. She was missing some connection. But *what*?

"Sorry, Lee. What will you do now?" he asked as he handed the phone back to her.

"Keep following up on leads. I do have the names of the other kids… It's interesting that San Pedro has had four kids go missing in a short span of time." She didn't mention the kid from last night since he might not be aware of her yet. Lee didn't want to give up the fact that they'd found those kids.

"Well, one was killed and the cops think it might have been motivated by her mom's stance on the three-strikes-and-you're-out policy."

Lee hadn't heard that but would follow up with Detective Monroe. "But then Sam and Harry and Isabell? I mean…that's a big coincidence."

"Yeah, that's why I called you in," Boyd said. "You're good at finding people."

"Not sure that I am this time…" She looked up from her phone to meet his eyes. "Did you ever meet her parents?"

"Her dad came to parents' night. She was a good student, so we didn't have much to talk about."

At least one parent was interested in her. Isabell being a runaway was making less sense as far as Lee could tell. "Where was the mom?"

"Oh, they schedule the night so that sometimes two classes that a student is in might be presenting at the same time. She was in an English class, I believe."

So both parents were interested in Isabell. Why then was her room empty? The house ransacked?

Lee needed answers before she could move forward with her investigation. Aaron was busy infiltrating the Cachorros and she wasn't due behind the bar at Mistral's until eight. Which meant it was time to head back to Price Tower and do some real digging.

She thought better when she was in her place.

But as she got in her car after saying goodbye to Boyd, and started heading toward the tower, she realized that part of the reason she had a clearer head there was that it was just *her* place.

Aaron had never been there. It was where she'd started the search for Isabell. Clear of any and all distractions, and right now she needed that.

Between working with Boyd and the memories of Hannah's disappearance all those years ago, and Aaron making her feel all the emotions she hadn't realized she was capable of, her mind was sort of a chaos center.

There was more to what she'd learned so far. She just needed a quiet space to figure it out. And though a part of her felt like she was running away when she did it, she wasn't ready to share this information with Hammond and his task force.

Or Aaron.

Lee was used to being very good at her job and lately it felt like she had been spinning her wheels. It was time to get her mojo back.

Chapter Eighteen

Walking into the first task force meeting wasn't what Aaron had expected. Lee had been distant and at Price Tower all day. He worried seeing him as Quinn was starting to make her realize the potential in him for aggravated behavior. But she smiled when she saw him and motioned for him to take a seat near her.

Denis and Jayne were sitting on the other side of the empty chair, so he hurried toward it. Once seated, he recognized Van and Rick Stone and knew Hammond from reputation and the video call. His boss had sent a warning to him and Denis to not mouth off to him.

But as his gaze moved down the line, Aaron froze. Steve from Jako's gang was there. Their eyes met. Steve shook his head. "You were too good. I should have suspected you were a government agent. I thought you were connected to Perses."

"And I figured you for a Chacal trying to move up. You were going to be my ace in the hole," Aaron said wryly. "Guess I can't turn you in now that we're on the same team."

"Probably not," Jayne interjected. "Would have been nice to know about this op, Hammond."

Hammond just arched his eyebrows at her. "The same could be said of yours. But Perses has his hands in a lot of things, so we should have expected our paths to cross."

"He does. We know he is tied to the biggest drug gangs in

the US. This is part of a multiregional operation," Jayne said. "What about you?"

"We're running multiple locations, as well, for trafficking. So far, we've found a concentration in border states and economically deprived areas," Hammond replied before addressing Lee. "So what did you find at the high school?"

"I sent the information that four kids were taken from San Pedro," she said. "Both of Isabell's parents work for a company called WINgate."

"What do they do?" Aaron asked her.

Lee turned to him. "Defense subcontractor that provides border security."

That was a lead that they had been waiting for. Finally a break to bring them closer to Perses. Though Aaron was pretty sure he'd met the man earlier today.

"Did anyone have a chance to run the description of the man I encountered at the mansion?"

"We did. So far, we haven't found a positive match but a few possibles. The thing is, if they are controlling the borders then his photo isn't going to show up on security cameras," Jayne said. "Right?"

Hammond nodded then looked over at Lee. "Did you find out what WINgate is providing?"

"It is biometric scans, and as far as I can tell, they control the repository of all the scans. They then screen for known criminals. It would be very easy to black out selected people, as well, and make them invisible."

"Easy, how?" Aaron asked her. Loving seeing this side of Lee, who was in her element talking about tech and using it to help solve this case.

"It's just a simple code. They would put in the faces that they don't want to show up. From what I can tell, WINgate is the US company handling our borders, but there are similar tech companies in countries around the world. So moving drugs, people or whatever they want would be controllable if they had leverage."

"Do you believe they do?" Hammond asked.

Lee shrugged. "It's too soon to tell. Maybe WINgate is the

trial to see if they can get in and control it. Given that we think Cate O'Dell is working with Perses and we know what she did, I think, yes, it is believable."

Hammond's face tightened. Aaron wasn't sure if he was upset that she'd mentioned Cate or if he was peeved about the fact that this had been happening under all their noses. Aaron's operation with Denis was focused domestically, but he knew that Jayne would be concerned about the wider implications.

They had teams who worked the border, and if they couldn't trust their partners who were building smarter defenses, then the DEA was going to be ineffectual.

"That sucks. How do we find the people in WINgate who are helping them?" Aaron asked.

"We start with the kids from San Pedro. My guess is there must be someone else on the inside as well. But they will be harder to find," Lee said.

He was going to ask how she knew that but realized she was speaking from experience and what Cate had done to her and Van. "We'll find them. So what's the plan?"

"What *is* the plan indeed?" Hammond demanded.

"I can get some guys in WINgate... We've just started a corporate security arm, so I'll send them in to make a pitch and get the layout of the place," Van said.

"Good. Jayne, what do you need?" Hammond asked.

As the ranking government agent, he was sort of in charge of this entire operation and clearly felt comfortable in this role.

"Aaron will continue trying to get closer to Perses and Denis will keep his eye on the bagmen that are moving around the city," Jayne said. "If we disrupt them enough, they will get sloppy. They always do."

Aaron agreed. He'd experienced that in the past. The more that a crime boss felt like things were moving out of control, the more they started to move pieces around. "I'll see if I can stir up something else. It seems to me that they are transporting teens in every three days or so."

"So that gives us a day and a half to get ready for a bust," Hammond said.

"The Chacals heard there is a big shipment for the Cachorros coming into the port on the same day," Steve interjected. "You might want to check that out with your gang. I got the feeling that Chico's death pissed them off."

That was good information and Aaron would make sure he was there. "Did you suspect the gang was trafficking?"

"We knew one of the LA gangs was but didn't know which one so I was placed with both," Steve confirmed.

"Dangerous for you," Aaron said.

"Not until you came along."

Aaron and Denis were in a confab with their boss, so Lee and Rick went out to the parking lot together. She had been told to keep on doing what she had been. And Rick had already talked to both Jayne and Hammond.

He leaned against her car, putting his head up toward the sun. "Cases like this are why I got out of the DEA."

Same, she thought. "It's frustrating to learn that no matter how many avenues we shut down, the syndicates always find a new one."

"Sort of the nature of the beast. And this time...maybe they are using the kids as leverage."

No *maybe* about it in Lee's mind. "I keep thinking about the cleaned-out bedroom at Isabell's house. I thought maybe she'd run from a bad home situation, but Boyd told me her parents were involved in her life."

"Doesn't mean it wasn't a bad home sitch," Rick said. "But yeah, I'm starting to think the kids are key. How did they think they were going to keep that quiet?"

"Probably got a local cop as well," Lee guessed. She hadn't gone back to Detective Monroe to be on the safe side. She really hated this feeling of not being able to trust anyone. It reminded her so much of how she'd felt after Hannah disappeared and after Cate betrayed them.

Two completely different women and situations but that same feeling of helplessness and fury. For her, rage always made her irrational, so she was trying to stay calm and keep working the problem with a clear head.

That was the only way she was going to find answers...and

the girl. But it was hard when they were in a meeting like that one. Learning that Perses was more than likely controlling the border biometrics made finding lost kids near impossible. If one of his gangs had taken them, those kids' faces were never going to pop up at any border. What if they had access to CCTV footage as well?

Then she remembered she'd been accessing a government database to try to track Isabell and her parents. She pulled her phone from her pocket to verify who controlled the database. A few minutes later, she shook her head. "WINgate has the contract for all facial recognition tied to the US government."

Rick cursed under his breath. "We need to stop that—well, you do. That's not really my area of expertise."

"No, but the port will be. Thanks for helping on this. I know it's not—"

"You don't have to thank me, Lee. We're *family*. Besides, I needed this to remind me that I don't want to go back."

That surprised her. "Had you been considering it?"

He shrugged, pulling a cigarette out of his back pocket. It was well-worn and he turned it over in his fingers before shoving it away. Rick had quit smoking five years ago, but she knew he struggled every day not to.

"Sort of. Bodyguarding is fine, but I miss the action sometimes—well, not recently between Luna, Xander and now you."

She smiled at the way he said it. "I prefer the quiet."

"I know. You doing okay with this undercover thing?" he asked.

"Of course." But her colleague just looked at her like he saw through that. The truth was, she *wasn't* okay with this. She had hoped this kid would be like the others she'd found for Boyd in the past. Runaways who she'd tracked down in a few days. But in this case, it was like Isabell was hiding. Trying not to be found.

That was it!

The girl *was* hiding. She and her parents must have guessed that the syndicate would use her to make them do something. "I just thought of something."

Lee raced back into the meeting room with Rick on her heels.

Hammond was on his phone and Aaron looked up as she entered, from the other corner. He and Steve had been talking.

"What if they don't have everything in place at WINgate yet? What if Isabell's parents need to do something?" Lee asked breathlessly.

Everyone looked at her, then Jayne and Hammond both moved forward.

"Like what?" Hammond asked.

"Like the actual computer part. Both of her parents are in informational technology. Isabell's room had been stripped bare. There was nothing left in it to identify her at all."

"You're thinking they got her out first. Sent her somewhere to hide," Aaron said. "That makes sense. If she's gone, they can't harm their daughter to force them to work for them."

"Exactly," Lee replied. "So where did she go?"

"Do you have any ideas?" Hammond asked.

"I have this photo. I can't identify the background," she said, holding it out to share with the team.

Everyone studied it and it was Steve who figured it out. "That's a hamburger joint across the street from San Pedro High. The Chacals work the parking lot next to it. All the students and teachers go there."

All of them... Then how had Boyd not recognized it? Or maybe he *had* and he wasn't telling her. "Is there any place she could hide there?"

Steve shook his head. "I don't think so. But it's not far from the Old Mission Trail and there are a lot of hiding places up there."

"I've got some time to kill before I have to be at the club," Aaron said, winking at Lee. "Fancy a hike?"

"You bet," she said.

The Old Mission Trail had been created by the monks who had come to California with the Spanish during the Inquisition. They'd created the missions all along the Pacific coast. A lot of the old churches had fallen into disrepair and were now in ruins. But there was a nice hiking path that had different edible herbs and plants growing along the sides, thanks to those monks.

Lee and Aaron had parked his van at the hamburger joint, and he sensed that Lee wanted to go confront Boyd by the way she'd glared at the high school. But he'd guided her around the back and up the slight hill that led to the trail.

"How well do you know Boyd?"

"In high school, we were sort of close because of Hannah, but I don't really know him very well now."

"Hannah. That's your friend who disappeared?"

"Yeah. We sort of kept in touch and he still sends me a card every Christmas, and every five years, he's reached out to see if I could help out a kid who he thought was in trouble. He was usually right," she said.

Grabbing her hand, he pulled her toward him and locked eyes with her as they climbed the trail. "So that's what you think is going on with Isabell?"

"I did," she admitted. "I will literally never trust another soul on this planet if he turns out to be a rat bastard who used me to try to find Isabell for nefarious reasons."

Aaron couldn't help laughing at that sentence. She had to be really ticked off to say that. "If he is, I'll take care of him for you."

She shook her head. "Really?"

"Yeah. I'm supposed to be a thug anyway. And I do like fighting."

"I've noticed," she said, withdrawing her hands from his and clearly trying to change the subject.

"You know the problem isn't that you trust people, it's that people don't trust themselves and they are weak and make dumb decisions?"

"It doesn't feel that way to me," she confessed as they reached the ruins of an old mission.

Lee paused and Aaron took the lead as they walked into what was left of the crumbling building. No one was inside, but they both spread out looking for any sign that someone had been there. Aaron moved along the left wall while she took the right. He worked slowly, making sure to look for any remains.

If Isabell was on the run as Lee suspected, she'd be trying to leave no signs behind. He noticed indentations in the ground in the far corner. Like someone had been sitting and sleeping against the wall. Getting down on his knees, he shifted the sand around and found an earring. He picked it up as Lee joined him.

"What did you find?"

He held it up and she gasped.

She pulled her phone out with shaking fingers and flipped through the pictures, stopping on a yearbook photo of Isabell where the teenager had her hair in a ponytail and was wearing the earring. "So she owned a pair of them. Let me see if they are super popular."

Lee leaned against the wall, tapping away on the screen of her phone. Aaron left her doing what she did best and moved out the back of the ruin to search for a trail. A few minutes later, he found one. This time there were no signs of anyone trying to hide their steps. It looked like the hiker had slid down the side of the hill. He carefully made his way down there and found a backpack along with two sets of footprints. One smaller, probably a teen or a woman, and one definitely larger, and Aaron's gut said it was male.

He grabbed the backpack as he heard Lee calling for him.

"Down here! I stumbled upon some things," he said.

She made her way down to him. He was turned-on watching her work. There was something inherently sexy about Lee. "Those earrings were from Etsy and no two pairs are the same. I think these were definitely hers."

"Great work."

"Thanks." She smiled, then lifted an inquiring brow. "So what did *you* discover?"

He held up the backpack and then pointed at the ground. "These tracks look like they came from two different people," he said. "I might be reaching, but those larger prints look like a man's to me."

"Boyd's?"

"We don't know. Seems like he wouldn't have hired you and then taken her," Aaron said.

Lee didn't respond for several long moments. "Let's look in the backpack," she said, taking it from him.

She opened it up, pulling out a notebook and handing the

bag back to him. The first page had Isabell's name written in it and a sketch at the bottom. "This was hers." She grew silent for several moments, just looking down at the notebook, flipping the pages. She shook her head. "Isabell was hiding from Perses's people. She doesn't know who they are, but her parents told her to trust no one and to stay hidden."

"That's solid, so you can use that."

"Trust no one...not even Boyd? What if he couldn't find her? I showed him that picture yesterday and he didn't recognize it."

"Now you're thinking he did?" Aaron asked. His gut was telling him that she was right. That there was more to this than either of them knew. "Do you think he's part of Perses's organization?"

"I'm not sure." Lee sighed heavily. "His marriage is in trouble and his wife said he's been odd. So perhaps. I don't want to believe that Boyd would hurt a teenager the way that Hannah had been hurt. That he would be complicit in taking a young girl's future from her. But right now, everything is pointing to him," she said.

"Do you want to ignore it?"

"I can't. You know I can't," she said.

"I know. Like I said, people make dumb decisions sometimes."

"That sounds like Boyd. Maybe he's given up on saving kids to make up for the loss of Hannah," she said.

"Maybe he's stopped blaming the world and himself and started to blame you," Aaron said.

"Whatever. If he's involved, he's going to regret it for the rest of his life."

Chapter Nineteen

The club was almost quiet for the next two days. Van and Kenji had gone to WINgate to try to sell them corporate security and had gotten a nice tour. The two of them looked the part and Lee wasn't at all surprised by the friendly welcome the men had received.

Kenji had also been able to slip a small routing device onto the main security computer that Lee tapped into from her computer back at the apartment. As she worked, Aaron was showering and getting ready to head to Mistral's.

The both of them knew that this gig wasn't going to last for much longer. A part of her wanted to ask him about the future, but everything with Boyd and his possibly working with Cate had thrown Lee.

She had thought she'd changed and grown stronger over the last fifteen years but turns out she hadn't. She'd just kept trusting the wrong people hoping they'd be decent. Had she done the same thing with Aaron?

He walked into the room, looking at her carefully. "What's up?"

She shrugged, not really wanting to answer that. Right now, she was in her head and that wasn't a good place to be. Not at all. In her head, it was too easy to spot that Aaron was a chameleon changing to suit his environment.

The caring, understanding lover with her. One of the guys who liked to fight with Jorge. The charming manager at the club. He changed his skin so easily, slipping from role to role.

She had thought she'd had a glimpse of the real man but now…she wasn't so sure. Had she just been fooling herself again?

The way she had with Cate and now Boyd?

There was no clear-cut way to that answer. There was only the doubt and fear that she might make a huge mistake by believing in someone.

As if her childhood hadn't taught her anything. She could feel the crack of her old man's hand against her face and his cruel laughter when she'd cried. Telling her to toughen up and be smart.

Looking over at Aaron she wasn't sure. She didn't know the smart thing to do.

"What is going on in that beautiful head of yours?"

"Too much," she choked out.

"Talk to me," he replied, coming closer. Smelling so deliciously yummy with his aftershave and just that scent that was uniquely Aaron.

She closed her eyes, forcing herself to picture Boyd telling her he didn't recognize the burger place across from the school's wall.

"I don't really know what to say," she said.

He arched an eyebrow at her. "Undercover getting to you?"

"Yes. It is. What we found at the ruins pushed me over the edge," she admitted.

"I thought so. We don't know that your friend—"

"Acquaintance," Lee corrected. The Boyd she'd thought had been her friend wasn't the man he was today. They hadn't been close—it had been Hannah's disappearance that had caused her to think of him as a friend.

Aaron ran his hand through his hair as he turned the chair next to her backward and sat down. "I'm sorry."

"Why? You didn't trust him."

"Because *you* did and I think there aren't a lot of people who you do trust. Because this might be connected to a woman who betrayed you. Because Tony says life isn't fair, but dammit, it should be."

She almost smiled. Aaron was cheering her up. A new part of his persona she hadn't seen before. Now she was analyzing him instead of just taking him at face value.

"What's going on, love?" he asked again.

"I can't stop seeing everything as a lie," she confessed.

"Even me?"

She didn't answer him. But the truth was there between them.

"I knew this would happen. We have to live that lie every time we leave this apartment. Lines get blurred. But I've been straight with you from the moment we met, Lee. You know me."

She closed her eyes, wishing it were that easy. That she could just say yes, she knew him. But right now she felt so low…so stupid for not having seen Boyd's play for what it was.

"What if I'm the reason that girl gets killed?"

The words were torn from her. The real thing that was going on just ripped from her soul and her darkest fears. "That's on me."

Aaron stood up and came over to her, pulled her to her feet and into his arms. "That's on Boyd and Cate—or Diana…whatever name she is going by. Right now, we are going to do everything we can to find Isabell before she's hurt."

"She was taken… Those prints—"

He put his hands on the side of her face and kissed her hard. "She's smart and she's strong. Boyd had to hire you to find her. That tells me that he was getting desperate. Tonight we are going to capture Perses and Cate and find the girl. I know it."

"You can't guarantee that," she pointed out.

"You're right, I can't. But until we know otherwise, let's not kill her off. Let's bet on her outwitting them again," Aaron said.

His words were finally starting to sink in. She'd let herself get to a bad place…no doubt because she was tired and so much of this case was forcing her back to the past. A place she thought she'd exorcised from her memories but it turned out still had an emotional hold on her.

"You're right. Thanks for that. I was just—"

"You don't have to explain. I get it. I've been there. Remem-

ber when I sent Obie into danger and almost got her killed?"
Aaron mentioned the case that Xander had gone on to rescue
Obie and to help save Aaron himself.

"That must have been hard to handle."

"You have no idea what it's like to be sitting in jail while your
brother and friend are being hunted in a swamp. And I really
have no idea what you're experiencing right now but we both can
appreciate it and understand where the other is coming from."

She hugged him, resting her head on his shoulder and trying to steal a little of his confidence for a teenage girl going up
against a known human trafficker.

Aaron didn't want to let Lee out of his arms. He wanted to
keep her close, but the burner phone in his pocket that he used
as Quinn was vibrating.

She slid her hand down his butt and squeezed before she took
the phone from his pocket and handed it to him. "Life is calling."

"The *job* is calling. It's not more important than making
sure you are okay."

"I am. Now. That really helped," she said.

He looked into her gorgeous brown eyes and wasn't sure if
that was entirely true. His phone went off again and he glanced
down at the screen.

Jorge wanted him to come ride along this morning. Nice. He
was getting deeper into the gang and felt like they were starting to trust him.

"I'm going to have to go in early," Aaron said. "We are still
waiting for more information on the shipment that's coming in
tonight. Once we have it confirmed, call Flo and tell her you
can't come in tonight. I don't want you at the club alone."

She frowned. "Why would I be alone?"

"Because I'm definitely going to be wherever this is going
down," he told her. "I want a second crack at Perses."

"Fine. I won't go into the club." She blew out a breath. "I'll
just work from here and then try to catch up with Denis since
he knows all the drop houses. I'll see if I can find a location
that Isabell might be held."

"Good. Stay safe," he said gruffly.

"I'll be fine. You're the one I'm worried about."

He kissed her long and deep, groaning when he pulled back because he wanted so much more. "Love, I always come back."

"Make sure you do," she whispered.

He walked out of the apartment a few minutes later. It was the kind of gorgeous Los Angeles day that Californians bragged about. He put his sunglasses on and headed toward the van.

The traffic wasn't too bad and he was at Mistral's in no time. Jorge waited in his Camaro with a box of doughnuts and two coffees. "Thanks for riding along today. Might need some extra muscle."

"Trouble?" Aaron asked as he got in and took a chocolate doughnut from the box.

"Not sure yet, but I don't want to risk my boys," Jorge said.

So much for building trust. But Aaron got it. Quinn was tough and strong and wouldn't back down; he was the kind of man Jorge could count on in a tough situation. And Aaron also knew that as Quinn, in Jorge's eyes, he was expendable.

He definitely admired the man's loyalty. When they started making the run, Jorge relaxed and Aaron decided it was time to start digging for more information. They'd need everything that he could find before the shipment tonight.

"Do you know much about this shipment?"

"Yeah. Why?"

"Figured this is my chance to show Ramos what I'm made of," Aaron said.

"He knows. The big man mentioned you were at the house. You're part of the crew going tonight. Ramos said to make sure you were solid and ready."

So that was why he got the invite this morning. "I am."

Jorge just sort of nodded at him. "Jako and his crew will be there too. Your old boss vouched for you again. That went a long way with Ramos. He wasn't too happy that you were in the mansion."

"Can't help what happened," Aaron said matter-of-factly. He had zero regrets about it either. What he'd found at the house had changed what they knew about Perses.

"Don't do it again," Jorge warned.

He nodded. "Are we going back there?"

"Not with you in the car."

The run was pretty much a duplicate of the last one that Aaron had been on until Jorge turned away and clicked on a new address on the GPS. One that he hadn't seen on Denis's tracking map either.

"New place?"

"Overflow. Business has been good lately," Jorge said.

"Overflow?"

"Normally it's Diana's house, but we use it when necessary," the man explained.

Aha. Diana's house meant that there would be kids there. Maybe it was on the map of locations they'd tracked the teens to earlier. This could be the break that Lee had been waiting for.

He hoped they found her girl today. Lee needed that. She was working hard to find Isabell, and the connection between her and WINgate was strong, so it might lead them to more than just the teen.

Finally getting a glimpse into this other part of the operation made him realize that this could be the break he'd been waiting for too.

He suspected that Denis and Lee were listening in and hoped they'd relay this information to the rest of the task force. Jayne had been clear that they weren't to lose focus on identifying Perses, and if possible, capture him.

Because Hammond was focused on the kids and human trafficking, Jayne didn't want them to let Perses slip away. She knew that Diana was important too and counted on Hammond, Lee and the rest of the team to take her down.

Their primary focus was the head of the international crime syndicate. Now that they had a rough sketch of the man, and for the first time in years of searching, an actual *sighting* of the man, everyone wanted him.

No one was going to be satisfied if he slipped away as he had so many times in the past. Aaron was determined not to let that happen.

The next time he saw Perses, he was going to stay on the man. Jorge pulled into a neighborhood that had largish houses and seemed to be well maintained. A bit more upmarket than the other homes in the area. The house he stopped at had a large driveway that fit four cars and there were already two parked there.

The home looked ordinary from the front but there was a guy in surf shorts and sunglasses sitting in a lawn chair on the porch. When they got closer, Aaron noticed he had a semiautomatic weapon in his lap.

Denis stopped to pick Lee up in his van, which was equipped with computer and surveillance equipment. Between Denis and Jayne and the FBI task force, they had two sketches of the man that Aaron had described. Lee put them into the international database, searching for a match, and it was running a list of possibles as they drove toward the location that Aaron was at.

It was interesting listening to him without being in the same room. His conversation changed based on who he spoke to and how he wanted to be perceived. He'd sounded like a hired gun when he'd been in the mansion the other day. Lee hadn't been able to see the woman he'd been talking to, but having been the backup for Cate and Van all those years ago, she was more certain than ever that they were dealing with Cate.

Was Perses, the shadowy head of the crime organization, her father? They'd all suspected after she'd turned on them that her connection to La Fortunata had to be a personal one and someone very high up. It took a kind of deliberate dedication to give up a child and raise them to infiltrate the government.

Only someone who ran an organization like La Fortunata would do that. Or that was Lee's thinking.

Meanwhile, she'd gotten some hits on the kids and realized something she should have sooner. They were all members of a new social app that had launched about a year ago. It targeted high school students, and the registration restrictions were hard to crack. A new member had to scan their high school ID if they wanted to join. Then it was matched against the school's database.

The app had been touted as a safer online experience, making sure that it was only for students, and allegedly, it was monitored for bullying behavior. The back-end programming for the app was tight and Lee concentrated on trying to find a hack to get into it.

But she had the feeling it was going to take her more than a few days to do it. She looked at the developer information. Seaview Programs. She turned to her phone and used the internet app to search for them. The address was in Silicon Valley but when she used Google Maps it showed a Taco Viva.

"Anyone ever hear of Seaview Programs?" Lee asked in her headset. She was linked in with Denis and his boss as well as the FBI task force.

"It rings a bell. Is that the one that has that social app aimed at teenagers?" Hal, from the task force, asked. He was the computer expert and monitored all social media for online grooming and patterns between kids who were trafficked.

"Yup, that's the one. All the kids that have been taken from the same high school as Montez and the others that Aaron identified were on it." She hesitated. "Do you have a way into it?"

"It's hard to crack. I've been trying the back end," Hal said.

"I'm running that too. We need to get in," she insisted. "I might be able to get a fake ID."

"They run it against the high school database and so far no one has been able to grant us access to that."

"Hammond, you there?" Lee asked. Knowing her old boss was always listening in.

"Yes. I'm on it. I'll see if I can get permission today. Work with Hal on this," he told her.

Good. That was one thing down. She turned back to the sketch of the man. "Did we ever identify Cate O'Dell's family? That voice sounded like hers again and there is something familiar about the man in the sketch. Maybe they share the same eyes?"

"It did sound like her," Hammond agreed. "You have access to all of the old files. I don't recall that we got any further than La Fortunata."

"Which is a dead end," Denis said. "It all leads to Perses and we've never been able to get more than that nickname."

"I'm floating a theory that Aaron's guy is him," Jayne chimed in. "We'll have to wait to hear more from Aaron, but that guy didn't seem like he was reporting to anyone else. And Jorge sounded *scared*...or was that just my take?"

Lee concurred as did everyone else on the call that Jorge had seemed afraid of the man in the house. Was he the elusive Perses or just another heavy hitter in the crime syndicates? It was hard to know just how interwoven these gangs were.

There wasn't much for her to do but keep looking at the same information again and again. She had the feeling that she was looking too hard. If she could just relax, maybe the solution was right in front of her. But she couldn't ease up.

The chances of finding Isabell Montez alive and well were dwindling, and no one knew that better than Lee did. She rubbed the back of her neck and took a deep breath, forcing herself to move on to the next thing.

Cate.

A family connection, some clue that would give them a name they could search for. A name they could run against the face in the sketch. She opened the files and had to force herself to stay in the present as she read her own reports and remembered the woman she'd been. That Lee Oscar had been trusting and open. She'd thought her work was changing the world.

Having no idea that she'd been playing right into the hands of a criminal mastermind.

Not anymore. She was determined that this time she was going to find the missing high school girl, catch Cate or Diana or whatever name she was going by, and put an end to the crime syndicate that had been trafficking teens for too long.

It was a big ask and she knew it might not all be achievable, but she wasn't going to stop until she tried.

Chapter Twenty

Aaron followed Jorge into the house and the other man talked to the workers. There was a group of women in their underwear at the money-counting machines. A pretty similar setup to the one that he and Denis had taken down the day that Lee had come back into his life. It seemed as if a lifetime had passed since that day.

So much had changed and unraveled and then restitched itself. Which was sort of the story of his life. But now he had a new version of the tale. One that very much involved Lee. He drifted out of the main room down the hallway, which no one seemed to notice. The hallway was empty and not too long. There was a bathroom to the right, with no door on it, and the window had been covered over with a piece of plywood.

Typical of this type of house. He moved farther and tried the door on the left, but it was locked. Fortunately it seemed to be a standard type of lock and he turned the handle with all his strength until he heard it pop. He pushed the door in, scanning the room, and noticed that the kids he'd seen the other night were inside with about twenty or so others.

"Kids in the room to the left down the hallway," Aaron said under his breath and then stepped back into the hallway, closing the door behind him.

He was pretty sure, given Hammond's insistence, that they

were going to get the teens out. But Aaron had a short clock to depart the premises before the raid took place. He went into the bathroom and flushed the toilet and then headed into the main room, where Jorge was talking to one of the guards.

"Ready?"

"Yeah," Jorge said, doing some sort of fist bump with the other guy before leading the way back to the car.

Aaron glanced up and down the street, noticing Denis's work van, and knew that his partner was no doubt waiting until Aaron was clear before raiding this place. Jorge wasn't talkative on the way back to Mistral's, which left him with too much time to think.

He had no doubt the raid would be successful, but what if that put an end to the trail they'd been following? There was a chance that this would spook Perses—if that was even who Aaron had met—to postpone whatever plan the big man had.

Aaron also wondered if Lee would find her missing girl in that mass of teenagers. He wasn't sure what the endgame was for the kids he'd seen in that room. Though he did know usually they were moved out of their home country to make them more pliable and afraid of running away once they were transported to wherever they were going.

Isabell Montez needed to be rescued in time. Lee wasn't going to be able to live with the fallout if that girl didn't. As much as Lee had seen in her career, there was still a part of her that believed good triumphed over evil. All the time.

But as much as he wished he could help, that was for Hammond and his task force to figure out. Getting closer to Perses was Aaron's primary goal. He'd gotten a good look at the different drop houses around the city and most of them lined up with the Old Mission Trail. Everyone was on edge with the big shipment coming in tonight. Which made an odd sort of sense given that most of the missions were ruins now and only accessible by walking trails. It was a nice way to move product without being seen.

When they got to Mistral's, Ramos was waiting for them and he looked pissed. He exploded as they walked into the club, punching Jorge and then turning to hit Aaron square in the jaw.

Which Aaron countered with an uppercut to Ramos's chin followed with a solid jab to his gut. The other man was solid and didn't flinch but sort of stepped back.

"What the hell?" Jorge sputtered.

"The new house was raided. Were you followed?" Ramos demanded.

"No, we weren't," Jorge said. "I never am."

"What about Quinn? I told you to stay put."

Aaron rubbed his jaw. "I don't take orders that well. Jorge and I needed to know we could trust each other."

Ramos moved closer and Aaron got ready to fight, if needed, to prove himself in the gang. To let Ramos know that he might be the big fish in the operation but Aaron didn't bow to anyone.

Standing his ground as Ramos got closer, Aaron took a deep breath and was ready to throw the next punch.

Ramos shook his head and looked back at Aaron. "The big man wants to meet you again."

"Big man? The guy from the mansion?" This was the break he'd been waiting for.

Aaron felt the tension in the other man. He was suspicious of everyone and everything. Aaron had seen this happen before when things were about to break big on a case. Everything was unraveling and that made the situation more dangerous.

"Jorge, take care of the bags and get out of here. I'll see you tonight," Ramos said.

Jorge didn't say anything, just went up the stairs. After he was gone, Ramos tilted his head toward the door of the club. "Let's go."

Aaron followed him, not sure what to expect or what he was going to have to do. This wasn't something they had planned for. Denis and Lee were both busy with the raid and Aaron realized he was on his own.

Which had never bothered him before. But being with Lee had changed his thinking. She considered him part of her family now, and that meant that she might do something reckless if she thought he was in danger.

There was a part of him that cherished that thought, but he knew that it might lead to her getting hurt or killed. Which was probably why he shouldn't have started a relationship with her during this mission.

But it was too late to go back. He'd play the hand that he was dealt, and this time, he wasn't leaving wherever Ramos was taking him without the identity of the man in charge.

Lee waited in the surveillance van while the DEA/FBI task force went in to raid. She was known to the gang who worked in the club, and as much as she wanted to be part of the group taking them down, she knew it was dangerous if she was identified.

She listened to Aaron bullshitting with Jorge on his ride back to Mistral's and smiled to herself. He had a nice, sexy voice and she could listen to it all day, but he was also clever at portraying the type of man that Jorge expected him to be on the ride along. Aaron was smart like Xander but he combined that sharp intelligence with a suave charm that his brother didn't usually bother with.

While she waited, she checked the progress of a piece of code she'd written to find any similarities between the kids that had all gone missing from San Pedro High School. There was only that Seaview Programs app as a connection between any of the kids, which left the not-so-apparent ones. Her first thought was that it was a fruitless search. The honor student's parents were a local politician and her catering-company-owning husband, the "dropout's" father worked for a cleaning and maintenance company, and Isabell's parents both worked for WINgate, which had a large campus just north of the high school.

She'd contacted the defense contracting company, which had confirmed what she'd learned before about both of them being on a month-long vacation. Which still made no sense, given the time of year. But that was the company stance.

She dug a little deeper on the politician, wondering if she had any connections to WINgate. Nope. Not a thing, but her husband's catering company staffed the employee cafeteria.

Lee opened another window on her laptop and put that information into a note. Then she checked on the maintenance guy and discovered his company was subcontracted to WINgate. So all roads *were* leading back to that company after all.

Opening the feed that Kenji had placed in the WINgate security offices, she didn't notice anything and thought maybe they'd found her bug. All of the rooms were empty. Odd for the middle of a workday.

Then she saw Cate/Diana walking through the building with two men behind her. They were dragging a teenager behind them. Lee leaned in as she hit Zoom, which made the video grainy but not too clouded that she couldn't make out Isabell Montez.

The girl had been found.

Lee didn't recognize either of the men as being Boyd, so maybe he had nothing to do with her capture, but deep down Lee didn't believe that. She'd been played by Boyd and maybe Cate again.

Lee was ticked off and ready to storm WINgate, but they were already taking Isabell out of the building. So instead, she tried to find the camera feed for the parking lot, then she noticed that two more kids and a group of adults were being moved out of the building as well.

"Something's going down at WINgate. I can't find the parking lot feed," she said into her comms.

She paused in her search, listening for the "all clear" from Denis. Originally she was meant to search for Isabell but the girl was at WINgate.

Aaron was making a joke about LA traffic to Jorge, so he was good. She went back to her search. All contracts awarded to WINgate would be public record so she sent a query and then waited for them to come back.

"I've got eyes on the parking lot," Van said. He gave the description and the plate number of the vehicle as well.

"Tracking it," Hammond replied. "Let them move. We'll make an arrest when the time is right."

There was silence on the comms. "You hear me, Price?"

"I heard you. I'm not going to let anyone get away this time," he muttered.

Neither of them spoke of Cate, but Lee knew both men were driven by their mutual desire to see her caught and brought to justice. There was a definite resemblance between Cate and Perses, and it wasn't a huge stretch to think he was her father. She'd always been close to her dad and had said more than once she wanted his respect.

Lee had been envious of the other woman, who seemed to have a close-knit family. Given that her own had been anything but. "How did I miss that Cate and her family were all criminals back in the day?" she asked Van on a private comm channel.

"We both did," Van said dryly.

"You're right, but the way she talked about it... Looking back it seems so obvious."

"Looking back, everything seems obvious because you know the whole story, Lee, but when you're living it every day you only see what's pertinent to the situation. This isn't on you. It never was," he said.

"But I'm the intel woman."

That had been her secret shame for so long. Information had flowed into her fingers from all places, and she was usually so good at finding patterns and uncovering secrets. How had she overlooked something so big?

She'd determined to never let that happen again but she wasn't 100 percent sure she was achieving it. There were still moments, even now, when she missed things.

Like the WINgate connection. She'd had those kids' names for a few days. Was she once again letting personal relationships get in the way of her job? Was Aaron distracting her?

Van hung up and she went back to listening in, ready for some action, and then everything sort of happened at once. The raid was over and Denis gave her the all clear to come and help with the teenagers.

Before she could get to him, she got a second message.

Aaron was confronted by Ramos and is being taken somewhere.

Holy hell. Her stomach was in knots. Aaron could handle himself. She'd seen him do it so many times, but it didn't stop the fear that was eating her up inside. She had to stay focused. Help these kids first, then... Then she was going after Aaron.

* * *

The teens that had been rescued were transported to hospitals.

"Aaron's being taken to meet the big guy, according to Ramos," Lee updated Denis when he got back in the van.

"Come back to the office and so we can regroup. We can listen in on Aaron and figure out our next move," Jayne said on comms.

"I saw the sketch and am trying to run it through facial recognition, but so far, nothing," Lee told Hammond as they walked back to the van.

"He's stayed off-grid, so I'm not surprised. We're running it as well. I assume you're tapping into other organizations' systems?"

"I am. He's too big to not get a lead on," she said. "But I did also send a request for permission…so eventually the search will be legal."

"I don't need to know," he warned.

"I don't like Aaron alone at that mansion or wherever the big guy is," Denis said. "I know we need a plan, but he's a bit of a loose cannon on his own…"

"Want me to catch a ride with Hammond?" Lee asked him.

Denis looked uncomfortable for a moment and then seemed to make up his mind about something. "I want you to come with me."

Lee knew that Hammond and the rest of the task force were expecting them, but this was Denis's op, and if he thought Aaron needed them, she was going to trust his instinct. "Yeah, I'm good with that."

It made it easier to go along with the plan since Denis had been the one to bring it up. She was worried about Aaron as well. They didn't know the man he'd seen but Lee *did* know Cate. She might look all glamorous, calm and serene on the outside, but underneath that polished exterior, she was lethal. And if she suspected Aaron of anything, she'd kill him without asking any questions.

"Good. There's vests in the storage container, and weapons," Denis said as he got behind the wheel.

Lee climbed into the back again to monitor the listening device Aaron had planted. There was no witty banter with Ramos the way there had been with Jorge, and she wondered if Aaron was nervous.

But then she shook her head. That was the opposite of the man she'd come to know and love. He didn't get nervous. If he was quiet he was strategizing. She suspected he'd be ready for anything that he encountered at the mansion.

Being ready didn't mean that he'd be safe. He was still just a man, even though he seemed invincible, and she knew he could be hurt.

She wished they'd had more time together, wished she'd told him how she felt about him and hadn't been trying to keep the fake relationship for their cover separate from her feelings. Because now that he was going into an unknown situation on his own, it was painfully obvious that her feelings had been real from the start. That she hadn't ever been playing a part when she was with Aaron.

But then, emotions were the hardest thing for her to admit to. She could see other people's weaknesses and their bonds to each other, but for herself, she *hated* them. She hated how weak they made her feel. There was no denying that she was falling for Aaron and she was scared for him.

She wasn't sure what they were going to encounter, but she only hoped they were close enough to him when he got to the mansion. It would kill her to hear him in trouble and know that she couldn't help.

Hammond messaged that his border force contact said WINgate had won the contract approximately nine months ago. When the first kid had gone missing from San Pedro.

She called him back. "That's when the maintenance guy's kid went missing. I'm going to find out if he was issued a backup ID. He filed a missing person's case, but the kid was known for skipping school, so the police wrote it off as a runaway."

"Where are you?"

Oh yeah. "So about that… Denis thinks we need to be close to Aaron in case anything goes down."

"I always trust my field guys' guts. Keep me posted. We'll move in once everyone has been debriefed."

"Thanks. Will do."

She disconnected the call, and trying her best to tamp down her gnawing worry, started to compile all the information together that she'd pulled from the web and from Hammond. The patterns were all pointing to drugs and human trafficking and a way to make them both easier.

The San Pedro kids had been taken as leverage, Lee realized. And if the camera footage from WINgate was to be believed, Perses and Cate had gotten everything they needed from them, which meant that Isabell Montez might be dead.

Chapter Twenty-One

Aaron leaned back and put his sunglasses on as they sat in the LA traffic, heading back toward the mansion he'd visited earlier. He wished he'd had a minute to talk to Denis and Jayne. He wanted to know if they'd gotten any leads on the man he'd described.

Ramos didn't seem inclined to talk and Aaron wasn't sure what the right lead-in was to get the other man chatting. It was somehow easier with Jorge after he'd started that fight. It had broken the tension.

"You don't like me much," he said at last. In a way Ramos reminded him of his brother Tony, who just sat back and observed. Of course, with Tony, everything had changed when he'd become a paraplegic. He'd had to look at life differently and part of that was watching everyone else's reaction to him. That had been one of the many reasons that Aaron had struggled to forgive himself for the past.

These last few years, he was getting closer to moving on. Tony had trained and gone up Kilimanjaro last summer with a team. His brother hadn't been changed as much as Aaron had once believed.

"Nope," Ramos said in a short tone that didn't really invite more conversation.

Aaron looked around them at the other cars in the traffic. "You from Los Angeles originally?"

The man nodded.

It was too sunny here. He knew a lot of Brits craved sunshine, but there was a part of him that missed the rain and cloudy skies. Here, everything was too bright, too…well, it felt fake sometimes. Not lately. Not since Lee had started working the operation with him. But he didn't want to let his mind drift to that. He had to try again to get Ramos talking.

"Mate, we're stuck in traffic—"

"Listen to the radio."

Aaron flipped on the radio. The lead story was breaking news that a drug-and-human-trafficking house had been raided and more than twenty kids had been rescued. Ramos clicked off the radio.

"Wonder how that happened," Aaron mused. "The operation is usually tight."

Ramos turned that big head of his and said, "Someone got sloppy."

The movement was slow and deliberate, meant to intimidate. But Aaron just shrugged. He wasn't afraid of Ramos. He wasn't 100 percent sure he could take him in a fight, but Aaron knew he'd give it a good go. "Jorge?"

Ramos shrugged, looking back at the road. "He did bring you with him today."

"You accusing me of something?" Aaron asked. Was his cover blown? It was a question he had been afraid to even think as soon as he saw Ramos. But he was new in the organization and a lot of shit had been going down since he'd been moved to the club. Everything was pointing toward him.

Ramos didn't respond at first as the traffic slowly inched forward. "Not yet. You see anything unusual at the house?"

Right now, there were two choices. Give up Jorge and make it seem like the other man was sloppy. Or…just stay silent. He was going to see the big boss so he wanted to go in with as much ammo as he could.

The team was listening as he debated how to answer. He was sure that Lee and Denis would be on their way to his location as soon as they could get there. So he knew he had backup, but there was also that feeling of being alone. That maybe this time he'd bitten off more than he could chew. Took one too many chances. Fate had been waiting for him since that cold, wet day playing rugby with his brothers when he'd hit too hard and hurt Tony. Had it finally caught up with him?

"I'm not sure. There was a van parked on the street when we left... Maybe they were watching the house."

"What'd it look like?"

"Standard service van. I think it was a pool cleaning service. White with blue letters," he said. Which was true. It was the one that Denis used when he was in the field.

"Could be nothing," Ramos said.

"Maybe. But the homes in that neighborhood don't have pools," Aaron mentioned. It was time to get Ramos's support.

The man did that nodding thing again as the traffic inched forward a little more. They were less than half a mile from their exit, but it was taking forever.

"You're good at details," Ramos said after a few minutes had passed.

"You have to be when you're the odd man out."

"How do you figure?" Ramos asked.

"The rest of you all know each other. I know the game, but I don't know the players here. I'm watching and learning to make sure I don't get burned," Aaron stated. Knowing that those words were probably the most truthful he'd given Ramos since he'd met the other man. There was an aura of danger around him.

He wasn't Perses but he was high up in the organization and Aaron could tell just from being around him that the man had sacrificed and killed to get where he was. They passed the exit for the mansion and seemed to be heading toward the port.

"I feel that."

"What can I expect when we get there?" Aaron asked. No use pretending he wasn't nervous about meeting this big fish in the gangs. He didn't even have a name, which increased his tension.

"Not sure. I got a call asking to meet you and telling me to get it done."

"Do you always deliver?" Aaron asked.

"I'm still alive."

Ramos's answer gave Aaron the information he needed. This was the man that no one said no to. It could have been from his earlier run-in or maybe the raid on a house that the gang had thought was secure, but whatever it was, he was now in the spotlight and there was no amount of talking that was going to get him out of it.

He didn't say anything else as they eventually got off the freeway. Instead, he just started to get ready for a fight. It was going to take all of his skill, muscle and wits to get out of this alive.

The back of Aaron's neck was itchy as they were cleared into the port without showing any ID. Ramos followed instructions on his phone and pulled up next to a stack of shipping containers that had two other cars and a van parked in front of it.

When they got out of the car, Aaron bent to tie his shoe and relayed the plate numbers for the other vehicles to the team. Then took the small semiautomatic handgun from his ankle holster and tucked it into the back of his pants under his T-shirt. He stood, rolling his neck and shoulders, loosening up for whatever was coming.

His gut was telling him that the missing kids from San Pedro might have come to this big meetup in the van with the blacked-out windows.

Ramos watched him with a slight grin on his face before leading the way to a small warehouse off to the side of the shipping crates. There was a guy out front that Aaron recognized from Jako's crew. The other man lifted his chin at Aaron in acknowledgment as they walked past.

Moments later, Ramos opened the door and went in first. Aaron followed him in.

Diana was there, standing next to Javier, who worked for her, and two men he'd never seen before were with Steve. Aaron stared at the redhead, wondering what her part in this was. From what he'd learned from Lee, she'd used her spot in the FBI to learn the inner workings of the US government and their task force. That had to be a key reason why Perses had been so hard to locate and identify.

He glanced around, looking for Perses. Where was he?

There were four adults all bound, tied to chairs with gags over their mouths. Next to them was Lee's contact Boyd. Aaron knew that Lee wasn't going to like it, but she'd suspected he must be involved.

The teenagers… He immediately recognized the Montez girl Lee had been trying to find. She looked like she'd been in a fight and her hands were tied in front of her. Next to her were two boys about the same age. They had similar bruises on their bodies and were also bound.

"I didn't think there would be kids here," he said clearly so that Denis and Lee would know.

Ramos just made a grunting noise, which Aaron didn't know how to take.

"Quinn, Boyd tells me your girlfriend works for a private security firm and she's been investigating our operation," Diana said.

"WTF. She's a bartender I met at Madness when I first got to LA. Who's making the accusation? I'll take him out," Aaron growled, moving aggressively forward. Not giving away that he knew who Boyd was.

"I am," Boyd said, stepping toward him.

The other man obviously worked out and had some muscles. Aaron walked straight up to him and punched him hard in the throat. He used an uppercut to the jaw to send Boyd spinning backward.

Blood spurted from his nose as he fell in front of the teens, and Isabell kicked him as hard as she could.

"Enough," a deep voice boomed.

Aaron glanced over his shoulder to see the older man he'd met at the mansion. He wore a blue linen suit and had left the buttons of the shirt open halfway down his chest. Earlier Aaron had been busy studying the other man's face, but this time, he noticed the medallion and it was the confirmation that he really hadn't needed. A medallion of Perses.

Chapter Twenty-Two

Lee was in a bulletproof vest with the rest of the task force as she heard the accusation from Boyd and Aaron's response. Aaron was good at what he did, and now that all the power players were in one place, there was a palpable energy within the team.

They were all ready to go in and take down Perses. Hammond's eyes were glowing with the prospect of being the one to crush him. And Van's were hooded. She had wanted to keep him from having to confront Cate again, but there had been no stopping him from coming along.

As soon as the sketch and grainy video from WINgate had confirmed Cate's identity, Lee knew her boss would be here. He wanted answers and justice. She got that. She wanted the same with Boyd. How dare he use her to find a kid to be used and exploited?

Jayne stepped to the front. "We will be moving in as teams. Denis and I will go first. Hammond and Lee second. Price's sniper is in position and the other three will be covering the side and rear entrances."

"Our objective is to arrest Perses and Diana and get the kids and their parents out," Hammond reminded them all.

"But we also need to know what the shipment is and where it's coming from," Jayne said. "So keep that in mind as we move in."

Lee nodded. She wanted answers too, and she wasn't going to rest until she got them.

"As soon as Lee walks in, things will kick off," Hammond said. "I think she should stay at the side entrance and I'll take Rick with me."

Lee agreed with the plan, and she and Rick swapped places. Rick was buzzing with energy but was calm as could be. She understood why he'd considered going back in the field. It seemed to really suit him.

The longer they waited, the tenser Lee was becoming. She'd only been on one raid before...the disastrous one where Cate had gotten away from them. Normally she was the eyes advising everyone where to go. But Jayne had a person on her team who was more familiar with all the players and the decision had been made that Lee would be on the ground.

Van looked over at her and arched one eyebrow. Lee nodded a couple of times to let him know she was okay. She might not have done this very often, but she was motivated to make sure that Boyd and Cate were caught.

"Move into position and we will go on my signal."

Lee followed Xander and Van around the building. Xander took the back entrance, Van the right. Lee was by herself, her comms on but silent as everyone waited for the signal. Aaron's and Steve's comms were being broadcast to the team. She heard the deep voice yell, *"Enough!"*

Then Jayne's voice came through. "Go."

"Guard at front down. Teams one and two are moving into position and breaching the building...now."

Seconds later, she heard the sound of the door being blown open and then screams and gunshots rang out. She was meant to wait and catch anyone who tried to leave, but she couldn't. There was too much at stake. She went in through the window that she'd been watching. Scraping her stomach as she fell through it. Then, rolling into a shooter's stance, she was on the move.

No one was alerted to her entrance. She scanned the room near her and saw that Aaron and Steve were both fighting with gang members. Boyd was flat on the floor and the kids and parents she'd seen in the grainy security footage were all bound and gagged, clearly frightened out of their wits.

Moving carefully and trying to stay to the shadows, she slid behind the boxes until she was close enough to the teens. She had a pocketknife and pulled it out so she could cut the kids free.

Tucking her gun into her waistband, she ran toward them. She worked quickly, freeing their hands, and then went to work on their feet. It felt like time was moving way too slowly. Every second counted, and when she freed the last kid, they all turned to look at her.

There was fear and uncertainty but also, Lee thought, a bit of grit in their gazes. She wanted to reassure them but with gunshots and fighting going on around them, she doubted anything she said would help.

"Go out the back door. There is a big man waiting who will keep you safe."

The kids took off without a second's hesitation, and Lee stood to cover them in case anyone went after them. Cate noticed them and started to go after them, but Lee raised her gun and shot the other woman in the leg.

Cate fired back, hitting Lee in the side as she twisted her body and dove for the floor. "Cate's on her way out the back after the kids. Injured in one leg."

Lee knew that Van or Xander would get her. Adrenaline rushed through her, but the gunshot wound in her side burned, and she felt the warmth of the blood dripping down her side as she made her way to the adults, cutting one of the men free first. He took the knife from her and freed the others. "Go out the back."

The first man wanted to stay with her, but Lee pushed him. "Go! I'll be fine."

They hurried toward the back of the warehouse.

"Kids and adults are safe with Xander. Van is in pursuit of Cate and out of my sight."

Lee turned to try to find Aaron in the mix. He was still standing but locked in fierce battle with a tall, older man in a pale blue linen suit.

Perses.

Aaron wasn't giving an inch, but the man was built like Aaron, and the fight was too evenly matched. Lee was trying to find her gun when she felt the barrel of it pressed to the back of her neck.

"Stand up," Boyd said. "It's time for you to be useful again."

As soon as Perses stepped into the room, the air changed. Aaron looked over at Steve and saw the man had moved to separate himself from the other gang members who Aaron didn't know.

Aaron knew the team would be coming in at any moment, given that Jayne and Hammond both wanted Perses. Meanwhile, he pummeled Boyd one more time, knocking him to the ground, and then kicked him hard enough in the head to knock him out. He pivoted to face the rest of the room. The hostages were all terrified, and the woman hostage was crying behind her gag.

"What's going on?" Perses demanded of Diana.

"Quinn's girlfriend is Lee Oscar. She was on the team I worked on with the FBI," the woman said.

"Why didn't you know that?" Perses demanded of her.

"I never met her while she was bartending at the club."

Perses turned toward Aaron and Ramos, and the guys from Jako's crew were all moving toward him as well. "You working with the FBI?"

"Fuck no. I'm a British citizen," Aaron said.

That didn't seem to stop them from rushing at him. Aaron rolled away to give himself some space before dropping into a fighting stance and moving toward the man closest to him.

The doors burst open as he did, and he saw Steve come to fight back-to-back with him. Ramos came straight for Aaron and hit him hard enough in the gut to wind him and probably break his ribs.

Aaron countered by kicking the other man's legs out from under him and then pounding him hard in the stomach while he was down. Ramos grabbed Aaron's leg and jerked him off balance, but he rolled into the momentum of his fall and came up in time to dodge a kick from Ramos aimed at his head.

Noticing Denis moving behind Ramos, Aaron hit the other

man in the face with a solid upward punch that broke his nose as Denis tased him and put cuffs on him.

"I had him," Aaron muttered.

"Yeah, sure," Denis said as they both turned to take on more of the men in the room.

In the midst of everyone fighting, Aaron noticed Perses making a move for the front entrance. He threw himself at the other man, tackling him to the ground. Aaron's entire body ached from the contact, but he ignored it, lurching to his feet as Perses stood as well.

A gunshot and the sound of Lee crying out made Aaron almost turn, but he knew better than to give Perses any opening. So instead, he pulled his gun from the back of his trousers and lifted it to fire at the other man, who was prepared to fight back. He backhanded Aaron in the jaw, making his head snap around.

Aaron was dazed for a moment, but instinct had him slamming Perses hard in the face with the butt of his pistol. He hit the other man three times before his head cleared and he was able to start thinking more strategically about fighting. He didn't want to draw this out. He wanted Perses down and captured.

Hammond was moving in, as was Jayne, and Aaron lowered his gun, hitting Perses in the kneecap, which took the other man to his knees. But he was still dangerous. His hits landing with enough force to knock Aaron off balance again, but Hammond and Jayne were both there as Denis tased Perses and they moved in to cuff him.

Aaron turned to find Boyd holding a gun to the back of Lee's head.

"Back off or she's dead," Boyd snarled.

Everyone stopped what they were doing. All of the gang members were in cuffs or knocked out and Jayne and Hammond were still next to Perses. Who was nodding at Boyd. "Get me out of here," Perses said.

Fear roiling through him, Aaron was weighing his next move to disarm Boyd. There was no room for hesitation or error. Never in his life had his actions had so much weight. If he made the wrong decision, Lee could end up dead. Something he wasn't going to allow to happen, now that he'd found her.

"Duck!" Denis yelled.

Aaron dropped as a bullet whizzed past him and hit Boyd in the forehead and the other man fell backward to the ground. Lee was trembling and pale, blood seeping down the side of her body, as Aaron ran to her. Pulling her into his arms as she fainted. He lowered her to the ground as emergency vehicles started to pour into the port.

He held her close, whispering softly in her ear. "I love you, babe."

Aaron knew the task force was taking care of the arrests, but he just stayed with Lee, riding with her to the hospital. He was checked for a concussion and released from the hospital but sat in a waiting room with Xander next to him.

It felt so much like that night when they'd waited for Tony. Hoping, praying, racked with guilt.

"She's going to be okay," Xander said.

"Yeah."

But Aaron wasn't entirely sure. She would recover from her physical injuries, but her emotional wounds might run deep. Lee had been betrayed *again* by someone she'd trusted. Aaron's hold on her was based around this mission, and the couple they'd created was fiction, but the truth was that nothing about his time with Lee had been a lie. He loved her and wanted her by his side.

What if she wasn't ready to hear that from him? Regardless, there was no other possibility for him but to try to convince her.

However, it might take time and Aaron had never been good at waiting. Finally the others from Price Security showed up, even Van, who had tracked down Cate and captured her, seeing her arrested.

They were all quiet, their concern for Lee was almost palpable, and Aaron wondered if she knew how much she mattered to this family she'd created for herself. And if there would be a place for him in it or if it would be better for her if he let her go.

Lee woke with a start in the hospital room. There was the steady beating of her heart on the monitor and her mouth was dry. She tried to sit up and someone was there.

Aaron.

He put his hand on her shoulder. "What do you need?"

"Water, please," she croaked out.

He poured it for her and handed it to her. "Take it slow."

She nodded as she drank and tried to remember everything that had happened. "Boyd?"

"Dead."

She had mixed feelings about that. She had wanted to question him and find out why he'd been working with Cate and for how long.

"Cate?"

"Van got her and she's being questioned," Aaron said, looking down at her with an expression that Lee hadn't seen on his face before and struggled to identify. "Perses was arrested as well and is being transported to DC for questioning. Your team is all here. We've been taking turns watching you and they went to dinner a few minutes ago. I'll text them that you're awake."

He reached for his phone, but she stopped him with her hand on his wrist. "Are you okay?"

"Yeah. A concussion and broken ribs, but that's nothing new for me. This hard head has saved me more than once," he said. "Why didn't you wait outside?"

"I was needed inside. Those kids and their parents had seen enough... Are they okay? God, I can't believe I didn't ask about them."

Leaning closer, Aaron gently brushed his hand over her forehead. "You wanted to make sure the danger was gone first. They are all good. Some minor injuries and they are all being debriefed. They had been forced to work for Cate and make adjustments to the biometric software. The kids were used for leverage."

"And Isabell?"

"Her parents caught on to what was happening and told her to be on her guard. According to Isabell, Mr. Chiseck tried to get her to go somewhere off school property with him, which creeped her out. When she told her parents, they gave her cash and told her to hide on the Old Mission Trail until she heard from them."

"Good for them. I was worried they were abusing her and that had made her run away." Lee sighed. "So she was fine until Boyd asked me to find her?"

"Yes and no. Her parents were taken and the house ransacked, so Isabell was scared but sticking to the plan. When you showed Boyd the picture, it was all he needed to search the hills behind the burger place. He was the one who found her."

"I can't believe Boyd would do something like this," Lee said, tears filling her eyes. "Do we know why?"

"He had a lot of debt from online gambling, according to Daniella. She suspects he did it for the money," Aaron told her. "We might get more from Cate when they are done interrogating her."

"Maybe. She can be very tight-lipped, but then again, Hammond can be very persuasive," Lee said.

She sort of drifted off and when she woke again, Van and Luna were in the room.

"Hey, you awake?" Van asked.

"I am. You okay?"

"I'm not the one in a hospital bed," he said as Luna handed her some water to drink.

She took the cup and drank it as Luna helped her raise her bed up to sit. "Where's Aaron?"

"In the hall. He went for a debrief and has been here since. Said he won't go home until you do," Van said.

Now that she knew Isabell was safe and Cate and Perses had been arrested, she felt like she could finally breathe and think about the future. A future she wanted with Aaron, but he was an undercover man who moved around the country going where the DEA needed him.

She sensed that Van wasn't ready to talk about Cate and Lee was okay with that. She wanted to talk to Aaron and find out if his feelings had changed now that they weren't undercover, or if, like her, he wanted...well, more.

"Thanks for staying with me."

"You're family," Luna said. "Of course we're going to be here."

Lee smiled at them both. One thing that was different about

being betrayed by someone she trusted was *this family* and having the self-confidence to know that she hadn't messed anything up. Boyd was playing a different game and he'd used her, but he'd paid for it.

"You guys can go home now if you want," Lee said after a few more minutes had passed.

"Or maybe just go to the hall and send Aaron in?" Luna asked with a smirk. "Come on, Van, let's go."

Van kissed her forehead and Luna gave her a gentle hug before they both left. Lee was nervous as she waited for Aaron to come in, and it seemed he was too. He entered the room and then leaned against the wall, just watching her.

He'd had time to change, wearing one of his fancy vests with pants that were tailored to fit him perfectly. His hair was perfectly styled, the sleeves of his dress shirt rolled up to reveal his muscled forearms.

She lifted her hand out to him and he rushed to her side. Their eyes met, and she sensed he was feeling the same wild cocktail of emotions she was.

"I love you," he said. "That's probably not what you expected to hear from me. But I do."

"I love you too," she whispered. "I don't know how to make this work, or if it even will work out, but I want to try."

He leaned over her, careful not to nudge her side, resting his forehead against hers. "I'm so horrible at relationships, and a part of me knows I shouldn't risk it, but I can't *not* risk it. I am not letting you go."

Her heart beat faster, and she felt warm and fuzzy inside in a way that she'd never experienced before. She could think of no better man to be with than Aaron. He had weathered so much in his life and kept moving through it and getting stronger.

She had no doubts he'd do the same with his relationship with her.

"I'm not great at relationships either. We'll figure it out as we go along and make one that works for us."

Us.

She loved the sound of that almost as much as she loved him. He climbed up onto the bed with her, pulling her gently into his arms. The way he held her made her feel safe, cherished even. Two things she hadn't felt in a long time, maybe ever, until she'd stumbled into his undercover op and started fake dating him.

There was nothing fake about the way he kissed her or the emotions in his eyes as he held her until she drifted off to sleep, secure that she'd finally found a home of her own with this man she loved so much.

* * * * *

Romantic Suspense

Danger. Passion. Drama.

Available Next Month

Colton's Deadly Trap Patricia Sargeant
The Twin's Bodyguard Veronica Forand

....

Hostage Security Lisa Childs
Breaking The Code Maria Lokken

....

LOVE INSPIRED

K-9 Alaskan Defence Sarah Varland
Uncovering The Truth Carol J. Post

Larger Print

....

LOVE INSPIRED

Defending The Child Sharon Dunn
Lethal Wilderness Trap Susan Furlong

....

LOVE INSPIRED

Cold Case Mountain Murder Rhonda Starnes
Christmas In The Crosshairs Deena Alexander

6 brand new stories each month

Romantic **Suspense**

Danger. Passion. Drama.

MILLS & BOON

Keep reading for an excerpt of a new title
from the Intrigue series,
Cold Case Protection by Nicole Helm

Chapter One

Carlyle Daniels had grown up in a tight-knit family. Dysfunctional, trauma-bonded—no doubt—but close. She supposed that's why she loved being absorbed into the Hudson clan. Their tight-knit was familiar, but bigger—because there were so many more of them.

So, yeah, a few more overprotective males in the mix, but she had *sisters* now—both honorary and in-law, because her oldest brother, Walker, had married Mary Hudson last fall.

Carlyle liked to talk a big game. She *really* liked to tease her oldest brother about how lame it was he'd gotten old and settled down, but deep down she could not have been happier for him. After spending most of his adult life trying to keep *her* safe while they tried to figure out who killed their mother, he now got to settle into just...normal. He worked as a cold case investigator for Hudson Sibling Solutions and helped out on the Hudson Ranch and was going to be a *dad* in a few months.

Her heart nearly burst from all the happy. Not that she admitted that to anyone.

She'd been working as Cash Hudson's assistant at his dog-training business on the ranch for almost a year now. She'd settled into life on the Hudson Ranch and in Sunrise, Wyoming. It was still weird to stay put, to not always have to look over her shoulder, to know she just got to…make a life, but she was handling it.

What she was not handling so well was a very inappropriate crush on her boss—who was also her sister-in-law's brother, which meant she probably *shouldn't* ever fantasize about kissing him.

But she did. Far too often. And normally she was an act-first-and-think-later type of woman, but there were two problems with that. First, she no longer got to bail if she didn't like her circumstances. She was building a life and all that, and bailing would bum Walker out which just felt mean and ungrateful.

Second, Cash had a daughter, who Carlyle adored. Izzy Hudson was twelve, smart as a whip, sweet and funny. She also had a little flash of something Carlyle recognized. Carlyle didn't know how to explain it, but she knew Cash didn't see it. She didn't think any of Izzy's family saw it, because the girl didn't *want* them to see it.

Carlyle saw through Izzy's masks all too well. She'd been the same all those years ago, keeping secrets so big and so well, her brothers hadn't found out until last year. So, she felt honor bound to keep an eye on the girl, because no doubt one of these days she was going to run headfirst into trouble.

Carlyle knew the lifelong bruises that could come from that, so she wanted to be…well, if not the thing that stopped the girl, the cushion to any catastrophic falls. She considered herself something of a been-there-done-that guardian angel.

Carlyle looked up from the obstacle course she'd been setting up for the level-one dogs and surveyed her work. She was satisfied and knew Cash would be too. He hadn't been super excited about hiring her. The fact he'd even done it had been because Mary had insisted or persuaded him to—but Carlyle knew that was more about him being a control freak than anything *against* her.

She liked to think she'd proved herself the past year—as a hard worker, as someone he could trust. She glanced over at the cabin that was Cash and Izzy's residence, while everyone else lived up in the main house. Palmer and Louisa were just a few weeks out from a wedding and finishing up their house on the other end of the property, but everyone else seemed content to stay in the main house. It was certainly big enough.

Carlyle sometimes felt like the odd man out. She wanted to be like Zeke, her other brother, and have her own place in town, but staying on the property made a lot more sense for what her work schedule was like.

And for keeping an eye on Izzy.

Who, speak of the devil, stepped out of the front door of her cabin, followed by her father and then Copper, one of the dogs retired from cold case and search and rescue work.

Carlyle sighed, in spite of herself. There was something *really* detrimental to a woman's sense when watching a man be good with animals and a really good dad whose top priority, always, was his daughter's safety.

Or maybe that was just her daddy issues. Considering her fathers—both the one she'd thought was hers, and the one who'd actually been hers—had tried to kill her. More than once.

But Don, the fake dad, was dead. Connor, the real dad, was in jail for the rest of his life. So, no dads. Just brothers who'd acted *like* fathers.

And now, for the first time in her life, safety. A place to stay. A place to put down roots. She had not just her brothers, but a whole network of people to belong to.

Copper pranced up to her and she crouched to pet his soft, silky face. "There's a boy," she murmured.

She glanced up as Cash and Izzy approached. Cash was a tall, dark mountain of a guy. All broad shoulders and cowboy swagger—down to the cowboy hat on his head and the boots on his feet. His dark eyes studied her in a way she had yet to figure out. Not assessing, exactly, but certainly not with the ease or warmth with which he looked at his family.

And still, it made silly little butterflies camp out in her stomach. She felt the heat of a blush warming her cheeks like she was some giggly, virginal teenager when she decidedly was *not*.

She was a hard-hearted, whirling dervish of a woman who'd grown up fast and hard and had somehow survived. Survival had led her here.

Things were good. She was happy. She wouldn't ruin that by throwing herself at Cash, and she wouldn't ruin it by failing at this job or messing up being part of this family network.

No, for the first time in her life, Carlyle was going to do things right.

CARLYLE DANIELS WAS a problem. Worse, Cash Hudson couldn't even admit that to *anyone* in his life. She was a good worker, Izzy *loved* her, the animals *loved* her and she was an even better assistant than he'd imagined she'd be.

But he found himself thinking about her way too much, long before he'd stepped out of the cabin this morning to see her across the yard getting work for the day set up.

He too often found himself trying to make her laugh, because she didn't do it often enough and the sound made him smile…which he also knew *he* didn't do enough. As his siblings and daughter routinely told him so.

But if anyone had *any* clue he smiled more around Carlyle than he did around anyone other than Izzy, he'd be flayed alive.

He was too old for her—in years and experience. He was a father, and he had one disastrous marriage under his belt. He could look back and give himself a break—he'd been sixteen, reckless enough to get his high school girlfriend pregnant, and foolish enough to think marriage would make everything okay.

Maybe he was older, wiser, more mature these days, but that didn't mean he could ever be *good* for anyone. Didn't mean he'd ever risk Izzy's feelings again when she already had oceans of hurt over the mother she hadn't gotten to choose.

He wasn't even interested in Carlyle. He just thought she was hot and all the settling down going on around the Hudson Ranch was getting to him. Grant and Mary were fine enough. They were calm, settle-down-type people. Mary might be younger than him, but he'd always figured her for the marriage-and-kids type—and even if he liked to play disapproving older brother, Walker Daniels was about as besotted with Mary as a brother could want for his sister.

Grant was older, far more serious, and he and Dahlia had taken what felt like forever to finally even get engaged, so that was all well and good. Cash could take all those little blows that reminded him time marched on.

But it was Palmer and Anna who *really* got to him. Younger than him. The reckless ones. The wild ones. He'd never have pinned Palmer for marriage, and he'd never thought anyone would want to put up with the tornado that was Anna.

But Palmer was getting married in a few weeks, and by all accounts Louisa was the answer to any wildness inside of him. Anna was a *mother* now, and a damn good one, and somehow she'd found a man who thought all her sharp edges were just the thing to shackle him down forever.

Someday, sooner than he'd ever want, Izzy would be an adult. Making her own choices like his siblings were doing. Izzy would go off into that dangerous world and *then what*?

Cash pushed out an irritated breath. Well, there was always Jack. Single forever, likely, being that he was the oldest and Cash couldn't remember the last time he'd been on a date, or even gone out for a night of fun.

They could be two old men bemoaning the future and the world together.

And no one would ever know he had an uncomfortable *thing* for Carlyle. He blew out a breath before they finally approached the obstacle course. "Morning," he offered gruffly.

"Good morning," she said brightly, grinning at Izzy as she stood up from petting Copper.

"I'm going to walk Izzy over to the main house, then we'll get started."

"Dad," Izzy groaned, making the simple word about ten syllables long. "I can walk to the house by myself. It's *right there*." She pointed at the house in question. Yes, within his sight, but...

Too much had happened. Too much *could* happen. As long as his ex-wife was out there, Izzy wouldn't leave his side, unless she was with one of his family members.

"I'll be right back," he said to Carlyle.

Izzy didn't groan or grumble any more. He supposed she was too used to it. Or knew he wasn't going to bend. He wished he could. He wished he could give her everything she wanted, but there'd been too many close calls.

They climbed up the porch to the main house in silence and he opened the back door that led into a mudroom.

"I'm not a baby," Izzy grumbled. Probably since she knew he would follow her right into the house until he found someone to keep an eye on her.

He didn't say what he wanted to. *You're* my *baby.* "I know, and I'm sorry." They walked into the dining room, and Mary was already situated at the table with her big agenda book and a couple different colored pens.

She looked up as they entered and smiled at Izzy.

Cash would never not feel guilty that Izzy ended up with such a terrible mom, but Mary as an aunt was the next best thing, he knew.

"I'm craving cookies. What do you think? Should we make chocolate chip or peanut butter?"

Izzy didn't smile at her aunt, she just gave Cash a kind of killing look and then sighed. "What do you think the baby wants?" She went over and took the seat next to Mary at the table.

Mary slung an arm around Izzy's shoulders, and Izzy leaned in, putting a hand over Mary's little bump.

Izzy didn't want to be treated like a baby, she didn't want him being so overprotective, but she also loved her family. She was excited about cousins after being the only kid on the ranch for so long, and she *liked* spending time with her aunts and uncles.

So this wasn't a punishment. He tried to remind himself of that as he retraced his steps back to where Carlyle was waiting. She'd brought out the level-one dogs, and they were lined up waiting for their orders.

Because they were level one, there was still some tail wagging, some whining, some irregular lining up, but they were good dogs getting close to moving to level two. They all kept their gazes trained on Carlyle, and she stood there looking like some kind of queen of dogs. Her long, dark ponytail dancing in the wind, chin slightly raised, gray-blue eyes surveying her kingdom of furry subjects.

He came to stand next to her and didn't say anything at first. Ignored the way his chest got a little tight when she glanced his way, like he was part of that array of subjects she ruled.

She could, he had no doubt. If he was someone else in a totally different situation, she no doubt would.

"She's tough," Carlyle said, not bothering to explain she was talking about Izzy.

As if he didn't know that about his daughter. As if he hadn't raised her to be tough. As if life hadn't forced her to be. "Yeah, and the world is mean."

"Take it from someone who's been there and done that, it doesn't matter how well-intentioned the protection is, at a certain point, it just chafes."

Cash knew she wasn't wrong, but it didn't matter. "I'd rather a little chafing than any of the other alternatives."

Carlyle sighed, but she didn't argue with him. She surveyed the lineup of dogs. "Well, you want to start or should I?"

Carlyle was good at this. A natural. "Take them through the whole thing."

She raised an eyebrow. He hadn't let her do that before all on her own, but…it was time. He couldn't give his daughter the space she needed to *breathe*, so he might as well unclench here where it didn't matter so much. "You can do it."

She grinned at him, eyes dancing with a mischief that was far too inviting, and completely not allowed in his life.

"I know," she said, then turned to the dogs and took them through the training course. Perfectly. A natural.

A *problem*.

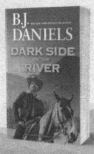

Subscribe and fall in love with a Mills & Boon series today!

You'll be among the first to read stories delivered to your door monthly and enjoy great savings.

WE SIMPLY LOVE ROMANCE

MILLS & BOON